WOLF MARKED

MAGIC SIDE: WOLF BOUND, BOOK 1

VERONICA DOUGLAS

MAGIC SIDE PRESS

For Carol and Ric, with all our love.

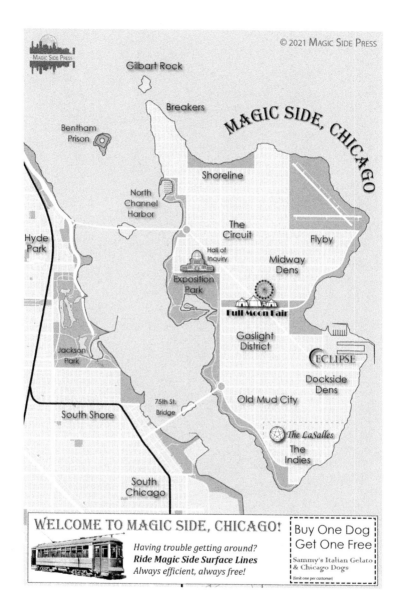

© 2021 Magic Side Press

MAGIC SIDE, CHICAGO

Gilbart Rock

Breakers

Bentham Prison

Shoreline

North Channel Harbor

Hyde Park

The Circuit

Flyby

Hall of Inquiry

Midway Dens

Exposition Park

Full Moon Fair

Gaslight District

ECLIPSE

Jackson Park

Dockside Dens

75th St. Bridge

Old Mud City

South Shore

The LaSalles

The Indies

South Chicago

1

"Find the red-haired woman with a tattoo on her left shoulder. Without her at your side, you will not discover the answers you need. But be warned—your adversaries hunt her, too. If you do not stop them, she will be dead before the full moon rises, and with her, the future of your pack."

-Prophecy given to Jaxson Laurent, first night of the Full Moon Fair.

Savannah

The woman at table five stared over my shoulder at the TV hanging above the bar, and I inwardly groaned, knowing what was coming. I'd been seeing it all week: the squint at the screen, the little wrinkles of concern between the eyebrows, the casual glance in my direction and double-take.

She didn't disappoint. "My gosh," she exclaimed as I mustered a polite smile, "you look exactly like that missing girl on the news! Madison Lee, you know? Doesn't she look like Madison, dear?" she asked her husband.

I didn't.

Well, to be fair, we shared a slender build, arm tattoo, and fire-orange hair that stood out like a lighthouse burning in a forest of pines. But I didn't *look* like her. I knew my own face—pretty enough, but hardened from having to make my own way. The girl on TV had a carefree smile and soft features that screamed, *I've had an easy life with parents and friends and money.*

But people didn't see my face, just my hair. I'd heard the same comment from nearly every table since the news broke four days ago: *You look like her.*

Thank God I'm not her, wherever she is.

The woman's husband flipped his menu and grumbled. "Six disappearances in two months. *In Wisconsin.* We came up here to get away from that kind of thing."

And yet, it was all that my customers wanted to talk about. It didn't help that the twenty-four-hour news cycle was doing its best to spread as much panic as possible. *Authorities baffled. No pattern. Anyone could be a target.*

Talk about milking the situation. Like I needed up-to-the-minute reminders that I, too, might end up in some wacko's basement someday.

I flipped open my waitress pad. "It's strange. I always thought this corner of Wisconsin was so safe."

The woman gave me a pitying smile. "Don't worry, honey, I'm sure they'll catch whoever is behind all this."

Her white shorts and bright pink top screamed *out-of-towner,* and clearly, she wasn't familiar with the capabilities of local law enforcement.

Really, I wasn't worried. The chance of getting abducted was like getting hit with a lightning bolt. I was just tired of having everyone's eyes on me and repeating the same conversation.

I took their order and headed toward the back.

While I could get out of conversations, I couldn't avoid the stares. The couple at table seven kept looking at me, so I headed over. "Can I get you anything else?"

They were backwoodsy sorts. The woman had long, tangled hair and wore a tank top, jeans, and a belt with a big brass buckle. Her arms were toned, and she had a barbed wire tattoo around her right bicep and a strange two-headed wolf tattoo above her collarbone. "Another round of Buds."

The man was ripped, and the buttons of his shirt strained at the seams. He had tattoos all over his arms, and he gestured to my left shoulder with his bottle. "Nice ink."

"Thanks. You, too." I'd designed the tattoo myself, but I wasn't about to share that fact with those folks. They smelled like bad news.

"You from around here?" the woman asked.

"Yes. Why?" They were probably looking for a local hustle.

The man rubbed his chin and nodded to the TV. "You know," he began, "you look—"

"I'll get those beers." I turned on my heel and grabbed the check from booth eight on the way. They'd left a four-buck tip on a fifty-five-dollar check. I slapped the leather check presenter down on the stack.

"Shit," I hissed. Had I really been here three years?

Stormy, the only other waitress on the clock, leaned against the wall. "You're in a mood."

"I'm too broke to get out of here, people tip like crap, and my tables won't stop comparing me to the missing girl on TV."

"You *do* look like her. What if you're *his* type?"

I rolled my eyes. "There is no type. The victims have been men and women, young and old. And she was the only one to disappear from our county."

As I headed to the bar for table seven's Buds, Jess, our bartender, grabbed my arm and pulled me toward the window. "Ho-ly heavens, Savannah. I think I'm in love."

A man stepped down from the cab of his shining black Ford F-150 pickup. The rolled-up sleeves of his gray shirt stretched over his thick, tanned forearms, and his blue jeans offset a pair of rugged biker boots. Somehow, he made the half-ton truck look small.

My knees locked as he turned toward the restaurant. Every movement spoke of restrained power, and his shirt clung to his chest in ways that made my mouth dry.

I licked my parched lips. *Definitely* an out-of-towner.

"I call dibs," Jess whispered, quiet and reverent as if speaking to the pope.

The man sniffed the air like he was searching for something, and a dark expression cut across his face.

I didn't blame him. Maybe it was my imagination, but I was certain I could smell the scents of grease and stale beer half a mile from the bar.

My apron and white Taphouse logo T-shirt suddenly felt dirty and constricting. This wasn't a place for a god like him. He was out-of-this-world gorgeous, with thick tousled hair and a trimmed beard that accentuated his strong jaw.

He approached, and my pulse quickened. Something about him screamed danger. When he pushed through the front door, the whole bar went silent—except for the idiots on TV still rambling about the abductions. Every eye trained on him, and we all knew we didn't measure up.

He scanned the room, not like a man who was lost, but like a hunter, assessing the two dozen faces all staring back. His search stopped on me, and though it must have been my imagination, just for a second, I swore his coffee eyes flashed gold.

I knew in that instant, that I should run. That I should flee. But his dark eyes had a magnetic hold on me, and I was torn between submission and flight. My legs wouldn't move, and my breath stilled as if all the air had been drawn from the room.

I'd seen this story before. He was the predator, and I was his prey—a deer transfixed while it stared into the beautiful face of its doom.

Luckily for my paralyzed brain, Jess jerked me behind the bar. "What are you doing? You're staring at him and practically drooling on the floor. I called dibs!"

"I..."

She spun me around toward the back of the restaurant. "Anyway, table seven just bolted out the back door. Did they pay? Because it's on you if they didn't."

That hit me like a bucket of ice water.

The only thing the backwoods couple had left at table seven were the empties, and their pile of unpaid beers would wipe out my wages for the day. The creepers had dined and dashed.

The death rattle of my pocketbook drove all thoughts of the man from my mind. I clenched my fists and slammed through the back door.

Those assholes were going to pay.

The backlot stank of grease and trash, and I scanned the area in vain for the two freeloaders. I strained my ears for any sign of movement, but the only sounds hanging in the air were the song of crickets and the buzzing overhead lights. I was about to head around the front of the building when the echoes of a hushed argument in the overflow lot broke the stillness.

Gotcha.

I fingered the bottle of mace in my apron as I headed through the trees down to the barren patch of dirt where employees and unlucky customers parked. I wouldn't have had to carry the stuff if the owner fixed the damn lights.

At least the moon was nearly full.

The couple was arguing in the shadows at the back of the lot. I slowed my pace. They looked as if they were about to come to blows, and I didn't want to get mixed up in that.

The woman got up in the man's face and jabbed a finger into his chest. "We gotta stick around. That's definitely the girl we're supposed to grab."

The heavily inked man shoved her back with a snarl. "No way. Did you see who just walked in? He'll scent me out in a second. We'll snatch the girl another time. We can't fuck this up again."

My pulse raced. *Holy crap.* They'd been staring at me all evening. I had to be the girl they were supposed to snatch.

I skidded to a halt in front of a car that was trying park. What the hell should I do?

Get inside. Call 911.

The car in front of me honked, and I jumped.

"Are you going to stand there like an idiot?" the guy inside yelled.

I glanced back at the couple. They'd stopped arguing and had trained their eyes on me.

Oh, no.

"She's the one! Get her!" the woman barked, and her eyes flashed red.

Shit, shit, shit.

Hands damp and shaking, I grabbed the mace out of my apron and darted toward the Taphouse. In a blur of motion, the man sprinted around the edge of the lot and blocked my path.

No one could move that fast.

Panic seized my mind. Keeping the cars between us, I dashed toward my Gran Fury, but I skidded to a halt as the woman stepped in my way.

"Don't scream, or I'll gut you." She glared at me with those haunting crimson eyes and drew a couple knives.

No. Not knives.

Her fingers erupted into *claws*.

Not possible.

The woman twitched, and I snapped my mace up and blasted it into her face. She screamed and hunched forward, rubbing her eyes and choking. "You bitch!"

I grabbed her hair, kneed her in the face, and tossed her to the ground. Then I leapt over her body and raced toward my car. At least life had taught me how to fight.

The tattooed man was on me in a second. I raised my mace, but he clamped his hand around my wrist. "I don't think so."

The driver who'd honked at me jumped out of his car. "Hey, let her go! I'm calling the cops!"

The tattooed psychopath released my hand, crossed the distance in a flash, and slammed his fist into the man's chest.

Not his fist, his *claws*. Blood sprayed over everything.

This is not happening, my mind insisted. Every part of my body started quaking. I ducked around the end of my car and fumbled with my keys as I jammed them into the lock.

Please, please, please.

I wrenched open the car door, jumped in, and slammed it shut behind me.

At the noise, the tattooed psycho wheeled around and hurled the body of the driver into the air. The poor victim's gurgling cry was cut short as he bounced off the hood of my car.

Screaming, I locked the doors and revved the engine.

Always park facing out—an underappreciated lesson from my dad. But before I could burn rubber, both attackers were at the windows, leering at me. The tattooed man punched through the passenger-side window, spraying glass everywhere. "You're not going anywhere," he growled, then thrust his arms through the window and strained to reach me with bloody claws, grazing my shoulder. I was too afraid to feel the pain.

I floored it, and my tires spun on the gravel. Then the car lurched forward, dragging the tattooed man with me. I swerved toward some small pines at the edge of the lot, and he grunted as I slammed him into the trees, breaking his hold.

With my heartbeat pounding in my ears, I fishtailed out of the lot onto the moonlit county highway and checked my rearview mirror just in time to see the woman haul the tattooed man to his feet. Then they started chasing me. On *foot*.

"What the hell is going on?" I screamed at the Gran Fury and pushed the gas pedal to the floor.

There was no way those wackos should have been able to keep up on the open road, but they were, and gaining.

My throat clenched. Four years of track, and I couldn't run half that fast.

I glanced down at my speedometer. Forty-five miles an hour? It had to be busted. Usain Bolt never broke thirty.

Wind whistled through the broken passenger window, and glass tinkled as it blew around the seats. I checked the rearview again.

The speed freaks had nearly closed the distance. The man suddenly disappeared, and something landed on the roof with a resounding thump. I jerked, swerving across the centerline, and my heart clenched. *This is not happening, this is not happening, this is—*

A hand—*with claws*—scraped the windshield above me, and I screamed.

My reflexes kicked in, and I slammed on my brakes. The car shuddered and swerved, and I fought the wheel to maintain control.

The thing on the roof launched forward onto the road. A second later, the running woman slammed full speed into the back of the car and flipped over the front.

My seatbelt dug into my ribs as the car came to a screeching halt. The body of the woman hit the pavement and bounced a couple times before rolling into a ditch, while the man's carcass skidded to a stop in the middle of the road.

No, no, no. It wasn't possible. There was no way that two clawed people just ran my car down on the open road.

My vision blurred as I started hyperventilating.

Ten feet ahead, the man pushed himself onto all fours. His arms bent and buckled, like the broken bones were snapping back into place. My chest heaved, but I couldn't seem to get any air.

He stood and faced me, raising a hand to block out the Gran Fury's headlights. His crimson eyes practically glowed in the high beams. When he glanced at the woman in the ditch, he let out a heart-wrenching howl like a goddamned animal.

Then he charged.

My mind spun, and I hit the gas. The car rocketed forward and jerked as I ran the bastard down. Once I bumped over him, I gasped and slammed on the brakes.

Everything was still. I could barely make out the moonlit form of his crumpled body in the rearview.

Had I just murdered someone with my car?

Apparently not. As the unkillable psycho rose, I could almost hear the echoes of his bones snapping back into place through the broken window. My chest seized as he turned toward me with those glowing eyes.

These were freaking monsters.

Adrenaline dumped into my veins. I threw the car into reverse and gunned it. His body disappeared beneath my bumper and skidded as he was dragged along beneath the undercarriage. I popped the Fury back into drive and rolled over him again.

Twice.

When I checked the mirror, his body lay motionless in the road.

Where was the damned woman? She wasn't in the ditch.

I let my survival instinct slip into the driver's seat, and I pushed the gas to the floor with only one thought in my mind: *Get the hell out of here.*

2

Savannah

My brain fog cleared after a minute, and I pulled over to the side of the road. Hands shaking, I grabbed my phone and dialed 911. I tried to explain things to the dispatcher but probably sounded like a lunatic.

Stay calm, Savannah.

I dusted the broken glass off my lap and kept checking the rearview mirror for movement along the moonlit road while I waited for the cops. Nothing seemed to be following me, but I kept the car idling and the headlights on, just in case.

After five minutes, a set of flashing lights pulled up behind me. A car door slammed, and a moment later, Sheriff Kepler tapped on my window. "Savannah? Is that you? Are you okay? Roll down your window."

I complied in a daze. "Hey, Sheriff Kep."

The sheriff leaned forward and aimed his flashlight around the interior of the car, illuminating the shattered remnants of my windows. "Jeez, what happened?"

I sat on my hands to keep them from shaking. My mouth was

drier than the Taphouse's fried chicken. "I think I just steam-rolled a guy with my car a mile back."

Kepler chuckled. "Honey, I saw that on the way over. You ran over a wolf. Splatted it real good, by the looks of it."

A wolf?

I rubbed my temples. "No, Sheriff. There were two people. They jumped me in the Taphouse parking lot and chased me down. I ran over one of them with my car just back there."

Kepler shone his flashlight into my eyes, and I looked away, using my hand to shield them. "Have you been drinking?" he asked. "Taking any substances?"

Heat lined my jaw. "No, sir. And don't talk to me like that. You know me, and I know what I saw. I was attacked."

The sheriff sighed. "All right. Tell you what, I'll call Randy's Towing to pick up your car, cause it sure as heck looks like it needs fixing. You and I can take a ride, and I'll show you what happened. Then I'll drop you back at your place. Okay?"

I nodded, shut the car off, and stepped out.

My head spun as I got a good look at the vehicle. The Gran Fury looked like it had been through hell and back. In addition to the broken window and the steam rising from the engine, huge claw marks streaked across the door, hood, and roof.

Holy hell.

The sheriff hung up his phone. "Randy's on his way. Just leave the keys in the glovebox. You can head over tomorrow morning to get things sorted out."

"Thanks," I murmured as I hid the keys.

I took one last look at my precious, wounded car and climbed into Kep's cruiser. How was I ever going to pay for all this?

Kepler made a U-turn, and we headed back to the scene of the accident. A mile down the way, his headlights illuminated a dark lump in the middle of the road. The sheriff pulled over and turned on his flashers.

Pulse racing, I climbed out and followed him across the road to the body. The beam of his flashlight swept over the crumpled form, and I froze.

A dead wolf. A giant, dead wolf.

"You're lucky you hit this animal straight on and didn't swerve into a tree," Kepler said. "A lot of people kill themselves trying to miss an animal."

Nausea caught me off guard, and I staggered over to the side of the road and threw up on the grass. Thankfully, I hadn't eaten before my shift, so most of what came up was iced tea.

Kepler laid a couple flares beside the wolf's body and joined me when the heaving finished. "You okay?" he asked, handing me a stick of gum.

I got off my knees, scraped the gravel out of my palms, and popped the gum in my mouth. "Yeah, just in shock."

"I'm sure. It's a hell of a sight. But it's good that it's dead, really. I was just over at the Taphouse responding to the attack there when I got your dispatch. This beastie mauled one of the customers pretty good. The man's all tore up and in a coma, but the paramedics think he'll live."

I shook my head in disbelief. "I was there. He wasn't attacked by a wolf. It was a man and a woman!"

Kepler tilted his head. "Savannah, you've been watching too much TV. The poor fellow was mauled by an animal." He kicked the corpse of the wolf with his boot. "*This* animal."

I started to protest when a pair of headlights swept over us. A truck rumbled around the bend and slowly pulled to a stop. The headlights stayed on, and a car door slammed.

The sheriff held one hand up to shield his eyes and put the other on his holster. "Hold on, there. Identify yourself."

A gruff baritone voice came out of the darkness. "Wisconsin

Department of Natural Resources. I see you have a dead wolf on your hands. Permission to approach?"

The voice was thick and rich, like honey, and made my skin tingle.

"DNR?" the sheriff asked. "Amazing you were alerted so fast."

"We were in the area. Been a lot of wolf activity," the voice said from the darkness.

"Well, come look at this thing, then. It's a monster."

A powerfully built man stepped into the beam of the headlights.

The man from the bar. What was he doing here?

My breath caught. It was one thing to see him walking into the crowded confines of the Taphouse. It was another to see him emerge from the darkness of the barren highway with only the sheriff at my side.

Unease coiled around me.

Backlit against the lights, the man was like a statue carved from obsidian. His long shadow swept over us as he approached. Light crept around the corners of his face, highlighting the edges of his strong features. I shouldn't have been able to see his eyes, but for a second, I thought there was a flash of honey gold in the dark. Then it was gone.

He stopped by the corpse of the wolf and looked down. "Big animal. What happened?"

His voice was practically a growl. My heart strained against my chest, and every fiber in my body urged me to bolt.

"This young lady ran it down," the sheriff offered.

I opened my mouth to speak but stopped short when I heard a truck door shut gently. I couldn't see anything beyond the glaring headlights. Had there been someone else with him? Why was DNR even on the scene at this time of night?

Something wasn't right.

The man stepped close, looming over me. *Ruggedly handsome* would be an understatement. *Breathtaking* was more like it. He was six-six at least, and his proximity made the hair on my neck stand on end. "You killed the wolf? What's your name?"

"Savannah Caine."

"You from around here?"

I crossed my arms. "Yes. Belmont."

"Grow up here?"

I narrowed my eyes. "What's with the interrogation? These are funny questions for someone from DNR."

His eyes glinted. "Just wondering if you're familiar with the local wildlife. We have a lot of wolves in these parts—keystone species. They've been acting erratic lately. Can you tell me what happened?"

Hey, Mr. Hot Wildlife Guy. I was just attacked by two people with savage claw hands and red eyes. They chased me down at forty-five miles an hour, and I ran them over with my car. Now there's just a dead wolf where the body should be.

Nope, that wouldn't sound crazy at all.

I glanced at the sheriff, suddenly doubting myself.

The DNR man followed my eyes, and he cleared his throat. "Sheriff, why don't you let us chat in private for a minute?"

Trepidation tugged at my chest. "I don't wa—"

The mysterious man's eyes flashed gold. "Give us a few minutes, Sheriff."

His deep voice vibrated with command, and a sense of his complete power and authority washed over me.

"Yes, of course." The sheriff nodded and stepped toward his cruiser.

What the hell was going on?

Run, the small voice in the back of my head shouted. I started to turn, but the DNR man locked me in place with his intense, unnatural gaze. "Don't worry, you're safe. I just need you to speak freely."

Inexplicably, the tension drained from my body, and I suddenly *knew* he was being honest. My godmother always said that I had a nose for the truth, but this was something else entirely.

"Tell me exactly what happened. Every detail, no matter how strange." His voice was low, like the roar of a distant waterfall. His eerie power washed over me again, but differently this time. All I wanted was to obey, to comply, to please him.

I tried to argue, but as soon as I opened my mouth, my story flooded out. I told him everything that I could remember about the attackers: the minute details of their appearance, their savage claws, unbelievable speed, and haunting crimson eyes. Eyes like his, but reddish orange, not honey gold...

The thought sent a shudder through me, and my mind cleared for a second. Was I really telling him all this?

"Please continue, Ms. Caine."

I clamped my mouth shut in resistance, but the man's pupils dilated, and I again succumbed to his will. I told him how I'd escaped, fled down the road, and finally run over the tattooed monster of a man, again and again.

At last, the pressure in the air eased up, and horror filled me.

Oh, God. Had I just confessed to vehicular manslaughter? Had I just ranted on and on about people with claws for hands? I shook my head, as if waking from a dream, and knew I needed to backpedal. "You must think I'm crazy. I mean, it's just a wolf here, lying in the middle of the road."

The mysterious man crossed his arms. "I don't think you're crazy. I think you were attacked, just as you described."

His eyes were a deep brown. Had I imagined the gold?

"What about..." I gestured to the bloody mess in the middle of the highway.

"It's a dead wolf."

"But..."

The man's posture softened. "Sometimes, during traumatic events, our mind mixes up memories. You were attacked. You fled and ran over a wolf. The cocktail of chemicals in your brain jumbled the events—it's called False Memory Syndrome. It's quite common."

I bit my lip and read his face. His smile was warm, confident, and inviting.

And he was lying. I could almost smell it. "But that's not what happened, is it?"

His smile wavered.

I knew it.

My skin turned cold and clammy as doubt crept in.

I'd heard a car door shut moments ago. Had someone else been in his truck? Or had someone else gotten in? Maybe the woman with the barbed wire tattoo? Her body hadn't been by the side of the road. And she'd had eyes kind of like the DNR man's, just a different shade.

I started to back up. "Who are you, anyway? There's no way you're from DNR. Are you in league with those people who attacked me? Is this a coverup?"

"No." His voice was so deep and guttural, it was close to a growl. My skin prickled. I could almost smell his sudden rage at the suggestion.

Truth.

The man's eyes flooded with honey. "Savannah, many things about tonight will seem strange. Impossible. Even our conversation. It's a byproduct of the attack and not real, do you understand?"

His presence surrounded me, soothing my doubts and fears.

"Yes." I nodded.

"As to who I am..." He handed me a black card with *Jaxson*

Laurent in bold white letters. I flipped it over. Just a black phone number on white. "I'm investigating the recent abductions, and I think you were targeted. Call me anytime, day or night, if you remember something more. Any detail, no matter how strange. The authorities aren't taking this seriously, but we are."

My head spun with what the man—whoever the heck he was—had confirmed. My attack was linked to the abductions.

"Who are you? A Fed?"

The man just smiled and looked down at the wolf. "I'm sure it's been a long night, and you must be exhausted." He turned and waved Sheriff Kepler over. "I think it's time to get Ms. Caine home."

"Wait," I hissed, "can't you tell me anything more? Why was I attacked? Why did they target me?"

He stepped back. "I'm sorry, but I'm not at liberty to disclose the details of the case."

Lie.

"I need to know."

"Good night, Ms. Caine."

My fists clenched. I deserved to know what was going on. I was the damn victim, after all.

Screw the creepy government man and his black truck. If he wasn't going to tell me why people were hunting me, then I'd figure it out on my own—even if I had to call every law enforcement agency in the state to get the details.

As I turned to leave, Jaxson caught my arm, and I gasped as a spark of electricity ran through my body. He jerked his hand back, and his expression darkened, then shifted toward surprise. "A word of advice, Ms. Caine: don't leave town. And don't talk about this to anyone. For your own good."

His eyes sparkled with gold, and his presence washed over me again. Somehow, the overwhelming sensation delivered a clear, unmistakable message: *Obey.*

3

Jaxson

Savannah Caine turned on her heel and strode back toward the sheriff's cruiser. Her bittersweet orange hair swayed back and forth hypnotically, and the way her long, pale legs disappeared into her high cutoff jean shorts amplified the alluring effect.

Heat raced up my neck, and I drank deeply of her lingering scent.

The red-haired woman with a tattoo on her left shoulder.

There was no doubt that Savannah was the woman the seer had sent me to find. The fortune teller's words still burned in my mind: *Your adversaries hunt her, too. If you do not stop them, she will be dead before the full moon rises, and with her, the future of your pack.*

I looked up at the moon-mother shining high overhead. Five days before full, and they'd nearly gotten to her before I had.

She was lucky. The abductors had attacked seven people so far. Forty-eight hours ago, I'd seen what happened to one of those who resisted. Utter carnage.

Yet Savannah had survived. Although she was Magica—a

person who had magic in their veins—the woman obviously had no idea what she was or how to use her magic, or that werewolves were real. But despite all odds, she'd managed to kill one of the wolves that ambushed her without using weapons or spells.

It was damned impressive. We were very difficult to kill.

Unfortunately, Savannah had slain only one of her attackers. The woman she'd described was still out there—a wounded she-wolf, judging by her scent.

Hopefully, Regina would catch her. My second in command was one of the best trackers in our pack. She'd slipped out of the truck to chase our prey while I'd distracted the cop and the woman. If we couldn't catch the she-wolf, there'd be blood. Savannah was wolf-marked now, and the she-wolf would hunt her until one of them was dead.

I motioned to the sheriff. He sauntered over and stuck out his hand. "Seems I'm lucky the DNR had people in the area tonight. This is one hell of a mess."

Rather than return the smile, I locked him in place with a cold stare. He froze like a deer caught in the headlights. His subconscious knew that I was in charge here, and that I could snap his arm like a twig.

I shook his hand for appearances. "The DNR will handle things from here, Sheriff. The woman ran over a wolf, that's all. The attack at the Lakeside Taphouse was an animal attack, too. Neither incident needs further investigation."

I let my alpha presence drown him into compliance. It wasn't mind control, just the force of raw, uncontestable authority. More than anything, most people just wanted to be told what to do, and this man would believe anything to make the monsters go away.

The befuddled sheriff nodded. "Of course, that's what I was thinking. Just an animal attack."

"And Sheriff, bury the report. We don't want the locals going around town with guns half-cocked, looking for stray wolves."

He shook my hand vigorously. "Of course. Happy to help. Can't have people around here all riled up. It's still the height of tourist season."

The man would do exactly what I'd told him to. He barely had a choice.

I released his hand. "Most importantly, make sure that woman gets home safely."

He rubbed his palm. "Of course."

The sheriff climbed in his SUV and started the engine. He switched off his flashers, did a U-turn, and headed back toward town. Savannah watched me suspiciously from the passenger-side window.

The red-haired woman with a tattoo on her left shoulder.

Why had the fortune teller sent me to her? How would she help me bring these killers to justice?

I picked up my phone and called Billy, my top enforcer and brother-in-law. "The county sheriff is headed your way. Follow him discreetly with your vehicle. A woman survived the attack, and he's dropping her off at home. Take two teams and stake out the place overnight. She's the first break we've gotten, and I'm betting that they'll come for her again. Make sure she doesn't get hurt."

I hung up and shoved my phone in my pocket, then headed toward the battered wolf lying on the asphalt. He'd been wolf-born like me. The wolf was our true form, and we shifted back at death. Not all shifters were like that. I knelt and examined the corpse.

Dane. I thought I had recognized the scent. I'd exiled him from the Dockside pack for inciting violence after my sister's death.

We needed to ditch the body and destroy the evidence. If we

didn't, we were going to be fucked. Another former pack member had already been implicated in one of the earlier abductions, though he'd never been found. Rumors were flying, and the Order of Magica—the body that governed all supernatural species—had threatened to revoke our pack's extralegal status unless we brought an end to the abductions. If this got out, we could lose our independence. It would be the end of pack law.

I stood and wiped my hands. Dane had been a cancer, and now he was roadkill. His actions had threatened our pack, and I had no pity for the bastard.

Regina stepped out of the woods, still half-dressed from shifting. Some shifters transformed clothes and all, but as wolfborn, Regina and I could not. We did it the real way—the original way—with snapping bones and growing claws.

From the expression on her face, she'd come up short. I asked anyway. "Any luck?"

She pulled her shirt back over her head. "None. I followed the she-wolf's trail to that crappy restaurant, but there were too many smells to track her closely. I'm betting she grabbed their car. Sorry."

"Did she smell like someone from our pack?"

Regina's eyes dilated in surprise. "No. Why?"

I nodded to the dead wolf lying on the side of the road. She crouched down and turned its head to the side. "Fuck, it's Dane."

I grimaced. "I know. Tell no one."

She stiffened. "He's got family in the pack. Surely they deserve to know."

"He's not part of our pack. I kicked him and his associates out to keep the peace in Magic Side. He's a rogue wolf, Regina. His family carries *that* burden already. They don't deserve the shame of being linked to these abductions as well. We can't have the pack implicated in this—not even our exiles. We could lose everything."

She fought back a pained expression and submitted. We had to do what was best for the reputation of his family and that of the pack.

Regina stood and looked around. "What do we do with the body?"

I grabbed the huge wolf by the scruff of the neck and heaved the corpse into the bed of our truck. "We'll bury him and say nothing."

She winced. "Should the Dockside alpha really be burying bodies in the backwoods of Wisconsin in the middle of the night?"

From some, that would have been insubordination, but she was doing her best to remind me that I wasn't my father's enforcer anymore. I was the alpha now—the master of our pack.

I wiped my hands on my pants and circled the truck. "I trust our team to a point, but someone might slip up. We can't risk anyone knowing that former Magic Side wolves were involved in this."

Regina shook her head as she opened the passenger door. "You did your father's dirty work, Jaxson. And your sister's. You need to find someone to do yours."

I grinned as I hopped in the cab. "You offering? Fine, you get to steal us a shovel."

With a snort, she buckled in. "Do we need to worry about the woman talking? How much does the dirty *wolf killer* know?"

Even if he'd been a bastard, Dane had been part of our pack once. Loyalty ran deep, and I was sure the pack would want justice. Once pack, always pack.

I started the engine. "The woman knows nothing—she doesn't even know she's got magic in her veins. Let's keep it that way."

"Do you think they'll come after her again?"

"I'm counting on it. The abductors targeted her for a reason. On top of that, she killed one wolf and can ID the other who attacked her. She's as good as dead if we can't protect her."

Regina cocked her head to the side. "Shouldn't we get her back to Magic Side? We have a safehouse, you know. We could prosecute her under pack law once this is over."

I growled, and she averted her eyes. "In an ideal world, yes. But right now, we don't have any clues to work from. We don't know why the abductions are happening or where the rogue wolves have set up their base of operations—if they even have one. The best chance we have of tracking them down is capturing one and getting it to talk. So we stay here and wait for the she-wolf to come back."

My second nodded. "You want to use the redhead as bait."

The dark, empty highway stretched ahead of us. Somewhere down the road, a small-town girl was heading home, completely ignorant of the monsters lurking in every shadow.

Savannah was going to lead me to answers, one way or another.

I tightened my jaw. "I'm going to find out who's behind these abductions and bring them down by whatever means necessary —even if I have to lure them with that woman."

4

Savannah

I was pretty damn sure that Jaxson Laurent had brainwashed the sheriff. How, I didn't know.

On our way home, I tried talking things over with Kep, but he was implausibly committed to the theory that it had been a wolf attack and that no abductors were involved. Worse, he wasn't going to investigate.

"I understand things seem muddled, Savannah," the sheriff explained, "so look at it this way—if you had actually run down someone on the road, that would be manslaughter. And jail time. So let's not dig too deeply, eh? It's better this way."

I sat on my hands to make sure I didn't strangle him. Kepler's point of view made perfect sense, but I knew what I'd seen standing in the middle of the highway, and it wasn't a furry dog. I *needed* the truth. I'd been assaulted and nearly abducted, and it could happen again.

Frustration near to boiling, I gave up trying to talk to Kep and replayed the events in my mind as we rumbled down the moonlit road. Some things I just couldn't make sense of—the claws, the glowing eyes, and the man in the black truck. But I understood a few things.

I'd been attacked by a couple. They were probably behind the other abductions. And they had targeted me, specifically.

Moreover, I was willing to bet that they'd grabbed Madison Lee—the red-haired woman on TV—by accident. They'd been looking for me. The tattooed man had even said, "We can't fuck this up again," right before they jumped me.

I sucked in a deep breath. Who the hell were they, and why were they after me? I had to find out. That was priority one. Unfortunately, it seemed like Laurent was whitewashing things over. He'd already gotten to the sheriff.

Who was he? Bad news, that was who.

He certainly wasn't from the Wisconsin DNR. I'd checked his plates—Illinois. So who did he work for, then? The FBI? CIA? The men in black?

My godmother, Alma, had always had crazy ideas about government spooks. Maybe her theories weren't so kooky after all.

And what was it with his eyes? The attackers' irises had turned crimson when they came after me. Laurent's had gone honey gold a couple of times while we were talking. I'd never seen anything like it until tonight.

My heart raced. Was he in league with my attackers? Either covering things up or working with them?

Probably not.

With those muscles and powerful frame, Laurent could have taken me then and there if he'd wanted. Just the thought of that sent shivers down my spine. There was no chance Kepler would've put up a fight. The sheriff was two years away from retiring—at least, everyone hoped so.

Then what was Laurent's game?

My stomach churned with the endless possibilities, and I

was nauseated by the time we finally pulled up in front of my godmother's house.

Our place was impossible to miss, even in the moonlight. The yard was decorated with all sorts of strange things. Pinwheels, chimes, too many hummingbird feeders. Sculptures with glass balls that didn't quite qualify as art but didn't really count as anything else. They were like flashing neon signs that screamed, *We are weird here.*

"This is you." The sheriff rapped his knuckles on the wheel. "Are you going to be all right?"

With a sigh, I heaved my tired bones out of the cruiser. "Thanks, Kep. Alma will set me right."

"I'm sure she will." He closed the door and waited for me to go in.

I picked my way along the meditation pathway that wound haphazardly around the house and up to the front porch. Alma walked it every day to realign her energy, but I was amazed that she hadn't broken an ankle. The path was strewn with tripping hazards: hoses, rakes, and potted plants that had migrated from where they belonged.

I took the stairs of our rickety wooden porch two at a time.

Alma was sitting on the living room couch, sipping a cup of tea with a giant twig in it that I didn't recognize. She brushed her long gray hair back from her face. "What's the matter, honey? Your energy is completely off."

I tried to speak but couldn't find the words to explain what had happened.

"Gosh, Savannah, you're hurt!" She jumped up and wrapped her arms around me, and the tension and terror drained from my body. If I ever needed my energy reset, her arms were the place to start. She was a font of goodness, calm, and inner beauty.

And she was all I had left in the world.

I looked down at my right arm. Blood had hardened along a set of claw-like scrapes. I snapped my gaze away, unable to think about how I had acquired those.

Alma got hot water and a washcloth and started fussing over my wound. My sweet godmother had taken care of me ever since my parents died six years ago, when our house had burned down. The ignorant local newspaper speculated that it had been a meth lab explosion, but I didn't believe it for a second.

The night of their death, Alma had grabbed me from a friend's house and brought me to live in Belmont. *People might be coming for you*, she'd warned. She wouldn't say why, but I'd known my parents were mixed up in something. I'd even changed my name to hers—Caine—and we'd never gone back up north.

Alma forced the cup of tea into my hands. "Drink this. It will realign your chakras. And tell me everything."

I breathed in the earthy scent and took a sip. It tasted like dirt and smelled like cow patties, but if it could clear my head, I'd drink a gallon of it.

Alma sat and wrung her hands as I filled her in on every detail. The claws and scarlet eyes she took in stride, but when I mentioned Jaxson Laurent and his effect on the sheriff, she went ashen. "A government man. Oh gosh, Savy, this is *dire*."

My godmother lived in fear of the shadowy government men lurking in the corners of her imagination. I'd always assumed it was simply tin-hat paranoia, but now I pictured the man with the black truck stepping out into the headlights, a mysterious silhouette.

"What do I do?" I mumbled, too exhausted to think.

"You gotta get out of town, Savy!"

Then she darted from the room, leaving my jaw flapping in the wind.

A moment later, Alma rushed back in, dragging an empty, oversized suitcase. "I was always afraid this day would come."

"What do you mean?"

"Well, it's gotta be the sins of your parents coming back on you. When I brought you here, I knew it was only a matter of time before someone came looking."

Had my parents really been so deep in the shit that people would come hunting me six years later? "It can't be my parents' mess," I protested. "There've been four other abductions."

Alma pressed a slip of paper into my hand. "Honey, I don't know if it was related to the explosion that killed them, but they knew someone would come."

I unfolded the paper to find a note—to my surprise, one written in my father's hand: *If anything happens to us, watch over Savannah. Get her away. If you think there is danger, or if anyone comes looking, send her to Laurel LaSalle, 7546 Wildhaven Ave, Magic Side, Chicago.*

Confusion tore through me, and I had to steady myself against the doorframe. My parents had known. What in God's name had they been wrapped up in?

I looked up from the note. "Who is Laurel LaSalle?"

"Your aunt."

The world spun, and I shook my head, not quite comprehending. "I have an aunt? And you *knew*?"

My heart raced. I tried to steady my emotions, but it was impossible, and anger crept under my skin. As long as I'd lived, my family had just been me, my folks, and Alma. I clenched my jaw. Why had she kept this from me?

The old woman sat on the low couch and looked down at her entwined fingers. "I knew you had family in Illinois, but that's neither here nor there. Your parents always said that if anything happened to them, they wanted me to raise you here in this town. That no one else was to be involved."

The reality of the situation rolled over me as I reasoned things out.

I'd never met an aunt. Never even heard of one. My folks had died when I was sixteen, and Chicago wasn't far. There had been plenty of opportunities to meet in those sixteen years.

This wasn't Alma's deception.

I let the note droop in my hand. "They didn't want me to know."

She nodded. "Your folks never told me much. They were wrapped up in some kind of bad business, though I'm not sure what it was. They went up north to disappear. The only thing your mom ever told me is that your dad came from extremely dangerous people. Deadly people."

I dropped down on the couch beside her. *I have an aunt.*

Alma sat quietly, perched rigidly on the edge of the cushion. I could almost taste her emotions—a bitter chicory taste, like dandelion root.

"Why didn't my aunt come for me? After Mom and Dad died?"

She shook her gray hair and took my hand. "All I know is that your folks loved you more than anything in the world. And if they didn't want you to know about your family in Chicago, then it was for your own protection."

"So what about now?"

"It sounds like the boogeyman has come to town."

I swallowed hard, and we sat silently, hand in hand, with only the sound of the wooden chimes clacking outside.

Finally, I stood. "I'm being hunted. The backwoods couple targeted me."

Alma nodded. "Sounds like."

"I have no idea why they're after me, but I need to figure it out. The local authorities think I'm a nutter, and the whole thing is being whitewashed by a government man in a black truck."

"Typical."

"There's a chance that this could be linked to my parents, and they left a note that if ever someone came looking for me, I should go—"

"Don't tell me!" Alma interjected.

"What?"

"Ah, ah, ah." Alma plugged her ears. "If a government man comes asking me where you've gone, I sure as hell don't want to know the truth. As far as I know, you've gone off to Tuscaloosa for art school, like you always planned."

"But you already—"

Alma shoved me toward my room. "Get your butt in gear and get packing for art school!"

I shook my head in a daze. I loved Alma, but she was a certified, tin-hat nutter.

Man, I hoped it hadn't worn off on me.

Suddenly, my stomach sank. "My car is in the shop. Randy had to tow it."

Alma pulled a wad of cash out of her pocket and held it out. "Get him to fix it, fast."

I pushed the money back. "I can't take that."

"I've been saving it up. You'll need it to get that hunk of rubbish to wherever you're going."

Surrendering, I accepted her gift, then yanked a small bag from under my bed—the sleepover bag I'd had the night our house burned down. It was full of unmentionables and dust, but also a few things I'd need if I ever had to run. My stomach twisted. All these years, I'd kept a bug-out-bag under my bed, as if some part of me knew that I'd never be safe.

I started haphazardly hurling underwear and socks inside. Was I really going to split town?

I'd never been one to run from my problems. Usually, I just kicked them in the nuts and made them pay their tab.

These aren't your typical kick-em-in-the-nuts problems, Savy.

But the man with the black truck had warned me not to leave town. More than anything, that told me shit was going down. In my experience, when someone told you to stand still and close your eyes, you needed to duck the hell out of the way.

Maybe a dangerous family was just what I needed right now.

"I'm not running," I said to my socks and unmentionables. "I'm going to figure out why the hell people are hunting me."

To do that, I needed to find out about my family in Chicago, and why they were so dangerous that my parents never risked telling me about them.

Out of the frying pan and into the fire.

Too bad I didn't like to cook.

5

Jaxson

I checked my watch and knotted my fists. One p.m.

The she-wolf was out there hunting, while I was stuck in my hotel room, renegotiating every single deal we had with the scattered Great Lakes packs. They were using the abductions and rumors to damage our reputation and to squeeze me for concessions.

I growled at the werewolf on the laptop screen. "We've had the same right-of-passage deal with your pack for thirty years. The deal should stay. Nothing's changed."

Mac, the alpha of the Upper Peninsula pack, stroked his grizzled beard. "But it has. We don't want your city wolves anywhere near our territory, not until these abductions stop. Sorry, Jax, but that's the way it is."

"We have nothing to do with the abductions."

Mac leaned forward. "From what I hear, CCTV caught the license plate of the abductors' truck after an attack last month. It was registered to one of your wolves."

Fuck. The Order leaked information like a sieve. Was that detail what had initially started all the rumors about our pack?

Regina shifted uncomfortably beside me. She could smell my rage. "It was a stolen vehicle belonging to an ex-member of the pack. Nothing to do with us," she interjected.

Mac ignored the comment and moved closer to the camera. "Then, I hear that three days ago, a trio of wolves killed a witch while trying to abduct him. Two were shifters, but one was *wolf-born*. That sort of cooperation doesn't happen up here. But in Dockside...yuh guys are a bit of a mixed breed."

And I'm pretty sure that that wolfborn was Dane.

I had to restrain my claws and keep calm. Mac couldn't smell me lying, though Regina would. "These are rumors and speculations. No one from Dockside is involved. But clearly, you want to renegotiate deals. Fine. Good luck getting your fucking product distributed in Magic Side without us."

Did he really expect me to roll over? I would cripple his pack first and watch them come begging on their bellies.

My old friend raised his hands. "Hold on, Jax. Are you serious? I'm just talking concessions, here."

My phone rang. *Tony.*

"I have to take this." I slammed the laptop shut and strode out onto the concrete balcony of the shitty motel—the only one in Belmont—then answered the call. "What do you have?"

"The woman is on the move," Tony said. "We assume she's going to check on her car. Should we pursue?"

More trouble. "Don't pursue," I replied. "I should be the main point of contact. Is she in a vehicle? On foot?"

Tony paused. "Rollerblades."

My eyebrows shot up. "What?"

"Skates. Moving fast."

I shook my head. Rollerblades? Who was this woman?

"Okay, I'll go after her. You swing by the Taphouse. See if anyone shows up." I hung up and summoned Regina. "We need to go. Now."

She locked the door behind us. "What's up?"

I pulled my keys from my pocket as we walked to the truck. "Caine seems to be going for her car. We need to make sure it's not fixed for a while, not until the she-wolf shows up again."

"Can't you send someone else? That was an important meeting you just shut down."

The Upper Peninsula assholes were the least of my worries, and I growled as I unlocked the F-250. "*This* is important. Stopping the abductions is important. Caine's attackers probably know that you and I are in town. Word travels fast in places like this. I don't want anyone else on our team breaking cover."

We loaded up and rumbled out of the parking lot. My palms itched. Something told me the woman was going to be a problem.

Once we turned onto the county road, we overtook her quickly. Between our truck and her bright blue rollerblades, it was no contest. Still, I stared in fascination as we approached. She bent low and thrust her long, lean legs side to side as she glided down the road with a pair of white sneakers slung over her shoulder. Her motions were so fluid and elegant, it was like a dance, and the way her ass flexed beneath those cut-off shorts stoked a heat deep within me.

I slowed as we drove around her. For safety.

Regina glared at the woman as we passed. "That wolf killer should be standing trial before pack law, not skating around town."

Disgust tinged her words, but I understood. Savannah had killed a pack member. I'd kicked Dane out, but once pack, always pack. Self-defense or not, there needed to be some sort of justice for his family.

Regina's eyes seemed to say, *Your sister wouldn't have hesitated to drag Savannah in by her long red hair.* Stephanie had believed in the Old Ways, just as plenty of the pack did.

She would have been the alpha one day.

I tightened my grip on the wheel. "The seer told me the woman will lead us to answers. We need her for now, and we'll protect her until we don't."

Regina stiffened. "You shouldn't have gone to that fortune teller. Divination is one of the dark arts."

I said nothing.

"Only the moon-mother knows the future," Regina pressed. "You should have at least warned me."

Our pack forbid the perverse practices of the occult. My sister would never have gone to a seer. But Stephanie was dead, I was in charge, and we were desperate.

Fuck the old rules.

"The seer got us this far," I muttered.

She snorted. "And what, are you going to start breaking all our taboos? Will you try scrying next?"

It was impossible for our kind to use that kind of magic, but I gave her a warning growl. "I'll do whatever it takes to protect the pack."

Regret tinged her eyes. "Which is why I worry, Jaxson. There will be a hidden cost. The fates take as much as they give."

"I know."

While I hadn't told Regina, the seer had already warned me. *If you find the woman, you will find the answers you seek. But those answers will destroy you.*

That didn't matter—the pack did, and I'd deal with my own destruction when the time came. For now, I needed to end this madness.

Regina checked her side mirror and crossed her arms. "So, what are we going to do with the woman, then? Just sit around and watch her skate?"

That would be a good view.

Regina would smell my arousal at that thought, so I growled

and took control of the conversation. "If you want to string her up for what she did to Dane, you can bet that his she-wolf partner will want to rip Caine to shreds."

"It's a good thing those two abductors weren't a mated pair."

She was right. If they'd been true mates, the she-wolf wouldn't have run. She'd have ripped her way through the car doors and torn Savannah limb from limb or died trying. I'd seen it happen before: Billy, my brother-in-law, had gone berserk when my sister died. It had taken all my strength—and my father's—to stop him from starting a war with the fucking sorcerers who'd killed her.

But even if those two weren't mates, the missing abductor was a wolf, and she would come looking for vengeance.

"Then what's our plan?" Regina asked, stirring me from the echoes of Stephanie's death.

"I'll make sure the mechanic doesn't fix Caine's car. Then you and I will pretend to head out of town this evening and circle back through the woods. I'm hoping the she-wolf will return as soon as we're gone, and the rest of the team can jump her and beat some answers out of her."

It didn't take long to pass through Belmont. The town was insignificant, and you could miss it if you blinked. I pulled into Randy's Auto Body and parked in front of one of the open bay doors. Savannah Caine's car sat in the second bay.

No one was in the dingy little office. I didn't have the time or patience to wait, so I ducked into the dark garage. My eyes adjusted after a second, and I saw a mechanic with his head down behind the open hood of Caine's Gran Fury. "Are you Randy?" I asked.

The man stood straight and grabbed a stained towel. "Yep. How can I help you?"

"My truck needs an oil change." It didn't need a thing, but humans couldn't smell lies like werewolves could.

Randy started wiping grime off his fingers. "How about this afternoon?"

"I'm in a hurry. I'll pay extra." It wasn't a request.

The mechanic glanced back at the woman's battered car, weighing his priorities. It was the perfect opening. "Hell, that thing looks like it's in pretty bad shape."

He nodded. "You can say that again. Poor girl ran over a wolf last night. Look at these claw marks—it's like the damn thing attacked the car. Thank the Lord that monster is dead. They should shoot them all."

Instead of ramming my claws into Randy's eyes, I forced my fist to relax. "How bad is it?"

"Well, that depends." The mechanic scratched his head with still-greasy fingers. "The owner wants it back pronto, and it's technically running. I just had to reconnect a few radiator hoses. How the radiator isn't cracked in half, I don't know. A surprising amount of the damage is cosmetic."

I stepped close and let my alpha presence wash over the man. "It seems like the damage is a lot worse. Are you comfortable sending the woman out on the road in a vehicle that isn't roadworthy? Does your insurance cover that?"

The reek of the mechanic's rising shame and guilt flooded my senses. He rubbed his chin. "I guess I hadn't really thought of it that way. I've known Savannah for a few years. Nice girl. I wouldn't be able to live with myself if something happened to her because I didn't fix her car right."

I nodded. My alpha presence worked best if I led people to conclusions that matched their beliefs. The sheriff hadn't wanted to believe that monsters could be in his Podunk town, so he'd readily accepted that everything was a wolf attack. The mechanic, on the other hand, probably prided himself on his work and reputation.

I fished a coil of bills out of my pocket and started counting hundreds. Randy's eyes widened as I thrust the wad of cash into his hand. "I'm sure it will take weeks if you're going to fix it right. This is a down payment. I'll pay the entire bill at twice the normal price, just make sure you take your time. And don't tell the woman about our arrangement."

He nodded slowly and took the money.

I tossed him the keys. "First, my oil change."

Randy caught them in cupped hands and headed out front to pull my F-250 into the empty bay, leaving me alone with the Gran Fury.

I checked over my shoulder and extended my claws, preparing to sabotage a few important components of the engine, but Regina gave a low whistle, and I froze.

Retracting my claws, I stepped to the edge of the garage just as Savannah came zipping down the street.

6

Savannah

Oof. Rollerblading was way harder than I remembered.

I hadn't been on skates since I was sixteen. A lot had changed since then, including my shoe size, and my feet were screaming expletives at the rest of my body.

Alma didn't have a car anymore, her old bird-shit-blue bike had a flat, and I didn't want to spring for a taxi—not that they were easy to get around here. As a last resort, I'd pulled my old blades out of the closet. I'd had them with me when Alma had whisked me off to Belmont, and I hadn't put them on since. Skates were for children, and after Mom and Dad died, I was no longer a child.

Once I pushed past the pain in my feet and legs, I embraced the euphoria of speed and being on the open road with the wind in my hair. I'd worked up a sweat and my blouse was damp, so the breeze felt divine.

Actually, these rollerblades were still pretty fun.

I whipped around a bend, and Randy's Auto Body appeared down the road. The parking lot out front was empty, but there was a black truck with Illinois plates in the left-hand bay. My stomach twisted, and bile rose in my throat. What the hell was that asshole doing here?

I glided into the lot and started applying the heel brake when a dark shape stepped out of the shadows of the garage. I jerked back, my foot caught some gravel, and I launched into the air.

Instead of hitting the pavement, I jerked as two strong arms grabbed me and hauled me up onto my unsteady feet. A jolt of electricity ran through my body, and a shiver danced across my skin.

Jaxson Laurent. A light breeze carried his forest-scented cologne, and heat rushed to my lower belly. His pupils dilated as his dark eyes penetrated mine.

Oh, God.

With my cheeks burning like I'd spent the day in the sun, I awkwardly disentangled myself from his strong arms and balanced ungracefully on my blades. I was a sweaty mess, and my blouse stuck to my body in awkward places.

Jaxson, on the other hand, was just as gorgeous as he'd been last night, only today he was wearing a business suit that contrasted well with his tousled hair and stubble-lined jaw. His deep brown eyes traced over my body, and his lips quirked into a smile. "You should keep your eyes on the road."

I drew in a ragged breath as his smoky voice skated over my nerve endings. "I hit a pebble."

Blood rushed to my already red face. That was all I could say? Desperate to rekindle my dignity, I snapped, "What the hell are you doing here?"

"Oil change. What are you doing here, Ms. Caine? Not planning to leave town, I hope?"

I sure the hell am.

Something about him made the hair on my neck stand on

end, though I couldn't quite put a finger on it. Power. Presence. An undercurrent of danger.

I dragged my gaze from his. "I'm checking on my car. I was in an accident last night, remember?"

He smiled, though it was nowhere near genuine. "I do. And as luck would have it, we've been wanting to ask you a few questions about what happened. Let me introduce Regina Martin."

A chestnut-haired woman stepped up to his side and held out her hand. Her smile didn't reach her eyes—not even close. While Jaxson's expression had been a pleasant façade, the one on her face was an abject lie. I could smell it on her. While her extended hand said, *Let's be friends*, everything else about her said, *I want to leave your body in a ditch*.

Nuh-uh. I knew better than to shake hands with people like that. "Sorry, I'm here for my car. Maybe another time." I leaned to the side so I could peek into the garage, only to find that Randy was busy working on Jaxson's ride, not mine.

That ass. Ignoring Regina's hand, I shoved off my right foot and skated around Jaxson and his sour-faced henchwoman and into the garage.

Jaxson's relentless gaze never left my back, and I couldn't stop thinking about how that made my skin feel flushed and sensitive.

It's hotter than a fish boil in here.

I stumbled over to Randy in my skates. "Hey! How's my car?"

Randy tilted his hat back on his head. "Pretty banged up. It's going to take me a couple of weeks to fix."

I couldn't have been more surprised if he'd thrown motor oil in my face. "What the shit, Randy? You told me it was running just thirty minutes ago!"

His eyes flicked over my shoulder and back. "I had a chance to take another look. If the cops don't bust you for a broken headlight, the tranny or radiator will leave you stranded somewhere you don't want to be. You need to get this fixed."

Anger boiled up inside of me, but it lacked a good outlet. While I had a nose for lies, Randy was telling the truth—my car was screwed.

The heat of Jaxson's stare was practically unbearable. I peeked over my shoulder, then leaned toward Randy and lowered my voice to a whisper. "You know I can't afford to fix all this. I'm broke, and my insurance is crap."

He smiled. "Well, there's good news. I called your insurance agency. Everything is covered, including the tranny. They won't even raise your rates."

There it was. *That* was the lie I was waiting for. Fury surged through my veins, and I fixed Randy with a soul-rending stare. "Is. That. So?"

His eyes darted over my shoulder again, telling me everything I needed to know. The goddamned spooks had gotten to him.

"You ass," I hissed, and skated out of the bay. Coasting over to the suspects, I shouted, "What did you tell him?"

"Nothing," the henchwoman said.

Truth.

I skidded to a stop in front of lying Mr. Laurent. "What did *you* tell him?"

He leaned back and shoved his hands in his pockets, a satisfied look on his face. "Why? Are you trying to go somewhere? Not with that vehicle, I hope. Especially after I asked you to stay in town last night."

"Why are you trying to keep me here?" I snapped.

He tilted his head. "Why do I have the feeling you're not going to stay put, Ms. Caine?"

I wanted to impale him with eye-daggers, but it was really difficult to be intimidating when I was barely balanced on my rollerblades. I leaned in carefully, trying not to flop on my face, and gave him the best glare I could muster. "Because people are trying to abduct me? That seems like a *damn* good reason."

The vixen chimed in. "Mr. Laurent and I are trying to stop these abductions. You're an important witness. We need you to stay in town until we can apprehend the people responsible."

I took a step back. "'Apprehend the people responsible'? Who *exactly* do you work for? I know it's not Wisconsin DNR. You have Illinois plates, so nice cover there, idiots. You're not cops, and I'm not telling you anything until you produce credentials."

"We represent an interested party," the woman said. It looked like she was interested in gutting me.

"FBI? CIA? ATF? Campbell's Soup?"

Jaxson inclined his head, and I thought I saw a flicker of gold in his eyes. Whoever he worked for had power. Control. I could practically feel it radiating off him. That, and a deep, intoxicating scent of forest and cedar.

He spoke with a voice so low and rough that it excited the nerves under my skin. "You don't need to worry about the details, Ms. Caine. While the authorities are doing nothing, we're hunting your attackers down. We just need your cooperation."

Honestly, when he said it like that, it made sense. Sheriff Kepler was a goddamned idiot, far past his prime and way out of his league. And so far, the state investigation had produced jackshit. If I wanted answers, I was going to have to cooperate with the spooks.

At least they seemed marginally competent, if exceedingly suspicious.

"I'm not blind," I said. "You showed up at the Taphouse right before I was attacked."

Jaxson looked around. "We're hunting the people who were hunting you."

Truth.

"Fine. You want my cooperation? I need answers first. Do you believe I was attacked yesterday by the same people who are responsible for the other abductions?"

He nodded. "Yes."

My heartbeat began to drown out the noise around me. Shit was getting *real.* "My assailants said, 'She's the one.' Am I being targeted?"

"That is a possibility, which is why it's safest if you just head home. We have people watching your back."

Holy hell. I was under surveillance? My heart raced, and my skin turned cold, even in the hot midday sun. These assholes had to be FBI or the actual damned men in black.

"Who's after me?" I whispered. "I need to know. Why am I being targeted?"

"I'm afraid we're not at liberty to disclose the details of the case," the woman said.

I glared at Jaxson. He'd said the same thing the night before —*lyingly.*

This was bullcrap.

I stepped forward on my blades, moving so close to Jaxson that I was sure he could hear my heartbeat. "If these psychopaths are hunting me, give me one good reason why I should stay put."

My mouth soured, and I could almost taste the frustration radiating off him. Behind those shadowy eyes, there was a man struggling to maintain control. A beast, lurking below the surface. My muscles tensed, and the hair on my neck stood on end.

Jaxson leaned down so that his mouth was next to my ear, and his breath danced over my skin. "You have no idea who or what you're dealing with, Ms. Caine, and you're not in possession of all the facts. Three people that we know of fought back, just like you did. The difference is, their entrails ended up splattered across the floor of their homes, and their bodies were ripped apart, piece by piece."

I jerked back, eyes wide.

He straightened and fixed me with a stern expression. "From your experience in the parking lot yesterday, you might imagine how."

I shook my head in denial as images of that tattooed psycho ramming his claws into the other man's chest flooded my brain. The monster had thrown the man's body onto the hood of my car like he was a rag doll. He'd grabbed my wrist—he could have just as easily gutted me and left my blood splattered across the parking lot like a Jackson Pollock painting.

Murderous psychos with claws for hands. I'd fallen into an episode of *The X-Files*.

"What the hell is going on?" I demanded. With a million questions whirling in my head, that was the only one with the strength to break free.

My vision swam, and I staggered back, but the man in black steadied me with his electric touch and raised my chin. His eyes went honey gold, and his voice turned gravelly. "Monsters are real, Ms. Caine. You can't outrun them, and wherever you go, they'll find you."

My adrenaline surged as inexplicable sensations washed over me. Cold. The scent of pine. And the taste of bitter chocolate.

Jaxson Laurent loomed over me, and I couldn't help but gaze into his glowing eyes. "You're in danger. I am the only one who can protect you, but only if you do as you're told. Stay in your house unless you're at work. Don't leave town. I will take care of everything else."

My mind whirled, and my stomach lurched. *Monsters are real, and they're hunting me.*

Somehow, part of me had known that all along. At least I finally had the answer I needed. I was in danger, and Jaxson Laurent was the only one who could protect me.

Truth.

Verging on tears, I backed away. "I've gotta get home."

He nodded.

I turned, pushed off with my skates, and raced toward the house. *Everything will be okay if I do as I'm told. Go home. Don't leave town.*

Jaxson would take care of the rest.

Each thrust of my legs took me one step closer to safety, one step further from the nightmare that had become my life. The wheels of my blades whirred, and I was one with the road.

That was, until I hit a pothole and spiraled head over heels.

The asphalt ripped into my knees and elbows, and fire coursed through my nerves. Tears formed in the corner of my eyes, and I rolled over to stare at the sun, now tilting far past noon.

What the hell are you doing, Savy?

Head throbbing, I staggered to my feet and glanced back at Randy's Auto Body in the distance. I'd gone to reclaim my car so I could skip town, and suddenly, I was running home like a frightened girl.

Who the hell was Jaxson Laurent, and what spell did he have over me? When he was near, I couldn't think or shake the overwhelming urge to *please* him.

He must have some pretty damn freaky pheromones.

I started skating again, slower now as lucidity returned to my thoughts.

Monsters were hunting me, and the spooks were hunting them. All I had to do was go home, close my eyes, and wait in ignorant bliss for the nightmare to be over. I just needed to obey the man with the honey eyes. But if I chose that path, I'd never get any straight answers. Jaxson wouldn't even tell me who he worked for.

What choice do I have?

My original plan? I could grab my piece of shit car, blow out of town, and hope that I could make it all the way to Chicago in order to...what? Get answers by hunting down a family that was so dangerous, my parents never told me about them?

Option two was utterly preposterous. No guarantees. High risk of failure.

But it was a chance for answers. Real answers.

I bit my lip and slammed on my heel brakes.

Screw it. I'd never been any good at doing what I was told.

I rounded the corner and raced down the alley until I reached the rear of Randy's shop. The back door was open to let the breeze through, so I sneaked in—well, as best I could on skates. Jaxson and his evil vixen were gone, so I stepped over the clutter of hoses and car parts, and smacked Randy on the shoulder.

He spun. "*Hell*, Savannah! You nearly gave me a heart attack! What are you doing?"

I grabbed his shirt. "Will my car run?"

His eyes went wide. "Y–y–yes."

"I'm taking it."

"Savannah," he said, finally getting a full word out, "these people are going to pay for all the fixes to your car. I can do anything, it's a blank check! It'll be better than before. I could make a lot of money. You could have a new ride."

My car was the most important thing I owned. The last thing my parents had given me. It was filled with promises and broken dreams. But I wasn't a rube, and I stuck my hip out. "Doesn't that sound sketchy to you? Nothing in life is free."

"But it's a lot of mon—"

I tightened my grip and gave him *the look*.

I didn't use it much, just on special occasions. In high school, people had called me "Crazy Eyes." That was fine by me because I loved *Orange is the New Black* and Uzo Aduba, and I didn't really care what people said—as long as I got what I wanted.

It wasn't like I'd had any friends to lose.

Randy, the hapless ass, was now on the receiving end of *the look*.

"Let me explain things to you, Rand-dee. I'm taking my car. You're not going to tell Jaxson or that mean-looking woman, and you're not going to fess up when they come asking. You don't know them. You know *me*. I designed your stupid auto body logo, for what it's worth. Help me now. I need to get out of town."

It was like I was a different person when I was angry. Like I had a snarling, raging force inside me that demanded to be free.

I guess that's what happened when your parents blew themselves to bits, and you had to spend the rest of your life walking with your head down.

Randy looked around nervously. "I'm sorry, but there's no way I'm going to help you. Those people seem like they leave bodies in places where they're never found. But I've really got to piss, and I'm going to go use the restroom. If you happened to go by the office and take your keys and leave while I'm gone, there'd be nothing I could do about that."

I let him go. He looked about ready to wet himself, so it was a pretty good call either way.

Randy hurried off to the restroom, and I staggered awkwardly to the office on my rollerblades. I was really glad there weren't cameras because I probably looked like an utter idiot.

My keys were hanging on a hook inside the door...right next to Jaxson Laurent's.

Sometimes, life gave you lemonade, and you didn't even need to squeeze the lemons.

A minute later, I was safe in the heavenly confines of my Gran Fury, desperately struggling to yank my rollerblades off. They'd been hell to get on, but this was worse. I didn't even bother putting on my tennies—I just chucked them on the passenger side along with the blades.

I fired up the engine, took one second to savor the low rumble of freedom, and rolled out of the garage as quietly as possible. Once I was a couple blocks away, I hit the gas and raced home.

Soon, doubt crept into my mind. The spooks might be watching me. But I was already committed, and I'd have to risk it.

I called Alma and explained the situation. As soon as I as screeched to a halt in front of our house, she dragged my bags down the front steps, and we threw them in the car. I kissed her and my familiar life goodbye in under a minute. Then I hit the open road.

I didn't bother throwing Jaxson's truck keys out the window until an hour later when I was in Illinois, roaring down US-20 on my way to Chicago.

Savannah

The trip to Chicago sucked.

My old Gran Fury struggled to stay over fifty, so I had to take side routes. With the summer heat and the passenger window broken, it was like I had a hair dryer blasting in my face the whole way. Heading to Chicago was probably a terrible plan, verging on horrendous. I shuddered as I recalled Jaxson's warning. *Monsters are real, Ms. Caine. You can't outrun them, and wherever you go, they'll find you.*

I dialed the old radio to 101.5 FM for a little rock. The speakers had a tendency to crackle and pop and sounded pretty hollow compared to my headphones, but I loved the hazy sound. "Werewolves of London" by Warren Zevon came on, and I started to sing along. The ridiculousness of it lifted my soul.

Monsters. Ha! What a bunch of bullshit. But something dangerous was definitely going on. I just had to figure out what it was.

Why had people attacked me? Did it have something to do with my parents? Or who I was? The questions kept looping through my mind like a broken record. I needed answers...but I also needed protection, and I hoped Laurel LaSalle could offer both.

My parents had kept my relatives a secret for a reason. If they were so dangerous, then maybe they were dangerous enough to keep the monsters at bay.

Of course, all of that hinged on whether Laurel LaSalle would be happy to see me, which was a pretty substantial assumption.

Hi. I'm your estranged batshit-crazy niece who thinks she's being hunted by people with scarlet eyes and clawed hands.

Maybe I wouldn't lead with the monsters bit.

I fingered the note in my pocket. It had to count for something.

There was just one tiny hitch in my plan to find my aunt: I couldn't pull her address up in Google Maps, which didn't seem to recognize a 7546 Wildhaven Avenue in a neighborhood called Magic Side. That wasn't entirely surprising. My phone was an old Walmart POS. But at least Chicago was on a grid, so I had a backup plan. I decided that I'd come into the city on 75th Street and drive west until I found Wildhaven Avenue.

Three hours later, the Gran Fury was dangerously close to overheating, and I'd nearly run out of 75th Street. I'd gone slowly, asked for directions twice, and checked the well-hidden signs at every cross-street, but there'd been no sign of Wildhaven or Magic Side.

Apparently, I'd made several flawed assumptions about how the Chicago grid system worked.

Pangs of hunger clawed at my stomach, and the stupidity of it all drove tears of frustration into my eyes. I rumbled over some train tracks and just kept driving because I didn't know what else to do. Businesses with gated windows gave way to apartment buildings, and just as I was about to cross South Shore Drive, I finally saw the sign: *Magic Side Exit.*

The arrow pointed straight ahead.

Goddamned Google Maps.

I wiped my runny eyes with the back of my wrist and drove along the tree-lined street with my pulse racing. The buildings stopped, replaced by Lake Michigan, a dark expanse of water that glistened in the setting sun. I took the exit onto a long bridge that stretched over the lake toward Magic Side. A wide channel separated the suburb from the rest of Chicago, and I spotted the faint outline of another long bridge to the north. Apparently, Magic Side was an island, like Manhattan.

Parks full of dark trees lined the lakefront, and the skyscrapers rising from the north end of the island mirrored those of downtown Chicago. The air over the whole city seemed to shimmer in the twilight.

I glanced at my phone. Google Maps showed me driving over a barren stretch of lake. I reached over and zoomed out. Still no island. I released a deep, exasperated sigh that felt like it contained all the frustration of the day. No wonder I couldn't find my aunt's address—the damn phone wasn't loading that part of the map.

The stress of the drive flooded out of me. Now that I'd found Magic Side, it should be easy to find my aunt's house, even in the dark—with or without stupid Google Maps. I flexed my hands on the wheel, feeling confident about my choices for the first time all day.

Then my car died.

The headlights went out, and I lost power completely. The car rolled to a halt smack dab in the middle of the bridge, probably half a mile from either end.

My stomach knotted. The Gran Fury was dead quiet.

I broke the silence by screaming at the top of my lungs and pounding on the steering wheel.

Headlights swept through the car, and a horn blared as a Jeep swerved around me, bringing me back to my senses. I was sitting in a dark-brown car with no lights on a dark bridge in the middle of a lake. I tried turning the ignition but didn't have any power at all, so I couldn't turn on the emergency flashers. I should have packed road flares, but who actually had road flares?

Should I get out and flag someone down? My imagination conjured up visions of me standing on the bridge and getting smashed against the guard rail when some idiot driver rammed into the rear end of my nearly invisible vehicle.

A truck raced by, honking furiously.

Hands trembling, I called roadside assistance and explained the situation.

"Where are you, ma'am?"

"I'm on the bridge between South Side Chicago and Magic Side."

There was a pause on the other end of the line. "Ma'am, right now your cell phone location is showing you in the middle of Lake Michigan. Can you help us pinpoint your actual location? Do you see any road signs?"

"I *am* in the middle of Lake Michigan. There's a bridge right off 75th Street that connects to the giant island."

The dispatcher paused again. "I'm not finding the island you're talking about."

"The one right off Chicago! With two bridges! I'm on the south bridge!"

"Ma'am, have you been drinking tonight?"

I hung up and squeezed my phone in rage, which accidently

prompted Google Assistant to pop up with a message: "Hi, how can I help?"

My eyes clouded with tears, but I was desperate. Maybe it would have an answer. "Where am I?" I muttered weakly.

"Your current location is Lake Michigan, Illinois," Google Assistant said in a cheerful voice.

Mid-curse, rolling blue and white lights flashed in my rearview mirror. The cops. Every muscle in my body relaxed. Apparently, the dispatcher had figured things out.

The white police cruiser rolled past and pulled to a stop in front of me. It had *Magic Side Police* written in big red letters beneath a blue stripe.

At least I was in the right place. I eagerly cranked down my window.

A female cop got out of the car, flicked on a flashlight, and sauntered over. She pointed it in my face, rather unnecessarily. "You're sitting in the dark with your lights off in the middle of a busy bridge. Are you in need of assistance?"

Pretty obvious, *yeah.*

I kept my hands on the steering wheel, not knowing what these city cops were like. Probably not like old Sheriff Kepler. "Yes, please. My car stalled, and I can't turn on the emergency flashers."

The cop nodded, returned to her car, and dug some flares out of the trunk. She made a perimeter around my car and came back to the window. "License and registration."

I had them ready and handed them over.

The cop looked at them and then handed them back. "I'll need to see your *other* ID."

"What other ID?"

She sighed. "I'm guessing this is your first time coming to Magic Side?"

I nodded.

She typed something into a tablet. "Reason for visit?"

God, it was like going to another country. Magic Side wasn't part of Canada, was it? Did I need a passport? I shrugged, searching for a response. "I have family here. I'm visiting my aunt."

The cop looked at her tablet. "Any weapons or dangerous concoctions in the vehicle?"

"What? No!"

"Ma'am, I'm going to have to ask you to stay in your car and hand over your keys. I've got an alert on your license plate, and I need to hold you here until the proper authorities arrive."

I handed my keys over in a daze. The Gran Fury wasn't even running. It didn't matter.

She walked back to her car, calling in something on her radio. I couldn't hear the words over the pounding of my heart.

What was happening?

Then the hard truth hit me like a brick.

Somehow, I'd just stumbled onto a government black site. It all added up. The city wasn't on the map. I needed another kind of ID, probably military. The cop was acting weird and asking strange questions. And they already had an alert on my license plate.

That meant one thing. They knew I was coming. The man in the black truck—Jaxson, if that was his real name—had tipped them off.

Holy shit. Alma's crazy tin-hat conspiracy theories had been right all along.

I had definitely seen something I shouldn't have. Who attacked me? Some kind of super soldier on the loose?

I was so in over my head.

My pulse raced. *I've got to run.*

But then again, if I did that, they would probably shoot me. I gripped the wheel in desperation and indecision.

Then a pair of high beam headlights rolled to a stop behind me, and a car door slammed.

I glanced in the rearview mirror as a well-built shadow stepped into the headlights. I'd know that silhouette anywhere.

Jaxson Laurent.

8

Savannah

I clenched the wheel with both hands and watched the black silhouette slowly approach in the rearview mirror.

I'm a goner.

He paused beside my window, placed both hands against the car, and bent low. I slowly turned my head to meet his gaze.

Gold flickered in his dark-brown eyes. "Ms. Caine, I thought I told you to stay in Belmont."

I was so scared that my hands trembled on the wheel, but his silvery voice still sent shivers down my spine. There were times for pride and there were times for figuring out how not to end up at the bottom of a lake. This was the latter, so I begged. "I'm sorry. I know that maybe I saw something I shouldn't have, and that I shouldn't be here. Just please let me go. I won't say anything. Please don't kill me."

A long pause hung in the air as the man stared, dumbfounded. "What in the hell are you talking about?"

I turned away and kept my gaze locked straight forward. "I know this definitely *isn't* some kind of secret facility, but if it was,

I sure as *hell* wouldn't be dumb enough to mention it to anyone. Ever. Swear to God. I just really want to live."

"What?"

I flicked my eyes toward the city at the far end of the bridge.

He leaned closer. "If you're implying that this is some kind of government black site, it's not. It's a city like any other. The police are here. You're safe."

His voice was calm and soothing, and a compulsion to meet his eyes again came over me. They were now a deep honey gold, and an inexplicable wave of relief relaxed my muscles.

Then a cascade of sensations overwhelmed my senses. The rich scent of moss and pine. The taste of fresh snow and smoke. And I could almost hear a brook running over smooth stones. It felt like my heart was trying to leap out of my chest.

What the shit was happening to me?

A part of me was suddenly certain that everything was going to be okay. I was safe, the cops were here. I was probably the safest I'd ever been. But the other part of my mind knew something wasn't quite right. "The city's not on the map."

Jaxson pulled out his cellphone and opened Waze. "It's on *my* map. You might need an update."

I wasn't sure if my bargain-basement cellphone could even be updated.

Reality sank in, and blood rushed to my face. I'd let Alma's paranoia make an ass out of me. *Again.* Shit like this was why high school had nearly driven me crazy and I didn't have friends.

I channeled my embarrassment into anger. "Then why are you here, stalking me? And why is there an alert on my plates?"

"Beside the fact that you stole my truck keys?" he growled, releasing a spark of restrained fury.

I blushed deeper. "If I had, which I didn't, that's not the reason why you're after me."

Jaxson gave a deep, *God-give-me-patience* sigh. "You're a witness. We need your help. You've been targeted. You could be in danger. All of which I explained when I told you not to leave town."

"But why me?"

"As for why you were targeted, I don't know. As for why we need you, you're the only person who can identify the assailants."

"So you tracked me all the way to Magic Side?"

He looked me up and down with a stony gaze. "I think the bigger question, Ms. Caine, is what are you doing here?"

Suspicion made the hair on my neck stand on end. There was a question beneath the question, but I didn't understand it.

This man seemed adept at discerning lies, so I hedged. "I'm visiting family. For the first time."

"Who?"

"None of your business," I snapped.

His eyes turned a deeper gold. "I have many friends here in Magic Side, Ms. Caine. Who are you visiting?"

I considered that for a moment as those eyes of his pulled me in. Alma had said my family was extremely dangerous, but it might be good to have a second opinion. He might know of them.

"I'm visiting my aunt, Laurel LaSalle."

Jaxson jerked back as if I'd slapped him in the face, and I yelped as the car tilted slightly. His eyes dilated and blazed like twin suns, and I could practically taste his emotion.

Abject hatred.

∾

Jaxson

Of course.

In the twenty-four hours since I'd laid eyes on Savannah Caine, she'd killed a werewolf, disobeyed every request I'd made, stolen my keys, and led me on a two-hundred-mile wild-goose chase.

Of *course* she was a LaSalle.

I should have known just from the bittersweet-orange hair. To think that I'd found it beautiful at first sight. Now the only thing I could see in it were the flames that had consumed my sister as she'd choked to death on wolfsbane.

Fucking LaSalles.

"Is everything okay?" the bridge cop began, approaching.

I sucked in a sharp breath and looked at where my hands rested on the edge of the roof. They'd shifted to claws, and I was pushing so hard against the car that I'd inadvertently tilted the driver's side so that the wheels were three inches off the ground.

"We're fine," I growled out of the corner of my mouth.

She halted and averted her eyes in submission. She was from my pack and would do exactly as ordered.

Unlike the LaSalle woman.

Savannah stared up at me with wide eyes. She couldn't have seen my claws on the roof, but she knew something was up... probably because I had the car tilted off the ground. I fought to rein in my emotions, relaxed my arms, and let it settle.

"What was that?" Savannah gasped.

I looked deep into her eyes. "Nothing to worry about. Just a gust of wind."

"A gust of wind?" she asked incredulously.

I intensified my signature. "We're on a bridge over Lake Michigan. The wind hits hard. No buildings to stop it."

It was the best I could come up with in the moment. Also, the winds could be hell.

She nodded slowly, her mind finally submitting to my intentions. "I guess that's why they call Chicago the Windy City."

Wrong.

Savannah was unusually resistant to my power. It still worked, but not as well, and not nearly as long as it should have. Maybe it was her accursed bloodline.

I drowned the hatred in my chest and forced my claws to retract. I couldn't let my disgust cloud my vision.

It wasn't her fault my sister was dead. She hadn't poisoned Stephanie with wolfsbane or caused the fire that burned her alive. Savannah wasn't *truly* a LaSalle, just a woman related to the monsters. I couldn't hold that against her.

She bit her lip in a way that made my heart miss a beat. "You looked like you knew my family. I don't. Can you tell me anything about them?"

They're murderers. Monsters and practitioners of the dark arts.

What was I going to do with this woman? Simple truths were best. "They're dangerous."

She turned forward and glared at the city ahead. "I've heard that. What does *dangerous* mean?"

"Do the names Dillinger or Capone mean anything to you?"

One eyebrow inched upward as she looked at me again. "You mean the gangsters?"

"That's what the name LaSalle means around here."

She swallowed. Trepidation, but not surprise. That was interesting.

Why Savannah was trying to get in touch with the LaSalles, if she already knew they were dangerous, was anyone's guess. But I couldn't let her meet with them—not before I'd had a chance to talk to her first. Not ever, if I could help it. They would twist her mind and turn her against my kind. They'd teach her hate and mistrust.

The moment Laurel LaSalle got her hooks in Savannah would be the moment she would never work with me again.

She'd disappear into the Indies—the neighborhood the LaSalles controlled—and she'd be out of my reach for good.

I needed to convince Savannah to help me before she looked up her family. And I'd need leverage in case she refused.

"You have to be very careful here, Ms. Caine. Those people might be your relations, but you're not their family. They'll use you. Reaching out to them would put you in far more danger than you're already in. They're wrapped up in a very bad line of business."

She studied my face, probably searching for any sign of a lie. She wouldn't find one, because I believed every word I'd said.

It was possible that the werewolves were hunting her simply because they'd discovered she was a LaSalle. Every pack around the Great Lakes region hated the family. It didn't explain the other abductions, but it could explain why she was targeted.

Savannah crossed her arms and slouched down in the seat. "Well, I'm not going back to Belmont. Not with those freaks running around hunting me."

I nodded in assent. I'd given up that plan the moment she'd split town. Not many had the power to resist me like she had, and apparently, she was very invested in being in Magic Side. I shouldn't be surprised. Magic Side was one of the largest supernatural cities in the world, and it called to its lost children with a siren song that few could resist. That might explain everything.

Maybe the fates wanted her here. With any luck, the wolves would come for her next, and I could spring a trap. I could control the entire situation. All I had to do was keep her in pack territory, out of the Indies, and away from her family.

The problem would be getting her to play along. So far, my power had worked on her when I pushed her in a direction she wanted to go. As a last resort, I could threaten to prosecute her for Dane's death under pack law. But that would make everything public, and I'd cede control of the situation to the elders.

That, and she'd never trust me again. Three things I couldn't afford right now.

I leaned close to the window and drew her in with my eyes. "I have no intention of preventing you from being here, Ms. Caine, but it's late. If you don't know the LaSalles, you definitely don't want to look in on them at night. A tow truck is already on the way. I'll set you up with a good mechanic and a decent motel in a safe part of town. It's a big city."

She considered my words. Her eyes were weary, and I could sense her exhaustion. Finally, she nodded, submitting at last.

I'd put her up in the Full Moon Motel on pack land and send her car to the pack repair shop, Savage Body. The truck was already on the way.

I took my hands off the car and leaned back. "It's been a hell of a day. How about I buy you dinner? You must be starving."

"I'm fine, thanks," she muttered, but her stomach grumbled, betraying her lie, and she blushed.

Gods. How obstinate could one person be? She didn't trust me—that much was clear—but she might trust a female cop. I turned to the patrolwoman and gave her a look. "Hey, what's the best place to eat in Magic Side?"

"Eclipse! Best food I've ever had," the cop shouted back. She'd known the answer I wanted. Eclipse was my restaurant, after all.

I looked back at the skeptical woman in the car. "How about Eclipse for dinner? It's the least I can do. Usually, it's impossible to get a table, but I can pull a few strings."

She gritted her teeth. "Fine, but only if you give me answers about the case. And tell me what you know about my family."

I nodded. "Not much about the case. But I'll tell you about your kin. And more. Far more than you ever imagined possible."

Her eyes blazed with hunger. Starving for information, not food. I could use that.

"Deal?" I asked. I didn't even have to use my power. She was hooked on the promise of answers.

It took a second, but she finally nodded. "Doesn't look like I'm going anywhere else."

Well, that was close enough to a yes. She was as prickly as a hedgehog and as stubborn as a badger.

I was glad I'd left Regina back in Belmont. This was a risky game, and she'd have been pissed that I was taking a LaSalle out to dinner in the heart of pack territory. If anyone found out, things could get violent. I leaned on the car. "Just a word of advice, Ms. Caine. Don't mention your family's name to anyone in this city. There'd be consequences, none of them good."

She tensed, and the scent of fear rose off her.

The Savage Body tow truck arrived, lights flashing. I walked away to make arrangements with the driver, but I had keen ears and could hear the LaSalle woman chatting with the patrolwoman.

"Look, I don't know anyone around here. Is Mr. Laurent, you know, to be trusted?" Savannah whispered.

The cop pitched her voice low and conspiratorial, but she knew that I'd hear. "I'd trust him more than any other man in Magic Side. If he says you'll be okay, you'll be okay. But I can give you a lift somewhere else if you need it."

There was a long pause, and I held my breath.

"I think I'll be okay," Savannah said at last.

"I know you will," the patrolwoman said.

I turned and nodded thanks to the cop, though I was certain she'd meant every word.

She started to walk away, but Savannah leaned out the window and hissed after her, "Hey! Is the food at Eclipse really that good?"

The patrolwoman winked. "It'll make you howl at the moon."

9

Savannah

Jaxson effortlessly heaved my suitcases into the back of his black SUV.

So much for running from my troubles. Now they were giving me a lift.

I gave a last forlorn glance at my Gran Fury as the tow truck driver loaded it onto his rig. He handed me a card. "Don't worry, ma'am. We're taking it to Savage Body, one of the best repair shops in Magic Side. It'll be up and running before you know it."

I thanked him and gave my poor car one last miserable look. I'd come so close, halfway over the bridge, with only a few more blocks to go. I'd pushed the car over its limit to cross the finish line, and it wasn't any wonder that it had conked out.

Sometimes you ran so fast, you wound up tripping over your own feet and landing on your face. That was me in a nutshell.

I sighed and hopped into Jaxson's vehicle. I didn't dare ask him about his keys, or where he'd gotten an SUV to chase me with. A sliver of guilt tugged at me. He could get new keys made, right?

He climbed in the vehicle and fired up the engine, and we rumbled across the bridge to Magic Side.

I took a deep breath, trying to calm my nerves. Was I really driving off into the middle of the night with a perfect stranger? The cop had vouched for him. Still, I kept my hand on the mace in my pocket, though something about Jaxson's demeanor told me I wasn't going to need it.

He brooded as he drove, clearly lost in thought, and didn't even glance at me. When I tried pressing him for information, he dodged at first, but finally, I wore him down.

"It seems like I'm being targeted," I said. "Do you know why?"

He kept his eyes on the road, avoiding my stare. "No. There's been no pattern in the abductions. We assume that those who were killed were the ones who fought back."

"How do you know?

"A woman witnessed an attack three days ago, but she didn't get a good enough look to identify the attackers. *You* did. Would you be willing to work with a sketch artist tomorrow?"

Hell, I had enough talent to draw them myself, but that probably wouldn't be official enough. "Sure."

Biting my lip, I silently watched the city lights roll by—illuminated old storefronts, artsy shops, restaurants, and blocks of tightly packed red brick walk-up apartments. I racked my brain as to why those monsters might be after me.

The answer I kept coming back to was my parents.

"You said my family—the LaSalles—are dangerous and wrapped up in bad business."

"Yeah, they deal in illegal arms and materials."

Crap. Were my parents gun runners?

They sure as hell had made certain I could shoot. Mostly rifles, shotguns, and pistols, nothing heavy. Mainly, they'd hunted deer. My mother had spent a lot of time alone, hunting in the woods. She'd said it reminded her of who she was.

Then they'd died in an explosion. What if it had been ammo? Had I spent my childhood sleeping on a powder keg?

"My family...could that be why people are after me?"

He nodded. "Quite possibly. None of the other victims were related to the LaSalles, but there might be a connection. Your family is...not well liked in the region. You definitely shouldn't reach out to them, not until this is over."

Maybe I had gotten very, *very* lucky that my car gave out. I brooded silently, trying to imagine how badly things could've gone.

Ten minutes later, we pulled up in front of Eclipse. There was no parking, and the street was hopping and filled with all sorts of colorful people.

I slipped out of the SUV into the strangely dressed crowd. A woman with pointy ears slung her arm around a man who was wearing contact lenses that made his eyes look catlike. I'd always heard Chicago was wild, but this wasn't what I was expecting. Was there some sort of costume party going on?

"Do people in Chicago normally dress up like this?" I asked as Jaxson stepped around the front of the car.

He passed his keys to a valet. "Only in Magic Side. We tend to draw the most interesting people."

Great. He'd taken me to dinner in the middle of crazy town.

I followed Jaxson toward a solitary black door marked with the restaurant's name in bold white letters. We cut in front of the line of waiting patrons, and a handsome bouncer with rippling muscles opened the door for us. He tipped his head as we entered. What did Jaxson do around here to command so much respect?

The sound of jazz and the aroma of amber and spice over-whelmed my senses. Cocktail waitresses in red wove between candlelit tables occupied by people sipping fancy drinks. Waiters flitted around with trays of delicious-looking food, and my stomach groaned.

Toward the back of the room, several people were swinging their hips and twirling to the beat of the live band that I couldn't quite see on the stage. The pulse of the music was hypnotic. A sweet riff from the horns sent shivers down my spine. I'd never seen anything like it in my whole life, nor been anywhere even close.

Certainly not in Belmont.

The people were out of this world as well. Absolutely gorgeous, but to be fair, there were quite a few with strange costumes. I had to shimmy out of the way of a weirdo wearing a headband with horns. He'd gone so far as to paint his skin a pale shade of blue. Completely nuts.

I caught the eyes of a man dressed like a vampire, and suddenly, it all made sense: there had to be some kind of Comic Con going on. I knew they held a few big comic and gaming conventions in the city every year, but I wasn't a big enough fangirl to shell out the money to attend one.

I followed Jaxson to a dark marble bar illuminated with blue lights.

"How about a drink, Ms. Caine?" His smoky voice wrapped around me, whispering of mystery and power.

I nodded because my voice failed. I knew I should run from him—he was dangerous. But somehow, when he looked at me, I couldn't tear my eyes away.

He moved like he owned the place. People melted away around us until we were isolated at the bar.

Who *was* this man?

A tough-looking brunette bartender swung over. "What can I get you, hon?"

I tended to drink like my folks had: whiskey, add one glass.

Panicking, I tried to think of a fancy alternative and managed, "A Manhattan?"

"Two," Jaxson echoed.

She nodded and grabbed a lowball glass, eying Jaxson with a raised brow.

I caught my reflection in the mirror behind the liquor bottles. I was grossly underdressed in my wrinkled sundress, and my hair had seen better days. I was obviously small town in the big city, all the while standing next to the hottest guy in the bar.

God, how could a man like *that* stomach being seen in public with a bedraggled girl like me? Embarrassment bored through my remaining confidence like a swarm of termites.

Why, for heaven's sake, had the cop recommended this place? There was something almost magical about the atmosphere. It had to be insanely exclusive, and I couldn't be more out of my element.

I made a couple of stealthy adjustments to my dress and looked up. Half a dozen women were shooting daggers at me with their eyes, probably wondering how I had the gall to be with *him*—the man the whole place seemed to revolve around.

Like a slap in the face, that hardened my resolve real fast.

Screw them.

I'd been attacked by some kind psycho super-soldiers the night before, and I'd killed one of them. I could handle a couple of bar bitches. I tossed my hair to let them know that I'd killed better folk and that I could wear whatever I damn well pleased.

Then I gave the one on my left *the look.*

To my surprise, she backed off with a shocked expression, then quickly averted her eyes.

Chicago was so weird.

I looked up at Jaxson and froze. He was studying me.

Intensely. Heat warmed my cheeks, and I lowered my eyes, just like the woman had.

The bartender slid a couple Manhattans in front of us, and I welcomed the interruption. I took a sip and savored the sweet and smoky flavors, delighting in the way the whiskey warmed my stomach, then followed Jaxson to a table. Several women shot inviting glances at him, but he didn't seem to notice.

He wouldn't notice you, either, if you weren't a witness.

I adjusted my hair—my best characteristic—as I sat. For a second, Jaxson's full lips twitched downward, as if somehow, my hair was an insult.

I buried my face in the menu to hide my shame. Whatever moment of confidence I'd experienced at the bar was over—clearly, the only reason he'd brought me here was to buy my cooperation.

Well, he'd soon learn that my cooperation had a steep price.

The menu was all small plates, so I didn't feel overly embarrassed when we wound up practically ordering one of everything, along with another round of drinks.

Soon enough, a waitress swept over with plates of bacon-topped figs, charred brussel sprouts, and endive cups filled with some kind of cheese and herbs. By the time I was halfway through, I was thankful I was wearing something flowy and comfortable.

I kept trying to get tidbits of information out of Jaxson, but he delayed or deflected, instead responding with prying questions I didn't want to answer. Stymied, I mostly kept my head down and focused on the food.

Just sitting across from Jaxson was intimidating. I could feel everyone's eyes on us. He drew attention to himself like a black hole, all the light and color of the room swirling around him, slowly being pulled in.

So was I.

He was beyond eye candy with his sleeves rolled up, lightly circling the rim of his glass with his thumb and index finger. I'd never seen a man built like him before. So much strength, tightly bound. His jaw set as if he were holding back a great force in his chest.

"Who are you?" I finally asked as I watched the room study him.

"I'm the man who's hunting your attackers."

"That's not an answer. Who *are* you? Who do you work for?"

He set his glass down as if dropping a heavy burden. "I run Dockside, this section of the city."

That explained a lot—he was a king in his petty kingdom. Probably a powerful politician. No wonder everyone seemed to bend before him.

I opened my mouth to press him, but Jaxson leaned back and traced me head to toe with his eyes. They flashed gold for a second, and heat rushed through me.

"Why don't you tell me who *you* are?" he asked.

"You know who I am." I prickled. He seemed to know a lot about too many things.

"Who were your parents?"

That killed whatever heat had built up in me. "Nobodies. They're dead," I snapped. "It's time to stop delaying and tell me what's going on."

I shoved the last bacon-topped fig in my mouth to make a point.

Jaxson inclined his head with a look of amusement in his eyes. "You have a healthy appetite."

Was he judging me? I wiped my sticky fingers on my napkin. "My only appetite is for information. Dish."

"What do you want to know?"

"Who attacked me? You said you believed my story—that I

was attacked by people with claws for hands. That they'd chased me down on the road. What the hell were they?"

Jaxson looked around the room, then rose. "We should discuss these things discreetly. Why don't you join me on the terrace?"

I nodded. At last, I was going to get some real answers—and they were going to be good ones, because Jaxson didn't want people eavesdropping.

We took our drinks, left the table, and headed to the rooftop terrace. It was packed with revelers when we arrived, but Jaxson gave the waitstaff a look, and the place emptied in a few minutes.

Holy smokes, he'd just kicked everyone out like it was nothing.

The terrace offered a view of the entire island. The skyscrapers of downtown sparkled to the northwest, and the whole city was a sea of light, with the nearly full moon floating high overhead. A light breeze stirred the leaves of potted plants, and I sighed, for some strange reason feeling at home here overlooking the city below.

I joined Jaxson at a small table positioned next to the railing. "Okay, you've used your mojo to clear the deck somehow," I said. "You need to start giving me some straight answers. Who attacked me? None of it makes sense."

He leaned casually against the railing, disarmingly handsome and dangerous. "Ms. Caine, when you set foot in Magic Side, you entered a world very different from the one that you thought you knew. You're going to need to open your mind to possibilities you've never imagined."

"Fine. I'm used to batshit-crazy discussions with my aunt. Who attacked me?"

Jaxson fixed me with a long, serious gaze.

"Werewolves."

10

Jaxson

Savannah shot whiskey out of her nose and snorted with laughter. After a minute, she paused, took one look at my growing grimace, and started cackling again.

Frustration wormed its way beneath my skin.

Finally, she wiped her eyes with the back of her wrist. "Sorry about that." She sighed. "That was way funnier than it should have been. It's just been a long twenty-four hours. I've been so scared. I needed that."

This was going to be an uphill battle. I rubbed my temples and muttered, "I'm being serious."

"Yeah. And I'm Buffy the Vampire Slayer."

"Not likely. A vampire would kill you in an instant. You're weak and slow. But most vampires, like werewolves, wouldn't attack you unless provoked."

She started chuckling again, and I sat my drink on the table and glared. What was it about her that got under my skin? Had she been anyone else, I would have let her family explain all of this. But not the LaSalles. I needed to control the messaging about werewolves.

Finally, Savannah settled down, and her expression of mirth turned into bewilderment as she studied my face. She slowly pushed her drink aside and whispered, "Oh, my God. You actually believe what you're saying."

At least we were getting somewhere. "Because it's true. You're being hunted by werewolves."

She placed her hands over her face. "Oh, no, you're not from some government agency. You're a lunatic who thinks he's David Duchovny in *The X-Files*."

Irritation rippled through me. This was going nowhere. "Savannah, look at me," I commanded.

She put her hands down, and I let my presence wash over her. "You are going to listen. You are going to have an open mind. You need to forget everything you thought you knew about the world. All your preconceptions."

She nodded meekly.

"I want you to describe your assailants. What stood out as strange about them?"

Savannah swallowed, looked down at the table, and mumbled, "They had claws for hands and glowing eyes. They could run faster than a car. I ran one over and killed him, but there was just a wolf left on the road."

She was exaggerating. Wolves couldn't run faster than cars.

"Tell me, what were they? What makes sense? What fits the things you saw with your own eyes? Speak the truth, not just the truth you want to believe," I commanded.

She started shaking her head. "This is crazy. You're telling me that I was attacked by people who transform into wolves? That werewolves are real and they're hunting me?"

When she staggered back from the table, I caught her hand and felt the electricity in her body. It was magnetic, and I didn't want to let go. "Yes. But you don't need to be afraid."

"I don't need to be afraid? How is that a reasonable statement? Either A, werewolves are real and they're trying to kill me, or B, I'm having casual cocktails with a madman!"

"Everything is going to be fine. Calm down." I unleashed my full presence and pressed her into submission with my magic, pushing the terror from her mind. She needed to think clearly and not panic.

At least it was easier to control her with my presence after she'd had a few drinks.

She pulled away and wrapped her arms around her chest, looking over the city. "I can't believe any of this."

Even forlorn, she was beautiful, and for some reason, her pain made my heart clench. Guilt, probably. She shouldn't have to hear this from me...but then again, she shouldn't hear it from her family.

Finally, she stopped shaking. "I think I need another cocktail."

I motioned to the waiter, who was standing far off to the side.

Savannah started pacing back and forth on the empty terrace and put her hands to her forehead. "Okay, nutcase. For argument's sake, let's assume you're telling the truth and aren't a deranged lunatic. What *are* werewolves? Monsters?"

My jaw ticked at her impudence. No one spoke to me like that. "Not everything you don't understand is a monster. Were-wolves are people who can turn into wolves, and vice versa. They are quite common."

"They're *common*?" she squeaked, looking around in wide-eyed panic.

"There are thousands in this city, living normal lives, like you or me."

Savannah gripped the railing, struggling not to hyperventilate. I touched her back and pushed a little of my power into her, calming her with my presence. She shivered beneath my touch, which sent a current through my fingers and...well, somewhere else.

Her breathing calmed. "I'm not sure that I understand. There are thousands of these monsters just roaming free in the city?"

"Not monsters. Businesswomen, doctors—quite a lot of firemen, if that's your cup of tea." I tried a smile, but the joke fell flat.

She spun toward the terrace doors. "You mean there could be werewolves here? Lurking and watching me?"

I turned her chin to me and let my eyes glow. There was something about her that was mesmerizing. Intoxicating. Maybe it was the innocence and naïveté underneath that hard exterior. Or maybe my wolf just liked a challenge. "You don't have to worry. There are, but it's safe. *You're* safe, and they're not going to hurt you."

She pulled away. "But I was attacked."

"You were assaulted by two very bad people who just happened to be werewolves. Most werewolves are kind, helpful, upstanding citizens, just as most humans are good. In either case, a few are bad."

I surrounded her with my presence, calming, protecting. If she were going to stay in Magic Side, the most important thing I could do was convince her that she didn't have to be afraid of us.

"This is a lot," she mumbled.

"I know. But you're now part of something very special." I turned and looked out over the sparkling lights of the city. "This is Magic Side. It's one of the largest supernatural cities in the world. Werewolves, vampires, witches—you name it, they all live here in the thousands."

"A supernatural city? Full of witches and vamp..." She petered out.

I was finally beginning to break through her denial. "Yes. All those things and more. We're known as Magica—it means people with magic in their veins. You can't actually see the city unless you're Magica."

"But I could."

"Exactly. You're like us, and you belong here." I studied her closely, unable to take my eyes off her damned red hair.

Why had the fates brought this woman into my life?

To torment me, no doubt.

~

Savannah

It was all too much.

I pressed my hand to my pounding chest, willing it to slow down. Wooziness settled over me, and I bent over with my head between my legs.

I didn't care that Jaxson Laurent was looking. I could barely stand, and it had nothing to do with the drinks I'd just downed.

"What do you mean, I'm like you, like everyone here? Magic?"

He sighed with a hint of exasperation. "Yes."

What did he expect? That I would accept his words without question?

Probably. Jaxson was an arrogant bastard who seemed to get his way.

I took a breath and straightened my spine. "Like, I have powers?"

"Yes, but I don't know what kind."

I shook my head. It was impossible to believe, but there wasn't a hint of deceit in his eyes.

"And my family here, the LaSalles. Are they magic, too? You talk about them like they're monsters. What, are they were-wolves? Or something worse?"

Jaxson's eyes blazed with fury, and I had the sudden urge to flee.

"They're practitioners of the dark arts. Black magic."

His words were laced with venom, and I froze as information poured into my mind. My family was magical, and they practiced the dark arts—whatever the hell *that* was. What had they done to deserve this man's ire?

I regarded him carefully as he moved close, his posture commanding. "Stay away from them. And don't mention your relation to the LaSalles to anyone in this city. They may be the reason you were targeted."

"So where am I supposed to go?" I asked, nearly in tears.

He laid a hand on my shoulder, and as a soft current of electricity flowed between us, I shivered. Was that part of his magic? I sucked in a breath and met his honey-gold eyes—eyes that penetrated straight through me, leaving my soul naked before him.

"It will all be fine as long as you stay away from your family. I'll arrange a motel here for you. You have nothing to worry about. You're in a new world. Magic is real, and your potential here is limitless."

Jaxson's gaze drew me in like a black hole, and his voice soothed me. The anxiety in my chest evaporated, replaced by a cool, flowing undercurrent of calm.

Just like that, my worries vanished like smoke rising from a candle. Some part of me—maybe a magical part of me—knew that I didn't have to worry because finally, I was where I belonged.

When Jaxson escorted me downstairs, everything I saw, I saw anew.

The bartender wasn't just flaring cocktails and flipping bottles. He floated them in midair, grabbing the ones he wanted and spinning the others like pinwheels. He sent drinks sliding down the bar, hovering an inch above the marble surface.

In the back, another band was playing—but it wasn't a band, just one girl singing along to five instruments suspended around her.

"I think I've had a lot to drink," I muttered.

Jaxson pressed his palm to my lower back. "You have a lot to take in."

I nodded, too exhausted, confused, and inebriated to register the goosebumps that his touch elicited.

His eyes had lost their honey tone, and they bored into me. "Will you meet with the sketch artist tomorrow?"

I gulped and nodded. "I want to help."

I'd expected my aunt to help me figure out why I was being targeted, but if Jaxson could do it, so much the better. I'd come to Magic Side for answers, after all. I'd take what I could get.

His gaze landed behind me, and his jaw tensed before his eyes returned to mine. I was no idiot—I could read the distaste written all over his face. My family revolted him, and by association, so did I.

"It's late, and I have a prior engagement." Jaxson's voice was as cold as his sudden demeanor. Or maybe it had always been that way, and I'd just been too foolish to notice. "Samantha will get you set up with a place tonight. I'll send a car to collect you from your motel at noon tomorrow."

He was ditching me?

"Fine." I was too overwhelmed and affronted to think. What had I expected? It wasn't like we'd been on a date, but still, after bombarding me with all of that information, I never expected him to just leave me here. My cheeks burned from my foolishness.

Without another word, Jaxson turned and strode out, leaving me high and dry. *Bastard.*

Suddenly, I heard a woman's voice behind me. "I'm Samantha. You're Savannah, right?"

Turning, I recognized the female bartender I'd seen earlier. I nodded again, because I was pretty sure that if I tried to speak, the floodgates would open.

She raised her brow. "You okay?"

I'm alone in a magical city, and my car is broken. My only family here apparently dabbles with the dark arts and gun running, and werewolves are hunting me down.

I shrugged.

"Don't worry, Jaxson's made arrangements. I'm taking you over to the Magic Moon Motel. It's not the Four Seasons, but it's clean and safe and cheap. The valets will grab your bags."

Suspicion and curiosity crept under my skin. "Is Jaxson your friend?"

The bartender smirked. "You could say that."

I felt like a complete idiot. She was probably his girlfriend, or at least his ex, because attractive people like them couldn't just be friends. I rubbed my throbbing temples, and whatever willpower I had was gone. I was like water, going with the flow.

"Thanks, Samantha," I mumbled.

"Call me Sam."

We loaded up in the back of a waiting Jeep and drifted off through the moonlit city. I was too dazed to think, to ask questions, to do anything but watch the lights go by.

For a second, I thought a black SUV was following us, but it drove past as we pulled up in front of the two-story motel. I craned my head to look up at the giant angular sign and its logo, a big yellow crescent that kept flickering.

Definitely not the Four Seasons.

"This is my uncle's place," Sam said as we got out of the car, perhaps sensing my sudden trepidation. She helped me check in and even lugged my bug-out bag to my room while I dragged Alma's oversized suitcase up the stairs.

Sam winked as she turned to leave. "Don't worry, hon. Tomorrow, everything will be better, I promise."

I triple-locked the door with the deadbolt and chain, and then pulled off my sundress and collapsed on the bed, utterly overwhelmed by the world that had just sucked me in. Scared and exhausted though I was, I was blessed with the ability to sleep almost anywhere, and the bed was good enough.

Tomorrow would be better.

11

Savannah

The nightmare coiled around me, a python slowly crushing the breath from my lungs.

The tattooed woman from Belmont chased me through the crowded bar. I shoved left and right, but people with horns and fangs pressed in around me. I could barely breathe, let alone move. In desperation, I dove over the bar, dodging flying cocktails and bottles. But I wasn't fast enough. The woman lashed out with long claws and dug them into my skin. My blood poured down her fingers, and her eyes blazed with crimson light. "You won't escape! You'll give us what we need!"

When I pulled away, I slipped in my own blood and crashed to the floor. She leapt through the air, face contorting and twisting into that of a wolf. Then she was on me, clawing and biting my neck like a savage animal.

In the midst of all the chaos, *he* was there. With one swift move, Jaxson slammed his fist into her chest and sent her flying off my body and onto the bar—just as that tattooed werewolf had done to the driver at the Taphouse.

I staggered to my feet. The woman lunged for me, but Jaxson

finished her with a savage blow. He turned to me, muscles taut and chest heaving. His eyes glowed with golden light, drawing me in, heart and soul.

But my breathing faltered as my gaze drifted to his hands. They were bloody claws.

"They're everywhere, Savannah." He put his head back and howled, then his whole body began shifting into a wolf.

I screamed and turned to flee, but everyone in the bar began shifting and howling. The bartender, the musicians, all the staff and patrons, one by one, until there was only one woman left alone, a woman with dark black braids and a jean jacket. I'd never seen her before, but there was something oddly familiar about her face.

Darkness swirled around her, as if she were gazing through a whirling maelstrom. She smiled at me. "You cannot outrun your fate, Savannah. They're coming for you. Beware the wheel of fortune. It does not stop. Time is ticking. You need to learn who you truly are so that you can stop the ones who are coming."

I screamed and thrashed against my covers, then sat bolt upright, lungs heaving and sweat rolling down my chest.

A nightmare.

I ran my fingers through my damp, tangled hair. I wasn't in my bed. Where was I? A hotel.

The memories of the previous day rushed back. The bartender, Sam, had sent me here. She'd said that tomorrow, everything would be better.

Sam was a goddamned liar.

My skull was pounding, and I regretted everything. My stomach and thoughts churned like Lake Michigan in heavy weather. Too many cocktails. Too many varieties of food. Too much weird city.

Too much Jaxson Laurent.

I sat up and rubbed my forehead. I remembered talking with

him on the rooftop terrace of Eclipse. About magic and were-wolves—which was insane. No wonder I'd had nightmares.

How much did we have to drink?

Hazy memories danced through my mind—the bartender flying bottles and cocktails around the room, people with horns and fangs, and an entire jazz band played by one lady.

I put my head in my hands. God, I must have gotten absolutely plastered.

Worse, I couldn't really remember the details of my conversation with Jaxson. Had I really told him that I was attacked by werewolves? Or wait, had he said that?

Either way, it was bad news. One of us was off our rocker.

Had he really claimed that magic was real and that were-wolves were after me? The logical half of my brain took control. Impossible. I'd had too much to drink and mixed a lot of things up. That sucked, because I was going to have to start weaseling information out of him all over again, and I really didn't want to be near him.

Lie.

What the hell was I going to do?

Take a freaking shower, that's what. Because I was gross.

As soon as I'd gotten into my room last night, I'd stripped off my sundress and face-planted into the bed. Normally, I'd shower before crawling between the sheets, but the day had just knocked me out cold.

I staggered out of bed and retrieved my crumpled dress from the back of the chair. It smelled faintly of sweat, car exhaust, and burning coolant. Man, I'd been some date—underdressed and over-fragrant.

I sighed. Not that it'd been a date. More like information gathering.

I peeled off my threadbare undies and slipped into the shower, letting the warm water relax my mind and muscles.

To be honest, I wouldn't have minded if it had been a date, even if it had ended weirdly. The place was amazing, and Jaxson was unbelievably hot—burn-your-fingers-if-you-got-too-close hot. He'd been studying me all night, though he'd tried to hide it.

Unfortunately, Jaxson wasn't interested, especially not after he'd learned who my relations were. The look on his face on the bridge and in the restaurant had made my skin crawl. Pure hatred. He'd said they were into weapons trafficking.

And dark magic.

What did that even mean? I couldn't be remembering things correctly.

It was possible that they were the reason I'd been targeted. I needed to find out more about them, to figure out why. Obviously, I'd need to be careful.

It didn't help that I was stranded. I didn't even want to think how much it would cost to repair the Gran Fury. Thousands, for sure, which was more than I had and probably more than the old car was worth. If my family turned out to be sociopaths, I could probably sell it for a bus ticket out of here, but otherwise, I couldn't leave it behind. That meant I needed a job and a place to stay.

Panic crept in, and I decided to focus on the short term as I rinsed the soap off, along with any remaining illusions I'd created about Jaxson Laurent. He was a means to an end, a way to get the information I needed. That was all.

I recalled that I'd agreed to meet with a sketch artist, and that Jaxson was going to send a car at noon. That was something, at least, even if the rest was a blur.

I got out, dried off, and wrapped the towel around me. Feeling a bit guilty, I texted Alma: *I'm ok. Spent the night at a motel. Had a little car trouble, but I'm getting it fixed. On my way soon. Love you. I'll call you when I get to my destination.*

I didn't like stretching the truth with her, but it was a lot easier by text.

The return text had probably taken her four minutes to type on her old brick phone: *Love you, too. Don't worry, no sign of feds.*

That was because they'd already found me, and I was going to meet with one in under two hours. At least it would be a good chance to talk things over, because there was no way that anything I remembered about last night could be real.

I had no idea what to wear. What casually said, *I'm hot and want answers, but I won't be pushed around*? Not like I needed or cared to look hot for Jaxson. I was pretty sure that he all but despised me, and I wasn't the kind of girl who tried to impress guys. Normally.

Biting my lip, I selected some gray jeans that made my butt look great and an airy button-down short-sleeved blouse. I examined myself in the mirror and popped a few buttons to nice effect. It was summer, after all.

I opened the door to my room and stepped out onto the concrete walkway. A cleaning lady moved her cart out of my way, and her broom scooted along after. Then it began sweeping off the walk.

All by itself.

I stepped back into my room, shut the door, and leaned against the wall.

Savy, you're not in Kansas anymore.

I cracked the door and peeked out, making sure not to look at the possessed broom. The lady was cleaning the adjacent room, and I slunk around the corner to spy through the open door. She pointed a stick—*a wand*—at the bed. The sheets flew off, and a new set zipped off her cart and onto the mattress, followed by a pair of towels that folded into a swan.

I squeaked in surprise.

She turned and put her hand on her chest. "Sorry, I didn't see you there. Can I help you?"

My mouth worked for a while before I finally spoke. "How are you doing that?" I lamely made folding gestures.

"Oh, just a little hocus-pocus. Nothing special." She waved her wand like a conductor, and a couple of mints levitated off the cart and landed gently on the pillows. "Is there anything I can get you? How about a mint?"

She flicked her wand, and it skipped into the air, hovering.

I gingerly plucked it from the air and munched it.

Minty.

Holy crap. Magic was real.

The rational part of my mind—which had been screaming in denial against everything I'd seen over the last twelve hours—finally packed up its bags and went on holiday, leaving the clearly insane part of my mind in the driver's seat.

I needed something to drink. Probably not alcohol. Espresso.

"Where can I get some decent coffee?" I asked the cleaning lady.

"Try Moon Bean, two blocks south."

I nodded as if cleaning ladies with telekinetic powers were perfectly normal. "Kay, thanks."

With that, I locked my room, strolled down the concrete stairs in a bewildered daze, and headed south to Moon Bean.

All around me, the city bustled with signs of magic. A shop selling potions. People with horns. Empty dresses sashaying in store windows. It all meant one thing: what Jaxson had told me was true. Magic. My family. Werewolves.

The hair on my neck stood on end, and I glanced around nervously. They literally could be anywhere. *Anyone* could be a werewolf. The backwoods couple had looked normal until their eyes turned blood-red and their hands grew claws.

I jogged the last couple of steps to Moon Bean.

As soon as I pushed through the door, the scent of freshly ground coffee and toasted pastries wafted over me. A short, gangly creature with wings pulled a shot of espresso from the machine and then started frothing milk.

I immediately turned away, trying not to hyperventilate. Too much, too soon. Instead, I studied the overhead menu and discretely avoided the creature that was actually making the coffee.

A nerdy kid in a dark yellow apron smiled from behind the counter. "Hi, welcome to Moon Bean. What can I get you today?"

I kept my eyes locked on the menu. "Uh...a latte?"

"Anything else?"

What I needed was information, more than I'd needed anything in my whole life. I could risk making an ass out myself. "So, um, this city is full of magic. And werewolves?"

He blinked. "Yeah. That's why it's called Magic Side."

Right. I met his eyes. "Have you heard of a family called the LaSalles?"

Everyone in the coffeeshop went quiet.

Damn it.

The kid leaned forward and gave me a conspiratorial whisper. "Look, lady, you seem new here, but I wouldn't go poking into their business unless you want to get cursed. They say one look from Laurel LaSalle can turn a man to stone, and I believe it."

Okay, dark magic. Check. Jaxson had been telling the truth.

"What about a man named Jaxson Laurent?"

The kid made a funny face. "Duh. He's the Dockside Boss."

"What does that mean?"

The kid looked around the room, clearly uncomfortable, as if he were dealing with a crazy woman—which was a distinct possibility at that point. Barista boy scratched his head. "Uh, it means that he's the alpha. Leader of the local pack."

The sinking feeling in my gut felt like the *Titanic* had sprung a leak. "He's the leader of the local pack of...?"

The kid shot me a bewildered look. "Shifters? Werewolves? Wow, you're really not from around here, are you?"

I had to ask, though I knew the answer already. "And that makes Jaxson Laurent a..."

"Werewolf. He's, like, the king of the Chicago werewolves."

That asshole.

My fists clenched as my vision blurred. He'd been playing me the whole time.

Forgetting my coffee, I stormed out the front door but stopped dead in my tracks. A sandy-haired man was watching me from beneath the shade of a trolley stop across the street. He looked down at his phone as soon as I met his eyes, but I recognized that face. I'd seen him chatting with Jaxson last night.

Was he a werewolf? Were there others following me?

Panic dumped into my veins.

There are werewolves everywhere.

I had no idea who was friend or foe. In fact, I didn't really know which of the two Jaxson was, either. It was time for a new plan.

I flagged a passing cab and hopped in. The sandy-haired man looked up and started heading in my direction, and my chest constricted as my heartrate skyrocketed.

"7546 Wildhaven Avenue," I told the driver. "And would you please lock the doors?"

The man on the street slowed and raised his phone to his ear as the cab pulled away.

A minute later, my phone vibrated with a number I didn't

recognize. I had a sneaking suspicion it was Jaxson *freaking* Laurent, and I didn't answer.

I had no idea what was going on, but I knew one thing. My parents had left a note that if anyone ever came for me, if I was ever in trouble, that I should go to my Aunt Laurel. No asterisk with a note that she might turn me to stone. Just the instruction to go.

And that's what I was going to do.

Ten minutes later, the driver pulled onto a tree-lined street and stopped in front of 7546 Wildhaven Avenue. It was a big red brick house with a wide porch, green trim, and white scalloped siding on the second floor. It looked like it had been built over a century ago and bordered on being a mansion. Sure, the house seemed a little shabby in places, but it was fancier than most of the closely packed apartments that I'd seen so far. It even had a yard.

Laying eyes on the place set my nerves on end. I had no idea who my family really was. Jaxson had said they were dangerous, but then he was also playing games with information. Withholding. Manipulating.

I recalled the words of the woman in my dreams: *You need to learn who you truly are so that you can stop the ones who are coming.*

I wasn't about to start believing in dreams, but with everything I'd seen, I wasn't going to not believe in them either. Whether she was just some manifestation of my subconscious, or the face of fate, she was right that I needed to figure out who I was and how I fit into this world. The LaSalles' seemed like the place to start looking for answers.

Maybe they were into bad business, but my aunt might know

why I was being targeted. Jaxson certainly didn't—at least not answers he was going to share.

I paid the driver. "Can you stay for a few minutes? I'm not sure if anyone is home."

"Uh..." The cabbie looked around nervously, and then started counting the cash in his hand.

I gave him another ten.

"Sure. I can stay a second."

I got out of the cab, headed up the walk to the front steps, and triple-checked the address on the envelope.

This was it. No going back.

12

Savannah

Straightening my shoulders, I took a deep breath and climbed the stairs. I didn't see a doorbell, so I slammed the iron knocker three times. The metallic clang reverberated unnaturally through the air.

Tires squealed as the cabbie peeled away, which didn't do wonders for my confidence.

No one responded, but the cab was out of sight, so I was stuck.

I slammed the knocker twice more before the door suddenly jerked open. An attractive dark-haired man in his mid-twenties opened the door. "Hey, what are you doing?"

He had broad shoulders and a Van Dyke, and bore just the slightest resemblance to my father. Not that my father would have been caught dead with facial hair. The similarity was possibly a coincidence.

My voice hitched when I tried to speak. "I'm looking for a Laurel LaSalle."

The man's eyes narrowed. "And who are you?"

I sure as hell wasn't giving that information away for free.

"None of your business. I'm here to see Mrs. LaSalle. I have a note for her."

He scrunched his nose and held out his hand. "I can give it to her."

"No," I said, stepping back and using the same tone I'd used when I had to tell guys *no* for the last time.

His pupils dilated a bit, and he stepped back. "Hey, no need to use your hocus-pocus on me. One minute." He turned back. "Mom! Some chick is here to see you! She says she's got a note, and she's a little sassy."

My stomach swam. Holy shit. My aunt was in there. That made the irritating obstruction my cousin—a thought that was a little too much to take.

Footsteps echoed on wooden floors inside. The man—my cousin—moved out of the way, replaced by a silver-haired woman with a penetrating stare and rings on most of her fingers. "You have something for me?" She held out a bejeweled hand.

She was wearing so much perfume, I could feel it with all my senses. Her scent was of nutmeg and hot wax, and the sweet taste of honey. My skin prickled from a sensation that felt like smoke curling over my skin, and as I focused my mind, I could hear a faint buzzing like bees. It felt like happy bees, for some reason.

It was overwhelming.

She raised an expectant eyebrow.

"Uh..." My voice broke.

"Yes?"

It was now or never. "My name is Savannah Caine. I grew up in Wisconsin—I think you might be my aunt."

The overwhelming sensation in the air intensified, and I felt it wrapping around me like an invisible serpent. The woman's voice was hard. "Is this some kind of joke?"

I fought to keep my breathing steady. Something about her terrified me to my core.

Practitioners of the dark arts. Black magic. Could turn a man to stone with her stare.

But it wasn't the things people had said. Instead, it was that feeling of raw, barely restrained power all around me. I'd never felt anything like it, except maybe near Jaxson.

I pulled out the note my father had left and thrust it forward with a trembling hand, barely able to speak. She snatched it and opened it.

Brushing my hair back, I steadied my breath. "No, it's not a joke. I didn't know about you until yesterday. I'm sorry to bother you, but my father passed away five years ago, and I never knew I had an aunt. I don't think I'm supposed to know, and I'm not trying to cause trouble."

The woman looked at me with hard, penetrating eyes, and then glanced back at the letter. "How do I know you're my niece and this isn't some sort of trick?"

"Uh..." I hadn't really expected the third degree.

"Hold out your hand," she commanded, fury simmering in her voice.

"What, why?"

"I will test your blood." She gestured to my hand.

"I'm sorry, what?"

She gritted her teeth. "Silas and his family all died. You are either a charlatan trying to make use of your looks and hair to worm your way into some sort of scam, or you are telling the truth, and the fates have been very cruel to me indeed. Either way, I will test your blood for the truth."

These people were nutcases. "Sorry, I think I've made a mistake," I said, and turned to leave.

"Please."

The tone of her voice stopped me in my tracks—no longer

imperious but pleading. I looked over my shoulder. Her jaw was set hard, as if she were on the verge of tears. "I need to know. Please. A drop of blood for the truth."

Apparently, she needed answers just as much as I did. But a blood test? What the hell kind of world had I gotten myself into?

I sighed and stuck out my hand. When in Oz...

She grasped it and swiftly pricked my palm with a pin she'd drawn from somewhere. I tried to pull away, but she held my hand in a vice grip. "Who was your father?"

"Silas LaSalle," I hissed.

Another strange, overwhelming sensation surged around me, like a violent storm in the still summer air. A current of electricity rippled through my hand. Then the tiny bead of blood in my palm burst into blue flame, and just as quickly turned into a trail of smoke.

I jumped back. "Holy crap!"

Laurel LaSalle met my accusatory gaze with wide eyes. "You're telling the truth."

Before I could react, my aunt threw her arms around me and started weeping into my hair. "Oh, my fates, my fates."

She nearly crushed the breath out of me. I'd never had anyone hug me like that.

I stood there, absolutely petrified, until crazy Aunt Laurel finally disentangled herself. She wiped her eyes and hollered at the top of her lungs, "Casey!"

The man—my cousin—poked his head out. "What now?"

Aunt Laurel wrung her hands. "Meet your cousin. Silas's girl."

His eye went wide. "Ho-ly shit. Seriously? We thought you were dead."

I arched my eyebrows. "Uh, no. I'm here."

Before I could protest, Laurel grabbed me by the hand and pulled me into the house. "Come, come, come."

Within seconds, she'd shoved me down on a big, red, over-stuffed couch with carved wooden ornamentation. The room was large, with dark wooden floors and molding and lots of big oil paintings hanging on the walls. Laurel sat down beside me, and Casey leaned in the doorway. "I can't believe you found your way to us, thank fates," she said. "You must have a million questions."

I did. Too many to sort out, but I knew I needed to get the elephant out of the room first. "My parents kept you a secret from me. Why? Why didn't you come for me when they died? You said you knew about it."

She nodded eagerly. "We thought that you'd died in the accident along with your parents. It was hard to resist looking you up, but they said in the event of an emergency, you'd be taken care of. I should have done some digging, even though I wasn't supposed to..."

"Why?" That was the biggest question of it all.

She hesitated for a second. "Your folks wanted to give you a normal life away from Magic Side. Our family is entangled in many things, and when you were born, we didn't think you would be safe here. Or happy. We didn't want to jeopardize the world they'd built for you by making contact after their death. But none of that matters now because the die is cast. You're back with us."

I had an uncanny knack for sniffing out the truth, and this was it—but not all of it. I crossed my arms. "What else aren't you telling me."

She paused, contemplating how to proceed. "How much do you know about our family? And about Magic Side?"

I bit my lip. "Um, that it's magic?"

She nodded, waiting for more. At least that suggested I wasn't entirely delusional.

I shrugged. "I'm not even sure what that really means. I've

seen...well, a lot of stuff floating around. To be honest, it's a little hard to believe. I didn't know that you or magic or this city existed until yesterday."

"Yes, it's clear that you are unfamiliar with the arcane arts. No one in their right mind would have willingly given their blood to me. Just putting your hand out practically proved you weren't a charlatan."

I raised my eyebrows. Practitioners of the dark arts. What could she have done?

Aunt Laurel took my wrist. "First lesson you need to learn: never give your blood to anyone. On any account. *Ever.*"

My gaze darted between her and Casey. "So...are you both like witches or wizards or something?"

"Wizards? Are you crazy?" Casey laughed and flopped down onto the other couch. "Wizards are lame. We're fucking sorcerers. It's awesome, pew, pew," he said, making gun hands at the ceiling.

I raised an eyebrow. "Pew, pew?"

He lifted his hands, and a billowing ball of flame rocketed upward and dissipated just before it hit the ceiling.

I screamed and then slapped my hands over my mouth.

"Casey!" Aunt Laurel shouted. "Not in the house!"

Cousin Casey rolled his eyes. "Yeah, yeah, yeah. Remember the fire of 1871 and all that. But she needed to see something cool. Like, proof of awesomeness." Turning back to me, he summed everything up like I was braindead, which didn't feel far from the truth at the moment. "Mom's a sorceress. I'm a sorcerer. We do magic. Maybe you can, too."

My brain was still trying to catch up with the whole fireball thing, but slowly my thoughts forced their way through the shock and confusion.

"And my father, was he...?" I swallowed, my mouth parched.

Aunt Laurel laughed softly, as if suddenly touched by a long-forgotten memory. "Yes. Silas was a sorcerer. A very talented one too—though he was prone to mischief." She glared at Casey. "That also runs in the family."

My mind reeled like a child who'd spent too much time on a merry-go-round. *My father was a sorcerer. He could do magic.*

It was a preposterous thought on every level, but I'd just seen my cousin lob a fireball into the ceiling. Proof of awesomeness. That left a glaring question. "What about my mother?"

My aunt's expression darkened, just for a moment, and then she gave me warm smile. "No. She wasn't a sorceress—she didn't have it in her blood. I'm sure you're curious, but I'm afraid we only met her a few times."

A little shadow passed over my heart, but I shook it off.

Aunt Laurel adjusted her dress and leaned forward. "Let's not bury the lead though my dear. You can do magic. I can feel it in my bones."

My breath caught as my stomach tumbled. The woman in the dream had told me to find out what I was. Was this the answer? That I was a sorceress? It was definitely a step up from waiting tables.

I looked at my hand's wondering where the fireballs would come out. "How can you be certain?"

"It's obvious." Casey snarked. "You'd have to be blind not to see it."

"What do you mean, obvious?"

He waved his hand to encompass all the room. "Everybody who can do magic has a unique signature. It's something that tickles your senses. The more powerful you are, the more other people can feel. For instance, Mom always smells like nutmeg and sounds like bees. And a lot more when she shows off."

I blinked. That checked out, bizarrely. "And do I have a signature?"

He nodded. "Yeah. It smells a little like sushi, tastes like garlic, and feels a bit like swimsuit rash."

My jaw dropped in horror.

A heavy tome flew off the shelf and smacked Casey in the face hard enough to slam him into the back of the couch. "Ah, shit! My nose!" he cried, then held his head forward as blood trickled over his lip.

My aunt stared at him impassively. "That was rude."

He stood, keeping his head forward, and protested, "I was joking. She's my cousin, and I just met her. I can't say she smells nice. That's creepy."

Aunt Laurel flicked her hand, and the leather-bound book flew into the air and reshelved itself. "Sometimes, Casey, the best thing is to say nothing at all."

Casey left to stop the bleeding, and Aunt Laurel took my hand and closed her eyes as I tensed. "Your magical signature feels like sunlight and tastes like cold spring water," she said. "It's quite strong for someone who has never practiced magic. I suspect you've inherited the gift of sorcery. You might be a natural."

"What does that mean?"

My aunt smiled. She twisted her hands, and a rainbow of light drifted through the room. The upholstery changed from red to a pale lime, the dark wooden floors turned to bright pine, and the walls became a cheery shade of white. The curtains brightened and rearranged themselves, and the clutter around the room tidied itself up.

Her signature of nutmeg and happy bees whirled around me.

My aunt leaned back. "It means endless possibility, Savannah. For you. Whatever your life was before, it will never be the same. Whatever you had dreamed of doing, so much more is possible."

13

Savannah

My aunt waved her hand, and the room changed again. "Magic is very strong in our family. It rarely comes naturally— though sorcery can be an exception to that rule. Still, it requires practice. And struggle."

She leaned forward and took my hands. "Would you like to learn?"

My breath caught. What could I say to that? No? Of course not. A day and a half ago, I'd nearly been killed by werewolves.

"Can I learn to throw fireballs?"

She smiled. "Let's find out."

My aunt turned to Casey, who'd just returned from washing his face. "Casey! Bring the Sphere of Devouring!"

I jumped from my seat. "The *what*?"

"Don't worry. It's well contained."

None of those words made me feel any more confident. Quite the opposite. I wrung my hands. "Whatever happens next, I think I'm going to need an explanation first."

"Magic takes a long time to emerge in children and cultivate.

I'm assuming you don't want to spend years. In adults, it often manifests in response to a traumatic event."

I started shaking my head. Time to run.

She laughed. "Oh, don't worry. We're not going to do anything traumatic to you. But we're going to speed up the process of you getting acquainted with your magic by sucking it out of you. As I always say, why take the long way, when you can get there faster?"

Maybe because the shortcut involves a thing called a Sphere of Devouring?

I didn't have the strength to make a quip. My fight or flight response was, at this point, just a petrified flight response.

"Got it!" Casey chirped. Aunt Laurel used her magic to rapidly clear the coffee table, and he set down a heavy wooden platter inscribed with a nine-pointed star and a ring of runes. Some sort of object sat in the middle under a velvet cloth—the Sphere of Devouring, I presumed.

This wasn't ominous at all.

She pulled the velvet cloth away, revealing a floating black sphere. "This little monster," my aunt said affectionately, "sucks in magical energy and devours it."

Casey crossed his arms and leaned back against the wall—notably, on the far opposite side of the room, practically out the door. "We use it mainly when spells go haywire."

Aunt Laurel waved her hand at him dismissively. "We're going to use it to draw your magic out. I'll turn it on real low, though this little beastie could eat a pretty big hole in this part of Magic Side if I cranked it all the way up."

I shook my head.

She gave me a warm smile that did nothing to ease my nerves. "I know this seems scary, but you can do it."

"What am I supposed to do?"

My aunt straightened her back and raised her hand in front

of the orb. "Put your hand out. Let the sphere draw your magic from you. Memorize every sensation. Learn how your magic *feels* when it's flowing from you."

Casey leaned in. "Also, don't touch the ball. It's like a portable black hole and will drain you dry."

Laurel nodded calmly.

This was insanity. I didn't trust these people. I sure as hell didn't trust the werewolves. But I trusted my instincts, and they said I wasn't going to survive long in this world unless I mastered my magic—whatever that meant—and learned who I really was.

I stuck my hand out and prepared to die.

Only I didn't. "Nothing's happening."

"It's not on yet." Laurel traced her fingers along the runes, and a few started to glow blue.

Suddenly, a vortex of power surrounded me, a whirlpool drawing me toward the sphere. I felt vertigo, like I was falling through the limitless sky.

"What's going on?" I stammered.

"The Sphere wants your magic. Let it have it. Relax. Concentrate on what you're feeling."

Pain.

No, not pain, *cold*. Like ice water trickling over my skin and through my veins. Cold that burned. I gritted my teeth as they began to chatter, and the skin of my arm turned pale. I tried to focus on the other sensations around me, but I could only think about the pain, because that's what everything had become.

Beads of sweat stung my eye, but I blinked back the tears that pooled in the corners and stared down at the black orb, willing my magic to come.

Then like a dam breaking somewhere deep inside, cold water poured though my body. Tendrils of bluish-black smoke streamed off my arm, spiraling down into the orb. I gasped with fear and relief. Was that my magic?

It wasn't fiery like Casey's, but shadowy and sinister. *Black magic. The dark arts.* Maybe I didn't want to find out what I was. Everything about this felt wrong. Dangerous.

Fear took root in my chest, and I tried to pull my hand back, but it wouldn't budge. "That's enough!"

The swirling sensations of cold and burning only intensified as my magic spiraled down into the ravenous orb. Panic gripped me, and my eyes flew to Aunt Laurel and Casey. What I saw on their faces chilled me to my core—disbelief and terror. Laurel started messing with the device, and Casey was shouting something I couldn't hear.

A heart-crushing tightness grew in my chest, and I pressed my eyelids together, feeling tears wetting my cheeks. "*Stop!*"

Suddenly, a stinging pain exploded through my palm, and my body jerked backward. The couch I was sitting on screeched across the floor, colliding with the bookshelf behind us.

My body trembled from shock, and I heaved in a lungful of air. Apart from my gasps and the sound of a book dropping to the floor, the space was eerily silent. "What the hell was that?"

"Yeah. What the *fuck*, mom?" Casey snapped.

Laurel covered the orb. "That wasn't supposed to happen like that. I'm sorry. You're new to this and haven't used your magic before. It was foolish of me to think this might work."

She darted out of the room with the floating black orb and its platform, leaving Casey and me staring blankly at each other.

"It didn't work? What would have happened if it had?" I shivered at the thought.

"No, it worked, all right." Casey grinned. "You've just got a shit ton of crazy magic."

"Is that supposed to be reassuring? Because it isn't, you ass."

I shot to my feet and hugged my chest. "Did I just use my magic?"

Casey drew a hand through his hair. "Technically, you had it vacuumed out of you. But yeah."

"What did it feel like?" Laurel asked. I hadn't seen her return.

"Unpleasant. Like ice water flowing over my body."

"Hmm." Her brows knit, and she seemed lost in thought. I couldn't decide if it was worry or perplexity on her face. "When you call your magic, you're going to focus on that sensation."

I choked back a laugh. "On the pain? Great. Is it like that for everyone?"

"No. Everyone is different, and the sensation would depend on their magic."

"And what *is* my magic? Because it sure felt dark and freaky."

Laurel took my hand and smiled. Her signature wrapped around me, calming my nerves. "You've got a lot of raw power, my dear. But it's not dark, I promise you that. It will be a long time before you can control your magic and create things, but for now, it might just manifest in little uncontrolled bursts, like electric shocks."

I gaped, not sure how to feel.

Remnants of my magic still prickled my skin like water dripping from an icicle. Having it ripped from my hand felt unnatural and was frankly terrifying. But suddenly, I felt alert to the world around me in a way I had never been before.

My skin was sensitive, and I could feel Casey and Laurel's signatures permeating the room. It was like a part of me I didn't know existed was awake and staring at the world for the first time.

Fireballs and floating brooms.

My stomach knotted. Why had my parents hidden this from me? Was there something wrong with my magic?

Jaxson had called sorcery the dark arts, black magic.

Was that what was inside of me?

Over the next hour, Laurel peppered me with questions about my childhood and my parents. I think she was trying to get my mind off of what had happened with the freaky orb that had probably nearly killed me. Luckily, reminiscing about the happy times in my life did clear my mind and raise my spirits.

Finally, Laurel gave me a coy glance out of the corner of her eye. "With all this excitement, you haven't mentioned what brought you to us so suddenly, after all these years."

There it was. The bombshell, ready to detonate. She'd left the question lying in wait, like a crocodile on the riverbank, and I didn't really have a plan to get out of its jaws.

How would they feel about me if they knew I had trouble on my heels?

I pushed that thought down. I was here for answers. About myself, about my parents, and about why someone might be after me. If it had something to do with the LaSalles, then they would be the ones to ask.

"I was attacked by werewolves. My father gave my godmother the note I brought to you, saying that if anyone ever came looking for me, I should seek you out."

Casey jumped to his feet. "Werewolves? Are you kidding me? Where?"

He'd been remarkably quiet this whole time, and now he looked like he wanted to step into a fighting ring.

Laurel motioned for Casey to sit, but her eyes blazed. No one had ever looked that intensely at me, ever. It was like she was trying to bore into my mind, kind of like Jaxson did. "Explain. *Everything.*"

Somewhat shakily, I laid out the facts for them. Laurel's eyes dilated when I said that I'd been targeted, and both of them stiff-ened when I mentioned Jaxson. She folded her hands and leaned forward. "Jaxson Laurent was investigating your attack? Don't be fooled by his handsome appearance. He's lethal. Are you aware that—"

"He's a werewolf?" I interrupted. "The alpha—whatever that means. I found out this morning. After we went out to dinner at Eclipse." I blushed, suddenly embarrassed.

Casey's eyes nearly popped out of his head. "You went on a date with the Dockside alpha? Are you crazy?"

I slapped my hands on the table. "I didn't know what he was or that werewolves even existed! That *any* of this existed!"

Casey wandered over to the sidebar and poured himself a whiskey. "Yeah, okay. Well, hopefully you didn't tell him who you were or that you're related to us."

"I did. My car broke down on the bridge. He had it towed to a shop and bought me dinner at some place called Eclipse. Then he told me about werewolves."

Casey's eyes ballooned. "Holy shit. Do you realize that Eclipse is one of the pack's main headquarters? A third of the crowd was probably werewolves. I'm surprised they didn't eat you alive."

My voice spiked an octave. "They eat people?"

Laurel put a hand on my arm. "Casey means metaphorically. They hate our family."

"I gathered. Why? He said you were dangerous and told me not to contact you."

They're criminals. They deal in illegal arms and materials.

Laurel pressed her lips together. "Of course, we're dangerous. Casey can throw fireballs. I'm one of the most lethal people in Magic Side. It doesn't mean that I'm going to dump my long-lost niece in the lake the moment she shows up. He was using your ignorance about this place to manipulate you."

I had suspected as much, but for some reason, Jaxson's warning wouldn't quite go away.

"Considering Jaxson owns Eclipse, I hope he didn't make you pick up the tab," said Casey, snickering. I sat back against the couch and put my head in my hands, and Casey passed me a whiskey. "Welcome to Magic Side. Be prepared to get dicked over by wolves."

It was a little early to be drinking, but I took a sip anyway and let the cool liquid heat my throat, while Laurel stared across the room, lines of fury fixed on her face.

Had Jaxson been laughing at me the whole time? Of course he had.

And of course the cop would recommend *his* restaurant. He'd played with my obvious ignorance of magic and werewolves.

"He was toying with me," I muttered.

Casey swirled his whiskey, then clinked his glass against mine. "Yep. They like to do that shit. I'm betting he neglected to explain why your car stalled out."

"I've got transmission problems. I'm just lucky it got me as far as it did."

"Nah. He let you believe that. The bridge is enchanted with a spell that knocks out the engine and electrical systems of any car that drives over it unless it's got a thing called a magic regulator installed. It's supposed to help keep normal people out, though since they can't even see the island, I don't know what the big deal is. The wolves run the bridges and give a cut to the mages who maintain the spells. It's a total racket."

I set my glass on the table so I wasn't tempted to throw it across the room. "So my car *didn't* break down?"

Casey shook his head. "It just needs a doohickey installed. But that's wolves for you. They like to shake your hand with their right while they dig their claws in with the left."

"He had it towed to Savage Body, which—"

Casey rapped his knuckles on the chair. "Belongs to the pack. He's got your car hostage."

I rocketed to my feet. That bastard.

He'd paid off Randy at the auto body shop to trap me in Belmont. I'd stolen his keys, and now he'd stolen my car right from under my nose.

"You're leaving?" Aunt Laurel rose in surprise. "You just got here!"

I tightened my fists and headed toward the door. "I'm going back to Dockside to skin me a werewolf king."

14

Jaxson

The loading cranes whirred and ground as they lifted the containers off the ship and onto the dock.

I shouted at my brother-in-law, Billy, over the noise. "Everything accounted for?"

He held up the manifest. "So far. Still waiting on that last batch of parts."

We'd have to unload those discreetly. They'd been procured by the lower Michigan pack, and we had to make them disappear. Thankfully, Magic Side had a number of vendors that were happy to overlook a few details for a better deal.

"Good."

He stepped close. "I've been watching what's going on here. You've been distracted by that LaSalle woman. Unfocused."

I gave a warning growl. "Thankfully, I know I can rely on you."

"Always have. But people are beginning to talk, Jaxson. You should distance yourself from her."

"Not until I can clear the pack's name. Getting tied to these abductions and murders affects our business, not just our pride."

"I know. But you should get that girl out of town. None of us like having her around."

I'd told my inner circle who Savannah was related to, thinking they could handle it. Clearly not.

I gave a laugh that was a half growl. "That might be difficult. The woman isn't compliant."

"Then get her to comply and get rid of her."

My wolf snarled in my chest. I kept it in check, but I let myself partially shift—slowly and deliberately. Hair slowly covered the backs of my hands as my claws and canines emerged, millimeter by millimeter. A slow shift demonstrated control, power, and mastery of the beast within, and not many could manage it.

Billy inched back but froze under my glare.

I stepped closer, looming over him. He was big. I was bigger. "Savannah Caine is mine. No one touches her. She's staying here, and there will be no further discussion until the pack's name is clear. Then we can figure out what to do with her."

He bared his teeth but nodded. He ran the docks. I ran the pack.

I retracted my claws and headed to the on-site manager's office. Halfway there, my phone vibrated.

Savannah. Speak of the devil. I'd called a half-dozen times, and my irritation flared.

The moment she'd left her motel room, she'd gone off script, ditched our meeting, and headed south, presumably to meet with her family—though my people couldn't follow her all the way into LaSalle territory. It was the *one* thing I'd implored her not to do.

What was it that compelled the woman to do the exact opposite of everything I asked?

I stepped into the dock manager's office, pulled off my safety hat, and picked up. "Ms. Caine. You were supposed to meet with the sketch artist. Instead, you headed to the Indies after I explicitly warned you against it. What the hell do you think you're doing?"

"Avoiding werewolves. How is it that you conveniently forgot to mention you were the damned alpha when you were scaring me out of my mind last night?" Her voice was terse and bitter.

Wasn't it obvious? "Can you blame me? You would have run screaming out of the building. You were barely holding on as it was."

She exhaled noisily. "I deserved to know what I was walking into. You're playing games with information, Jaxson. Like, for instance, you failed to mention that the only thing my car needed was a magic regulator, and it would run just fine. The funny thing is, I'm over at Savage Body, and your goons won't release my vehicle."

"It needs repairs. You can have it back once you've finished helping me."

At least she was in pack territory again. I just had to find a way to keep her there, which was unlikely, considering her current mood.

"Why do I have a feeling one sketch isn't going to be enough? What else are you expecting?"

"It's a start."

"Here's the deal: I'll make the sketch, but you get your ass over here and give my car back."

She hung up, and I tried to call her. No response.

I jammed my phone in my pocket and cursed violently enough that the clerk in the back corner of the office whimpered.

Storming out of the dockyard, I jumped into my ride, and five minutes later, I pulled up outside Savage Body. I slammed the door of the truck and grabbed the nearest mechanic. "Where is she?"

"In the office," he said, wide-eyed, "drawing something."

I pushed through the door and waved the manager out. There sat the obstinate LaSalle woman, bent over a sheet of paper on a table, sketching furiously with a stubby pencil. I could almost feel her anger with each stroke. Her energy was vibrant and alive. Something about her called to me—her fierce focus, or maybe her reckless resistance. I couldn't stand her stubbornness, couldn't stand the reminder of what had happened to my sister, but being around her was like a drug.

Then she broke the spell by speaking.

"You have some explaining to do, Laurent." She didn't even look up. "I was attacked by werewolves, and the very first thing you did when you brought me into the city was take me to the damn werewolf den."

I growled. "Because it was safe. You were *safe* with us. Yet the first thing you did this morning was prance over to the LaSalles. I made it clear that they're extremely dangerous, and I warned you to stay away."

"Yeah, so did others. The thing is, the LaSalles didn't spend all evening playing mind games and lying to me."

So she *had* gone to them.

I put my hands on the table. "If the LaSalles are talking, they're lying. You don't know them or this city. Like sugar, they'll rot you from the inside out."

"Funny. They said similar things about you. So who am I to believe? My own family, or one of these?"

She flipped the paper around and shoved it across the small table so I could see.

I sucked in a sharp breath. Fates, could she draw.

Savannah's illustration depicted a rough, tattooed woman, partially shifted. Her muscles were tensed, and her arm had retracted as if she was going to rip free of the page with her long, savage claws. Her lips were pulled back in a contemptuous snarl, revealing her erupting canines.

I let out an imperceptible sigh of relief. I didn't recognize the she-wolf, so she wasn't from our pack.

Picking up the paper, I studied the details. Somehow, working with just pencil, Savannah had even captured the glow of the she-wolf's eyes and the rage in the contours of her face. It was so lifelike—and filled with hate.

"It's extraordinary." I met Savannah's eyes. "This is far better than the sketch artist could have done."

"It's what I saw." She scowled, but I could smell her pride simmering beneath the surface.

My wolf shoved against my chest, excited by the scent. I glared at the drawing. Was this how Savannah saw us? Saw me? Neither human nor monster, but a savage half-beast, forged from violence and hatred?

I laid the extraordinary illustration back down. "I'm sorry for what happened to you. This is not what or how we are."

"I figured that much, or I would've been dead already. You didn't need to lure me to a bar. If you wanted to take me, you could have done it anytime."

Heat shot through me, and my wolf shifted. "Is that so?"

The words left my mouth without thinking and carried a tone that I hadn't intended. I could sense her surprise, and beneath that, the sweet scent of her arousal. It began to do inappropriate things to me.

Her cheeks flushed, and she put her hand on her mouth. "That came out wrong, I mean that if—"

"You never mentioned this tattoo," I said, and pointed to the woman's neck, trying to cover for the both of us. I shouldn't have said that sort of thing to a LaSalle, nor felt this way. It was wrong and dangerous.

The tattoo was a two-headed wolf, small, and just above the collar bone.

Savannah grabbed the page and inspected it. "I didn't really notice it much while they were trying to murder me. But I saw her in the bar earlier. The tat kind of came back to me. Does it mean something?"

"I'm not sure. Did the other man have one, too?"

Dane hadn't had a tattoo like that when I'd kicked him out of the pack, so maybe it was a sign he'd joined a gang or something. The problem was that Dane was wolfborn and turned into a wolf at death. There was no way to inspect his human form for tattoos. They didn't transfer.

Savannah bit her lip. "I can't remember if he had one. Let me draw."

The flowing lines of her sketch pulled me in: quick bursts of pencil, jagged marks, the scratch of shading. Soon, I found myself standing next to her, breathing in the heady aroma of her tangerine signature. It was like standing in warm sunlight.

There was something about this woman beneath the fire and anger and stubbornness.

She leaned slightly against my side, and then froze. Her cheeks reddened, and her pencil quivered. "You're breathing on me, wolf man."

I stiffened, chagrined, while my inner wolf howled with humiliating laughter.

"Do you have to draw it all? It's taking forever," I snapped.

Her partially completed illustration revealed a huge, tattooed man lunging forward in the high beams of a car.

"Yes." Savannah pointed with her pencil. "Sit. Over there. I don't need you looming over my shoulder. He's got a lot of tattoos. They're hard to remember."

Sit? Did she just command me like a dog?

My jaw ticked, and I leaned against the wall, staring out the window.

Her talent was remarkable. She could find work as an illustrator in the city, even without magic. I studied her out of the corner of my eye. Pencil in hand, she seemed calm for the first time since I'd met her, as if the images provided catharsis, or the sketching was meditation.

I smiled, pleased.

Finally, she slid the paper across the table and jabbed her finger down. "There, on his neck. I hadn't really noticed it. There are so many other tattoos, it blended in."

I rubbed the stubble of my chin. The double-headed wolf, same design, same location. Savannah's recall was amazing. "They both had one. It must be important, but I don't know exactly what it might indicate."

She leaned back and crossed her arms. "But you know something?"

I shifted the paper in my hands, uncertain how much to say. "There are dark legends in werewolf lore and religion of a twin-headed wolf—stories that were told to haunt the moonless nights. Maybe it's a reference to that."

Savannah tensed. I could smell the dread creeping across her.

I took both illustrations. "This is excellent work. I'll circulate it to all the packs around the Great Lakes and see if we get a hit. Also, I'll have someone look into those tattoos."

She stood. "Right. You've got what you wanted. Now give me my car back. I'll pay for the magic regulator, but I didn't authorize any other work."

I shook my head. "Not a chance. Your car needs help. It's on the verge of death and not safe to drive. I can't believe it made it here. It's like a zombie, shambling down the road."

She tensed and looked up. "Wait. Are zombies real?"

"Yes."

"I want my car back."

"When this is over, I'll return it to you better than new."

Her eyes flashed. "You're holding my car hostage, just so I'll cooperate?"

Why was this even a discussion? The jalopy barely ran.

I glared, temper rising. "So far, you haven't cooperated much, even when it's in your best interest. Think of it as payment for you, insurance for me."

Savannah jutted out a hip and crossed her arms. "Why are you investigating if you're the werewolf king? To cover things up? Also, why am I talking to you instead of the magic cops, or whatever it is they have around here?"

Werewolf king? I wanted to ram my claws into the wall. Why did she have to make everything so difficult?

Our pack's position was perilous. Just because a few exiled dockside wolves might be involved, the Order was tightening the screws. If I couldn't stop these abductions, they were going to invalidate our extra-legal status. We'd lose the right to practice pack law and prosecute crimes on our lands. The shame would be too much to bear.

But I sure as hell wasn't going to share any of that information with a LaSalle.

I steadied my breathing and fixed her with an impassive stare. "It's not a cover-up. Werewolves were involved. I have jurisdiction to pursue and punish them under the laws of our pack. Who better to hunt wolves than other wolves?"

"But why you? Shouldn't you be sitting on some kind of throne, getting your claws manicured?"

I snarled. "Because I'm the best. Because I'll see it done right. Or would you prefer your highly competent sheriff to handle the investigation going forward?"

She glared, clearly untrusting, but at least she seemed

partially mollified. "Fine. So you're a natural bloodhound. What more do you want from me, Jaxson? I did your sketch."

I shrugged. "The sketch is just a start. Even if someone recognizes her, that doesn't mean we'll be able to track her down. At this point, we need to consider other ways of moving forward."

"Like?" she snapped. The fire in her eyes matched her hair.

I glanced through the window into the garage bays to make sure no wolves were eavesdropping. "I'd like you to drink a scrying potion to help us locate her."

Savannah gave me a *You've got to be shitting me* stare. "What the hell is a scrying potion? I'm not drinking any crazy concoction from a damned werewolf, that's for sure."

"Hear me out. Magica drink potions all the time to boost their abilities, heal, or give themselves temporary powers. If we don't get a match for the sketch, it may be our best shot." I nonchalantly leafed through the illustrations, trying to act unconcerned, as if this were an everyday request. I hoped no one was listening.

Curiosity got the better of her. "What does it do?"

I gestured to the security cameras. "Drinking a scrying potion gives you clairvoyance for a short time—remote seeing. You take a sip of the potion, close your eyes, and concentrate on the person you need to find. Then you see a hazy picture of them, like you're an old video camera, floating in the air."

She looked into the lens of the security cam. "It's like spying on them with a drone?"

I leaned back against the office desk. "Pretty much. Scrying can give you details of their location or clues to what they're doing."

Savannah pointed to her illustration. "Can't *you* just do it, then, using the sketch? Why me?"

"Because I'm a wolf. The power to scry isn't in my blood, but it might be in yours. Plus, scrying only works if you've met the person and had a really strong impression of them. That's key. The stronger your impression, the clearer the picture, and the further the reach of the spell. You would have gotten a very strong impression of your abductors, even if you only saw them briefly."

She bit her lip as she considered. Every time she did that, it lit an inexplicable heat within me.

The woman was wavering, so I pushed. "Think about it. Just one sip of a potion, and you could help us locate that she-wolf. She'd never know we were watching, and we'd be able to ambush her before she got to anyone else. You could have justice. For yourself, and for all the others."

Savannah studied my face with a piercing gaze that was beyond her years. It made the hair on my neck stand on end. Those eyes, what was it about her eyes?

"What's the catch?" she snapped.

She was shrewd. And smart.

"No catch." I kept my expression steady. "Scrying potions are complicated to make, and each potion has to be attuned to its user. Therefore, it requires a little of your blood as a component."

She grabbed her purse from the table. "Nuh-uh, mister. Are you insane? I'm not giving you my blood for crazy magic. Do you know what someone could do with that if it fell into the wrong hands?"

"Do you?" I retorted.

She blustered. She didn't know what she was talking about, but it was clear that the LaSalles had gotten to her already.

I spoke calmly, trying to diffuse the situation and undo the damage, but my temper simmered. "Look, you don't have to be afraid. We'll use a potion maker with a stellar reputation—Alia, up in the Midway Dens. You can be there for the whole process. When she takes your blood and when she makes the potion."

She bared her teeth. "No deal. It's totally off the table. We're done here."

I grabbed her arm. "Where do you think you're going? This conversation isn't over."

"Yes, it is. I'm going back to the LaSalles, you're going to call me when my car is ready, and on no account am I giving you any of my blood."

Her signature surged, and I could feel the heat of her anger like the rays of the sun, burning my skin. But my wolf liked her spirit.

"You shouldn't go back there. It's not safe."

She narrowed her eyes at me, her dislike for me palpable. "Well, *I* feel safe there. Something tells me they have ways of keeping werewolves out."

I growled. "I can put guards at the Magic Moon Motel. You'll be safe. I'll give you an escort."

"Why are you so desperate to keep me in your territory?" she asked, regarding me closely.

The seer's prophecy echoed in my mind: *Without her at your side, you will not discover the answers you need. But be warned —your adversaries hunt her, too. If you do not stop them, she will be dead before the full moon rises, and with her, the future of your pack.*

If I wanted answers, if I wanted to protect her, I had to keep her close and under control. They were coming for her. If I wasn't there to stop them, we'd lose everything. I was tempted to tell Savannah what the seer had told me, the details of the cards she had turned. But the prophecy was for my ears only—that was the way of the magic. The fates gave you a glimpse of the future, then made you face it alone—and I wasn't going to cross the fates.

"You're an asset," I said. "I'm going to protect you, but I can't do that when you're with them. I want you close."

Her eyes dilated. Arousal? Definitely fury. An interesting cocktail.

Savannah stepped so close that I could feel her breath on my chest, then looked up to meet my eyes. "You want to put me in a box, Jaxson. To lock me in a hotel and strand me here without my car. You want control, but you're not going to get it. I'm not going to be in some creepy werewolf witness protection program, sitting in a motel room with guards outside. I'm *not* going to be beholden to *you*."

I could practically feel my wolf pacing back and forth in my soul. It liked the challenge. Wanted to fight. I, however, was tired of Savannah's obstinance, her constant resistance to logical requests. She'd steer off a bridge just to prove to everyone that she didn't have to drive straight.

I'd had it.

"Here's the truth, Savannah: you *are* beholden to me. You want your car back? Then you're working with me. You want any information about why those werewolves attacked you or what these tattoos mean? Then you're working with me—and working *with me* means going back to your motel and staying on pack land so that I can keep these rogue wolves from ripping your entrails out, like they've already done to three others."

I left her there, shaking in rage and fear, but turned back before I stepped out the door. "Tomorrow afternoon. One p.m. We go to meet the potion maker, and you're going to figure out what these people are up to. Until then, motel."

I slammed the door on the way out.

15

Savannah

A cab dropped me off at the LaSalles' and sped away. I sure as hell wasn't going straight back to the motel. I was too pissed, too confused, and I didn't know what else to do.

Casey answered the door. "Where's your wolf pelt?"

"What?"

He grinned. "You said you were going to go skin yourself a werewolf king. I don't see a car, either, so things apparently didn't go according to plan."

How much should I tell him?

I grimaced. "Jaxson's holding my car hostage, just like you said. He's not going to give it back unless I agree to work with him."

Casey ushered me in. "That's some serious bullshit. No way can you let a wolf leverage you like that. We should steal your car tonight."

"Are you kidding? Like, break into the auto body shop and just take the car?"

He closed the door and fastened four locks, one of which started to glow. "Yeah. You gotta stand up to wolves—otherwise, they'll walk all over you. It's a dominance game. You can't let him win. Trust me, we've been dealing with this kind of shit for years."

I had the distinct feeling that Casey and Jaxson were drawing me into a feud that I wanted nothing to do with, and I shook my head. "Look, breaking in is crazy. I'm just pissed. I've got an unknown number of bloodthirsty werewolves after me, and I want to bring them down. Clearly, Jaxson does, too. I just —I just hate him using my car against me. It's the only thing I've got left from my folks."

Casey rolled his eyes. "They're wolves, Savannah. If you submit, they'll expect you to submit every time. And if you try to negotiate, it'll turn into a game of keep away. He's toying with you to see if you have a backbone. It's their way."

I'd pulled off a similar car heist when I'd grabbed the Gran Fury from Randy's shop. That had gone okay. But then again, I hadn't had to break in that time, and the car was paid for. It would be a lot different smashing our way into a shop owned by werewolves in the middle of pack land.

Nope. It would feel good, but it was reckless. I sighed and leaned against the hallway wall with my arms crossed.

Aunt Laurel came home an hour later with bags of groceries. She wanted to get the extended family together for a big welcome dinner, but I talked her down. I'd had too many new things today, and I didn't have room for anything more.

I was tempted to ask her about a scrying potion, but the moment I mentioned Jaxson, she grew cold. "You shouldn't have gone to meet him. I'm not telling you what to do, but hear this—no sane woman would risk working with that man."

My Uncle Pete—Laurel's husband—came home soon after. His signature had the scent of fresh tobacco and tasted like bread cooked in a wood-fired oven. I joined him for a whiskey in the living room. While Laurel and Casey were chatterboxes, he was quiet and reserved, for which I was deeply thankful.

We ended up with Chinese takeout for dinner. I'd braced myself for greasy noodles, but it was actually pretty good, though I didn't have much chance to eat. Laurel bombarded me with questions, mainly about my dad. I hadn't really considered that when I'd lost my parents, she'd lost a brother. They'd obviously been close, but after I'd been born, he'd left Magic Side and dropped out of her life. Then he'd died. I was probably her last chance to connect to him and those lost years.

She was forthcoming with information about my father—an older sister who adored her younger brother. He was the best painter. A wonderful potion maker. His runes were precise—whatever that meant—and he could grill a good piece of meat.

Laurel was much less forthcoming about my mother.

"You never knew her at all?" I pried.

"Your father fell in love when he was at college in Georgia, and we never visited. When they moved back here, she was already pregnant with you. We were ecstatic. I thought Casey was going to have another cousin to play with, but then they moved up to Wisconsin soon after. She wasn't happy here, and they decided that this wasn't the life they wanted for you."

"Why? Because of the magic? The werewolves? Something else?"

My aunt looked to her husband. The unspoken answers between them hung in the air. Finally, she turned back to me. "It was all of it, really. It broke our hearts to have them leave, but I would have given up a little of my soul to keep them and you safe and happy."

Truth.

I bit my lip as sorrow washed over me. I tried to muster the strength to ask her more, but my cell rang. Alma. She wouldn't call unless it was important.

"Sorry, I've got to take this," I said, then rose and ducked into the other room. "Hey, Alma. Everything okay?"

"Absolutely, honey. Are you all right? Someone put posters all over town that say, *Missing: Savannah Caine, last seen on her way to Chicago.*"

"What? Is the sheriff an idiot? I'm not missing." I pushed my palm to my head. Could he be more incompetent?

"He said he didn't put them up. I asked him to take them down, but he hasn't yet. I just don't understand how he knew where you were headed. I didn't tell anyone you'd left."

"Okay, thanks for letting me know." I rubbed my forehead. Just what I needed: a bunch of road signs pointing the werewolves right to me, if they hadn't already figured out where I'd gone. Since my attackers had been hunting Magica, they'd probably assumed that I'd flee to the biggest magical city around. This didn't help the situation.

I would have chatted longer, but Alma hung up quickly in case someone was tracking our phone call.

"Everything okay?" Laurel asked when I slipped back to the table.

"Just my godmother checking in on me."

"She must be worried. You haven't told her the truth, I assume. Magic Side is a secret, and it is forbidden to tell outsiders who aren't Magica."

"She thinks I'm being chased by the men in black. Honestly, I'm probably more worried about her. If those werewolves go after her to get to me…"

My breath stilled, and my heartbeat picked up. I hadn't really considered the risk Alma might be in.

"I'm sure she'll be fine," my aunt said unconvincingly.

Concern wormed into me, but the problem sparked an idea. An opening.

It was time for a gambit.

I set down my chopsticks and muttered, "I wish there were a way I could check in on her. She doesn't always answer her phone, and I get worried. Is there any form of magic that, oh, I don't know, lets you look in on someone?"

I tried to keep my breathing steady.

Laurel raised an eyebrow.

"Yeah," said Casey, chewing noodles. "It's called scrying. Like peeping without permission. It's totally illegal, probably immoral, and you can get in big trouble."

"It's also dangerous," Laurel noted.

Damn it all, Jaxson.

"Oh," I said, and dejectedly turned back to my dinner.

"Hey, don't give up so easily," Casey leaned forward, whispering, though everyone could still hear him. "Our family happens to be really good at scrying. Kind of one of the things we do."

I bit my lip, trying to restrain my excitement. "Is it something you could teach me?"

I looked to Laurel, who raised both eyebrows this time and gave me a satisfied smile. "You know, that sounds like an excellent idea. Pete could help you make a scrying potion so you could look in on your godmother. It would be an excellent way to begin practicing your magic."

I looked to my uncle. "You make potions?"

He didn't even bother opening his mouth—Aunt Laurel just butted in. "He's quite talented with potions. That's how he ensorcelled me. A *love* potion." She gave her husband an absolutely licentious look.

"Mom!" Casey blanched and slammed down his chopsticks.

I turned to my uncle, excitement dancing across my skin. "Would you help me?"

Uncle Pete grinned. "How about tomorrow morning?"

I matched his broad smile. "I can't wait."

Things were finally coming together. I'd found my family,

and while they were clearly into shady shit, my parents had been, too. It almost felt natural to have someone claim to be really good at illegal stuff.

Moreover, I'd learned that I had magic. I'd learned that despite years of being beaten down by work and school and a backwoods upbringing, there might be something special about me after all. I still had no idea why I'd been attacked, but with a scrying potion, I might be able to get some answers without having to rely on Jaxson Laurent.

16

Savannah

After dinner, we cleared the table, and then my uncle came into the room with a tray of beautiful purple flowers with roots, leaves, and all. "If I'm going to help you make a potion, you'll need to work. Time to prep some potion components."

Casey snickered. "Welcome to my childhood. And adulthood."

Uncle Pete set the tray down and tossed me some plastic gloves.

My eyes widened. "Is this for the scrying potion?"

"No, this is just for the family business. This place is a sweatshop. Get used to it," Casey said.

I pointed to the flowers. "What are these? They're beautiful."

"Aconitum," my uncle said. "We mostly import it, but this is locally grown. It's a good component for potions, but toxic. Be careful while you're handling it."

He showed me how to delicately remove the beautiful, hood-shaped blossoms without damaging them, and then how to clip the leaves and roots. We separated them into little jars. He wasn't kidding when he'd said they were toxic. My eyes were itchy and began to water.

Laurel joined us, pulling apart the flowers. She regarded me closely, then handed me a box of tissues. "I assume you were unable to get your car back today?"

The thought of Jaxson killed the sense of peace I'd gotten from plucking blossoms. "What's the deal with you and the Laurents, anyway?"

My aunt and uncle paused. Apparently, this was not an after-dinner conversation, or at least not a flower-plucking conversation.

"They're furry, and they suck," Casey said from the sink, where he was half-assing the dishes.

I figured I'd crossed into forbidden territory, so I looked down and began to pick at the pretty purple flowers again.

"There's a lot of bad blood," my aunt finally murmured. "But we don't need to talk about that tonight."

My uncle leaned forward and put his arms on the table. His voice was bold. "Three centuries ago, Magic Side was a cluster of little islands in Lake Michigan. People filled in the spaces and created a unified city. But our island stayed separate. Ultimately, the city council, which was largely made up of wolves, forced us to join them. They got rid of our harbor so that we'd be beholden to the city. Then they tried a land grab." He waved a flower defiantly. "We taught them a lesson about what's ours and what's theirs."

My eyes darted between my aunt and uncle, unsure if I should encourage him. It was better I had the information, though, so I blurted, "But that was so long ago."

"They control all the bridges and the harbor, and they haven't stopped trying to squeeze us. You'll learn. Give them what they want, and they'll take more."

Didn't I know it. "But why do they hate you? Jaxson...seems angry."

My uncle leaned back and drummed his fingers on the table. "Because we provide people with the means to stand up for themselves."

"We shouldn't talk about this tonight," my aunt commanded. "Let's speak of brighter things."

I swallowed.

During the drive to Eclipse, Jaxson had told me the LaSalles dealt in illegal arms and materials. I looked down at the flowers so I wouldn't stare at my hosts, but my mind was churning. What did the LaSalles actually do? Was it just trafficking weapons, or did they make them, too? Were they guns like the ones I'd grown up shooting, or something worse? Something magical? Something to do with dark magic?

Jaxson had pushed me hard into staying at the motel, but when I thought about it, this was probably the safest place for me to be—with people who'd been in a standoff with werewolves for centuries.

He wants control.

But things were spiraling out of control. Some idiot had posted pictures of me all around Belmont, letting my assailants know exactly where I'd gone. Worse, Jaxson had paraded me through pack headquarters. Tons of werewolves had seen me and knew that a red-haired girl with a tattoo had just shown up in town. If one of them were in cahoots with my attackers, they'd know exactly where I was. It was practically a slam dunk.

I dropped the flower I was holding.

It couldn't be.

But something clawed from within my chest, and my pulse quickened. Was Jaxson using me as *bait*?

He'd had people keeping an eye on me. He'd tried to keep me in Belmont, where they could strike again. Now he was keeping me in town, holding my car. I was a sitting duck, and he knew they'd be back.

He's planning on it.

I jumped up from the table, my heart thundering.

"Everything okay?" Laurel asked.

"I just remembered I have to make a call," I stammered, then hurried out the front door and scrolled through my phonebook to find the entry for *Asshole.*

Jaxson picked up after the first ring. "Savannah. Good to get a call. Have you changed your mind?"

"You ass, have you lost yours?" I snapped, keeping my voice low in case anyone inside was listening.

"What are you talking about?"

For all my anger, the sound of his whiskey voice still lit a fire in me, but I fought to keep myself focused. "Are you using me as bait?"

"What? No." He scoffed. Was it genuine?

Shit.

I should have confronted him face to face. I had a good sense of when people were lying to me, but it only worked when I was right there, looking them in the eyes and making them sweat.

I pushed on anyway. "Apparently, someone plastered posters all over Belmont that said I was last seen heading to Chicago. The sheriff didn't know where I was headed, nor did anyone else in town. Did you have your people post those signs?"

"Absolutely not."

Was he lying? I couldn't tell, and it made my palms itch.

"You've tried pinning me down. You've got your stalkers watching me wherever I go. You wanted me to stay in your motel, on your lands."

"I'm doing my best to protect you while you're doing your best to get yourself killed," he said coldly.

I'd bet money his eyes had turned honey-gold, like they always did when he was pissed.

"You posted those signs. This isn't werewolf witness protection! You're using me as goddamned bait!"

His breath caught, and when he spoke, it was practically a growl. "I would never put you at risk. I'm doing everything I can to stop these people."

Was he picking his words carefully? God, I wished I could see him now. I'd be able to smell the lies on him.

"Screw you, Laurent." I jammed my finger on the end call button, as if he could feel it. He immediately called back, so I pressed the power icon until the phone turned completely off.

"Fuck," I said to the rising moon and dark summer night air. It was a filthy word that I reserved for rare circumstances. For when I was good and truly fucked, like now.

One thing I knew—I wasn't going to be staying on pack land tonight. The LaSalles were perfect strangers, but they weren't actively trying to get me killed. Plus, Laurel had offered to put me up twice.

I slammed the door out of habit on my way back inside, then blushed and remembered I was a guest.

Casey poked his head around the corner. "Everything okay?"

I glared. I was pissed at Jaxson but okay with settling for Casey as a target of my ire.

He threw his hands up. "Whoa, hey there, Medusa, point those viper eyes somewhere else. Remember, I'm the guy who's going to help you get your ride back."

I shook my head vehemently. "No, you're not. But it'd be great if you'd be willing to give me a lift to get my things. I think I'll stay here, if that's still okay."

"Of course! Mom will be thrilled. We'll get your things and your car."

"Stealing my car back from a werewolf is a terrible plan," I replied, though it would give me a hell of a lot of satisfaction to see the look on Jaxson's face. And I'd be out from under his thumb, free to make my own decisions.

Casey waved a hand dismissively. "It's a great plan, and it's already in motion. We're going to meet Zara up near the Midway in three hours."

"In motion? Who's Zara?"

"She's the gal that drives the truck that's going to tow your car out of Jaxson's auto body shop and into glorious freedom."

I crossed my arms, raised an eyebrow, and gave him a deeply skeptical look. "So what, we just break in, steal the car, and escape without consequences?" I didn't see Aunt Laurel or Uncle Pete, but I whispered anyway.

"Don't worry, I'm a pro at shenanigans like this."

I rubbed my temple. "Casey, I appreciate it, I do. But this sounds unnecessarily risky. Let's say we pull this off and don't die. Won't Jaxson just come take the car back?"

"No way. You'll have made your point and demonstrated that you've got a backbone. Plus, we'll stash it in the Midway Dens, which are run by devils and demons. Wolves respect that line in the sand, if not much else."

The world spun a bit, and I had to brace myself against the wall. "Devils and demons?"

"Ah, shit, right. You just learned about magic and were-wolves. Devils and demons are more like day-two material. On the other hand, Zara is half demon, so there's that little thing."

"You want me to work with a demon?" Who *were* these insane people?

"Not a demon, a half-demon. The other half is mage or something like that. She's cool." He grinned. "And hot. Get it?"

There wasn't much more I could really take. I was way past the point of keeping up, so I just slumped against the wall and sank down on my butt.

Casey crouched beside me. "You don't want to be beholden to this asshole, right?"

My stomach soured. I was up to my eyeballs in trouble. Jaxson had taken my only option for escape and might actually be using me as werewolf bait. I rested my arms on my knees. "Jaxson can shove it, for all I care."

"I fully agree. He's an alpha and accustomed to just taking what he wants. To having everyone around him defer. He's going to expect that of you. Do you want him bossing you around for the rest of the time you're here?"

"I want my goddamned freedom back, that's what."

Casey stood and slapped his hands on his pants. "Well, let's go get it back, then."

17

Savannah

Three hours later, the moon was high, and we were on our way to play grand theft auto in real life. We drove the long way out of LaSalle territory to make sure we weren't followed by any of Jaxson's goons waiting to stalk me at the border. Eventually, we parked Casey's RAV-4 a few blocks off the Midway, and my adrenaline was humming.

Stealing my car was an insane idea. I knew that.

Old Savannah wouldn't have done anything of the sort. But Old Savannah hadn't been attacked by werewolves, didn't know her parents had hidden her magic and family from her, and hadn't had her car essentially stolen by a mob boss who was using her as a pawn.

New Savannah was kinda having her teeth kicked in and needed a win. Also, I needed to teach Jaxson a lesson. Thus, I was going to break into his auto body shop and steal my car back.

What could go wrong?

Our plan involved three conspirators—Casey, me, and Zara, who owned a truck with a dolly trailer to tow my car. She looked almost normal, if not for the horns and the purple streaks in her dark hair.

"What are you looking at?" she snapped.

"Your horns." I was past caring at that point. This place was so weird, and *it* needed to accept the fact that I thought so. "They're cute," I quickly added, because she was also driving the truck that would be towing my car to freedom, and I didn't want to start off on a bad foot.

Zara shrugged and leaned back against the pickup with a nonchalance that shouted outward confidence but whispered, *I'm ready to bolt the moment the cops show up.*

I turned to Casey. "So, what's the plan? There is one, right?"

He waved a hand dismissively. "Pretty simple. We all hop in Zara's truck, then we break in, grab the car, load it on the dolly, and escape. The whole thing should take five to ten minutes."

I narrowed my eyes. "You seem to be skipping important details. How do we get in? How do we not trip alarms? And crucially, how do we not get caught?"

"Don't worry, cousin. I've got this handled."

I put a hand on his shoulder. "I'm worried."

"Fine. First step, we climb in the car. Second step, Zara turns the ignition. Third—"

That was just too much lip, so I kicked him in the shin. "Real details."

Casey winced and rubbed his leg. "Jeez! I was teasing!"

"We'll go through the back," said Zara. "Casey will disable the alarm spells, and I'll unlock the door. You find your keys in the office while he opens the garage bay door and I pull up out front. We'll all push your car onto the dolly and drive away. Simple."

"And if wolves show up?"

Casey shrugged. "We won't trip any alarms, so they won't.

But if they do, we get in the truck and go. There's no way to outrun them on foot."

"Won't they just chase down our car? The wolves that attacked me caught up with me on the open road."

Casey's eyes got big. "Really? Shit. I didn't think they could run that fast. I haven't seen them do that around here, but maybe they're holding back. They don't like us to know much about them. Still, that's freaky fast. Let's not get caught."

"Watertight plan, Case." I sighed.

"Also, if they catch you, no lethal force." Casey fixed Zara with a stern look, then turned to me. "This is Magic Side, not Chicago. There are rules of engagement. That's why I'm giving you this." He pressed a little bottle into my hand. "I know you can't control your magic worth crap, so if someone looks like they're going to eat you, just point this at them, close your eyes, and spray."

"Yeah. I'm familiar with the application."

He shook his head. "No, you're not. Only use this in *dire* emergencies. The wolves will try to scare you because they think it's fun. They might rough you up. Roll with the punches and get them back later. Only use this if you're staring down a wolf, it's out of its mind, and it's getting ready to bite. That's some serious weapons-grade shit in your hand."

I swallowed hard. None of these scenarios sounded great.

Casey paused as he opened the truck door and glanced between Zara and me. "And, uh, don't tell anyone where you got that if they ask."

I rolled my eyes. "I won't."

"And cousin, really, really, *really* try not spray yourself in the face."

I pocketed the bottle of what I assumed to be some kind of mace and stuck out my hip. "Casey, you're a complete ass."

He hopped in the passenger side, leaving me the suicide seats in the back. "Strange. A lot of people tell me that."

Five minutes later, we pulled to a halt a couple blocks from Savage Body.

"Why are we stopping?" I asked.

"Disguises for the cameras," Casey said as he handed out black gloves and fuzzy masks.

I held one up. "Oh, God, what is this?"

In answer, Casey put his on. They were furry wolf masks.

I groaned. "You've got to be kidding."

Zara put hers on, too. "Suit up. Let's go, rookie."

I acquiesced as the pickup rumbled down the road. The eye holes in the mask limited my vision. Was trolling the wolves like this really worth it?

Before I could decide if it was better to call things off, the truck stopped right around the corner from Savage Body. Adrenaline surged through my veins as my mind tried to come to grips with this lunacy.

Casey and Zara jumped out and darted up the alley behind the restored brick building, and I followed after. As soon as we got to the back door, Casey began whispering and waving his fingers like an abject madman.

Was this what it meant to be a sorcerer?

My doubts vanished as he formed a little glowing ball of light in his gloved palm. He blew, and the light drifted outward like a feather on the wind. It brushed gently against the door, and in a crackle of power, the whole doorway lit up with glowing magical runes.

My breath caught at the beauty of it.

Then the magic symbols dissolved into sparks and faded

into nothingness.

"That should do it," Casey whispered. "Wolves don't do magic, so they buy off-the-shelf stuff from mages. Not too hard to crack."

Zara knelt beside the doorknob, touched it, and closed her eyes. It clicked. She carefully turned the knob and swung the door in, revealing a pitch-black room.

"What did you do?" I whispered.

"I'm part Iron Mage. I control metal."

"Cool." I couldn't quite wrap my mind around what all that entailed, but it sounded awesome.

Casey pulled a tiny flashlight out of his back pocket and flicked it around the room. Within a few seconds, he'd found the lights and switched them on.

My heart seized. My Gran Fury sat on a lift in the middle of the second bay, hood up and totally in pieces.

"What did he do?" I gasped as I dashed over to the car.

The seat back had been removed and lay to the side, along with several parts that I assumed made the car go.

This was bad.

Zara flicked a switch on the wall, and the hydraulic lift roared to life, slowly lowering the car to the ground.

Casey grabbed my shoulder. "Don't worry, your ride's probably okay. We'll just need to take everything with us. Go get your keys from the office."

Tears swam in the corners of my eyes as I darted for the office. That asshole had ripped apart the one thing that mattered to me.

I tried the office door. "It's locked!"

"Give me a sec, I'll get it!" Zara shouted from the lift.

I shook the doorknob as my mind spun with worry. There could be a silent alarm. They could be on their way. Jaxson could be here any second.

My skin began to prickle, and my arm hair stood on end. Then a shock of cold raced down my arm and blasted the doorknob out of my hand. I yelped as the office door blew off its hinges, and the detached doorknob clattered to the floor somewhere in the office.

"Damn," Zara called from her post. "I thought you didn't know magic."

I looked down at my hand in shock. "I don't."

A big red light in the interior of the office started blinking.

Well, crap.

As a new layer of panic seeped into my voice, I shouted to Casey, "I think I screwed up!"

"Get the keys," Zara hissed. "I'll get the truck. We gotta work fast."

I flicked on the office lights and found the cabinet with the car keys, which was also locked. Zara was gone, so I tried focusing my mind and doing the magic thing.

Nothing. No explosion, no icy skin, no juice.

With nothing else to do, I rampaged through the desk until I found a key hanging on a hidden hook. I jammed it in the lock and popped the cabinet open. My keys were on a chain with a bunch of tiny silver paint brushes, so they were easy to find. I snagged them and dashed out of the office.

When I emerged, Casey had the car down and the bay door open, and Zara had expertly backed the truck up so the tow dolly was aligned.

We were so close.

Casey waved me over. "Hop in and put her in neutral! Zara and I will push."

I slid into the driver's seat, and my heart wrenched. My radio was gone, leaving only a big black hole in the faux wood paneling.

I was going to murder Jaxson Laurent.

But first, we had to get out of here. I threw the car in neutral and gripped the wheel. "Okay!"

Casey grunted and pushed the car with all his might. Zara rolled her eyes and waved her hand, and the car slowly rolled forward. When Casey grunted and fell on his knees, she grinned.

Apparently, mastery over metal meant she could shove half-ton cars around. Cool.

The metal ramps of the trailer grated on the pavement as the Fury's wheels rolled on up. Then the pickup lurched forward an inch as the car thumped against the end of the dolly and settled down in the wheel sockets.

"Nice! Let's get the other shit!" Casey shouted.

I scrambled out of the car as Zara secured straps around the wheels, barely believing our luck. Casey was struggling with the loose back of the seat, so I grabbed hold, and we dumped it in the bed of the pickup.

I ran around the pile of car parts. "What is all this stuff? Does it even belong to my car?"

"No idea!" Casey yelled, picking up a few pipe-like objects. "Just grab it and go. You can give it back later if it doesn't belong!"

"This is insane!" I snatched a few things I thought I recognized, ran back to the truck, and dumped them in the bed.

Zara had finished securing the Fury and climbed up into the cab of the truck. "Let's go, you two!"

"Wait! There's more stuff!" I darted back into the garage.

Casey held up a couple of bits and bobs. "I'm not actually sure that any of this is yours."

"That's my radio." I grabbed it and clutched it close to my chest. The open socket in the dashboard had been like a hole in my heart.

Shouts erupted from behind us, and I spun around. At the

commotion, the pickup's tires screeched on the pavement, and it lurched forward. "She's leaving us!" I shouted in disbelief.

Casey and I raced toward the open garage as the truck peeled away, my Gran Fury in tow. We staggered to a halt as shadows appeared in the street outside. Werewolves.

"Back door! Run!" Casey shouted.

We barreled out the rear into the alley. He slammed the door shut and wove a quick spell, and sparks erupted from the door-knob. "Go! They'll just run around the outside of the building. Or over the top—they can jump really far!"

We tore down the alley. I looked back as a dark shadow leapt onto the roof of the garage, then sprung high into the air. With the obscured vision of the mask, I couldn't see where it landed. I could barely see where we were going.

"Are they going to kill us?" I screamed.

"Probably not! Don't use any hocus-pocus unless absolutely necessary. We're on their turf, and that would be bad," Casey panted, surprisingly out of shape.

"I don't have any goddamned hocus-pocus left to use!" I yelled back as we rounded a corner.

"You'll be fine!" he replied, but then the shadowy form of a woman slammed into his chest, and he flew into the wall.

Sam. Jaxson's bartender.

I skidded to a halt.

Jaxson stood at the far end of the alley, silhouetted against the streetlights. My breath caught, and my knees locked.

"Run, Savannah!" Casey screamed as he scrambled up from the ground.

Sam swept his feet out from under him, which knocked him on his ass and knocked me to my senses. I bolted back down the alley with Jaxson on my heels.

18

Savannah

My heart hammered in my chest as I sprinted between the brick buildings. I'd run track in high school and had a little speed, so maybe I could get a lucky turn and lose him.

I checked over my shoulder. Nope.

Jaxson was almost on me. He was too damned fast.

Not that I was surprised. The wolves that had attacked me had run my car down, and Jaxson was several magnitudes more powerful.

I ran anyway. A part of my soul leapt at the exhilaration, while the rest of my mind rebelled against the sheer insanity of it all.

I gave it everything I had.

Gravel scuffed, and a shadow flew through the air. Jaxson slammed into the side of a building and hung there with his fingers—no, his *claws*—embedded into the old, crumbling brick.

I darted right down a side street. Jaxson leapt again and landed on the adjacent wall above me, sending mortar raining down.

Holy hell. His hands could dig straight into brick.

He sprang upward and landed on the rooftop. I spun around a corner, but he hurled himself through the air and onto another rooftop right ahead.

He could outrun a car and leap thirty feet.

He's toying with me.

With that realization, I skidded to a halt, clutched the old radio to my chest, and yanked the bottle of mace out of my back pocket. Arm extended, I pointed it up at the black shadow on the roof. "Stay back, Jaxson!"

He leapt overhead, rebounded off the wall, and landed square in front of me with a low growl.

I pointed the mace directly at his glowing honey eyes. "I mean it, I—"

The bottle flew from my hand. I shook my wrist in shock. He'd struck the mace out of my grip so fast that I'd barely seen his arm move.

Jaxson let out a deep, animalistic growl. His hands were claws, and his body quaked with restrained power. "Don't you ever bring that stuff onto pack land ever again."

There was something almost feral in his voice.

I pressed my back against the bricks. My heart pounded so hard in my chest that it was about to rip its way out.

Two other werewolves rushed into the alley, but he stopped them with a flick of his clawed hand as he took another step forward. "How dare you break into my shop, LaSalle? I thought it might take longer before your family corrupted you, but it hasn't even been a day. The apple doesn't fall far from the tree, it seems."

His signature—I knew it for what it was now—overwhelmed me, like he was letting it all out. Pine and moss and smoke and snow and the sound of running water. I couldn't resist breathing it in. All of it. It called to me like a drug. The werewolf before me was terrifying and intoxicating, like the urge to jump at the edge of a cliff. But I was too scared to go over. I could barely find my voice. "Please—"

Jaxson met my petrified gaze with his honey-colored eyes. They seemed to be drinking me in, reading every thought in my head. He loomed over me, chest heaving, though I was sure he hadn't broken a sweat chasing me down.

Finally, he gave me a half smile and brushed the side of my masked cheek with a claw. I didn't move a millimeter as it dragged over my skin, but my heart felt like it was going to explode out of my body.

When he withdrew his hand, it was human again. I let out a fraction of the breath pent up in my lungs.

"Don't worry, Savannah. You're safe." Then he grabbed my mask by the snout and pulled it up over my head. "And I must say, I quite like you as a wolf."

The rich, silvery tone of his voice made goosebumps rise on my skin. His amber eyes flicked to my heaving breast and back. I could almost smell...his desire?

Impossible. He hated me. This was *so* screwed up.

Jaxson was close enough that I could almost taste him. Part of me wanted to, and heat pooled in my belly.

What's wrong with you, Savy?

My phone rang in my pocket. I squeezed it through my jeans to silence it and fixed Jaxson with my best *Don't screw with me* look. "You need to back off."

Amusement flashed through his eyes, but his features were still hardened. He leaned in and softly whispered. "Why? I caught you. You're not very fast."

I bared my teeth, suddenly and inexplicably offended. It wasn't like I was an Olympian, but I had plenty of giddy-up and high school trophies to prove I was fast enough. He was just stupid fast.

Casey had said I needed to hold my ground, so I raised my chin. "I do *not* like being toyed with."

"But you're such a pretty toy," he growled, low and rough.

Anger shot through my veins like ice water. I reared back and slapped the Dockside alpha as hard as I could. Electricity cracked through my arm, and my fingers went numb from the cold.

Jaxson staggered back a single step. His pupils dilated, and his claws erupted from his hands. He touched his cheek, where the faint streaks from my nails were beginning to turn pink.

Did I just slap the Dockside alpha?

I looked at his claws. I'd seen ones just like them nearly rip the guts out of a man and hurl him onto the hood of my car. But it was too late. Jaxson was on his back foot, and I couldn't back down.

So I stepped up, moving so close that we were only an inch apart. He was tall, so I had to crane my neck back to stare him down, but I wasn't going to let this slide. "I am not a toy, Jaxson. You don't get to boss me around, and you don't get to dangle me as bait."

Jaxson

Savannah Caine was an inch from my chest and as close to meeting my wolf as she had ever been. He fought to be released, but I held him down with difficulty.

Her aromas intoxicated my senses. A cocktail of terror and anger, and hidden beneath it all, a faint whisp of arousal.

Her nails had left scratches where her hand had hit, and my skin was tender.

The taste of cold spring water mixed with a trace of blood in my mouth, and I could smell the scent of tangerines. Her magic?

While her touch stung like frostbite, fire burned in her eyes. Everything about her in this moment made me feel alive.

"I'm the Dockside Boss, and you're in my territory, causing trouble. That means I get to boss you around."

"Get over yourself!" Savannah almost snarled, and my wolf liked it.

"You broke into my shop. I expect an apology."

"No way am I apologizing. You screwed with my car—after holding it for ransom! Why was it in pieces?" Her eyes flicked to the two werewolves hanging back down the alley. As if they would be any threat, compared to me.

"It was a wreck. Your tranny is shot. Your radiator hoses are cracked. Your upholstery is disintegrating, and your radio is over thirty years old. I was installing upgrades."

"Never, *ever* touch my shit without my permission. Or me." She smacked my chest with the heel of her palm, to no effect. No magic this time.

"Says the woman who broke into my property and slapped me with her magic."

Her eyes widened. "Your scratches are gone!"

"We heal quickly. How else do you think your attacker got up again after you ran him over? He only stayed down after you snapped his neck."

She trembled with shock, surprise, and simmering fury, but she wouldn't be put off the warpath. "I have half a mind to run *you* over. You're using me as bait to catch the psychos behind the abductions!" She looked so furious, I wondered if claws would rip out of her hands.

"You don't know what you're talking about," I snarled, but she wasn't entirely wrong.

"You paraded me through Eclipse on purpose, you plastered signs all over Belmont to point the wolves my way, and you've tried to keep me on lockdown. You knew they would come back, and you're using me to catch them. Deny it."

"I knew that they were coming for you, and I told you as much. I'm trying to protect you as best I can. The moment they show their faces, I'll drop a hammer on them. But you keep running straight into danger."

"Those are justifications, not denials!"

I considered her words. She'd caught my lies before, but since wolves could smell lies, I was used to word play. "Look, Savannah, I'm not going to use you as bait."

That plan was dead, anyway.

"I don't trust you," she hissed.

"I don't care. But know this: I will protect you. You are important to me, and I'm not going to let you fall into their hands."

Every word was true.

Her eyes burned into me, and she gritted her teeth. She didn't believe me, but she finally relaxed.

"You might think that, Jaxson, but you're still going to get me killed."

I stiffened as the seer's prophecy burned in my mind. *Your adversaries hunt her, too. If you do not stop them, she will be dead before the full moon rises, and with her, the future of your pack.*

I looked up at the moon. Three nights left.

"I need you to work with me," I told her.

"I don't give a shit about you or your needs. Is that clear?" She pushed on my chest with her free hand, but it didn't budge me a millimeter.

I grabbed her wrist. "You need to stop playing games, LaSalle. People are disappearing. Three have been murdered, and you're next on their list."

She struggled in my grip. "I want to figure this out as much as you do. More so because I'm trying to live through it. But you gotta back off, or you get nothing."

When I pulled her to my chest, she resisted, but it was nothing for me to hold her close. Her warmth pressed against my body, and I could smell her hate and desire. I spoke low in words for her ears alone. "I'll make you a deal. I'll let you go. I'll let your idiotic cousin go. And I'll let the car go. You're going to help me, and you're going to do what I say. And you're going to stop running around, getting into fucking trouble."

"Or what?" she snapped, voice held at a whisper.

Why. Is. She. So. Damned. Obstinate?

I lowered my head to her ear. "You killed a werewolf. That means you're subject to werewolf law. Many of my wolves want to make you stand trial before the pack, and the consequences could be dire."

Savannah jerked back, and I could feel the anger radiating off her. "Stand trial? Where do you get off? For the wolf I ran down? I was freaking attacked! That's self-defense."

"We don't take the killing of our members lightly—even if they're exiled, they're still wolves, and the Old Laws call for an eye for an eye. Maybe in another case, the pack elders would be fair, but every single one of them hates your family and will want to see you bleed. So far, I've intervened on your behalf and will continue to do so as long as you're an asset. But if you don't help me, I won't help you."

She shook with rage.

I stepped away and issued one final command. "My men will escort you out of pack territory for tonight. You have my permission to return tomorrow. Your cousin doesn't. Meet me at Eclipse at one."

19

Savannah

The Dockside asshole turned and walked away.

Clutching my radio, I leaned my head back against the rough red brick and let out a deep sigh of relief as he turned the corner, though the world seemed less vibrant with his signature gone.

Get your head screwed on straight, Savy.

I hated the way my body felt around him. Excited. Aroused. The man was a wolf. He'd stolen my car and threatened me with a murder charge. He'd chased me down a dark alley at night. Not to mention he loathed everything about me. I could see it in his face whenever he set those damn honey eyes on me.

Also, the noble werewolf king had just left me standing there with a couple of his thugs.

"Let's go, LaSalle." Goon One shoved me hard and gestured down the alley.

"I'm not a LaSalle." I bent to grab the bottle of mace I'd dropped, but Goon Two put his foot on it.

Fine.

I raised my chin and strode down the alley with the goons in tow. My phone rang for the third time, and I pulled it out and answered, "Hey, Case."

"Are you okay? Do I need to call in the troops?"

"Yeah, I'm fine. I'm being marched out of pack territory by a couple of Jaxson's thugs."

"Thank fates. I was getting nervous," Casey clucked like a mother hen.

"Are you okay? What happened?"

He sighed. "Well, I just got my ass kicked by a chick."

I wrinkled my nose in annoyance. "And what's wrong with that?"

"Nothing," he huffed. "I've got lots of chicks who are friends, so it happens a lot. I'm just saying I *literally* got my ass kicked by a woman, and it's gonna be uncomfortable sitting down for a few days. Where are you?"

"An alley somewhere. Probably headed in your direction."

"Cool. I'm just chilling across the street from my new wolf *pals*, so I guess I'll see you in a few minutes."

I hung up as we exited the alley and followed the sidewalk along the street. Everything was closed aside from a couple of dive bars, though the road was well lit with the deep golden glow of sodium streetlamps. A few late-night drinkers staggered down the sidewalk, and I brushed my hand along the bars of a pawnshop window, quite happy to have bodyguards at my side for the walk through this part of Magic Side.

This wasn't small-town Wisconsin anymore.

As my fight-or-flight instinct began to relax, a spark of elation built in my chest. Sure, I was forcibly getting escorted out of the neighborhood, but we'd gotten my car back, and it'd been a rush. I'd been chased down by the alpha, but I'd stood my ground at the end and showed him I wouldn't back down. And that felt good.

Sort of. He *had* made me nearly piss myself.

Despite that, by the time we reached the edge of the pack's territory, I'd gotten my mojo back.

Casey sat on the hood of a car across the street, under the close supervision of Sam and another wolf. I opened my mouth to apologize to her, but she tossed her hair, turned away, and climbed into a black SUV.

Goon One gave me a final unnecessary shove. "Stay on your side of the street, LaSalle."

"Hands off," I snapped, and then I marched across the road, head held high.

Casey grinned, and flipped off the wolves as they drove away. "Hey, we did it!" he crowed. "And I'm glad you're okay. How are you feeling about your first car heist?"

"Well, short of injury, I'm not sure how much worse that could have gone. We got busted. I thought you were a pro at this."

He shrugged apologetically. "Maybe not a pro, but in all fairness, I didn't think they'd disassemble it. That was bullshit. Anyway, we got the car and the parts, and that's what matters."

I pointed the radio at him accusingly. "Your asshole friend ditched us. God knows where the car is."

He shook his head. "Rules say every man for himself, but yeah, she's an ass. Still, she did her job. I called her, and your car is at the shop now under lock and key. The wolves won't risk a confrontation up in the Midway Dens. Mission accomplished. Also, don't tell Mom. Ever."

Great. That basically confirmed how idiotic this had been.

I took a deep, chest-stretching breath and scanned the nearly empty street. "Mission-critical question: how do we get home? That's not your car, too, is it?" I gestured to the Honda Civic that Casey was sitting on.

He glanced down. "No. Why? I already summoned a cab. It'll be here in a couple minutes, and we'll grab my RAV-4."

I shrugged and leaned back against the Civic. "I thought your ass hurt so much, you wouldn't be able to sit for a week."

Casey kicked his legs out. "Yeah, but my legs are tired. That was a lot of running."

He'd made it all of five hundred feet before getting tackled. Casey was oddly out of shape for his build.

I released a long, low breath that felt like it had been pent up in my chest for hours. "I can't believe we did that. It was so stupid. And dangerous."

"Totally stupid, but not *that* dangerous. These things don't generally end up with fatalities. I can throw fireballs. They can gut us with their hands. Generally, everybody is so deadly, we make sure things don't escalate. The most important thing is that we had a fun time."

I closed my eyes and slowly shook my head. My cousin was clearly bonkers. One hundred percent a nutter. But I couldn't deny that I'd had fun. Breaking magical locks, sneaking in, getting what was mine...even getting caught, though I was scared at the time. My instincts told me Jaxson wouldn't hurt me, but *damn* was he intimidating.

And I'd wanted to run. To have him chase. That made no fricking sense at all.

I cracked a smile at my lunatic cousin. "I think hanging out with you is making me crazy."

He kicked his heels softly against the side of the car. "Oh, we're crazy for sure. But that probably wouldn't wear off on you so quickly unless you were nuts to begin with."

"Maybe. But strangely, I didn't notice it before coming here."

Casey slid off the hood as our cab pulled up. "We're all more than what we suspect we are. In this case, I'm willing to bet you were nuts long before you met us."

Fair enough.

We walked our tired asses back to Casey's RAV-4, then immediately violated Jaxson's explicit orders by going to the Magic Moon Motel.

It was a risk, but I needed fresh undies, clothes, and a toothbrush. I was a civilized person, and I was going to get my stuff back.

Casey parked out front and shook his head. "You're shitting me. You actually stayed here? The name wasn't a dead giveaway?"

Magic Moon. That made a lot more sense now.

"How was I supposed to know? At the time, I was drunk and didn't really know about magic. Now come on, help me pack."

"Hold up." He reached under his seat and pulled out another bottle of mace and handed it to me. "Try not to lose this one this time."

"How many bottles of this stuff do you have?"

Casey smirked. "More than I can count. I wouldn't go on pack lands without it. Just remember, emergency use only."

The guy at the front desk was gone, thank God, so we darted up the stairs two at a time.

"This place isn't half bad," Casey said as we reached the first-floor landing.

"Just because they're animals doesn't mean they can't run a good business. I mean, have you been to Eclipse?"

"Girl, did I just hear what I think I did? Rewind. Werewolves are bastards, and any business they run is shifty. Don't you forget that."

I rolled my eyes and pulled out my room key, but I paused before slipping it into the lock.

The door was already slightly ajar.

"Motherfuckers," I whispered. I'd raided the shop, and now

the werewolves had raided my room. Was Jaxson going to hold my underwear ransom?

My instincts held me back. Maybe it wasn't Jaxson.

"Let's get out of here," I whispered to Casey.

Before I could turn around, the door whipped open, and a meaty hand grabbed my arm and pulled me inside. I twisted and came face to face with a six-and-a-half-foot-tall grinning shifter. He wore a ski mask that hid everything but his erupted canines and glowing crimson eyes.

Fear sunk its claws into chest, and my pulse shot through the roof.

Red eyes. It's them. The people hunting me.

I wrenched back, but when he wouldn't release me, I pulled out Casey's mace and gave him a good spray. A cloud of mist enveloped the man's masked face, and a heart-wrenching snarl erupted from him. He stumbled back into the wall, clawing at his eyes and roaring in pain.

Tears streamed down my cheeks, and I coughed, suddenly unable to breathe.

"Don't spray that shit inside!" Casey yelled, too late.

A second shifter stepped out of the bathroom and let out a roar of rage. Casey stepped around me and unleashed a glowing fireball.

Flames billowed around the room and paralyzed me in place.

Was I breathing? No, because I was choking on mace.

A hand smacked me in the face, returning me to my senses. I stumbled back and clutched my stinging cheek, then snarled and kicked my attacker in the nuts. He was still fighting the effects of the mace and dropped to his knees, grimacing in pain.

"Didn't your mother ever tell you not to hit girls?" I managed between coughs.

Before I could react, his fist shot out, lightning fast, and struck me in the stomach. I flew several feet back and crashed into the opposite wall. Pain exploded in my abdomen, and I gasped for air.

"You okay?" Casey shouted over his shoulder. Another crimson-eyed man appeared through the door and leapt toward Casey, claws extended.

My eyes bugged out, and I tried to scream a warning, but only a croak came forth.

Casey spun away from the claws and flung a burst of glowing light at the man. It hit the shifter in the chest and pitched him back out through the door.

The shifter I'd dropped to the floor grabbed Casey's ankle and jerked him to the ground. He twisted, and Casey's ankle popped. My cousin unleashed a slew of curses that shocked even me and blasted the shifter with a stream of fire.

The shifter howled with pain as fire cascaded over him. His ski mask went up in flames, and the skin on his face sizzled off. I gagged from the smell of burnt flesh and polyester. He scrambled to his feet and charged out the door in a blur, followed by the other.

"You little sissies! Come back and fight!" Casey yelled after them.

Clutching my stomach and gagging from the aftershock of the mace, I got up and dragged Casey to his feet. "Come on, we can't let them get away."

He flinched and hobbled on one leg. "Are you nuts?"

"Probably, but this is a chance to nab one of these bastards. Let's go!"

I hauled him outside and down the stairs. His ankle was swollen, and I had to brace him the whole way. Luckily, the guy at the front desk was still gone. I hoped he hadn't been offed by the attackers.

Unless he was working with them.

"Keys!" I held out my hand and shoved Casey into the passenger seat. He rolled his eyes and tossed the keys to me, but as I started for the other door, I froze halfway around the car.

The three shifters who'd ambushed us were lurking across the street, their ruddy eyes on me. Fear and anger gripped me, each fighting for control. The one that Casey had fireballed strode toward us. His skin looked like it was almost healed, and I shivered.

These monsters were unstoppable.

Casey rolled down the window and held out his hand with a ball of fire floating above his palm.

The shifter paused, and then all three scrambled for an Oldsmobile parked on the side of the road.

Casey's fireball soared through the air and exploded on the pavement beside them, knocking one of them on his ass. The glass of the nearby storefront shattered with the blast.

"What the hell are you doing?" I yelled as I jumped into the front seat of the RAV-4 and turned the ignition.

The shifters scrambled into their car and tore down the road, weaving across the street.

I gunned it and raced after them.

Casey grinned at me, one hand holding the oh-shit handle. "Preparing the barbeque. I'm hungry for some shifter steaks."

"And *I'm* the one who's nuts? You are a certified wacko, Casey."

He was having way too much fun, and I was pretty sure that blowing up shit in the pack's territory was a no-no.

There was going to be hell to pay.

20

Jaxson

"And what about the Traverse City pack? Will they sign the deal?" I asked, thumbing through the papers on my desk.

I was working late because every other pack around was trying to squeeze my balls, and the LaSalle woman was eating up my time—even when she wasn't around.

Why couldn't I get that damn woman off my mind?

I couldn't believe that she'd had the gall to break into my shop to steal her car. Her boldness and utter disregard for my authority were infuriating.

"They'll sign if you agree to give them a ten percent share," Barb said over the line.

Sam and Regina raised their brows at me. Clearly, that was too much, given that we were taking all the risks hauling black market car parts over state lines.

"Five percent. And I'll throw in a crate of magic disablers," I said.

There was a pause on the end of the line. "Eight percent."

"Seven."

"Fine," Barb sighed. "I'll fax over the paperwork tonight. Good doing business with you, Jax, as always."

Sam grinned. "Not a bad deal. Way to get rid of those magic disablers."

She was in a cheery mood after getting to kick the LaSalle boy's punk ass. I deeply regretted not getting to see it myself. She could unleash hell when she had to, but generally, Sam fronted information for me. Everyone in town, whatever species, wanted into Eclipse, so her job at the bar allowed her to trade and barter with demons, devils, and fae all night long.

My cellphone rang, and I answered. "Yes?"

"Boss, there's been several explosions over on 67th Street. From the reports, it sounds like the sorcerers," Tony said.

You have got to be shitting me.

I growled. "The LaSalles?"

"No word. Heading over that way now."

That was right by the Magic Moon Motel.

Savannah fucking Caine. It had to be her and that fucking cousin of hers.

"We'll be right there. Don't let her get away." I hung up and clenched my fists.

This woman was a damned nuisance, and if I had it my way, I'd chain her to my desk where she couldn't cause any more destruction.

The image of that made my wolf stir and my muscles tighten. Fuck. I scrubbed a hand through my hair and stormed through Eclipse, Regina and Sam in my wake.

At least *they* could tell the difference between when to follow and when to ask questions.

My phone rang again.

Savannah. Speak of the devil herself.

I punched the screen and growled, "You're blowing up shit in my territory after my wolves escorted you out? Are you out of your goddamned mind?"

"Shut up and listen," she said.

Fury coursed through me, and I clenched my phone. Something cracked.

"I was attacked at the motel by red-eyed psycho wolves. We're chasing down the shifters now." I heard the screeching of tires and the curses of her cousin in the background.

Fuck. Why hadn't I been alerted that she'd been attacked in the motel? I had someone stationed there for just that reason, as I knew she'd be back sooner or later for her things.

"Stay on the fucking line and don't let them out of your sight!" I shouted at the phone.

We burst out the back door of Eclipse while Savannah screamed the details of what had happened over her speaker-phone. We jumped into my truck, and the beast roared to life. "Where are you right now?"

"Where are we, Casey?" There was a pause. "67th and Ironwood. Get your ass over here!"

I heard an explosion across the line, and it disconnected.

I hit the gas. The truck lurched forward, and the tires squealed against the pavement.

"If that asshole cousin of hers is throwing fireballs in downtown Dockside, I'm going to skin him and hang him on the wall," Regina snapped. I wouldn't put it past my second in command. She'd been my sister's best friend and still had a score to settle.

"I've got to hand it to her, Jax. First her car, and now this? Savannah is a damn wild card." Sam had a shit-eating-grin pasted on her face.

Did she actually like the red-headed monster? I growled and shot her a look. "Not now, Sam."

Darkness seeped into my mind, and I tried not to break the steering wheel.

I told Savannah to go to the motel. I had people watching it. She would be safe. She said no.

Fine. I could adapt, so I'd redeployed those people to watch the Indies. Then she went to the motel.

One of us was going to be the death of the other.

Red brake lights filled the street ahead, so I veered into a back alley, swerving around a dumpster. A flash, followed by an explosion, echoed from the south.

"What the hell do they think they're doing?" Regina yelled.

My phone rang again, and Sam answered it on speaker.

"Hello?" a man's voice said. Savannah's *cousin*. We had a mile-long dossier on the creep. "Where the hell are you guys? I knew you were slow, but come on."

I tightened my grip on the wheel, wishing it were his neck.

"We're right behind you, asshole," said Sam. "We just heard the explosion. Pro tip: stop unleashing a firestorm on our town, or we'll return the favor."

"Message received. They turned right and we're heading north on Razorback. Just passed Donahue's Grill House. Hey, they opened one over here?"

"Casey, focus!" Savannah's voice cut across the line.

"What are they driving?" I asked.

"Tan Oldsmobile. Looks like a real piece of shit. Maybe you should steal it and hold it for ransom in your shop," her cousin said.

To my wolf, that man was just a mouthy steak with a bad attitude.

I gunned it down 64th Street. If my calculations were correct, we might be able to cut them off. Regina cursed as we sped through a red light, narrowly missing a collision with a Beamer.

Two blocks ahead was the Diagonal—our shortcut to intercept. Adrenaline pumped through my veins, distracting me from the anger that clawed in my chest. I had to put it aside for now. If we could catch one of the rogue wolves, it would solve most of our immediate problems. I'd beat the information out of them. We'd hunt down their allies. And once it was done, I would be mercifully free of Savannah Caine.

The truck careened right as we peeled through the intersection onto the Diagonal.

"Tell me where you are, Savannah," I growled.

"This is Casey here. Savannah's busy driving like a bat outta hell. We're just passing 64th Street and Louie's Strip Joint. That looks promising."

Just where I needed them.

"Seatbelts on," I said as I shifted gears and hit the accelerator. Two blocks, and we'd be coming right up—

A tan Oldsmobile came into view as the lights in the six-way intersection turned red.

I hit the gas, and we rocketed forward. Shock crossed the face of the shifter in the passenger seat of the Oldsmobile just before my truck T-boned them.

The grating of metal was deafening, and I braced myself against the wheel. The Oldsmobile slid across the intersection sideways before stopping. Steam rose from the hood of the truck, but the grates on the front had absorbed most of the impact.

I sucked in air and felt around my neck. A broken clavicle.

I glanced over at Sam and Regina, who were smiling wildly. Sam popped her arm back in its socket and hopped out.

It was good to be a wolf.

I ripped my crushed door off its hinges and extracted myself from the wreckage.

Screeching tires echoed behind us.

"Holy shit!" Savannah's cousin was hanging halfway out the

passenger-side window, pumping his fist into air. He was a fucking lunatic. Then again, he was Laurel's son. The apple didn't fall far from the tree.

Two masked male shifters climbed out of the crumpled Oldsmobile, and with a burst of speed, I circled around the rear. The one in the front seat was dead. Neck broken.

The rogue shifters put their backs together as Regina and Sam closed in around the wreckage, their claws extended.

The two shifters took one look at them and me, and then sprinted down the street, heading north.

I grinned and tore off after them. I liked a good chase, and tonight, I had some steam to blow off before ripping Savannah a new one.

But they ran fucking fast. Faster than possible.

What the hell was going on?

Sam and Regina shifted into wolves but still couldn't catch up.

My wolf roared with rage as they rapidly pulled away from us. I started to shift, and my shirt ripped, but Sam growled and snapped.

I understood her intent, as I could speak without words to the wolves of my inner circle: *We'll hunt. Don't let the LaSalles blow anything else up.*

I snarled but slowed. She was right. I had to get the LaSalles out of pack territory before they were spotted. The destruction Savannah's cousin had likely caused was sure to draw attention.

Savannah was peering into the smashed Oldsmobile. Her cousin hobbled out of the car and leaned against the hood as I approached. His foot was injured, and I could smell the repressed pain streaming off him. He deserved more for unleashing hellfire on my city.

"You were told to leave, and yet, you came back," I growled, smelling the faint traces of wolfsbane on her.

Did this woman have a death wish?

Savannah spun and met my gaze, her eyes blazing. The skin on her cheek was red and swollen where she'd been struck. Rage and protectiveness flooded me, threatening to spill out.

I'd beat the hell out of the shifter who'd hit her.

"What are you doing here?" I roared.

Savannah flinched and I could smell her fear, but she planted her feet and stared me down, giving me that ridiculous *look* she used when she thought she could make me bend. "I needed my stuff, so I came back and was jumped. In. Your. Territory."

Anger burned through me, and my claws itched to come out. How did this woman know exactly how to drive me over the edge?

I strode up to her, my body shaking as I fought for composure. My wolf wanted control. He wanted her to submit. *I* wanted her to submit.

And something else.

Her heat flooded into me, and her pulse pounded in my ears. I could taste her sweat from here, so fucking sweet. "I told you to stay out of my territory tonight. When I tell you something, you'd better listen."

Her cousin scoffed as he limped around the car. Broken ankle, I noted. I'd have liked to break the other.

"I do what I want. I'm not a wolf. I'm not beholden to you," Savannah hissed, though I could sense her trepidation.

"Apparently, you want to fuck up as much shit as possible."

She grabbed my partly torn shirt. "Well, I guess we know one thing: your plan to use me as bait would have worked. Except without my cousin, they would have grabbed me and been long gone before you knew what had happened."

My body shook. She had no idea how close I was to shifting. Nor how close I was to picking her up over my shoulder and dragging her back to my place to lock her in my spare bedroom. At least I'd be sure she wouldn't be causing trouble.

I closed my eyes and asked my wolf for patience. "If I would have known you were going to go to the motel, I would have guarded the goddamned place. How am I going to fucking protect you if you always do the exact opposite of everything that you're told?"

She crossed her arms. "Well, I lived. And it looks like they got away. I thought you were fast, but..."

I had to step away. Just for a second. Just until I could get my wolf under control. Now was not the time for them to meet.

My chest rose and fell as I sucked in a deep, calming breath. I knew in my gut that the masked wolves were going to escape. They were amped up on something and moving far faster than a werewolf could.

The one in the car was dead. That meant that as much as Savannah infuriated me to the core of my being, I needed her.

I turned back and stepped up into her face. "Your situation is perilous. You need to help me. Scry on the she-wolf that attacked you. *Tomorrow.*"

"I'll scry for you on the she-wolf, but"—she paused and narrowed her eyes, like that would somehow have some effect on me—"*I'll* bring the scrying potion."

My mind reeled. She agreed? If I'd known that all it would take to get Savannah to work with me was a little fright, I'd have done it sooner. Myself.

It was time to press. I shoved my hand in my pockets and loomed over the red-haired woman. "I'm glad you found your senses. You'll meet me at Eclipse tomorrow at one p.m. We'll scry, and if that doesn't pan out with enough information, you'll come with me to meet a seer."

"Wait a sec, I didn't agree to meeting a seer. Why would I do that?" She cocked her hip out and frowned. Even with a welt on her cheek and her hair a mess, she looked delicious.

But my patience was thin. "Because scrying might not give us the answers we need. We must do everything we can to stop these rogue wolves, for your sake and my pack's." I leaned close, whispering, although no one who would care was close enough to hear. "The seer is how I found you. She warned me that I had to protect you. She's available tomorrow night. You'll go."

Savannah glanced over her shoulder at her cousin, who was resting his busted foot on the bumper of their car, looking amused. He shrugged.

"Fine. I'll see you tomorrow. Until then, I'm going back to the motel to get my stuff. I assume I won't be jumped there again, but feel free to tail along." Her eyes lingered on me for a second, and then she spun and headed toward her cousin's car.

Protectiveness surged inside me. "You should stay here tonight. I'll put you up in a different hotel, somewhere safe."

She opened the driver's door and paused, regarding me with obstinance. "Not a chance. I'm safest with my people. My family."

My wolf rose, and my claws extended. "I can't protect you there."

"You can't protect me *here*, Jaxson. Nobody can. I've been on my own for a while now. I'll take care of myself."

Her sadness and anger hit me like a punch to the gut. She was alone and had no one she trusted in this new world.

Savannah slammed the door and drove off, and my emotions ripped into me like claws. Frustration. Rage. Possessiveness.

Why did I fucking care if she was miserable? She was just a means to an end. The key to getting the answers I needed.

The seer's prophecy wound around me like a python strangling an unsuspecting victim in the night. *If you do not stop them, she will be dead before the full moon rises, and with her, the future of your pack.*

The moon was up, and nearly full. Three nights left.

I scrubbed a hand through my hair. The fortune teller had drawn three tarot cards to foresee my future. The Moon for our adversaries. Strength for the woman. And the third had been for me.

The Hanged Man.

That fate seemed inevitable now. Savannah Caine was going to be the end of me.

21

Savannah

The next morning, I awoke in another strange room far from Belmont.

Aunt Laurel's house.

I hadn't had nightmares. This time, the nightmares had been real.

In a vain attempt to get a little control over my life, I'd broken into Jaxson's auto body shop, stolen my car, and was chased by the damn werewolf alpha himself down the back alleys of Magic Side. To cap the night off, I'd gotten jumped by the very psychos I was trying to avoid. Not to mention, the horrifying image of Sam ripping through her clothes and shifting into a wolf was now burned into my memory forever. I'd never be able to look at her the same.

What a freaking mess.

Terror wasn't something I experienced anymore. It was just a part of my life.

I sat up and groaned. Every part of me ached. The mattress felt like it had seen a lot of use since the late eighteen-hundreds, and my ass and lower back missed the motel.

The LaSalles' guestroom had apparently been decorated by a blind person with a side job at a thrift store. There might have been a theme, but I was too overwhelmed to find the connection between framed antique sketches of pineapples and jaunty sailboat bookends.

God save me.

I'd learned about these people less than forty-eight hours ago, and now I was staying with them. Temporarily.

Still, it was insane. But so was this city. Either way, I would need to find my own place once the rogue wolves were behind bars. Or dead.

Maybe somewhere in southern France.

At least I had my car back.

Well, not technically, but kind of. In theory, the Gran Fury was currently sitting in another auto body shop in a part of the city run by demons. I assumed *that* was going to raise a whole new set of problems, but still, no one was holding it ransom at the moment. As soon as Zara installed the magic regulator and the Fury was up and running, I'd feel a bit more in control, and the extreme weirdness of the situation would be more bearable with a viable exit plan.

California. Texas. Cabo San Lucas. It didn't matter.

Until then, I would have to make the best of a bad situation.

It was like the woman in my dream had said: *You cannot outrun your fate, Savannah. They're coming for you. Beware the wheel of fortune. It does not stop. Time is ticking. You need to learn who you truly are so that you can stop the ones who are coming.*

Fate had nearly got me, this time.

I showered, and while the hot water ran over my skin, I tried to figure out what to do. No matter how much I disliked the idea of working with Jaxson, I needed to help him stop the damned rogue wolves. Clearly, they were hunting me, and I had to find out why. There were three things I could do.

One, I'd make a scrying potion with Uncle Pete and use it to spy on the wolves.

Two, I could go with Jaxson to the Seer. I would have scoffed at that notion three days ago, but apparently dream warnings and fortunes were a real thing.

And finally, I could mine the LaSalles for information about my parents and my magic. Maybe I could figure out why the wolves were hunting me from that.

In the worst case, I could probably learn to blast them.

I hopped out of the shower, dried off, and dug through my bags. At least, after everything that had happened, Casey and I had been able to go back and get my stuff. Jaxson would have probably agreed to just about anything to get us out of pack territory, especially after the hellfire Casey had unleashed.

Once I was dressed, I staggered down the stairs and wandered into the kitchen. Someone had left a yellow sticky note on the coffee pot: *Make yourself at home, and help yourself to anything.*

I shook my head in disbelief. Somehow, I had gone from having no family to having a dangerous and untrustworthy family entangled with dark secrets, and then straight to living in their house in under forty-eight hours.

Well, supposedly, adaptation was the key to survival.

I put a kettle on and rummaged around the kitchen for tea. The first cupboard I opened was loaded with boxes of sugar-coated kids' cereal. I smirked. Casey, one hundred percent.

How was he still eating this kids' stuff in his twenties? I hadn't had sugared cereal since I was fifteen, because it rotted your brain and teeth and attention span. I preferred donuts... which, okay, weren't much better, but at least my guilty pleasure didn't come with a prize in the box.

My fingers twitched. I grabbed a box of Count Chocula and poured myself a huge bowl and topped it with milk from the fridge. Then I plopped down at the table and dug into the sugary goodness.

I could adapt however I damned well wanted.

Halfway through the bowl, my stomach started to rebel against the sickly sweet milk and sodden marshmallows, but a rising sugar craze drove me on, spoonful after spoonful.

A waft of nutmeg drifted into the room, and shortly after, Aunt Laurel swept around the corner. "Savannah, you're up! And good, I see you've gotten breakfast. Count Chocula. You and Casey are so alike."

My stomach churned in protest, and I slowly set my spoon down.

Casey limped into the room seconds later, and Laurel looked from one of us to the other. "What have you done?"

"Nothing!" Casey protested.

Aunt Laurel rested her fists on the heavy wooden table in a gesture that reminded me of a silverback gorilla. "Are the cops involved?"

"I don't think so," he mumbled.

Her eyebrows rose. "Are we going to get sued?"

"Maybe? Probably not, actually."

"Did anyone die?"

I trained my eyes on my cereal. *Technically, yes.*

"Hey!" Casey exclaimed. "What's with the third degree? Everything is okay. And also, don't ask any more questions."

Laurel whipped out of the room in a rage.

"Uh-oh," I muttered.

She came back moments later and slammed a little glass vial full of red liquid down in front of him. "Drink."

"Ah, no, Mom. I'm gonna go to a doctor, and they'll heal me in—"

"You are not going to a doctor. We have perfectly fine healing potions here." She shoved the vial toward him.

"Oh, gods," he moaned.

"That potion will heal your ankle?" I asked.

"Well, it'll get most of the work done, though he'll have a bit of a limp for a while," Laurel said. "They're expensive and time-consuming to make, which I hope Casey *and you* will keep in mind on your next extracurricular adventure."

Casey looked at the potion with a dubious expression.

"Drink it," she ordered.

"Won't it make you better?" I asked, not understanding his hesitation.

"It's one of Dad's. He believes the worse a potion tastes, the better it works. His are legendary."

My uncle's low voice resonated from behind me. "It's true. The flavor is how you know it's going to work." I turned, and he beamed. "You ready to cook, Savannah? I've got everything ready."

"Absolutely." I leapt from my chair, leaving Casey to his fate, and poured the last of the cereal down the disposal, vowing never to eat it again. Then I followed my uncle to the back door with an eager bounce in my step.

Casey's gagging echoed off the hallway walls. "Oh, gods, it's so bad! The broken ankle was better!"

We headed out through the backyard to a shed. My uncle turned the key in the lock and did something with his hand like Casey had last night...perhaps disabling a spell?

"It's good to have the workshop away from the house," he said as he worked. "That way, if something goes wrong, the house will be left standing."

Holy crap.

I followed my uncle into the interior of the workshop, my stomach churning. My parents had died when the house burned down. Had one of them been making potions? Was that what had happened?

Wonder drove the intrusive thoughts away. My uncle's workshop was everything I'd imagined and more. The long workbenches that ran along the walls were covered with a bizarre assemblage of glass apparatuses—yellow curlicue tubes, beakers, flasks, and all assortments of devices. Potions—I assumed—bubbled on a few low burners at the back, slowly distilling into vials. Thousands of jars, boxes, and tins sat in racks on the wall, alongside dusty cupboards with long drawers and a couple of mini fridges. One was labeled *Beer*, the other *Not Beer*.

I'd wandered into the lab of a mad scientist. Or mad sorcerer. Or madman. I hadn't really asked my uncle what he was, and I needed to rectify that. "Are you a sorcerer like Casey and Aunt Laurel?"

"Yes, ma'am. We tend to stick together. Other people don't understand our magic." He started organizing a few trays on the table.

"How so? What's the difference between a sorcerer and, I don't know, a witch?"

He handed me a pair of heavy rubber gloves, and I put them on.

"Magic Side has every kind of spellcaster you can imagine," he explained in his low, earthy voice. "Witches, mages, druids, demons—you name it. What makes us all different is where we draw our power from. Mages are scholars. They cast spells using scrolls and books and formulas and learn their craft through intense study. Witches, on the other hand, draw power from their covens—from each other."

"What about sorcerers?"

"We draw power from ourselves, from within."

"Like our souls?

"Our bodies, our blood, our souls, all of it. It's a very personal art. A witch might make you a spell to go—you can carry it around and cast it later. We don't because we're not about to let people go waltzing around with a little bit of our soul in their pocket. I'd never sell one of my healing draughts, but I'd let Casey drink it. He's all the soul I've got."

I nodded, wondering if that's how my parents had felt about me. "So how do potions work? I don't know much about casting spells."

"Spells are one thing, and your aunt can teach you those. Potions are another. They're like a spell in suspension. You drink it, and it goes off. The ingredients don't entirely make the spell—they just hold it there, ready to be consumed."

My uncle lifted a tiny iron cauldron and set it on a burner, added a little clear liquid from a tin, and set the flames on high. Then he motioned to a tray of plants and boxes of powder. "I've got most of the ingredients here so you can look at them."

He listed them off. Some names I recognized—ginseng, ginkgo, amanita, cinnabar. Most, I did not.

Step by step, we measured each ingredient precisely with a scale, and dumped it into the cauldron. "You've got steady hands," he commented as I dusted some powder off a slip of paper into the brew.

"I shoot. And draw."

"That's good for making potions." He checked a list. "Always remember that the order of ingredients is important. If you add the amanita first instead of last, you make a hell of a potion. Instead of seeing whomever you're thinking about, they'll see you," he explained, and chuckled.

"We didn't mess up the order, right?" I hedged.

"I don't think so."

My trepidation checked in to see if I was going to need it again, but I shooed it away. Uncle Pete knew what he was doing.

I hoped.

Soon, the cauldron was frothing, and the workshop smelled

like so many repulsive things that it made my head spin. Sardines. Old rotting grass. Foot fungus.

"Just one more ingredient," said Uncle Pete. "Your blood."

I tensed. Jaxson had mentioned it, so I'd guessed it was coming, but the request made my stomach lurch. "Why?" I asked.

"A scrying potion has to be attuned to one person only. That requires a bit of blood."

Shit. Blood magic. Aunt Laurel had warned me about giving out my blood. Her first lesson. But Uncle Pete would be okay, right?

"Here." He pulled a knife out of a beaker with blue liquid. "Cut your palm a bit and fill up this vial."

I looked up with my trepidation suddenly in overdrive.

He smiled. "You're smart to be cautious. Always be careful with your blood. It's one of the most powerful components in spellcasting. Never give it out, or at least, never give it to someone you don't trust with your life."

"Why?"

"Blood is bonded to you. You can use it to make a potion that only you can use, like we are today. Alternately, you can use it to store a little of your power. And that means you can also use it maliciously to cast a spell on someone whose blood you have, though that's very difficult."

My stomach churned. Someone with my blood could cast a spell on me. Thank God I hadn't given any of it to Jaxson.

My uncle patiently waited, neither rushing nor coddling me.

Screw it. I was there for the potion and to learn. I pulled off my heavy glove and drew the knife along my palm, wincing at the bite of the blade. Tilting my hand over the vial, I flexed my palm, careful not to spill any blood on my clothes.

"That's enough." My uncle patted my hand and then grabbed a red potion from the shelf. He dabbed a bit on my cut, and my skin knit back together—though it stung quite a lot.

"Wow."

He chuckled again. "It's magic."

Still in wonder, I put my heavy glove back on.

He poured the blood into the flames until he had just the right amount left in the vial. "Now you know I'm not going to use your blood for any sinister hocus-pocus." With that, he handed me the vial. "All yours."

I grinned and tipped it into the cauldron.

A cloud of noxious gas exploded up out of the vat, and I started hacking. "Oh, Lord, I didn't think the smell could get worse!"

"It can always get worse." My uncle coughed. "Okay, time for the spell."

He stood over the little black cauldron and began to chant strange words in a language I didn't understand. Light swirled around the room, and I gasped. Suddenly, I was in whirlpool of vivid green flame, darkness, and my uncle's words. The workshop shook, and I grabbed the counter. Then there was a tiny puff from the cauldron, and the shadows of the world went back to their normal positions.

"Holy. Crap."

"Oh, right, I should have warned you it gets a little spooky."

An hour later, we'd distilled the potion and cooled it. My uncle set the flask on the table. Red droplets floated in the shiny, silvery solution, and I wondered if that was actually my blood. The thought creeped me out. "Are you sure this is safe to drink?"

"Safe? Perfectly. Appetizing? Absolutely not." My uncle dug around in the fridge marked *Beer*, pulled out a plastic bottle full of dark orange liquid, and shook it. "You're going to want a chaser."

"Great."

"I've found that carrot juice works best." He poured some in a beaker and set it on the workbench.

"Do I drink the whole thing?"

My uncle shook his head. "Not unless you want to be watching your godmother for hours at a time. Just a sip. It will last you a minute."

"How does it work? Do I have to do anything?"

"As soon as you've taken a sip, close your eyes and concentrate on your godmother. You'll see her in your mind, like a movie camera floating in air."

I held the flask up to the light. This really didn't feel safe.

I took the tiniest sip possible and instantly regretted all my life choices. The potion burned my tongue like acid, and my body jerked in protest. My uncle grabbed the flask before I dropped it and shoved the carrot juice into my hand.

I chugged it down and swished the last of it around in my mouth, trying to get rid of the residual taste. "Oh, my God! That tasted like electrocuted sardines! What the hell?"

"Forget the taste! Close your eyes. Think of your godmother."

I tried, but nothing came to mind. "I don't think it's working."

My uncle's tobacco-scented magic washed over me. "Focus on her face, the way she talks."

I felt the power of his magic guiding me. Suddenly the world started to spin, and I had to squeeze my eyes shut to combat the lurching vertigo. Then, out of the blackness, I saw my godmother. It was like I was looking through an unsteady handheld camera, but I could see her.

She shuffled about in her garden, tending to flowers. One of the lawn gnomes had fallen in the path, so she knocked it out of the way. Her lips moved, but I couldn't hear what she said.

I ignored my churning stomach and watched her go about

her garden chores. I'd always taken it for granted before, but now, the care with which she tended the flowers brought tears to my eyes. A glimpse of what normal had once been.

Then it was gone.

I jolted as the vision turned dark and I returned to my uncle's workshop. "Holy crap, I did it!" I cried.

He beamed and stuck a cork in the top of the potion, then he handed it to me. "First time's the charm! Now you can check in, but I'll warn you, I was able to give you a little nudge with my magic since I brewed the stuff. If you tried on your own, it would be a lot harder. So don't go trying without me. This stuff can be dangerous."

I nodded. "Of course."

A lie.

22

Savannah

I showed up at the back door of Eclipse at one p.m. and texted Jaxson. Part of me knew that coming to this den of wolves was insane, but I needed answers, and this was the road forward.

Clearly, I didn't belong here. Jaxson had asked me to use the back door like a girlfriend he was ashamed of. He probably was. I was a dirty LaSalle, and after last night, I was willing to bet everyone in Dockside knew—and was pissed.

Before he let me out of the house, Casey had insisted on me taking more of his crazy, military-grade mace. *Don't spray yourself in the face, and don't let the wolves know you have it, or they'll kick your ass.* I checked my purse. Still there.

The door opened. Jaxson was wearing jeans and a button-down that stretched across his chest. There was no trace of the monster I'd seen last night. No claws. No honey eyes.

I breathed a sigh of relief.

"You came. To say I'm shocked would be an understatement." His jaw was set as he stepped aside.

I pulled my sunglasses off and pushed through the door. "Here I am, ready to do your bidding."

He stiffened, and his eyes flashed, just for a second.

"Don't get any ideas. We're just scrying. I've got the stuff, so let's do this."

I marched through the kitchen, not quite sure where I was supposed to go but not wanting to give up the lead.

"Left," Jaxson prompted, as if he could read my mind.

I turned into the vacant bar, Jaxson following close behind. I could feel his eyes on me, unwavering. And I could almost smell the heat of his desire. Had I missed something?

Jaxson Laurent hated my guts, and after last night, probably even more so. I snapped him a look that put an end to his wandering eyes.

His signature filled the room. I knew, very clearly, that I had just walked into his lair—a place that was intimately a part of him. Everywhere I stepped, I felt his warmth around me, even though the bar was cool.

Then I remembered where I was, and my skin chilled. The wolf den.

The last time I'd been here, it had been with hundreds of werewolves, all staring at me for parading around with the alpha. At least they hadn't known who I was, or they would have torn me apart.

"You cleared the place?" I asked.

"Just for you, just for an hour."

I raised my eyebrows.

"We don't do lunch, so it was just the staff."

"But I thought you didn't think I'd show up."

He gave me a wry smile. "Well, I wouldn't have put money on it."

I plopped down at a raised cocktail table and pulled out a silver flask. Jaxson examined the potion and gave an appreciative grunt. "I'm impressed."

"I'm easy to underestimate. It's my compliant demeanor."

He actually chuckled at that. A little sunlight, peeking through.

"I'm guessing your people didn't catch those werewolves last night," I said.

The sunlight vanished. "No. They outran Sam and Regina in their wolf form. That shouldn't be possible."

"I told you they could go fast. They ran down my car on the open road. It was insane. I was assuming you all could do that."

He gave a low growl. "*I* might be able to catch your car, but they were even faster. They must be using some form of magic to boost their abilities. Or drugs. It might explain those red eyes—they're not typical, either."

I glanced at Jaxson's hands—hands I'd seen erupt into claws the night before.

"So how does it work?" I ventured.

"How does what work?"

I awkwardly twirled my hair, not quite sure what to say. "Shifting. I hadn't really seen it happen before last night. Sam—her body twisted and contorted, and her clothes just ripped to shreds like she had just *Hulked* out. It was crazy. Then she was a wolf and running. Is that what happens? I thought I could hear bones..."

Jaxson fixed me with a steady glare. "For some of us, yes. We change physically. Our bones shrink and snap, our claws and fangs erupt, and our bodies transform."

I shuddered, and his expression darkened. "Seems painful."

"Yes," he growled. "But it's also a release. Pain that's close to pleasure."

My breath hitched, and I flushed. "But not for all of you?"

He sighed. "No. Some shifters transform into their animal forms through magic, clothes and all. The rest of us transform physically. We're called wolfborn. It's what I am."

I imagined Jaxson's clothes ripping away, revealing a

snarling, savage monster. My pulse quickened as fear trickled through me—fear and the faintest hint of...lust?

Was I insane?

In my defense, it was rather easy to imagine what lay beneath Jaxson's shirt. The buttons were practically ripping off already. Did he have to wear rip-away stripper pants? *That* would be a view.

Jaxson's nostrils flared.

Suddenly embarrassed, I bit my lip and flushed. It wasn't like he could read my mind, but still, I pushed the conversation forward. "Sam and that other woman, they were wolfborn then?"

"Regina. Yes."

My brain spun and memories of the Taphouse flooded into my mind, killing whatever erotic thoughts had been lurking in the corners of my clearly disturbed head. "As was the man I ran over?"

Jaxson crossed his arms. "Yes. He was wolfborn, too. We turn back into wolves when we die. That's why it was so important you could draw his tattoos. We couldn't see them on the body."

I nodded slowly. Things were beginning to make a little more sense.

Jaxson placed a photo on the table and tapped it. "Lucky for us, the Oldsmobile driver from last night was a shifter. That means he stayed in human form at death. Note the two-headed wolf tattoo on his neck."

I briefly glanced at the bloody, burnt body in the photo and looked away, stomach churning. "Just like the others. What does it mean?"

"I'm working on that. Potentially, it has to do with the myth of a dark wolf god, so we could be dealing with some kind of cult. I've got people looking into it."

"That's all? What's the myth?"

Jaxson paused and gave me a stern look. "Some stories are for wolves only."

I bristled. For a minute, I'd had him on a roll, but now he was locked down again. Really, getting information out of Jaxson was like squeezing blood from a stone. "Fine. What do we know, then?"

He shrugged. "This suggests to me that they're part of a larger group—a gang, cult, or rogue pack—and not lone operators. They're coordinated, and they probably have a leader and a specific agenda. Somehow, you're part of that plan."

I fiddled with the potion. "Well, that's a start." At least he was sharing some information with me.

He put his hands on the table. "Time to see what you can do."

I glanced down apprehensively at the vile concoction. "Do you have carrot juice?"

He dug around behind the bar and produced a milky white plastic bottle full of orange liquid. "OJ okay?"

"I hope so." I wasn't looking forward to this.

He poured me a glass. I took it, but I didn't move toward the potion.

"You're nervous," he said.

I rolled my glass on the tabletop, willing the butterflies in my stomach to settle. "My uncle told me not to do this without him. My aunt said it was dangerous."

Jaxson regarded me closely. "I'm here."

That should have scared the heebie-jeebies out of me, but it didn't.

I took a sip.

The horrible brew burned my tongue, and I grabbed the orange juice and took a big gulp. "Oh, my God, that's worse!"

My stomach churned. Apparently, being orange wasn't enough.

I squeezed my eyes shut and tried to focus like my uncle had taught me. I thought about the she-wolf, her tattoo, the drawing I'd made, all of it.

"What do you see?" Jaxson inquired.

"My eyelids. Be quiet. I'm concentrating."

"Are you sure it works?"

"Shut up! I used it this morning to scry on my godmother!"

I gritted my teeth and tried to bring the she-wolf to mind. When I thought of her face, I could only remember the way she'd screamed and clawed at her eyes when I'd maced her. When I thought of how she was dressed, I only remembered the sound of her hitting my bumper, and then the image of her body rolling into the ditch. All I saw was darkness. "It's not working."

Suddenly, Jaxson was behind me. I felt his power vibrating inches away. I gasped as he touched me, and a shock jolted between us, just like the first time we'd touched. His aroma was a drug, and I felt myself melting beneath his fingers.

He could have anything he wanted.

"Focus on the woman," he grunted. "Describe her to me the way you saw her that night."

His voice vibrated with power, and as I wanted to do nothing more than please him, I concentrated as hard as I could. "She had long tangled hair, and an angular face. She was wiry, with sinewy muscles and a barbed-wire tattoo around her bicep."

I felt his presence around me, pushing me, guiding my mind. It calmed my emotions. Focused my thoughts on that woman who had sent my life tumbling into chaos.

"What was she wearing?" His breath was warm on my neck.

"A worn-out tank top. Ripped jeans. A belt with a shiny brass buckle."

"What about her eyes?" His hands rested on my shoulder, and I shivered.

"Crimson. Almost red, like blood."

Suddenly, the world swirled around me, and my stomach lurched with vertigo. I was hurtling through darkness, though I could feel myself in the chair and Jaxson's body pressed close behind mine. My vision blurred, but there she was, looking as vicious as I had ever seen her. Ripped jeans. Tank top. Barbed wire tattoo, and that two-headed wolf on her neck.

"It's working!" I gasped.

My gaze followed her as she moved around the room, as if I were tethered to her like a balloon.

"What do you see? Describe everything," Jaxson prompted. The sensations of his signature still wrapped around me.

"She's walking through a building with wooden walls. I can't clearly see what she's doing. Wait...there's someone else."

"Who?"

"It's a man. One of the abductees—I recognize him from the television. I think he's still alive. He's on a cot."

Jaxson squeezed my shoulder. "Now we're getting somewhere. Do you see any indication of where she is? Something out a window? A sign?"

"Nothing."

The woman swept around the cot where the man lay, and just for a second, I glimpsed a crimson circle on the floor. "There's a red ring with symbols all around it."

They reminded me of the ring of symbols that had helped contain my aunt's Sphere of Devouring.

"Can you look closer?"

"No, they're blurry, and she's moving away."

Then my stomach dropped, and I felt like I was being sucked backward through the air. Everything went dark. "Shit," I muttered, opening my eyes. "I lost it."

"Tell me about the ring," Jaxson growled. "Can you describe it any better?"

"No, it was just part of a ring with weird symbols. I don't know magic. Get me a pencil and paper."

He retrieved them, and I set about sketching furiously. I'd just glimpsed it out of the corner of my eye, and only part of the ring, but I reproduced it as best I could. Finally, I shoved the sketch toward him. It wasn't great, but it was all I could get. "What is this?"

He scrutinized the drawing. "I don't know, exactly, but it's some form of ring of containment."

I took the paper and traced it with my eyes, wishing I'd seen it more clearly or been able to make out the symbols. "What are they used for?"

Jaxson hesitated in a way that sent shivers down my spine. "They're used for summoning demons from the underworld. Not the ones you see here, working around town. Dangerous ones that have to be controlled."

Demons. I barely knew what that meant. Zara was a half-demon. I'd seen people with horns. But I could feel the tension in his body, so close to mine, and the thin line of his mouth told me that these were real demons. The things of nightmares.

My stomach knotted, and I looked up from my drawing. "Why would my attackers be summoning demons? What are they trying to do?"

"I don't know."

Truth.

"Another mystery, then. Did we learn anything?" I leaned back in my chair and slapped my hands on the table.

"Absolutely. We know at least one of the victims is still alive. That's something. Second, we know these wackos are part of cult associated with the myth of a twin-headed wolf and that they're summoning demons. That's a lot farther along than we were at this time yesterday. You did good work."

His eyes bored into me and flickered slightly gold. I could

almost sense his admiration, like an unidentifiable scent on the wind. Coming from him, that was a shock.

I blushed and ran my fingers through the ends of my hair, hoping he couldn't sense the heat forming in my center. I averted my eyes from his gaze. "What do we do next?"

"Tonight, we'll need to visit the seer at the Full Moon Fair. She's the one who pointed me to you. She told me that I wouldn't find the answers I was looking for without you at my side, so maybe she can point you the rest of the way. Perhaps the fates will intervene."

I swallowed. I hadn't ever put much stock in fate or fortune, but clearly, it had power here. It had sent Jaxson after me. The implications were dizzying, and my chest rose and fell as I tried to calm my breathing. What was my fate in all this? A sacrificial lamb?

I pursued a less loaded line of inquiry. "Tell me about this Full Moon Fair. Is it like a carnival?"

Carnivals had funnel cake, a potential bright point in the developing nightmare I was living.

Jaxson's eyes brightened, and he tilted his head. "It's best if you see it for yourself. It's hard to describe. The fair is held at the Midway at sunset. Until then, we need to figure out what the two-headed wolf tattoo means. And this." He tapped on the paper with the demon summoning circle.

I chewed on my lip as I studied my drawing. "Would my family know what the symbols mean?"

Jaxson raised an eyebrow. "Probably. Do you really want to ask them?"

My cheeks flushed. I'd stolen the scrying potion and used it without permission, and I did so to help their nemesis. I let my eyes drop.

He gave a knowing grunt. "I thought so. I'll send your illus-tration to some scholars I know downtown at the Order of Magica's research archives. Their people might be able to figure things out."

"What's the Order of Magica?"

"They're like our FBI and government all rolled into one. It's a corrupt mess that's mainly preoccupied with keeping our kind hidden from the world."

"So why aren't they handling this instead of you?"

Jaxson's jaw ticked. "They have their investigation, and we have ours, since werewolves are involved. They're looking for someone to blame, while I'm looking for the truth. Luckily, I have something they don't."

"What?"

He stepped close, and his heat melted into mine. "You."

23

Savannah

A half hour before sundown, we headed west toward the Midway Plaisance. Jaxson's contacts at the archives hadn't gotten back to him about the circle or the tattoo, and digging on the internet hadn't yielded any results either—not that it would. I'd considered asking Casey, but I figured we'd better hear what the seer had to say first. She might have all the answers we needed.

Jaxson parked along 62nd Street, and we walked north toward the Midway Plaisance, a long, grassy park that ran east-west through the heart of Magic Side. Police had barricaded off 60th, and it was packed with pedestrians and food trucks.

I couldn't help staring. I hadn't been out in public since my first visit to Eclipse. The place was packed, and everyone was...different.

A woman with horns and a tail caught my slack-jawed look and winked at me. I went deep red, then turned close to Jaxson to cover my embarrassment. "This is where we'll meet the seer?"

Jaxson scanned the crowd, barely registering my question. "The fair's not here yet. We have to wait until sundown."

Huh?

Jaxson seemed lost in thought, so I didn't bother asking for clarification. It wouldn't be a long wait, anyway. The sun was hovering just above the trees on the western end of the park.

Jaxson looked down, as if suddenly noticing me. "You need anything to eat?"

I was starving, but I snapped, "I'm fine." Then I noticed a truck selling deep-fried smores. "Actually, those."

If I was going to be held hostage all day, then I might as well live it up.

My fingers were irreparably sticky by the time the sun finally reached the horizon. Someone nearby hooted, and the crowd turned to watch.

"What's going on?" I asked as I tried to lick marshmallow off my finger.

"Follow me." Jaxson pushed through the milling crowd to the long stretch of grass that was blocked off by a line of red ribbon. I would never have made it through the press, but people seemed to melt away as if he were death walking among them.

A few car horns honked, and a couple people began chanting as the sun reached the tops of the distant buildings and trees. Soon, the chant swelled through the crowd: "*Sun— down. Sun—down. Sun—down.*" Over and over.

The words thundered like drums, and car horns erupted from the side streets. It felt like the whole city was chanting, and I couldn't help the euphoria rising in my chest.

"What's going on?" I shouted above the din.

Jaxson seemed mildly irritated. "Watch."

As the crown of the sun slipped below the horizon, the chant reached a fever pitch and cascaded into wild cheers as twilight took over the sky.

Then, as quickly as the din had started, a hush fell over the

Midway, and the last echoes of the car horns died away. The air vibrated with magic and anticipation.

I craned my neck, trying to understand what all the fuss was about. Then I saw it—a blue spark zipping down the Midway, leaving a crackling line of energy in its wake. With a burst of electricity that I could feel dancing across the crowd, thousands of sparkling lines spread outward, tracing patterns and squares above the expanse of grass. The earth shook, and a tsunami of sensations washed over me—a cacophony of color, noise, taste, and scent that my mind was too overwhelmed to separate.

A wave of pure magic.

My heart raced. I'd never felt anything like it.

All along the Midway, glowing blue pavilions sprang from the ground like mushrooms. Bursts of crackling magic exploded in the air like fireworks, and in the center of it all, a sparkling blue wheel formed, spinning on end—a floating Ferris wheel. With a crack of thunder, the pavilions turned solid and took on color, and where there had only been grass before, a massive carnival filled the Midway.

The crowd cheered and stampeded over the tape boundaries and into the fair.

"Ho-ly shit," I whispered as eager people shoved past me. "That was insane. *This* is insane."

"Try not to get crushed," Jaxson said. "And welcome to the Full Moon Fair."

We pushed our way into the fairgrounds, and my mind struggled to make sense of the riotous colors, sights, and sounds.

"This is all...magic? It just appears out of nowhere?"

"Seven nights every two months, right around the time of the full moon. Hence the name."

I shook my head, simply unable to wrap my mind around the idea of a whole fair disappearing and reappearing out of nothingness.

Food vendors, exhibits, rides, and shops packed the Midway edge to edge. Thousands of lightbulbs floated overhead independent of any wires. They bobbed gently in the breeze and bathed the fair with warm, cheery light.

I slowly turned. "What is all this?"

A column of smoke streamed up out of the ground, and a brightly dressed man popped into existence. He removed his hat and bowed. "Welcome to the Magic Side World's Fair, held continuously since 1893! Visit merchants representing every magical city in the world! Behold monsters from deep in the South American jungle!"

Jaxson motioned for me to follow. "Don't ask questions about the fair. It summons carnival barkers, a type of demon that thrives on attention. They're hard to shake. Don't make eye contact."

I hurried after him as the barker chased behind. "Excuse me, miss, if you are looking for wonder, you can find it here! Along with bizarre magic items, foods you never imagined, and entertainment around every bend!"

Jaxson growled at the barker and pointed at a long-haired man walking in the opposite direction. "That guy over there needs to know what booths are around here."

The barker hesitated for a second, then scuttled over to the unfortunate man and began pointing out nearby pavilions. "Hello, sir! Are you in need of assistance? Make sure you don't miss the fine cask ales from Guild City or the world's largest pumpkin from Magic's Bend!"

Jaxson locked me with his eyes. "Follow me. Don't run off, and don't ask questions. The fortune teller has a tent beside the Egyptian village."

Egyptian village?

A dozen questions died on my lips as I hurried in his wake past woodcarvers selling broomsticks and booths full of potions.

It was so unfair—there I was, at possibly the most amazing carnival on earth, and I was stuck with the self-appointed fun police.

We cut through the crowd with little trouble. It was almost as if they could feel Jaxson's dark aura coming and instinctually pressed out of the way.

All around, the cacophony of languages roared in my ears, too many to even begin guessing where everyone came from. But it wasn't only the languages—it was the people. A kaleidoscope of humanity surrounded me. Somehow, I'd never felt like I fit in Belmont, where everyone looked and acted so similar, yet among the unimaginable jumble of unfamiliar faces and horns and even tails, a deep sense of belonging welled up in my chest until I felt I would burst. All these ways of being human made me realize I was no longer alone. That there was a place I could fit in, no matter how strange or awkward or prickly I was.

But Jaxson pushed me onward.

We skirted the enormous Ferris wheel, and finally, I had to stop. How tall was it? Forty stories? Fifty? I craned my neck, my mind whirling as it slowly spun.

Crap. It wasn't resting on the ground. There were no legs or supports. It just spun there in the air, *fifty feet up.*

I really wasn't sure how much more my brain could hold. I opened my mouth to ask Jaxson a question, then remembered the barker demons and tried a statement instead. "It's gotta be hard to get on and off."

"It floats up and down," Jaxson said, not bothering to look at me. He was half-distracted, scanning the fair.

"Huh. This may be the craziest thing I've ever seen."

He grunted. "You haven't seen much. This is just classic one-upmanship. When Chicago held a World's Fair in 1893, Magic Side mirrored the event. They invented the Ferris wheel, so we built one twice the size. That flies. Mages have big egos."

"So this really is all part of the World's Fair, then, still going after a century," I whispered, really trying to make it not sound like a question.

"When the Chicago Exposition closed down, ours kept going. It brought a lot of business and outsiders to Magic Side, so we couldn't stop. But the whole thing's changed—anymore, it's a carnival of commerce. You can buy everything in the world you don't need at exorbitant prices."

Across the way, a man sat at an easel painting revelers. I pointed. "I need one of those."

Jaxson scowled. "A caricature? We don't have time."

"Ugh. Absolutely not. The last thing I want is a picture of me with my sullen, half-feral taskmaster. I want one of those *brushes*. They're...alive."

Jaxson's eyes narrowed on me, flooding a deep ochre color, but I ignored him and focused on the artist.

As the man worked, a pair of watercolor brushes helped fill in the details. When they finished a section, they jumped off the canvas and into his dirty water. They jiggled around, and once they were clean, they hopped out, shook off, and dipped themselves in the next color. "We should go," Jaxson said gruffly.

Life was deeply unfair. There were even red velvet funnel cakes nearby.

I really hated Jaxson Laurent. Unfortunately, without him, I would have been completely lost. The floating Ferris wheel was the only landmark, and there seemed to be no form of organization to the pavilions. Ducking behind a tent where Japanese chefs served seared slivers of beef and octopus from a grill, we turned down an alley between whitewashed buildings, then emerged onto a narrow avenue where men and women in robes haggled with passersby over trinkets and golden jewelry. Overhead, wooden balconies protruded over the streets, and scents of spices and sweet tobacco hung in the air.

The Egyptian village?

We passed a tent with racks of garments woven from exquisite iridescent cloth with golden threads running through it. I impulsively reached out to touch one of them.

"Helwani cloth from Egypt. Those garments sell for tens of thousands of dollars," Jaxson said nonchalantly.

I froze and let the luxurious material slip from my fingers.

Finally, we reached a small, dark red tent sitting at the base of an obelisk. Giant swirling letters spelled *Lady Fortune* on a large wooden sign. Beneath it, there was a second sign: *Palm Readings $20, Tarot $40, Dire Questions Answered $3000.*

Holy hell. $3000?

Jaxson had better damn well be paying.

His signature flared. The people around backed away, and we cut in line. Guilt crept along my skin, and I blushed. The whole city treated him as a king, but he was such a jerk.

Finally, a woman stepped out, an ashen expression on her face.

Jaxson held the tent flap open. "After you."

24

Savannah

I stepped into the tent, which smelled of cinnamon and incense. It took my eyes a couple seconds to adjust to the meager light shed by half a dozen dim candles floating in the air.

A young woman in a '90s jean jacket sat behind a table hung with purple and gold cloth. She gave a knowing smile. "Jaxson Laurent. I see you found your Strength. Let me see her." The woman motioned me over, and a dozen gold bracelets jingled around her arm.

I didn't move a muscle.

"What's the matter? I won't bite."

"I...saw you in a dream."

She swept the braids of her long black hair over her shoulder and extended a hand. "Oh, that's highly probable. The fates have been trying to lead you to me. I am Lady Fortune, after all. But you can call me Dominique. I've been looking forward to meeting you."

I cocked my head in confusion as I extended my hand to shake hers. "Savannah Caine. What do you mean?"

She started inspecting my palm. "The fates have plans for us all. Some of us need a push. You were in danger, so I sent Mr. Laurent to you after I read his fortune—though to be honest, I did not know if he would make it in time."

"Oh, he showed up. Right after I ran my attackers over with my car."

I glared at him, and he tensed. I could practically smell his irritation.

Lady Fortune raised her eyebrows and gave me a wide grin. "Well, the card I pulled for you certainly seems accurate, though maybe I should have pulled the Chariot."

My curiosity flared to life, burning away any apprehension I'd had. "What card did you pull for me?"

"Strength," Jaxson said, his voice low and hard, almost hitching.

Lady Fortune released my hand and flipped over the top card of the large tarot deck sitting on her table.

Strength. It showed a woman taming a lion.

"Don't let your success so far go to your head," she cautioned. "You are not out of danger. Far from it." She slid the card to the bottom of the deck. "Sit, and we will discuss your fate."

The seer pointed at the chair in front of her table and snapped her fingers. The chair shook itself like a wet dog, and suddenly, a duplicate chair sprang out and skittered over to me like a crab. I jumped back with a yelp.

She raised her eyebrows. "Sorry. I forgot that you're new to town. I should have warned you."

I nodded. The entire fair had been wondrous from a distance, but now that I was caught up in it, I was completely overwhelmed.

The seer gestured to sit, so I slowly lowered myself onto the chair, making sure it wasn't just an illusion. Solid. I breathed a sigh of relief. Not that I should be surprised by anything at this point.

Jaxson took the other chair and laid a stack of bills on the table. My heartbeat picked up, and my palms went damp. I hadn't ever seen so much cash in one place.

He just walked around with that in his pocket? Then again, he could rip someone's throat out in a second. He'd probably savor it.

Lady Fortune bowed her head slightly. "You have anticipated my next request. Perhaps you have a little seer in you, Mr. Laurent."

She went to snap her fingers, but she paused and looked at me. "Just to warn you, I'm going to do another magic thing. Okay?"

"Okay," I said.

She snapped twice. A little pink purse ran out of the back room, hopped up on her lap, and started wiggling like a small, over-excited dog. It popped open and trembled with restrained excitement. The seer plucked the cash from the table and dropped it in, and the pouch snapped shut, jumped down, and scampered back to the other room.

"He's very excitable," Lady Fortune mused.

My heart hammered with excitement. "Oh. My. God. How do I get one of those?"

"It's tough. They're very expensive and hard to train."

"Damn. I need a job," I muttered to myself.

She winked. "I recommend fortune-telling. The customers usually hate what you tell them, but it pays well. They don't call me Lady Fortune for nothing."

Jaxson grunted. "You didn't count the money this time."

Lady Fortune stuck a hand on her hip and raised her chin. "With a lady present? Never. Anyway, you tipped well enough last time that I don't think I have anything to worry about."

At least Jaxson was generous with his money, if nothing else.

She pushed a clipboard with a pen and contract across the table.

"What's this?" I narrowed my eyes.

"Liability release. Just in case you want to blame me for a bad fortune or any of the crazy things you're going to do once you hear it."

I glanced at Jaxson, becoming less certain of this plan every second. He nodded, so I skimmed the agreement and signed, hoping I hadn't just sold my soul.

The seer began shuffling her cards impossibly fast, then she slammed the deck down on the table. "Now, you've come a long way from Wisconsin. Tell me what it is that you want to know."

Hell, how much did she already know about me? I had so many questions eating at me that I could feel them trying to tear their way out of my chest. Could I only ask one? "Why are people hunting me, and who are they?"

Lady Fortune rested her long pink nails on the top of the tarot deck. "Two for the price of one? Cheeky, but I'll indulge you since you're new to town. Let us see what the fates have to say. Watch out. Magic is about to happen, and it scares the willies out of me every time."

Electricity crackled through the air. The candles dimmed, and the scent of fresh coffee filled the tent. I heard the sound of a heartbeat pounding deep in the earth, shaking the space around us. My own heart began to beat in time, faster and faster, and my breath caught as darkness swirled around the room. The shadows became serpents, constricting around us, squeezing the air from my lungs, and whirling like a hurricane. Darkness swallowed us, and my stomach lurched, as if falling from the sky. I grabbed the table to steady myself and to fight the rising nausea.

The only light left came from a single candle, flickering overhead.

I looked to Jaxson with frightened eyes, but he nodded calmly and touched my hand. Electricity jolted between us, and he pulled his fingers away as if stung. His eyes flashed honey gold.

But his weren't the only eyes watching me. The hair on my neck stood upright. There were other watchers in the darkness. Invisible. Waiting.

The seer cleared her throat.

"We draw three cards—one for each of the fates." She slid them off the top of the deck one at a time, keeping them face down. As soon as she was done, the deck vanished.

She flipped the first card over with her long pink nails and paused, her hand hanging in the air above.

"The Moon. Very strange." She glanced between us. "It was the first card I drew for him."

I leaned forward. The card showed two wolves sitting on opposite sides of a river, howling up at a smiling moon. As I looked, the image began to waver and move, as if the wolves were alive and the stream was flowing.

I blinked. It was just a card.

She flipped the second. "The Lovers."

Again, the seer looked between us and raised an inquiring eyebrow. I blushed. Hopefully, she hadn't drawn that card for him as well.

After a pregnant pause, the seer hooked a nail under that final card and flipped it over. "The Wheel."

Her magic swirled around me, and the distance between us seemed to fade. Soon, the only things left in the room were the cards and her brilliant eyes, which turned pure white. My heart clenched, and I sucked in a sharp breath.

The seer spoke in a voice that was not of this earth. It was hoarse, and infinitely old. "Your path ahead lies in peril, but the river of fortune draws you onward. You cannot run, and you cannot stop your fate. If you do not find those who are chasing you, they will find you. If you do not destroy them, they will destroy you. You must betray yourself to save yourself. You must betray us all to save us all. The end is inevitable. Darkness will fall."

A deep and unrelenting dread coiled in my stomach, and I reached sideways for Jaxson's hand but couldn't find it. I couldn't find him at all.

The seer's eyes flickered and returned to brown. I brushed Jaxson's hand and pulled my fingers away. It was like he hadn't been there at all for a moment, and then was.

I clenched my shaking hands into fists. "What does it mean?"

The seer shook her head. "Your prophecy arises from the cards I laid, but I do not know it or hear it. It is spoken by fate."

"Prophecy?" Jaxson asked, "I heard nothing."

"You would not. The fates speak directly. She would not have heard yours, had she joined you here four days ago. Those words were for your ears only."

I glanced at Jaxson, whose expression turned dark and brooding, and bit my lip. No one else had heard what I had been told, and I wished I'd written it down.

The seer adjusted her hands and placed her fingers gently on the Moon. "The prophecy is not all. I can still give you my reading of the cards." Tapping the first, she said, "You are being chased. But this is not just one card, but two."

She spread her fingers and slipped a second card from underneath where there had been none before. The Magician.

"You are being hunted by a wolf and a sorcerer. If you find the wolf, you will find the sorcerer. If you find the sorcerer, you will find the wolf."

Frustration bit into me. We knew that—or suspected it, at least. "But why?"

She moved her hand to the lovers. "Because of who you are —because of your parents and your bloodline. You are everything your adversary needs."

Panic rose in my throat. "But we don't have any leads. How do I find them?"

She placed her hand on the Wheel and tensed. Her eyes flashed white, and her voice croaked. "You do not need to. They are already here. Hunting."

25

Savannah

The darkness drained from the room.

I burst up out of my chair and stumbled back from the table. Jaxson, already on his feet, caught me.

Lady Fortune pointed at the door. "You need to run. They are close, at the Ferris wheel, but closing fast. Wolves and demons. Go."

I pulled the mace Casey had given me out of my purse and shoved it into my pocket as Jaxson grabbed my hand and pulled me from the tent. "Walk normally, but don't let go of me."

He pulled out his phone with his other hand and hit speed dial with his thumb. "They're by the Ferris wheel and headed our way—look for rogue wolves and some kind of demon. Sounds like there may be a lot of them. Send everyone in our direction but move discreetly. We're in the alley behind the Egyptian bazaar and will head toward the far end of the Midway, where someone can pick us up."

He hung up and, hand-in-hand, we pushed our way back the way we had come.

Confusion tore at me. "You have people here? Waiting?"

"Yes. A lot. As long as you're outside of the Indies, you're protected."

"Protected or bait?" I snapped. "Why aren't we running?"

"Because you're too slow. Stay with me, you'll be fine. If they pursue, they'll reveal their positions. With any luck, we can nab one of these bastards and make them talk."

Anger and terror thundered in my chest as we shoved our way through the Egyptian bazaar.

Suddenly, Sam was at my side, pushing me forward. "Everything will be all right, Savannah."

"You're in on this madness, too?" I snapped.

The three of us moved together through the fair. Goosebumps danced across my skin, and I surveyed the crowd as chills skittered down my spine. Everyone looked normal—just laughing, drinking, and playing carnival games.

Except for one. A man in a masquerade mask trailed on our left.

The mask was like those many people wore at the fair. But I caught his eyes, and they flashed red, for just a second. His predatory stare gave me no doubt that he was in league with the two who had attacked me at the Taphouse.

I squeezed Jaxson's hand. "On our left, someone is following."

He nodded. "I know. Don't make eye contact."

"On our right," Sam whispered.

Another masked werewolf—a woman. Was she the she-wolf from Belmont?

Dread clawed at my skin. It was like they were herding us.

Jaxson spoke so low that I could barely hear it over the clamor of the fair. "There's a gap between the pavilions up ahead. Turn right down that. I'll jump our pursuers when they come around the corner."

I trembled as we slowly walked forward. Jaxson was fishing

for sharks with me dangling like a mackerel on the end of the line.

Before we reached the junction, a woman in a half mask stepped out and smiled.

It was her. The bitch from Belmont.

I tensed, but before I could scream, she lifted the flap of a tent, and a large brown wolf leapt out and slammed into Jaxson.

Hand-in-hand, we tumbled to the ground.

Suddenly, Sam was pulling me to my feet, and we were running, shoving our way through the crowd. I whipped my head back to look for Jaxson just in time to see the she-wolf lunge at me. Claws burst from her hands, and she wrenched me back by my jacket. Sam shouted, spun, and rammed her fist into the woman's face.

My attacker staggered back, then jumped forward and kicked at Sam's knee. Before she could recover, the masked man who'd been following us earlier darted forward and shifted into a white wolf, clothes and all. With a savage growl, he pounced, and I screamed as he knocked Sam into a towering stack of French country marmalade. People panicked and fled, stampeding around us.

The bitch from Belmont grabbed my arm and pulled me to her. She fished a silver ball out of her pocket. I had no idea what it was, but it seemed bad. I struck her arm with my open hand, and it bounced away into the crowd. The she-wolf snarled and backhanded me, and stars danced in front of my eyes.

Fury coursed through my veins—and then magic. I could feel it burning me, like ice water rushing over my skin.

Hell, yes.

"You crazy psycho!" I grabbed the woman's face as magic poured from my palm. The she-wolf rocketed back and collapsed into a broomstick vendor's stand. Broomsticks erupted into the air like fireworks, and the she-wolf flopped to her knees, groaning.

Holy shit. I'd just face-blasted someone.

Sam heaved the white wolf off of her and started to stand, but it clamped its jaws on her leg, and she screamed. Then Jaxson was there. His hands erupted in long claws, and he ripped into the wolf as it yelped.

The she-wolf leapt to her feet, but Sam charged and body-checked her. They tumbled to the ground in a flurry of claws.

"Run!" Sam shouted.

I glanced at the broomsticks but ruled that out. It was the first time I'd ever seen them, and I sure as hell wasn't going to be able to ride off on one. Instead, I dashed past a pretzel salesman and into the alley, looking for somewhere smelly to hide. They might not find me if I could mask my scent. I needed to find a barbeque stand or a candle vendor.

Moments later, I stumbled to a halt at the intersection between four pavilions and spun.

No sign of Jaxson or Sam, or anyone I knew. No pursuers. Just a dozen people tending to their shops.

Which way should I go?

I pulled out my cell phone and froze. The tent to my right swayed, and a long black shadow lying across the grass moved.

I slowly looked up, and my heart stopped. There, silhouetted against the floating lights, a dark form balanced on the taut roof of the tent. Tall and gangly, it was like a body stretched hideously long and thin.

My mind blanked.

Holy shit. Monsters are real.

Faster than a viper's strike, its arm lashed out and gripped me by the throat, stifling my scream. When it lifted me into the air, I kicked and flailed and yanked at its claws, but its grip was unbreakable. Panic tore through me as the sinewy arm pulled me close. I couldn't turn my eyes away from the muscles visible beneath its translucent green skin. I didn't have the courage to look the thing in the eyes.

Its claws were too tight. I couldn't breathe.

The monster's hideous signature swirled around me, tasting like blood and copper, and feeling like oil trickling across my skin. I heard screams from below, but they were distant echoes. The floating lights began to bleed into a beautiful blur.

Suddenly, a dark shadow flew toward us. Then the lights spun around me, and I slammed back to earth. The wind trapped in my lungs exploded from my chest, and I rolled to my knees, gasping.

Ten feet ahead, two massive, snarling wolves pinned the fiend to the ground.

I staggered to my feet. To my horror, the monstrosity did so as well, flinging the wolves into the surrounding tents.

I ran as if the devil itself were after me. For all I knew, it was.

A wolf whipped around the corner ahead of me. I stumbled to the side and reached for my mace, but faster than I could react, it rushed back the way I had come. One of mine, I supposed.

With wolves running everywhere and no idea of who to trust or what to do, I turned right and darted for the edge of the fair. Someone had erected those barricades cordoning off the street. Maybe there were cops nearby. Surely they'd heard the screaming already, but the whole fair was in a panic, so they probably wouldn't know where to respond.

I looked both ways as I burst out of the fairgrounds and left the Midway behind. Racing along the edge of the pavilions, a white wolf bore down on me at unbelievable speed.

Jaxson? Another one of Jaxson's pack? Or an enemy?

I pulled the mace Casey had given me from my pocket and dashed toward the street, screaming, desperately trying to draw attention. Instead, loitering people melted out of my way in terror. So much for help.

I'd have to face this wolf alone. I whirled and raised my mace to find the white wolf almost upon me. Friend or foe, I would pull the trigger.

Then the white beast flew sideways as a giant gray wolf slammed into it. They tumbled to the side in a snarling blur.

I staggered back from the savage battle. Blood and fur flew as they growled and tore into each other. The grey wolf lunged and clamped its massive jaws around its opponent. With a single swift motion, it lifted the white wolf into the air and shook.

My stomach churned as something snapped.

In a swirl of magic, the white wolf turned into a fully clothed man, and the gray beast dropped the tattered corpse from its mouth. Then it looked at me with blood-reddened fangs and honey-colored eyes that seemed to pierce my soul. While the white wolf had been huge, the gray one was truly monstrous and rippling with power.

My scream choked in my throat, and my chest felt as if it might split in two.

The wolf took several menacing steps toward me, and I raised the mace in my trembling hand. "Stay back, asshole!"

The wolf's lips curled, revealing its sharp teeth. My body shook as I slowly backed up. *Maybe it'll let me walk away,* I desperately thought, but the gray wolf growled again.

Guess not.

"Savannah!" a woman's voice cut across the street, and I risked a glance out of the corner of my eye. Sam. She looked terrified, which only ratcheted up the panic shaking my body.

Wolves flooded out of the fair toward us. My heart was racing so fast, I was close to passing out. I staggered slightly.

Wolves everywhere. Two black ones circled my flanks, and panic choked all reason from my mind.

I'm surrounded.

"Put that down, Savannah!" Sam screamed, her voice close but eerily distant. "That's Jaxson! He's not himself. Don't make any sudden movements."

Jaxson.

Blood dripped from the gray beast's mouth. I dragged my gaze from the mauled corpse to the wolf's ruthless honey-gold eyes.

That was not Jaxson.

As it started to step forward, I shoved the mace in its face. "Don't take another fucking step toward me, or I'll blast you."

The wolf snarled at the canister, locked eyes with me, and took a step.

Fuck you.

I pushed the trigger all the way down, and a billowing cloud of gas exploded. The gray wolf reared back, roaring and snapping its teeth, and the black wolves whined as smoke rose from their skin. Sam screamed as well and doubled over, clawing at her face.

I tumbled back. My eyes and skin burned, and nausea rolled over me like a freight train. The gray wolf's snout wrinkled as he bared his teeth at me and released a hateful growl.

I could barely see him through my swollen eyes.

"Get the hell back!" I aimed the canister at him with my thumb held lightly over the trigger. His honey eyes narrowed, and his body trembled with rage. Then, in a flash, he took off, running impossibly fast back toward the fair.

Run, fucker.

I could barely see through the tears that were flowing from my puffy, stinging eyes. My lungs and skin also burned, and my breathing became ragged. It was worse this time than at the motel. *What the hell is this stuff? Sarin gas?*

Forcing my eyes open, I surveyed the chaos around me.

Sam had stumbled to her knees and kept cursing between coughs. The black wolves had retreated several dozen feet and were rubbing their snouts with their paws.

Police officers with glowing batons swarmed our position. I staggered away from the incapacitated wolves and into the arms of a patrolman.

For a glittering moment, the fair had been a dream. Now, I just wanted the nightmare to be over.

26

Jaxson

People dove out of my way as I barreled through the fair on all fours.

I had to get the wolfsbane off. Savannah might still be in danger from the rogue wolves and demons—or even my pack, after what she'd done.

I didn't have time for this.

Chemicals burned my skin, and my eyes stung so badly, it was nearly impossible to see. But that was nothing compared to the rage boiling in my veins.

Wolfsbane, of all things. After we'd saved her from the demon and the white wolf, she'd sprayed us with *that*.

Of course she did. She was a LaSalle. How could I imagine that she was any different?

Wolfsbane was toxic to werewolves. It blinded our senses, burned our flesh, and stopped our ability to shift and regenerate. It was a curse from the gods.

So was she.

I rounded a corner and growled as I spotted a dunk tank game. It would have to do.

The terrified dunkee jumped off his platform as I leapt through the air and dove into the water. From the instant relief, I knew that at least the version she'd blasted at me was water soluble.

Once I'd sufficiently thrashed around in the tank, I leapt out and shook, spraying water over anyone foolish enough to stand nearby. My wolf was pissed and wanted to bite the LaSalle woman.

They killed our sister. With wolfsbane.

My body trembled with fury. Just having the residual scent of it on me made my wolf want to rip throats. It had taken all my control to back off when I saw the canister in Savannah's hands. That shit had killed my sister. I would never forget. Never forgive.

And gods, I wanted revenge.

Yet, when my sister died, I'd been the one who'd had to bring the pack in line to prevent all-out war with the LaSalles. I'd had to swallow my anger to do the right thing. And I'd have to swallow it now. I needed the cursed woman alive.

I started running back toward where I'd left her. With my wolf enraged, I'd need to shift to get control.

That was going to be a problem. When I'd heard Savannah screaming earlier, I hadn't bothered to take my clothes off to shift—I'd just let them shred. I needed something to wear before I shifted so that I wasn't running around the fair stark naked. I'd never admit it to my wolf, but there were times I envied regular shifters.

I passed a vendor selling clothes. With a snap of my jaws, I yanked a pair of trousers off the rack and left the merchant woman screaming bloody murder behind. My wolf didn't care about ideas like property, just territory.

I slipped out of sight behind a tent and shifted back. My bones snapped and muscles stretched, my jaws shrank, and my fangs retracted. I gritted my teeth and gave a low growl. Shifting had never hurt like this.

Fucking LaSalles and their wolfsbane.

I snarled as I buttoned the trousers.

Human again, it was time to find the damned woman. Even with thousands of people milling around the fair, I could smell her. That was surprising, but clearly, the danger had attuned my human senses somehow.

Despite the rampaging wolves and demons, the fair hadn't descended into complete chaos. Magic-Siders were reasonably accustomed to demonic outbreaks and haywire magic. It was just a natural part of having a population made of spellcasters, shifters, vampires, demons, devils, and a dozen other magical species. Shit went crazy pretty often. It was a miracle that the city was still standing.

But there was no doubt about where everything had gone down. Blue lights flashed off the trees, and Order agents were swarming everywhere. One demon and one wolf were dead. Their accomplices would be long gone by now, including the she-wolf who had originally attacked Savannah.

We'd been so fucking close, both to triumph and disaster. Once again, Savannah Caine had gotten very lucky.

When I reached the flashing lights, I encountered a forlorn scene. Agitated cops. Miserable wolves. And in the midst of it all, the traumatized LaSalle woman, sitting on a curb.

She was a magnet for disaster, but I was relieved she was okay. I would do what was needed to protect her, but after what she'd done to us, I didn't feel one ounce of pity for her current predicament.

Well, perhaps a little pity. Three days ago, she'd had no idea that werewolves or demons were real. Tonight, she'd been nearly killed or abducted by both.

Savannah leapt to her feet as I approached. "That was you—the gray wolf that killed the man!"

Her eyes darted to my bloodied chest, and heat rose in her cheeks.

"The wolf that saved your ass," I snarled. "After which you sprayed me with wolfsbane!"

She bared her teeth almost like a wolf would. "I wasn't sure it was you! And it looked like you were about to attack me! You were snarling and had blood dripping from your goddamned mouth."

"I would never hurt you, but apparently, that doesn't go both ways."

She stepped up, but three cops intervened and pulled us apart. One started grilling me on the shifter that I had put down. What a disaster.

Sam had partially regained her senses. She was on the phone with my lawyer, by the sound of it. Thankfully, the dead man was a shifter, and we were subject to pack law. Still, there would be paperwork and interviews and reports, but they knew better than to restrain me.

It didn't matter. The Order was going to just squeeze us harder after this.

I glared at the body. I hadn't meant to kill him. But Savannah had been in danger, and I wasn't sure if more wolves were going to attack, or more demons. I'd made a quick decision—the wrong one—and we'd missed our chance to get answers. Now there was no way to get information out of him without a necromancer, and that was a line no one in the entire city was willing to cross. Not even the LaSalles, monsters that they were.

My nostrils flared. *Fear.*

I spun and spotted Savannah. Though flanked by two cops, she was as white as a ghost. Now what?

Leaving my own interrogator mid-interview, I headed over.

A cop waved the unmarked canister in her face. "This is wolfsbane. It's highly illegal, and we'll be confiscating it. How did you get it?"

She looked from one cop to the other. "I had no idea! I thought it was mace or some kind of pepper spray. I'm new to town...I didn't know any of this was real until a few nights ago! What the hell is wolfsbane?"

The cop clipped the bottle to his belt. "Wolfsbane is a chemical weapon and riot control agent. It is illegal for civilian use. I'm going to ask you once again, where did you get this?"

She shrugged. "Found it. Someone dropped it at the fair. I'd lost my mace, so I picked it up and kept it."

The second cop stepped up in her face. "This will go easier on you if you tell us the truth. Who gave it to you?"

The woman had authority problems and looked about ready to slap him, so I stepped in. "Her family."

Savannah shot daggers at me with her eyes, but as far as I was concerned, the LaSalles could collectively go to hell.

The overbearing cop crossed his arms. "Is that true, ma'am? If you don't tell us, we'll have to book you."

She set her jaw, and her eyes burned with hatred. At least she was loyal. That, I could admire.

"Okay, ma'am. We're going to need to take you downtown." The cop turned to me. "Do you and the pack want to press assault charges, Jax?"

Her eyes went wide. "Assault charges? I was the one who was attacked by a damn monster and that asshole over there!" She pointed at the body, trembling.

I could smell her rage and fear.

My wolves watched eagerly, waiting to see how this played out, hoping the cops threw the book at her. I could smell their hatred, and I owed my pack justice. Savannah should rot in jail for a month for what she'd just done.

But we needed her to stop these abductions and clear the pack's name. The seer had told me that Savannah would lead me to the answers I sought, and I hadn't gotten any yet.

I waved the cops away. "Let me talk with her."

The officers stepped back, and Savannah's body tensed as her eyes widened. I smiled as if to say, *Yes. I have sway here. They'll do as they're told.*

"Are you going to have your corrupt cops lock me up, Jaxson?" she spat.

"You'd be safer there, so I'm considering it."

She jabbed a finger into my chest. "Bastard. You're the one who murdered someone."

"Someone who was coming after you. Don't forget that."

Her lip curled up in frustration, and she balled her fists. "Fine, so you're my savior. What are you going to do with me?"

Such gall. "I need your help, so I'm not going to press charges. But there are conditions." It took all my restraint to spit out the words without growling. My wolf struggled in my chest in protest, and the way in which the other wolves slunk away told me the pack would be angry. Not surprising, but it wasn't the alpha's goddamn job to make everybody happy. It was my job to protect the pack.

The woman crossed her arms. "What conditions *now*? I'm already risking my life to help you."

I stepped close so she had to crane her neck to meet my gaze. "Never touch that shit again. Wolfsbane." Even the word burned my lips.

"And how do I protect myself, then, from the freaking werewolves trying to kill me?"

"Pepper spray. Something else. It's non-negotiable."

She ran her hands through her hair. "Fine. Whatever."

"Second, you have to make it up to the pack."

Her eyes widened. "How?"

"That's for you to figure out. But know this: they will hate you now if they didn't before." I turned to walk away.

"Jaxson!"

The pleading in her eyes stopped me in my tracks. "What?"

She wrapped her arms around herself and joined me. "What was that thing that attacked me? Did you kill it?"

"We killed it, yeah, but I have no idea what it was. A type of demon I haven't encountered."

She swallowed hard, and I could smell the terror rising from her. And determination. "I need to see it. If I'm going to have nightmares for the rest of my life, I want to see it for real."

Impressive. My wolf grudgingly agreed.

I shook my head. "Unfortunately, that's not possible. As soon as you kill a demon, their body melts away. This one left a sticky patch of black blood before it boiled away into nothingness. It's going to be difficult to identify off a description alone."

Her shoulders drooped. "At least it's dead."

It wasn't truly dead—demons just went back to the under-world. But I didn't want to explain that to her at this point, given what she'd faced that night, so I just shrugged. I was beginning to suspect she had a knack for knowing when I was lying. Perhaps I had some kind of tell. I'd need to work on that.

Before I could step away, she grabbed my arm. "Will there be more?"

"Maybe. Probably."

"Where do they even come from?"

I drew a long breath and met her eyes. "They're summoned from the hells. By sorcerers."

27

Savannah

My life had become a living nightmare.

Being hunted by werewolves seemed like a much smaller problem now that I knew demons were coming for me. Demons summoned by sorcerers.

Could Casey and Aunt Laurel summon creatures like these?

Jaxson had warned me the LaSalles practiced the dark arts. Was this what he'd meant?

I leaned against a tree and took stock of my situation. In addition to being hunted by a variety of supernatural beings, I was pretty sure that I'd just alienated and pissed off everyone in the local werewolf pack, and now the cops wanted to throw me in jail for using wolfsbane. At least Jaxson was able to persuade the cops to let me go—though I could tell that had infuriated his pack. Sam wouldn't even meet my eyes anymore.

The cab ride home was a dismal affair, and a black SUV full of werewolves followed me all the way back to the Indies.

Casey, as always, greeted me at the door. It was late. Had he been waiting?

He ran his fingers through his hair. "Jeez, Savannah, every

time you show up, you look worse off than you did the time before. What happened now?'

I didn't want Aunt Laurel to hear, so we headed upstairs. I explained everything while I sat at the tiny desk in my room and sketched the demon from the park to calm my nerves.

Casey rubbed his face with his palms. "That is fucking madness. You need to stay away from Laurent and his pack. He's going to get you killed."

I shook my head. "No. I have to put a stop to this. I can help."

My cousin frowned. "It's too dangerous."

"Jaxson may hate you, but I know he'll protect me—even after what I did to him tonight."

Jaxson had killed a man in front of me. Just to protect me.

Casey gave a half laugh. "Yeah, well, you're going to be working that one off for a while. Wolfsbaning the alpha. You're lucky he didn't kill you himself."

I set my jaw. "*You* gave me the wolfsbane! I nearly got thrown in jail just for having it on me!"

"Yeah, sorry about that. But I gave you it to use on assailants. Not the Dockside alpha," Casey said, chuckling. Clearly, the thought delighted him, but Casey hadn't seen Jaxson in his wolf form, glaring back with blood dripping from his mouth.

I flipped my sketch of the demon around and shoved it toward my cousin. "Can you tell me what this is?" While the demon's body had disappeared, its sinewy limbs and savage claws were going to be etched in my mind forever.

His eyes widened. "Holy shit, you're good at drawing. This picture actually scares the bejeebers out of me. Unfortunately, I have no idea what this is."

"Can you find out? You owe me."

"Yeah, we've got a few manuals of demonology stashed around here somewhere. And I know people I could ask."

"Discreetly."

For whatever reason, I didn't fully trust my aunt. Through the mild application of physical threats, I made Casey promise not to tell Aunt Laurel or Uncle Pete what had happened. While I trusted my cousin implicitly, I couldn't shake the feeling that his parents would try to stop me from working with Jaxson or that they'd keep me on lockdown until the threat had passed.

But I needed to figure out what was going on, and Jaxson Laurent seemed hell-bent on doing the same.

That night, I barely slept, and when I did, my dreams were filled with nightmares.

I woke exhausted, with a dark cloud hanging over my heart. Demons and werewolves were hunting me, and I'd just maced the one person who seemed the most invested in keeping me safe.

Not mace. *Wolfsbane*. I had no idea what exactly that was, but while it had burned my skin and eyes, it had practically incapacitated the other wolves. When I closed my eyes, I could see Sam staring back at me, filled with hate.

I put my hands over my face as I flopped back in bed. I had to make amends. The problem was, I'd never been particularly good at apologies or acting contrite. It was practically a foreign language.

At breakfast, I asked Casey how best to apologize to a werewolf, and he grinned. "Bring it a dead rabbit. Nice and rotten."

Thanks, Captain Helpful.

With little to be gained from my cousin, I kept to myself for the rest of the morning and had a cab drop me off at Eclipse at ten a.m.

A muscle-bound bouncer leaned against the wall of the restaurant, scrolling on his smartphone. He had a wolfy look about him, hot and menacing. Most of the werewolves I'd met in Magic Side were unbelievably good looking. There must have been some kind of sexy wolf gene in this pack.

The man slipped his phone into his pocket and stopped me with a meaty hand. "Hold up. Are you carrying?"

"Carrying what?"

He loomed over me. "Wolfsbane. I heard what you did at the Full Moon Fair. I can't have you bringing that in here."

"Nope, fresh out."

He growled and sniffed. Could he have smelled it if I'd had some on me?

"I was attacked by a demon and a bunch of werewolves," I snapped as I stepped back.

"Don't pull that excuse. You sprayed the alpha and the people trying to protect you. Don't *ever* try that shit when I'm around, or you'll regret it."

I pushed past him. "Well, everybody had fangs and claws out and was growling. How was I supposed to tell the difference?"

I stepped into the bar and immediately regretted my words. Four shifters sent me death glares, stopping me right in my tracks. I'd hoped the place would be empty that morning.

So much for putting off apologies.

The look of betrayal in Sam's eyes cut particularly deep. Three days ago, she'd taken care of me when I was drunk and adrift in a world I didn't understand. In return, I'd wolfsbaned her while she was trying to save my ass.

I straightened my spine and walked over to the bar. She turned her back to me and began stocking the liquor shelf.

I deserved that. And more.

I couldn't believe that this was the same place I'd gone out for dinner with Jaxson. That night, it had been rich, lively, and teeming with excitement and music and magic. Now, in the light of day, I could see the cracks and taste the bitterness in the air.

Placing a hand on the bar top, I murmured, "Look, I'm sorry you got caught in the crossfire yesterday, Sam. I didn't know what was in the canister, and I was really scared and fairly certain I was about to die."

She slowly turned with a deadpan look, then braced her arms against the bar. "Do you have any idea how badly that shit hurts? You should have listened to me. I told you to submit. Why don't you listen to anything anyone says?"

Her tone was cold and dismissive, and my temper flared. I lowered my voice so it was a knife-edge whisper. "When you first met me three days ago, I didn't know any of this existed. Since then, I've been attacked by more werewolves than I can count and nearly choked to death by a demon that looked like it walked straight out of a Tim Burton film. Excuse me if I wasn't ready to listen at that moment when Jaxson was about to rip my throat out. I'd just watched him snap another man's spine in front of me."

"He wasn't going to rip your throat out."

"Yeah, well, after being nearly shredded to pieces, I wasn't about to take any chances. Do you get my drift?" I emphasized those last words and glared at the other shifters around the room.

I was on the edge of a nervous breakdown, so they'd better cut me some slack.

A man seated at the bar slowly spun on his stool until he was facing me. Had I seen him last night? Several deep furrows cut his forehead, and his eyes sparked with pure hatred. "You need to keep in mind that LaSalles aren't welcome here before you go shooting your mouth off," he said, his voice almost a growl. "You're lucky the alpha needs you now, but as soon as that's through, don't you ever set your dirty feet in pack territory again, or I'll drag you out by your filthy red hair. Do you get *my* drift?"

My throat tightened.

Every look around the room was the same. They hated me

here, and it wasn't just the wolfsbane. They despised my family. This was a blood feud, and I was in the wrong part of town.

"I'm not a LaSalle," I said. "I'm a Caine. And I don't want anything to do with whatever feud you've got going. I assure you, I want nothing more than to get the hell out of here."

The sooner we tracked down whoever was hunting me, the sooner I could put these werewolves and their bullshit behind me.

The man slid off his seat and stepped up to me, towering over my head. His signature stormed around me. He was extremely powerful, reeked of vodka, and spoke with unstrained venom. "Blood is blood. You're a LaSalle, whether you like it or not. Consider this your warning, little witch. Next time, there won't be one." With that, he marched to the door and left.

I bared my teeth as he walked away—which was ridiculous, because I didn't have fangs—but it felt right. Tears of frustration threatened to creep out, so I clenched my fists.

What, exactly, had I done to be treated like this? To have drunks getting in my face and threatening me? I wasn't part of whatever shitty history they were caught up in, just collateral damage.

A glass of ice water slid across the granite bar top toward me, and I turned back. Sam had a sad expression on her face, but her voice had warmed a little. "Not many people stand up to Billy."

"He seems like a real jerk."

"He has good reasons for hating your family, but he won't cause you any trouble. Not with Jaxson as the alpha. *He* won't let any harm come to you."

The other werewolves in the bar turned away, as if even the sound of Jaxson's name could make them submit. There was so much I didn't understand about him or his position as the alpha. He held sway over his pack even when he wasn't around.

I considered the power he seemed to hold over me and shivered.

Every time I was around him, my mind fogged. He frustrated me to no end, and a part of me yearned to rage against him. But there was always a subversive undercurrent flowing through my thoughts, the desire to submit, to please, to obey. And when he was close, it was like I wanted to submit with my whole body. Judging from the heat between us, I *was* fairly certain he'd be amazing in the bedroom. God, why was I thinking about that?

Sam grinned widely and stacked several glasses that were still damp from the dishwasher.

"Is something funny?" I took a sip of the drink she'd given me.

"Oh, nothing. Just wondering how your thoughts went from Billy—the scariest wolf in our pack—to sex with Jaxson."

28

Savannah

I choked, and water sprayed from my mouth. I leaned forward, my cheeks burning like a Roman candle. She knew I was thinking about Jaxson? Sexually? "How...?"

Sam shook her head. "Honey, I'm a wolf. I can smell emotions. And FYI, arousal on you smells like a rare steak to a male wolf."

She winked at me, and I gasped, covering my mouth. "No, no, no."

One of the wolves who'd been setting up the stage for tonight appeared at the end of the bar. His eyes burned yellow, and he waggled his eyebrows at me. I planted my elbows on the bar and dropped my head into my hands, dying a little inside.

Jaxson, you son of a bitch.

That would have been good to know from the start. Possibly a good lesson number one about werewolves. Had he known every time I was angry or scared or turned on? I recalled the other night when he'd chased me down the alley. I'd been so frightened I'd nearly pissed myself, but something about having him close had lit a fire in me. Had I smelled like a rare steak to him then?

I wanted to crawl under the bar and die.

Sam's eyes sparkled. The goddamned wolves could probably all smell my humiliation, too, for all I knew. She certainly seemed to be in a better mood.

"Don't be too embarrassed. We're used to sensing emotions. It's how we communicate. While scenting feelings might seem odd to you, it's second nature to us and not surprising. Plus"—she handed me a napkin—"most women feel what you feel toward Jaxson, so we're used to it."

"I don't have feelings for Jaxson. He's good to look at, that's all."

Sure, he was gorgeous, powerful, and probably a good lay. But he was also a domineering monster who'd casually murdered a man—*werewolf*—in front of me the night before.

Then again, I'd killed a werewolf, too. Jaxson was just protecting me.

A perverse part of me found that pretty hot.

I rubbed my temples and whispered, "Is there a way I can mask it?"

Sam lowered her head and looked me straight in the eyes. "To mask when you're horny for Jaxson?"

My face turned as red as my hair, and I hissed, "Yes, but for God's sake, don't say that shit out loud!"

"Maybe you could try to control your reactions?" She shrugged and began scooping ice into a large bucket. "Then again, as the alpha, Jaxson has the keenest senses of us all. He'll know when a steak is on the grill. P.S., we also hear *really* well, so whispering in here isn't actually going to do you any good. Jaxson can probably hear everything going on in the whole building."

He'd heard all of that.

I dropped my head to the bar as my dignity died, and Sam gave my hair a soft, affectionate pat. She had to be loving this, and she actually started humming. Apparently, the best apology I could have offered was handing over my dignity like a dead, stinking rabbit.

Essentially, I was screwed when it came to hiding anything from Jaxson. Maybe Casey had something that could help with masking emotions.

Sam put her elbows on the bar and leaned close. "Jaxson wasn't going to hurt you, you know? His wolf was trying to protect you. To meet you."

What the hell did that mean? I gave her a skeptical glare. "Right. He was just saying hello with his teeth bared and snarling."

She shook her head. "Actually, he was sniffing you, but then you challenged his wolf by threatening him. Pro tip: don't challenge a wolf, let alone an alpha like Jaxson. It usually ends badly. When we're in wolf form, our wolves are in the driver's seat, so to speak, and can be unpredictable. You're lucky Jaxson was able to get control of his wolf after you sprayed him."

What the fuck? I was *lucky*? What would have happened if he hadn't gotten control of his wolf? A cold, creeping terror worked its way beneath my skin.

"Good to know." I took another sip of water with a shaky hand. "But I wasn't challenging him. I was protecting myself."

She lifted an eyebrow. "You were aiming wolfsbane at the man. That shit is bad, but for Jaxson, it's worse."

"Why worse?" He'd deserved what he'd gotten for wolfing out on me like that, but I couldn't help but feel a little remorse. If that stuff had stung my skin, I couldn't imagine what it was like for them.

"It's how his sister died." Sam looked down and started

stocking bottles in the cooler. I could practically smell the emotions coming off her.

Guilt hit me like a ten-pound brick. No wonder Jaxson had been growling at me. "I'm sorry, I didn't know. Really, I didn't even know what was in the canister."

"You'll have to tell him that." She headed to the side of the bar and lifted a full beer keg onto her shoulder like it was no heavier than a boombox, then nodded to a door at the back. "No time like the present."

The door had a *Do Not Enter* sign, which seemed particularly ominous in light of what I'd just learned. I forced myself to stand and slowly walk toward the door of doom, my cheeks still burning with a thousand emotions.

"Down the hall. Second door on the left," Sam suggested cheerfully as I pushed on through.

I knocked on the heavy wooden door to his office.

"Come in."

I opened the door and ventured inside. Jaxson was waiting with crossed arms and leaning against his large oak desk. Rather than a business suit, he wore jeans, biker boots, and a black T-shirt that showed off his rippling biceps.

Incredibly hunky.

He was framed by a large painting hanging on the wall, which depicted the moon rising over a still, forest-ringed lake.

I froze as Jaxson closed the door and stepped up behind me. Heat poured off him and mixed with my own. Shivers raked my skin, and I drew in an unsteady breath.

Calm yourself, Savannah. He knows what you're thinking.

He slowly circled me, his pupils dilated as he inspected every inch of me—a predator stalking his prey. Jaxson's power pressed against me, and his signature filled my senses. But there was something more than magic. Heat. Desire. An unseen force that drew me toward him like a magnet to its opposite pole.

I couldn't ignore the chemistry between us. Just being near him made the rivers of my body meet.

He *had* to know.

Did he enjoy his effect on me, or did I disgust him? His pack hated me and my family, and I had a sneaking suspicion they probably had many reasons to.

Finally, I couldn't take the awkward silence anymore, or his attention boring into me. "I'm sorry I sprayed you with wolfsbane yesterday," I blurted. "I was terrified, and I didn't know what was in the bottle."

His eyes blazed. "Wolfsbane is a chemical manufactured specifically to hurt our kind. Never use it again."

I shook my head. "I'm really sorry about everything. The wolfsbane, your sister, the fair. Everything."

He tensed. "We're not going to talk about my sister."

Obviously, *that* was the wrong thing to say. I looked at the ground. "Look, I'm not great at apologizing, and I'm not familiar with the rules here or your history with the LaSalles. But I'm here, and I want to help. So can we get past what happened last night?"

He narrowed his eyes and stepped closer so that I had to look up to meet his gaze. "I appreciate that, but you'll have to work for the pack's forgiveness before you get mine."

"Fine." I never backed down from a challenge.

The air vibrated between us for just a moment before he stepped away. "I'm sorry I scared you. Our meet shouldn't have happened like that. I shifted so I could protect you, but then my wolf took over and demanded to meet you."

Meet me? Sam had said the same thing. An unsettling fear crept into my chest. "Do you understand how creepy and weird

that sounds? Is your wolf different than you? Like, is it something that lives in you, or a split personality?"

There was so much I didn't know about werewolves—about
any of this world, for that matter. I was so in over my head, it was
scary.

"We don't really talk about it with outsiders. Suffice it to say
we're two sides of the same coin. When I'm in wolf form, I think
differently, and different aspects of my personality are heightened. We're one, but it's easier to talk about that part of me as
my wolf. We all speak that way."

Sam had talked about his wolf being in control when he'd
shifted, but what did that even mean? "Why would your wolf
want to meet me? You've already met me."

"Its senses are stronger than mine, and scenting you would
yield deep insights into what you are, your character, and what
you need. That would be enough, but my wolf is also drawn to
you, for some reason—it's intrigued. Always has been." Jaxson's
voice was low, almost a growl. Was that his wolf talking to me?

Something tugged in my breast, and heat began to pool in
my center. My skin flushed, and I could suddenly feel every
movement of my clothing across my skin. I had the overwhelming urge to sweep my hands over Jaxson's strong chest.
What the hell was happening to me?

I took an uncertain step forward, and Jaxson's expression
hardened. Anger? Distrust? But also something else—*desire.*

His heightened signature made me lightheaded, and I
faltered a little. He stepped closer so that he was just a breath
away, like we'd stood in the alley two nights before. Then, I'd
been trembling, too scared to run, but now I *wanted* to be
trapped between him and the wall.

Why was he looking at me like he wanted to taste me?

Everything about this was wrong.

I tore my gaze from his and slipped around him, suddenly

desperate to get control of the situation. Stopping in front of the couch, I hugged myself. "Look, I know you have heightened senses and can read my emotions. Don't make assumptions. I don't understand these feelings I have around you, and I'm not comfortable with them. So please give me a little space, no matter how intrigued you...or your wolf...are."

Jaxson tensed, and the honey color left his eyes. He regarded me for a long moment. "I can respect that."

My heartbeat slowed, returning to normal. "We want the same thing—to track down those bastards—and that's why I'm agreeing to work with you. This is a business arrangement and nothing more. Is that clear?"

"Yes, I understand."

"And one more thing, Jaxson. I appreciate your wolf saving me, but don't you *ever* let him try to sniff me or meet me without my permission."

That was definitely on my list as one of the weirdest requests I'd ever had to ask a man before.

His jaw twitched, and something flashed in his eyes, but he nodded.

"Good. Now that that's settled, what's the plan?" I asked, feeling a modicum of control return.

"You need to learn how to get away the next time you get jumped." He grabbed a set of keys from his desk and opened the door.

I set my jaw as heat rushed to my face. "I'd say I handled myself pretty well, all things considered."

"You got lucky. There's a difference. You're too weak to fight wolves and demons, and too slow to run away. We need to fix that."

My neck hair bristled as I stepped into the hall. *Weak? Slow?* I'd always prided myself on being able to hold my own.

Maybe I should have blasted Jaxson with more wolfsbane.

29

Jaxson

We left Eclipse through the back. My rental truck was parked in the alley, and I didn't want Regina or Billy or Sam wondering where we were going. My inner circle had been asking too many questions lately, and it was getting to the point that I would have to shut them down.

It was better to be discreet. Tensions throughout the pack were high, and parading around with the LaSalle woman wasn't helping matters.

Savannah was a crucial asset. She could scry, she could draw, and there was a possibility I could exploit her connections with her family. She'd already procured a scrying potion, after all. But she was also in far more danger than I'd originally thought and become a major liability. It was on me to rectify that.

I probably couldn't teach her to fight well enough to save her life, but I could help her run. A pair of enchanted boots would give her the speed she needed to get away.

Savannah climbed into the front seat. My gaze gravitated downward, and I couldn't help but notice her legs in those high-cut shorts. She had legs for days and was fast for a human. The boots I had in mind would enhance her natural abilities—heck, she might even be able to keep up with me.

I wanted to chase her. To hunt her.

Something about that image sent heat through me, and I scowled. To her, I was a monster, no different than the demon we'd killed. She wouldn't understand the chase.

Savannah was scrutinizing me closely, mildly annoyed. "Listen, if you're too busy to take me wherever it is we're going, don't worry about it. I'll be fine. I've handled myself well enough so far."

"You can't count on luck," I replied, putting the truck in gear. "This trip won't take long."

She huffed, and I sensed her disbelief as I pulled onto the main street that fronted Eclipse. Sometimes, she was intolerable.

As we passed my auto body shop, a slight smile tugged at her lips, and I suspected she was pleased with herself after her raid the other night.

For all her protests, she liked to play games, too.

My wolf liked that.

Savannah glanced at the signposts as we drove through the intersection. "So, the LaSalles are forbidden from entering your territory. Where, exactly, does your pack land begin?"

"*Now* you're interested in where you should and shouldn't go? Good. We generally claim everything up to 73rd. After that, you're in the Indies and on your own."

"Great. Just trying to figure out where I don't belong."

I looked over. "Billy got under your skin after all, huh?"

She shrugged.

"You handled yourself well. He has good reasons for hating your family, as Sam mentioned, but he'll keep his claws in check."

Savannah's cheeks flushed red, and she averted her eyes.

I grinned. If she'd had any doubts that I'd overheard everything in the bar, those were now gone. The next part of that conversation had been particularly interesting...and Savannah, whose thoughts had apparently drifted in that direction as well, was quite embarrassed but a little aroused nonetheless. That was gratifying after the hell she'd put me through last night.

The scents of her desire and mortification were intoxicating, and it was easy to imagine her fucking me. I shifted in my seat uncomfortably. She was a LaSalle. Besides, in her eyes, I was just another murderous monster.

Time to shift the subject.

"Over that way is Avery's Point." I gestured to the wooded area on the right. "That's one of the few forests on the island where we can shift and run our wolves." Slowing, I turned into the Flats. "The largest wooded area in Magic Side stretches south from Exposition Park and crosses into the Indies, your family's territory. It's not ideal, but it's been that way since the island was founded."

And yet another source of conflict between the pack and the LaSalles.

Savannah nodded but said nothing as we pulled onto the main drag of Market Street. I watched with curiosity as she took in the dozen or so storefronts, all specializing in different things —D's Witchcraft and Wizardry, Pure Potions, and a store called Updos with fancy wigs floating in the window. Her eyes rounded, and I could smell her excitement. "What is this place?" she asked.

"Market Street. The best place to find random stuff." I parked in front of Donahue's Hardware and Alchemical Supplies.

She turned to me with a look of confusion. "What are we doing here? Buying a magic hammer?"

"First, you need some new boots. You're too slow and need to run faster." Again, my eyes drifted to her long, lean legs.

Irritation colored her face. "I'll have you know I was the state champ in the four-hundred-meter in track. I *am* fast, just not four-legged fast."

A track champ. So that explained her speed—she was a natural.

"We'll have to do something about that," I replied.

She scowled at me. "What do you suggest, I grow an extra pair of legs?"

"That idea hadn't crossed my mind." I lifted my brows. "Why don't we start with boots?"

To my surprise, she shrank against the door. "Did you just flippantly imply that you could turn me into a werewolf? Are you infectious or something?"

I snarled at the impudent woman. "Lycanthropy is extremely rare. Maybe one in ten thousand wolves have the gene to pass it on. I could bite you a hundred times, and you'd be fine. If slightly tender." She definitely needed a good nip.

Savannah raised her hands defensively. "I didn't mean to offend. Just wondering if I should be worried. And please don't *bite* me."

Savannah would make a terrible wolf. Disobedient, hot-headed, infuriating.

"You have nothing to worry about," I said gruffly, swallowing my irritation.

"Good." She averted her eyes, and I sensed her relief.

I opened the door and stepped onto the sidewalk. "You did look nice in that wolf mask, if it's any consolation."

She snorted and slid out of the truck. "Not really."

A woman stepped out of Updos with a hairstyle that looked like an intricate bird's nest. Savannah did a double take when a live bluebird poked its head up from inside. "Wow."

"The things women do for beauty these days, I'll never understand."

It was true—real beauty was natural. Before I could stop myself, I glanced at Savannah.

"What now?" she asked, noticing my roving eyes.

I cleared my throat. "Nothing."

We walked down the street in silence. I relished the quiet as Savannah took in the sights around her. We passed an eyeglass shop that sold night-vision contact lenses, then a clothing store with dresses that flashed different colors in the window. I stopped in front of The Cordwainer's Curiosities. "And here we are."

Like its neighbors, the store's window held a selection of its wares—in this case, the finest shoes on offer. Rather than sitting on pedestals or boxes, however, each pair was levitating and engaged in some fashion of movement in place. The tennis shoes were jogging, the red flamenco heels stamped in a rhythmic dance, and the black stilettos sashayed like they were walking down a catwalk.

Savannah shot me a wide smile. "*Magic* shoes?"

"I told you you're too slow."

She rolled her eyes but stepped through the front door with a spring I hadn't seen since we entered the Fair the night before. I couldn't stop my smile as I followed her in.

Shelves of floating shoes filled every space along the walls, and Savannah's eyes landed on a pair of bright pink platform heels that were on display in the center of the shop.

"Ah, welcome." A stout, bald man appeared from out of a back room. He adjusted the apron tied around his front and flamboyantly gestured to the pink heels. "The new line from Andrea Todorova. Gorgeous, aren't they? You can walk miles in them, and they'll feel like you're dancing over clouds."

"Seriously? They're gorgeous." Savannah ran her fingers over the smooth leather.

I could easily imagine how those might look on her as she moved around a stage, her hair flying behind her.

Hair like flames.

She was an asset. That was all.

"We're in the market for a pair of running boots," I said, my voice rough.

The shopkeeper glanced at Savannah, then cast me a look over his glasses, and recognition dawned on his face. "I see. For the slow-footed."

Savannah shot me a deadly expression, and I forced a grin. "Exactly."

"A pair of Swiftleys might do." The shopkeeper waved his hand dismissively at her feet. "Could you remove...those things? For a fitting."

With a sigh, she shucked off her old tennis shoes and plopped down on a bench. The little man slipped out a long wooden wand and touched it to her right toe.

He closed his eyes. "What would you like? What fits, hmm?"

"Well, I'm generally a size nine," she answered.

"I'm not talking to you," the man muttered.

"Then who—"

"Your feet. I think it only makes sense to get their opinion on the matter." He touched the wand to her left foot and nodded, apparently listening intently. Savannah gaped, but without another word, the shopkeeper disappeared in the back.

"Was that for real?" she asked me, her eyes wide.

"Honestly, I have no idea, but I wouldn't get a fit anywhere else."

The bald man returned a minute later with a pair of black biker boots made of smooth leather with a buckle over the front and a one-inch heel. Savannah slid her feet into the boots and moaned, then circled the store twice. I could sense her joy. She'd witnessed unimaginable horrors in the past week, yet somehow, was still capable of experiencing delight.

She was strong hearted.

Savannah grinned. "These are amazing."

Watching her reaction to this new world was like seeing everything for the first time. A broad smile slowly spread across my face. "Just wait until you run in them."

"Can I really run in biker boots?"

The bald man made an irritated squeak and threw up his hands. "Of course you can. They're Swiftleys. It's literally what they're for! Why else would I bring them to you?"

She tensed and seemed about ready to dig into the man, but then she shook her head and turned her attention back to the boots with unabashed adoration in her eyes. "How fast can I go?"

"I cruise around forty miles an hour," I replied, "so that's your benchmark."

Her eyes widened. "Holy crap, that would easily double my speed at a *sprint*."

A glimmer of concern drifted into my mind. She'd need to be faster than me to outrun the rogue wolves. They must have been using some kind of enchantment or physical enhancement as well. I needed to know more.

As she admired the boots, doubt clouded her face. "How much—"

"Don't worry about it," I said. "I like the thought of you keeping up. Who knows, maybe you'll be my match."

30

Savannah

"When do I get to try these babies out?" I stared down at my new kicks with glee as we drove back through the Flats. They were the most gorgeous black biker boots I'd ever seen.

I caught Jaxson watching me from the corner of my eye. He seemed pleased, less like the weight of the world was hanging on his shoulders. His arm hung out the window, and the eternal tension in his frame had relaxed. Slightly. Maybe below that brooding and cold exterior, he had a fun side.

"Let's give them a spin now, if you're up to it," he said, turning into a parking lot beside the forested park he'd pointed out to me earlier. The lot was empty, and he pulled into a spot in front of the sign with *Avery's Point, Est. 1887* on it.

"Has your family been here that long?" I gestured to the date on the sign.

He got out of the truck. "You ask a lot of questions."

Nope, I was wrong. There was nothing fun about Jaxson. I sighed and climbed out.

"My family has been here since the early eighteen-hundreds, when the island was founded," he said. "Same as yours."

Right. The feud ran deep. I recalled what Uncle Pete had said about the wolves grabbing land from the LaSalles, and I wondered if Jaxson and the pack saw it that way.

"Ready to run?" Jaxson asked with a glint in his eyes.

"I was born to run." I tightened the laces and double-bowed them—no need to be tripping ass over tea kettle in front of him. "Anything I should know?"

"Start slow. They'll take some getting used to. If you go too fast, you might feel unbalanced and lose control."

Meaning I'll go ass over tea kettle.

I had no idea how these beautiful boots were going to make me run faster. Hell, I'd probably trip and break my nose, but I didn't care. They were the most comfortable shoes I'd ever stepped into. A soft-cushioned bed supported my arches, and my toes had room to spare. My heart had been sold the moment I'd slipped them on.

Jaxson took off into the woods at what seemed like a stroll for him, though for human legs, it was more like an Olympic sprint.

Here goes nothing.

I took two steps and surged forward, my feet moving like they had rockets attached to them. I stifled a shriek as I dodged a tree trunk and then a boulder, trying to wrap my mind around focusing on my feet while avoiding obstacles that were coming at me way faster than normal. Just as I thought I was getting the hang of it, I tripped over a fallen log and crashed into the mossy ground at high speed.

Pain ripped through my shoulder, and I gasped, stifling a shout.

Damn. That was going to leave a bruise or two.

"I told you, take it slow." Jaxson circled back and helped me to my feet.

"Yeah, easier said than done." I shrugged him off, plucking branches out of my hair.

Running in the boots wasn't actually that much different than skates—at least when the falling part came in. I should have had my rollerblading helmet and wrist guards. I'd look ridiculous, but it would be better than concussing myself or breaking a wrist.

It took about thirty minutes to finally get the hang of the things. We must have circled the park a dozen times, and I was pretty damn exhausted.

Jaxson, of course, seemed fresh as a daisy. He slowed and stepped through the trees onto a rocky beach. A light wind blew off the lake, and the water gently lapped at the shore. My shirt was sweaty, and a dip sounded divine.

"You've almost got the running down," he said, "but that's not going to be enough. These wolves are fast, and there's no knowing when they'll strike. You need to learn how to escape a grapple and chokehold. You panicked last night."

I planted myself in front of him and tilted my head to meet his gaze. "All things considered, I'd say I was pretty damn calm."

His eyes narrowed, and his jaw tensed. "You won't be armed with wolfsbane next time."

I said nothing, but I'd already asked Casey to get me another bottle as a fail-safe.

"You'd better not be thinking what I think you are." His voice was rough and gravelly, and an involuntary shiver worked its way down my spine.

"Never." I gave him *the look*, which usually made people back off. "Now teach me some moves, Jaxson, before I get bored."

Jaxson cocked his head and regarded me closely, looking confused. Amusement glinted in his eyes. "Where did you learn that?"

I frowned and put my hands on my hips. "What the hell are you talking about?"

"That look on your face." A faint smile ghosted his lips. "It doesn't work on me the way you think it does."

The look worked on everybody. I stared at him blankly, then shrugged. It must not have worked on him because he was an alpha or something.

"Ready?" he asked.

I nodded impatiently.

He moved so quickly, I barely had time to register his arm wrapping around my neck, constricting my airway.

I couldn't breathe. Flashbacks of last night swam before my eyes—the demon's claws around my throat. I fought them down. Jaxson was a man, not a demon.

I elbowed him in the stomach and brought my heel down on his foot.

He released me, though I knew it wasn't because of anything I'd done. He could probably take a knife to the chest without blinking an eye.

"Good. So you do know some basic self-defense."

My mom had brought me up to be scrappy. After my parents were gone, I'd just been a kid in a new school with a kooky godmother, which had made me fair game for bullies. I'd had to learn a few moves. Nothing standard—I mainly fought dirty. Whatever worked.

"I thought you were going to show me some moves, not attack me," I spat.

Without warning, he stepped forward and grabbed my neck. Heat pulsed through his palm and continued straight through me. His grip on my throat was gentle, but knowing that he could end me if he wanted to with just the faintest twist of his wrist sent a thrill through my body. Almost a turn-on, for some deranged reason.

What the hell was wrong with me?

I twisted and brought my elbow down on his arm *hard*, breaking his grip, then slipped behind him and struck him square in the back with my forearm.

Jaxson spun and grabbed my wrist, then yanked me backward into his chest in a bear hug. Heat flared where my form pressed against his, and my anger blossomed. Why was my body reacting this way?

I elbowed him in the ribs, and he growled in my ear as he pushed me forward. I stumbled on the rocks but stayed upright and twisted to face him. His eyes blazed a deep honey color, and his lips pulled into a twisted smile that was both a warning and an invitation.

Shivers raked my skin, and my pulse quickened. We circled each other. His stance was relaxed and loose, yet he was a predator waiting to strike.

When Jaxson lunged forward, I tried to dash to the side, but his arms wrapped around me, pulling me against his chest. His fingers were iron, digging into my flesh, and I knew that if he wanted, they could burst into claws. He leaned close and whispered, "You have fire."

His breath was hot on my neck, and quivers arced down my spine. I couldn't distinguish fear from desire.

He released his hold and gently pushed me away. "Relax your body and keep your knees bent. You have speed—use it to your advantage."

I glared at him but relaxed my shoulders and bounced lightly on my knees.

"Good. Now raise your arms." He positioned his body slightly askew and raised his fists. "One to block an attack, the other to strike."

He showed me the movements, and I watched closely, memorizing the way his body moved with grace and precision.

He was a natural fighter. It was easy to imagine him with claws bared, ripping into men and beasts. Savage. Lethal. Relentless.

Something about that bothered me in all the worst ways.

He'd fight for you. He did it last night.

My skin flushed, and I gritted my teeth, trying to focus on the moves that might save my life and not on all the ways that I wanted Jaxson. I could smell his sweat and power, a druglike combination I craved.

I stumbled, and Jaxson shot me a devilish grin and stepped back. "Focus, Savannah. I think your mind's on other things."

Oh, God, kill me now. What's wrong with me? Blood rushed to my face, and I died a little inside as we began circling each other again.

He taunted me a few times, which was good, as it helped me focus on punching that arrogant grin off his face. He attacked, and I met his strike with my forearm, then stepped to the side and brought my fist to his jaw. Before it made contact, he turned and caught my fist. I lost my footing on the loose rocks, but he steadied me before I could fall.

"You're a fast learner," he purred.

I probably wasn't much more than a toy in his hands. I steadied myself and pushed him away as my frustration bloomed. "What's next, Laurent?"

The air between us sparked with electricity, and Jaxson's eyes turned an even richer honey-gold.

He stepped forward slowly, like a predator stalking its prey, and leaned close. So close I could almost hear the rhythmic pulse of his heart. His breath caressed my skin. "I won't hurt you...but you better run."

Mid-sentence, his voice turned husky and almost bestial. My heart stalled for a couple beats.

What the fuck?

I bolted.

I knew Jaxson wouldn't hurt me, but I wasn't sure about the thing within him. The creature that I'd seen break a man in half.

Trees flew past. A root caught my foot, but I recovered.

Not too fast. Slow and steady wins the race.

Actually, I doubted that very much.

My feet thundered over the ground in a steady rhythm. I concentrated on each footstep, rebounding off solid logs and carefully dodging obstructions, trying not to faceplant into a tree.

A growl sounded behind me, and I glanced over my shoulder.

Jaxson was closing, *fast.*

He'd said he wouldn't hurt me, but my heart hammered in my chest all the same. I turned onto a game trail and ratcheted up to high speed.

A howl echoed through the forest, sending quakes of fear through my body.

That bastard. I'd told him I wasn't ready to meet his wolf, the monster I'd seen last night. Was Jaxson even in control?

Sam's words replayed in my mind: *When we're in wolf form, our wolves are in the driver's seat, so to speak, and can be unpredictable.*

I jumped at movement on my right. A blur flashed by, and my heartbeat thundered in my skull as another growl came from bushes on my other flank.

I was being hunted.

A ravine appeared ahead. I jumped over the edge and slid down the embankment, then booked it in the opposite direction, toward the beach. The euphoria of freedom and power flashed through me.

How do you like me now, alpha wolf?

A crash rang out above me, and I screamed as a blur moved down the embankment. Stumbling, I caught myself before colliding with a boulder. I cast a quick glance sideways and saw Jaxson—not in wolf form—with a wide grin on his damn face.

Cocky bastard.

I raced toward the shore, running as fast as my boots would take me. There weren't any trees in the ravine, so I only had to focus on the boulders and broken logs.

My adrenaline surged as the lake appeared a couple hundred feet ahead—the finish line.

Jaxson was on my heels, his feet ricocheting against the ground with impossible force. I swore I could feel his breath on my neck. My heart was thudding and my breathing ragged, and the thrill of the race coursed through my blood.

Suddenly, he was beside me. Startled, I caught my foot on a rock, and my thundering speed boots catapulted me into the air. I braced for impact, but instead of the ground, a hard body collided with mine, and arms wrapped around me. The air was driven from my lungs as we rolled several times, Jaxson's body shielding me from the brunt of the impact.

With a thump, we came to a stop. The man beneath me was staring back with deep, honey-gold eyes. His heat melded with mine, and my chest tightened. I struggled for air, grasping at my throat, but my lungs wouldn't respond.

Panic surged through me, but Jaxson gripped my hips and lifted me so that I was straddling him. "Breathe, Savannah." His hands gently cradled my back. His voice was calm and low and filled with power. I felt my fear melt into his golden eyes, and the tension in my body released.

Chest heaving, I sucked in steady gasps of air until my lungs no longer ached and the panic left me. Then I realized just how close Jaxson and I were.

The tightness in my chest grew, like something was trying to claw its way out. Heat pulsed through me, settling at the apex of my thighs, and all I could think of was his strength beneath me and the tenderness of my skin.

I began to move.

"Savannah." Jaxson's voice was thick, and he slid one hand up my back. His touch left a trail of tingles rippling down my spine, and I gasped. "We can't do this," he growled. His eyes flashed honey, and he gripped my butt with his other hand.

I felt his hardness beneath me, and I tipped my head back and moaned as I ground my hips into him.

He pressed against me, following my rhythm, "We need to stop."

Jaxson's words were the exact opposite of what his body was telling me, and I didn't care. My skin was flushed and sensitive, and I had the overwhelming urge to tear off my clothes. It made no sense at all, and yet there I was, pulling up the bottom of my shirt and—

Oh, my God. What was I doing?

My senses returned to me like a rogue wave slamming into the shore.

I looked down at the impossibly beautiful and dangerous man beneath me. Had I really been...*grinding* on him? Embarrassment, shock, and confusion rushed through me, and I scrambled off Jaxson's lap. "What the hell just happened?"

It had been like my body was overcome by a fever, and I was stuck sitting in the passenger seat, watching it all unfold.

Jaxson's shoulders rose and fell, and when he at last met my eyes, he looked just about as confused as I was. His silence spoke volumes.

Was there something he wasn't telling me? He looked distraught about what had just happened, and unease flooded through me.

"We should go," he said at last.

"Jaxson?"

It took him a second, and then he looked at me as if I'd just disturbed some deep inner thought. "I'm sorry. My wolf must have taken over back there. Are you all right?"

I nodded weakly as my mind reeled.

He forced a smile. "Everything is okay, I promise. It's getting late, and we should go."

He wasn't the same man from moments before. I'd let my guard down and almost forgotten that he was a damn *werewolf*. Had I lost my mind?

There was another Jaxson locked away inside of him—a savage creature with animal instincts. A Jaxson that I didn't know at all.

31

Savannah

I took a swig of Old Style, hoping the beer would relax me. Between our freak heat-filled encounter along the shore and the prospect of scrying again, I was on edge.

After our jaunt at Avery's Point, things had been pretty awkward, and we'd barely spoken a word on the drive back. Jaxson hadn't wanted to return to Eclipse, probably because he was afraid I'd make another scene, or maybe he was ashamed of what had just transpired between us. Probably both. I was just an unruly LaSalle, after all.

Ultimately, we needed somewhere private to scry, so we'd headed to The Boiler, a homely little corner bar in the southern part of Dockside. Jaxson had led me straight to a private room in the back like he owned the place. Maybe he did. Either way, no one asked a single question, and no one bothered us other than to drop off our drinks.

"Ready to give it another go?" Jaxson asked, nodding to the flask of silver and red liquid that I'd placed on the table between us.

I pushed the noxious scrying potion toward him. "Maybe you want to do it this time?"

He didn't touch the flask. "I'm a wolf. Your blood in that potion attunes it exclusively to you, but even if it didn't, our kind doesn't have the innate magic necessary to control the effects. Moreover, scrying is forbidden."

I crossed my arms and leaned back in the booth. "Forbidden? Or simply illegal and dangerous, which you neglected to tell me when you first asked."

Jaxson flinched slightly, but he kept his eyes trained on me. "Forbidden. Dabbling in the occult is taboo in our pack. Knowing the future, far-seeing, they're the domains of the moon-mother and not meant for mortals. She watches over us, and only she sees the future."

I leaned forward. "But you went to a seer."

"I was desperate. I needed answers."

I wondered how *that* went over with the rest of his pack. "What did she tell you about our adversaries? About me?"

"My prophecy is my own, just as yours belongs to you."

I scowled. "But you heard part of mine."

"Not the prophecy, just the fortune teller's interpretation of the cards. That's different."

I chewed on my lip and dug my nails into my palm to keep my frustration from boiling over. He was chintzier with information than Alma was with sweets. "Can't you tell me anything?"

Jaxson released a low, exasperated rumble from his throat, then leaned toward me. "The seer helped me find you and told me to protect you. She said you would lead me to answers, and that if anything happens to you, it'll mean ruin for my pack."

Of course—that was why he was so interested in me. The wellbeing of his pack. And to think I'd begun to believe he saw something in me.

I scowled and hoped he could smell my annoyance. "Fine,

let's do this. By which I mean I'll do it, seeing as you can't or won't."

My palms were wet from the condensation on the beer bottle, so I rubbed them on my jeans and uncorked the flask. "Bottoms up."

I screwed up my face as the bitter liquid burned my throat, making me feel slightly nauseated, and then I choked as I started laughing.

"What's so funny?" Jaxson asked, his eyes narrowing in on me like lasers.

"Honestly? I was thinking of throwing up on you. This tastes *so* bad."

He inclined his head, and a muscle in his jaw twitched. It was so easy to ruffle his fur. "Focus, Savannah. This is important." His voice was sharp and impatient.

I took a breath and closed my eyes, concentrating on the picture of the she-wolf I'd drawn. The potion began working its way through me like the tingle of a low-voltage current. My arms became leaden, and my fingers felt like they were merging with the wood. Black shadows and forms swirled in the darkness, drawing me in.

"Tell me what you see." Jaxson's voice was far off, like a dream.

I tried to speak, but the darkness tugged me in all directions and muddled my mind. I clenched my eyes shut as hard as I could and imagined the face of the bitch from Belmont. Her rage. Her hatred.

The shadows behind my closed eyes began circling me like wolves. Hungry. Impatient. The hair on my neck rose, and I had the distinct sensation of being watched by unseen eyes.

"Savannah. Is it working?"

"Something's different. I can't...it's not right. *Very* not right. I'm not alone..."

Jaxson's hand pressed against my back, and warmth poured through me, awakening a power deep within. He spoke in honey tones. "You're not alone. I'm here. Concentrate on the woman."

His signature washed over my body, and I wanted to drink it in. It filled my senses, and suddenly, despite the darkness around me, I felt like I was running through a cold and snowy forest with crisp air on my face. The stalking shadows in my mind peeled away and fled through the darkness. Light appeared. Suddenly, the forest wasn't just the scent of Jaxson's signature. It was there, bathed in summer sunlight, all around me.

I was moving through the woods, following the woman.

My pulse began to slow. "I see her."

"Tell me everything."

The vision was blurry, and I could only catch snippets of the images.

"She's entered a house, no, a cabin in the woods. It's got wooden walls, and it's really run-down. She's messing with something. I can't make it out—like red cables."

What the hell were those?

"Describe every detail. Is there a demon summoning circle?"

"I can't see, she's moving around the cabin. There's another person, but I can't identify them. Wait, she's picked something up and is heading outside. There's lots of trees. Tall pines, but I can see blue. It's a lake! She's walking to a lake."

"What's she carrying?"

I didn't have the right angle to see clearly. "A box of vials or bottles. Maybe potions? Okay, she's down at the lakeshore. It's all white limestone cobbles. There's a boat with someone in it. She's taking the box to a man in the boat!"

My heart pounded against my chest.

Jaxson's voice was low and controlled. "Savannah, look for

any landmarks. Could this be her home or a base of operations?"

I tried to look around, but I could barely control my vantage point, and my vision swirled like I was on a carousel. I suddenly felt sick to my stomach. Something caught my eyes, and I tried to focus. "There's a lighthouse nearby."

"Describe it, quick, before the vision ends."

"It's on a promontory or spit. I think it's abandoned—the light might be broken. It's tall, smooth, cylindrical...a white tower with a rusted red roof. There's a fence around the top."

"Excellent." Jaxson pressed his hand on the small of my back and gently squeezed, and elation shot through me. "Do you see who she's handed the box off to?

I pivoted my view, and the world spun. I felt myself sliding off my chair, but Jaxson's hands caught me and held me upright. The spinning stopped, and finally, I was able to get a fix on the boat.

My attacker waded into the lake, picking her way carefully over the slippery, greenish, algae-covered stones. When she reached the edge of the waiting boat, she lifted the box up. I held my breath and strained my mind. I needed to see who was there.

A man reached down and took the box. "I see him, but..."

My stomach dropped, and horror trickled through me.

"But what? Tell me, Savannah."

The man's face was a black hole. Swirling darkness leaked around from the edges of his body, distorting the air like grease over water. Confusion and panic tore through me as my mind tried to make sense of what I was seeing.

"His face is a blank. It's like he's got no face. Just darkness."

"He has an anti-scrying charm. Try to concentrate, try to break through. You can do this." Jaxson's breath was soft on my neck and sent power vibrating through my body. Every word of his was confident, cloaked in certainty. He believed in me without question.

I strained as hard as I could, imaging what my magic had felt like, trying to call the sensation forth, to force my way through the darkness. Suddenly, the man snapped his head up and looked directly at me with that horrifying, blurred-out face.

"Holy shit, he sees me!"

"Not possible," Jaxson said.

Adrenaline surged into my veins, and my heart hammered against my chest.

The faceless man slowly tilted his head, and words formed in my mind: *No peeking, Savannah.*

Then there was only pain.

32

Jaxson

Savannah screamed and tumbled from her chair.

I caught her and started to set her upright, but she clung to me, shaking and wide-eyed. "Oh, my God, Jaxson, I think he saw me! He spoke to me!"

The blood in my veins froze. "What?"

Her hands were trembling, and a trail of blood began to drip from her nose. Not good.

"Everything is okay," I said with more confidence than I felt. I kept my arms around her, unsure if I should pull her close. I had no idea how I should react after the incident in the woods, but I knew how my body wanted to react. The sweet tangerine scent of her signature brought water to my mouth. When her heartbeat against my chest began to slow, I set her back on the stool before my own heart could start racing. "Tell me what happened."

Panic shone through her watery eyes. "He looked at me and said, 'No peeking, Savannah.' But, like, in my mind. How could he see me?"

How, indeed?

I let my presence wash over her, calming her fears. I pitched my voice low and soft, holding back any sign of the alarms going off in my head. "He may not have actually seen you, just identified your presence. Some powerful spellcasters can protect themselves from clairvoyance and other forms of observation. I'm guessing he must be a sorcerer. Or a mage."

She shook her head slowly. "It felt like he was digging into my soul with his eyes, and I couldn't even see them. I couldn't see anything beyond that horrible darkness where his face should have been."

A bead of blood had pooled on the top of her lip and hung there, quivering. I had an inhuman urge to taste it. I was a predator, after all, and the scent of blood always climbed above the chorus of other aromas. But this was different. It smelled exotic, pungent, almost like a drug.

I dipped a napkin in my ice water and softly wiped the blood from her lip, wishing it was my mouth instead of my hand. "It's all right. You did great, and I think you got us the information we need."

After she'd calmed and repeated everything that she'd seen, I left her for a moment and had the bartender retrieve a pen and paper from the back. I placed them down in front of the shaken woman. "Draw the lighthouse."

She set about sketching, and as the dark lines appeared on the paper, the tension in her body melted away. The art had an almost magical hold over her. It centered her in a way that even my alpha presence could not.

Her hands flew over the page. "I bet this is in Wisconsin, or at least on the edge of Lake Michigan. The beach was white limestone cobbles. I went to a lot of beaches like that when I was a kid. We might be able to track down the lighthouse. They're all different."

I took a picture of her illustration and sent it to Regina, and then Savannah and I started scrolling through our phones, trying to identify the lighthouse. It took a half hour of searching through various historical society pages on the internet, but she finally found an obscure reference to the lighthouse, plus a couple of old photos. "This is it! It's the Jasper Point lighthouse in lower Door County."

Adrenaline surged through my body as I compared the images on her phone to her illustration of the lighthouse. "Well done. The location makes sense. Most of the disappearances have been isolated Magica living in eastern Wisconsin."

I dialed Regina. "We've got a location. Call Tony and have his Belmont team meet us at the Mobil station on Wisconsin Road 42. Tell them to plan on shifting, but bring guns as backup. Then grab Sam and a couple of others and meet us at the docks so we can arm up with Billy."

I hung up with her, grabbed Savannah, and headed for the truck.

Twenty minutes later, we pulled through the checkpoint into the docks and rumbled over the broken asphalt to a derelict section of the port. I parked beside a rusted container that appeared abandoned but was one of the secure places in which the pack stored firearms.

Regina and Sam were already on site, and Billy emerged from inside the container as we drove up. He dumped an armful of weapons into the bed of his truck and glared at us as we slipped out. "You brought a LaSalle into the docks?" he growled, giving Savannah a deathly stare.

I slammed the door and put a calming hand on the small of Savannah's back before she flew off the handle in response to Billy's challenge. "She'll know not to come here."

Savannah relaxed slightly beneath my touch, though she was shooting daggers at Billy with her eyes. She had a quick temper and no idea how to navigate pack hierarchy, an explosive combination that I didn't need going south, particularly with a pile of guns at hand.

"What's the situation?" Regina asked, grabbing a rifle and inspecting it. I could tell by her scent and the jut of her hip that she was also clearly at odds with having Savannah present, but unlike Billy, she wasn't going to push it.

"The rogue wolves are using a cabin on the shore of Lake Michigan as a base of operations. By Savannah's description, it sounds like a temporary arrangement, so we need to move quickly." I grabbed a pistol and a couple magazines of silver bullets.

Billy looked from me to Savannah. "A cabin? How did you find out about it?"

"Savannah has sorcery in her blood, so she scried."

Billy growled, and Regina sucked in a quick breath, even though she'd been in on my plans from the start. It was still taboo.

"You're messing with the fucking dark arts," Billy snarled, reeking of rage and hate. His eyes flashed yellow, and I could tell his wolf was getting near the surface.

Including him might have been a mistake, but Billy was part of my inner circle, and I couldn't just cut out the voices of my advisors when I felt like it. That would defeat the whole point of having them. I needed every perspective I could get, and Billy reflected the beliefs of many in my pack.

"I understand this isn't ideal, but we learned a great deal and confirmed that a sorcerer is involved. He was hidden from the spell, so we can't name him, but at least we know who summoned the demon."

Regina whistled low.

"Probably one of the LaSalles, forcing good wolves to do their evil work and shame our pack," Billy muttered.

"That doesn't make any fucking sense, and you know it," I snapped. Had my sister lived, he would have held rank. But she was dead, and he had trouble remembering that I was no longer his subordinate. I had to remind him from time to time.

Billy bared his teeth, but Regina stepped in before things could escalate. "This is good information, and at least we'll have the element of surprise if we go in."

I shook my head. "Probably not. I'm afraid that the scrying spell tipped off the sorcerer, so they'll know we're coming. Either they'll have turned their tails and run, or they'll be ready and waiting for us."

"Why are we attacking if they know we're coming?" Billy asked.

I panned my gaze across the members of my inner circle, reminding them who called the shots. "Because this is the best chance we've had. They appear out of nowhere, grab someone, and disappear. Now it's our turn. It's a risk, but we must stop them."

Regina nodded to Savannah. "You're not bringing the LaSalle with us, are you?"

I gave a warning growl. At least we were getting all the dissent out of the way in private, before we met the rest of the team. "She's the reason we know anything about these fuckers. And if they've split, she's the only shot we have at finding them again. She can scry, and we know that they want her. She'll find them, or they'll find her, and we'll bag the assholes."

I wasn't about to repeat the seer's words in current company: *Without her at your side, you will not discover the answers you need.*

Regina took a submissive stance but whispered, "She'll be a liability."

Savannah crossed her arms. "Then give me a gun. Problem solved."

"You can shoot?" she asked, surprised.

"Probably better than you, though I prefer a shotgun."

Truth. I could smell that it was more than truth—practically a point of pride.

Eyebrows raised, I handed her a Glock 19 and a couple of magazines. "This work?"

Savannah inspected the gun with expert grace and shoved the magazines in her back pocket. "It'll do."

The woman had moxie, that was for sure. I gave a half laugh. "They're silver bullets, so don't shoot me."

She grinned and winked. "Then don't get in my way."

Although I tried to fight it, a smile tugged at the corner of my lips. The backbone on this woman was a mile long.

A tortured snarl erupted behind us. Billy.

"I can't believe you're giving a gun with silver bullets to a LaSalle," he growled, ache in his voice.

Frustration tore at me. "She needs a weapon. End of conversation. Unless you'd like us to give her wolfsbane."

I could tell by his scent and fluctuations in his eyes that Billy was on the verge of losing it. "She's just as likely to shoot one of us as the enemy."

Savannah glared at Billy and bared her teeth in a surprisingly wolfish gesture. "If I shoot you, trust me, it'll be on purpose."

"I don't trust you—that's the problem. You're a fucking liability." Billy's fangs erupted, and Savannah flinched. I could smell her fear, but she stood her ground, jaw set and silent.

"I trust her," I said, putting my authority into each word.

Regina smirked. "I bet she can't hit the broad side of a barn."

Savannah whipped her arm up and pulled the trigger three times.

Gunshots echoed through the docks. Everyone ducked, and Billy started swearing as his claws came out. My ears rang, and I growled. "Fuck, Savannah!"

"She's a fucking lunatic, just like her cousin!" Billy shouted, his eyes burning bright like golden flames.

"I'm tired of your pack giving me grief. I'm not a liability. I can shoot, I can run, and I can scry, so screw anyone who has a problem with that." She gestured to a sign hanging at the edge of the water.

There were now three holes in the O in *Dockside*.

A siren sounded in the distance.

Gods damn it.

"Regina, call off the cops. Savannah, put the safety on and don't shoot Billy. Everybody else, get in line."

Billy stalked off to get control of his wolf. He was more enraged than I'd seen him in years. When he looked back, his voice was low and harsh. "You're on your own for this one, Jax. I'm not running with a LaSalle. Not one who's armed with wolf-killing bullets."

My neck hair bristled, and my claws slowly inched out. I'd deal with him later, but for now, his absence was probably for the best. "Fine. Stay. As you say, someone needs to watch the docks." I glared at the others assembled. "Anyone else have a problem?"

No one met my gaze.

33

Savannah

Jaxson's truck roared along highway 42.

It'd been nearly five hours since we'd left Chicago. I'd packed my backpack with an extra set of clothes and a tooth-brush—that, and a Glock.

Shit was getting serious.

Five days ago, I was worried about how I was going to pay for car repairs. Now I was worried about getting gutted by were-wolves while I shot demons in the face.

Casey was out, so I'd told Aunt Laurel that I was taking a bus to Belmont to help Alma with some urgent house repairs. I wasn't sure if she'd bought it, but she hadn't prodded.

In all likelihood, I should have stayed with the LaSalles while Jaxson did the dirty work. But he'd been pretty insistent on having me at his side, and I sure as hell didn't want to get left behind. Not when there was a chance for me to beat some answers out of the bitch from Belmont and her werewolf gang.

So now I was about to follow a bunch of unfamiliar shifters into a patch of woods that was going to be inevitably haunted by werewolves, demons, and a psycho sorcerer.

My life had changed a bit over the last week.

We'd passed a long, awkwardly quiet drive after everything that had gone down at the docks. Sam was in the front next to Jaxson. They were probably having weird wolf-scent-only conversations, because they sure hadn't been chatty with me. In Sam's defense, she'd offered me the front, but at the time, I'd figured that Jaxson and I could use all the space we could get.

Not that being a foot behind him was any different than being a foot beside him, but it somehow felt less close. I hadn't counted on him being able to watch me in the rearview mirror, though. He just couldn't seem to take his eyes off me—though I wasn't behaving any better in that department. It was frankly embarrassing to keep looking up and catching his eyes.

Thankfully, I'd passed out for two hours, missing the most boring part of the trip out of the city and suburbs. I was once again grateful for my mom's sleep-anywhere-anytime genes.

Adjusting my position in the back seat, I glanced at Jaxson in the rearview mirror. "What's the plan?"

"We'll meet with a few of our other pack members shortly, then head north to the cabin," he said.

"You have pack members living in Wisconsin? Does your territory extend all the way up here?"

Sam turned and shot me a suspicious look before staring at Jaxson. Could they speak telepathically? It sure seemed like they were exchanging thoughts. Creepy scent-speak, for sure.

"There are a number of other packs up here, but we have an inholding near their territory. Our pack is the largest in the Midwest, and Magic Side doesn't have nearly enough land for us, so some of our people come up here to run and get away," Jaxson explained.

"Is that why you were in Belmont when I was attacked? Wait a sec." I leaned forward and looked between them. "Is Belmont pack territory?"

"No," he said flatly.

"No what?"

Sam sighed, seemingly irritated. "You ask a lot of questions. You're a LaSalle. Details about our pack are really none of your business."

I scowled. "Just trying to make conversation."

Sam seemed pretty damned paranoid for a bartender. Why the hell was Jaxson even bringing a bartender along? For mixing cocktails after kicking ass?

Sam had shown up when we'd raided Jaxson's auto body and when I'd been attacked at the fair. She'd kicked Casey's butt and chased after those rogue wolves.

She ain't no bartender, I realized.

I settled quietly into my seat, and stared at the back of her head, just in case I had some sort of strange psychic powers and could read minds.

Apparently, I didn't.

Since reading minds and polite conversation were both out of the question, I watched the houses go by. I recognized some of the towns we passed through and couldn't help the rising lump of homesickness for Belmont. Alma was probably reading a palm or cleaning her crystals right now. A melancholy smile fluttered at the edge of my lips.

Jaxson kept looking at me in the rearview mirror. Was that remorse in his eyes?

He was reading my emotions again.

I leaned back and rested my forehead against the window, letting the late day sun warm my face and watching the blur of trees pass by. I didn't want his remorse or pity. The attack at the Taphouse might have changed the course of my life, but I refused to be a victim.

I buried myself in my phone and found a text from Casey: *Hey cuz. Where are you? Not in your room. I'm there now.*

Irritation pricked my skin. Damn it, Casey. I wasn't used to having people checking up on me and prying into my business. I typed out a reply: *Why are you in my room?*

Seconds later, my phone buzzed. *Looking for someone to get drinks with. Apparently, you're still out herding werewolves. Let me know when you get back.*

On my way home for a few days to help my godmother, I responded. *Sorry I didn't give you a heads-up, but it was an emergency.*

His response came back quickly. *Are you crazy? Without me?*

A sigh sloughed off my shoulders. I hated people keeping tabs on me. *Don't worry. I have hairy bodyguards. I promised not to wolfsbane them again, and they promised not to eat me.*

After a long pause, which I imagined was filled with cursing, Casey wrote back. *Stay safe. Call me if you need anything. If they look peckish, feed them some bacon and rub their bellies.*

"What's so funny?" Sam asked.

"Nothing." I stifled my giggle and buried my head in my phone again.

I felt bad about the chain of lies, but I was pretty sure that if Casey got a whiff of what I was up to, he'd have an aneurism. I would have taken him along in a heartbeat, but I knew the werewolves would never work with him. The blood was bad.

Twenty long minutes of brooding later, Jaxson finally pulled into a Mobil gas station, and I silently rejoiced. I had to pee like nobody's business.

He parked next to the pump. Across the lot, three well-built guys were leaning against a pair of Jeeps. They nodded subtly in our direction—Jaxson's reinforcements, no doubt.

Regina—the sour-faced woman who'd called me a liability at the docks—pulled up behind us with a young, dark-haired woman.

"Be right back." I slipped out of the car and hightailed it into the convenience store, clenching my muscles for dear life.

Two people were ahead of me. Dressed in jeans and biker boots, and they had the athletic, all-too-hot-for-my-own good *shifter* look to them. The man opened the door for the woman, but as I neared, he stepped in front of me and let the door close.

Definitely shifters. Apparently, my reputation preceded me —*LaSalle.*

I glared at the two as I speed-walked to the bathroom in the back.

When I came out of the ladies' room, Sam scooped up several plastic bags from the checkout counter full of pop, chips, and candy. "Eat up, Savy. You're going to need to keep up with us." She tossed me a bag of potato chips and a Coke, which I nearly fumbled as I followed her out of the store.

"Right, because sugar and salt are what your body needs before a run," I replied. This was a pretty sketchy way to carb-load, and it raised a lot of questions. Could werewolves eat carbs? Jaxson had eaten normally at Eclipse, but wolves in the wild ate mostly protein...God, I hoped Jaxson didn't wolf out and eat deer and rabbits. *Live.*

That train of thinking was derailed as I crossed the lot, replaced by the hot-and-sexy express.

I couldn't help it, but my eyes were drawn to Jaxson like a moth to flame. He had some maps spread out on the hood of one of the Jeeps and was going over details with the five new members of our team. Their eyes were locked on him just as firmly as mine were. Jaxson had a presence that absolutely commanded attention.

I took a deep breath. His *ass* commanded my attention. Jaxson's blue jeans and plaid shirt had my mind playing out all kinds of fantasies. Seeing him standing there, I suddenly felt slightly less embarrassed about what had happened in the woods. How was a girl supposed to control herself around a pair of buns like those?

He shot me a look as I approached. After a moment of butterflies, I remembered that these shifters would be reading my scents the moment I was near.

I blushed and tried to remind myself of how terrifying he'd been the night before in his wolf form, his fangs dripping with another man's blood.

That did the job.

Jaxson gestured to the five gathered shifters. "Savannah, this is Tony and several of our Wisconsin operatives."

I nodded. "Hi. Nice to meet you guys."

Only Tony acknowledged my presence. The others glared. If it hadn't been clear before, I was certain they knew I was a LaSalle—I could practically smell their revulsion. It didn't bother me. I was used to being the odd one out. As long as they played nice and didn't try to kill me, we'd be cool.

Jaxson glanced in my direction, and I was certain he could read my mind, or at least everyone else's.

"Savannah is the reason we know anything about these fucking rogue wolves." Jaxson's voice vibrated with power, and the Wisconsin shifters looked down and focused intently on the map.

I found myself inexplicably looking at my shoes.

Overall, it was one hell of an improvement from my encounter with Billy. He'd looked like he'd been ready to gut me. Thank God that asshole had stayed home.

Jaxson jabbed his finger on the map. "This is the area around the Jasper Point lighthouse, and this is the cabin Savannah saw in her vision. As soon as we pull along the road here, we'll break into three teams and converge from the north, west, and south. They know we're coming, so we'll go in eyes wide and ready to kill. Keep in mind that we're not up against normal wolves. They've got some kind of enchantments or enhancements, so chances are they'll be faster and stronger than us. And they may have demons under their control. That means you'll have to be smarter."

Jaxson divided the group into hunters and shooters, and then we loaded back up in the vehicles and continued north.

Ten minutes later, we turned onto a dirt road that wound through a forest. We continued for another ten minutes before the cars ahead stopped along the shoulder.

Go time.

I stepped out and stretched my aching leg muscles. My stomach growled, and immediately, nine pairs of eyes locked on me. *Holy werewolf hearing.*

Jaxson reached into the car and handed me a protein bar, which I took reluctantly and scarfed down. At least it was better than the junk Sam had bought.

Then he unzipped a black bag in the bed and pulled out a bulletproof vest for me.

Yeah. Shit was getting serious.

I slipped my arms through, and Jaxson deftly adjusted the straps. His fingers brushed against my side, and I could smell the deep musk of his body. "Okay fit?"

I nodded, not trusting myself to speak without my voice shaking. Tightness constricted my chest, but not from the vest.

Jaxson, Tony, and one of the other shifters slipped into vests of their own.

"You can heal, right?" I whispered, "your scratches went away in the alley..."

He smiled, warm and confident. "Yes, but it helps to have fewer holes in you."

When his eyes flickered gold, an unreasonable sense of comfort and security washed over me. At least Jaxson was going to be by my side.

He distributed guns to the shifters in vests, but most of his crew were going to go in as wolves and fight tooth and claw.

The jitters started to invade my belly, but they didn't stick around long before they were replaced by shock as Sam stripped off her clothes.

"Whoa. A little heads-up?" I laughed awkwardly.

Right. She was wolfborn, so stripping made sense. I guess she didn't want to shred her fancy Rock Revival jeans every time she shifted.

Sam shot me a gleeful grin and shook her buns as a couple of the Wisconsin guys shucked off their pants. I quickly averted my eyes...well, *reasonably* quickly.

Shifter guys had nice butts, so sue me.

Two of the clothed shifters transformed in a swirl of light and magic, and their signatures filled the air. That seemed a lot simpler.

I gave an involuntary shudder at the sounds of bones popping and flesh stretching as Sam and the other wolfborns transformed. The beds of my nails itched, and I dug them into my palms. I knew which I'd rather be, if I had to choose.

The bushes rustled, and I turned to see six large, fully transformed wolves disappearing into the trees. Tony and the other shifter raced north on foot with inhuman speed.

We were suddenly alone, and I was relieved that Jaxson wasn't going to shift. I wasn't ready to meet his wolf again.

"Ready?" he asked, concern flickering in his face.

"Hell, yes," I said, with a lot more confidence than I felt. I slipped the Glock into the back of my jeans and gave him a wink. "Remember, just stay out of my way."

His jaw went rigid, and he narrowed his eyes. "Let's go."

We took off into the forest at a jog, but with my boots and Jaxson's speed, it was more like a sprint by my old standards. I was still a little sore from earlier that day, but the practice had helped.

The low sun cast long shadows through the trees, making it a little difficult to find my footing, but adrenaline focused my mind, and I was able to wind through the trees like a pro. Okay, perhaps a semi-pro.

A wild sense of exhilaration filled my heart. I'd always loved running, but this was something more, almost like flying. I would never get bored of this. With that thought in my mind, my foot caught on a root. I lurched forward and landed hard, scuffing my hands and knees in the dirt.

"Getting a little cocky?" Jaxson stood above me, his hand extended.

My irritation flared, but I took his hand, and he pulled me up. "The pot calling the kettle black?"

I took a step forward, but Jaxson gently grabbed my arm. "Hey—hold on." His body tensed, and he tilted his head, breathing deeply.

I scanned the woods, desperately trying to catch a glimpse of whatever had alerted his wolf senses. The trees were still. Light filtered in through the canopy, illuminating the moss and lichen-covered forest floor that grew in these parts. Nothing seemed out of the ordinary.

Then a shadow moved.

My body strained.

"What did you see?" Jaxson whispered.

I pointed at where the shadow had been, but there was nothing there besides trees and dangling ivy.

And then I saw it: an eight-foot shadow, almost invisible in the patches of light and darkness of the forest canopy.

It moved a step, and my heart skipped four beats.

A twisted and monstrous demon, like the one that had attacked me at the fair. Its skin was a sickly, translucent dark green, and though it was humanoid in form, its legs and arms were unnaturally long and sinuous. It wore no clothes, and its muscles were just visible beneath the skin. The thing was even more horrifying in the fading remains of daylight.

I slipped the Glock out of my jeans.

Time to get even.

34

Savannah

I slowly raised my Glock and tried to steady my breathing. *Don't freak Savy,* I tried to reassure myself. *It's just like shooting beer bottles.*

The demon—which was distinctly not a bottle—shifted again, moving from shadow to shadow. Its cavernous eyes peered out at me from between two trunks.

I exhaled slowly and squeezed the trigger, and the Glock cracked and recoiled hard. The bullet ripped into the monster's skull, right between the eyes, slamming its head back. But though the creature staggered, it remained upright.

My blood curdled as the demon slowly turned its head and glared at me with those dark eyes. Ooze dripped from the bullet hole. Then the monster's mouth unhinged and spread in a silent, ghastly wail that vibrated my body and raised goosebumps on my skin.

I reeled, suddenly nauseated, and bile rose in my throat. What was it doing?

Jaxson shook his head and started firing as the creature

lumbered forward. Despite the bullets digging into its chest, the monster didn't slow.

My breathing turned ragged as my heart raced.

"Go back to hell!" I shouted, pulling the trigger three times. The demon's head snapped right as a bullet sank into the side of its skull and another in its chest, squarely where its heart would have been, had it had one. At that, the monster stumbled. Jaxson kept shooting, and finally, under our combined weight of fire, the demon jerked and collapsed onto the forest floor. Black smoke poured out of a dozen or so bullet wounds, and its body slowly dissolved into a pool of dark blood.

Jaxson pivoted, gun raised, scanning the forest. "You weren't kidding when you said you could shoot."

"Those things don't go down easy," I muttered, trying to calculate my ammunition in reserve. The magazines he'd given me held fifteen rounds each.

A burst of gunfire echoed from the north, but for a moment, the forest around us was still.

And then, deep among the trees, shadows moved. With keening shrieks that made my intestines churn, two more demons burst out of the underbrush and charged.

I raised my pistol and started firing wildly at the one coming from my left. Three bullets found their mark, but more lodged in the trees as it wove between them. The thing kept running, moving on two legs, then on all fours.

I tried to steady my breath and pick my shots. My magazine had to be nearly empty.

Bursts of gunfire erupted from Jaxson on my right and then a crash sounded through the trees. I glanced over quickly as the demon before him stumbled to its knees, then leapt up again.

"Run! I'll cover," Jaxson ordered, putting two more bullets in the demon on the right.

I hesitated.

"Go!" he growled. His eyes turned a vivid gold, and his fangs descended.

I clicked on the safety and slipped my gun into my jeans. Then I ran.

The demon on the left was on me in an instant, but it flipped sideways as Jaxson ripped into its shoulder with claws that had sprung from his hands—just like the shifter who'd attacked me at the Taphouse.

I didn't have time to wrestle with that image. I poured every ounce of energy I had into running. *Concentrate. Just like we practiced this morning.*

My feet pounded against the forest floor as I sprinted through the trees and sprang over downed logs. Within a few heartbeats, I was at a gully. A fallen tree made a bridge across, and I ran up the trunk, trying to get far enough to jump to the other side. My boot slipped, but I pushed off with my other foot and launched into the air.

I'd aimed for the far side, but the boots turbo-charged my leap, and I flew into the lower boughs of a tree. Branches lacerated my arms and face, but I clung on for dear life.

The sound of crashing brush from below told me the demon was nearly on me, and out of instinct and sheer panic, I climbed. Fortunately, there were several low branches that I could use to hoist myself up. Growls, snarls, and other inhuman sounds came from below, but I just kept climbing. No fricking way was I going to look down.

But then I did.

Black, cavernous eyes stared up at me from the foot of the tree. I lost my footing and slipped. Reaching out, I managed to partially land on the branch below, expelling the air from my lungs. I gasped and struggled to keep my grip as I watched my gun cartwheel down.

With the sound of tearing bark, the tree shook as the monster started climbing.

This isn't happening.

Desperation set in, and I swung my body back and forth, gaining enough momentum to latch one of my legs over the branch. Maybe the demon would be too heavy to climb very high.

Howls echoed through the forest nearby, but not near enough.

I heaved myself up and looked down, and I was suddenly face to face with the creature. It scrambled upward impossibly fast, and I screamed with all my soul.

The demon's eyes rounded, revealing tinges of red. *Blood.* Horror streaked through me, and my heart felt like it was going to explode.

A spindly hand reached up for me, inches from my shoulder.

Then a snarl boomed from the base of the tree, and the creature shot downward, towed by something.

I craned my neck to make out the forest floor below. Jaxson had ripped the monstrosity out of the tree and was slashing at its throat with claws on his hands.

I pulled myself onto the branch, and straddling it like a gymnast, I inched my way to the trunk. The terrifying noises from below suddenly quieted, and I dared a peek.

The creature lay motionless—a tattered pile of blood and sinew that began melting into a smoking pool of blood—and Jaxson was gone.

A screech rang out from nearby. A hundred feet, maybe more. I pivoted to look, but my boot slipped, and I had to cling to the trunk to stop myself from falling.

I should have bought boots for climbing if I was going to spend my days cowering in the treetops. The monsters could climb faster than me, so I was just a sitting duck up here. I needed to get down and find my gun before I broke my neck.

I slung myself downward through the branches as quickly as I could. Noises nearby indicated that whatever was coming was getting closer and heading my way.

Go, go, go.

I reached the lowest branch and dropped to the ground, landing in a crouch.

Where was my damn gun?

Where was Jaxson?

I waited, searching the trees, and listened. Silence, and the thudding of my heart.

Leaves rustled to my left. I panicked and broke into a run, leaving the Glock lost somewhere among the brush. My boots accelerated my body forward at lightning speed. Dodging a tree, I lost control, tripping and tumbling down an embankment. I hit the bottom and came to a stop, gasping from the pain. Thankfully, I'd landed on dirt and decaying leaves, and I sat up with nothing broken.

I'd fallen into a ravine a hundred feet wide. To my left, the space narrowed between a pile of boulders, but to my right, it was clear, and a small stream trickled slightly downhill. Was that the way to the lake?

Panting and pushing down the pain in my back, I climbed to my feet. Then I froze as something moved on the embankment above me. Snarls and shrieks rang out in the distance. The wolves must have been engaged with more of those monsters. Or other wolves.

Stay calm, Savy. Get out of the ravine.

The sides of the embankment were steep. I might be able to crawl out, but if one of those demons attacked again, I'd be a sitting duck.

Okay, change of plan. I'd follow the ravine to the lake. There, I could go along the beach and get my bearings.

A sickly feeling overwhelmed my senses. Time to go.

When I turned to follow the ravine down to the shore, the bitch from Belmont stood twenty feet ahead, blocking my path, with her claws extended. Fear iced my skin.

I was trapped.

"I was hoping we'd meet again." A sinister grin cut her face as she rushed toward me.

I darted left, the boots accelerating me forward. Hope sprung in my chest as I wheeled around her, but then her claws sank into my arm. Blinding agony shot through me, and my body jerked to a sudden stop. I careened onto my back, towing the she-wolf along with me, then kicked her in the face and scrambled backward. She growled and crawled toward me, grasping at my legs with her claws.

My back hit a boulder. I panicked and flailed about for any kind of weapon—a loose stone, a branch, *anything*. The she-wolf gripped my ankle, and I screamed as her claws dug into my skin.

She pulled me toward her in one swift motion. A rock ripped into my back, and the world spun as she loomed over me, fangs out.

She's going to gut me alive, I distantly realized.

I rammed my arms upward, trying to throw her off. The sensation of ice water trickled over my skin, and a jolt of energy shot out of my palm, blasting into the woman's shoulder. She flew several feet and let out a blood-curdling scream. But in a split second, she had clambered back toward me. "You're going to die."

"Eat me!" I shouted as I raised my palm and tried to release my magic again. Nothing came, and I immediately regretted my choice of words.

In a blur of motion, the she-wolf pounced on me. She

pinned my legs and gripped my neck, her claws pricking my skin. With her bloody hand, she grasped my hair and slammed my head against the boulder.

My vision swam with stars. I tried to scream, but only a gurgle came out.

She pulled my head back again, but before she could crush my skull, she hesitated for a split second as a blur appeared in the corner of my darkening vision. The woman screamed, and blood splattered across my face as a massive gray wolf sank its jaws into her neck and dragged her off of me.

Jaxson.

He threw the she-wolf's body through the air like a rag doll, and she crashed into the ravine's embankment. Leaping onto her, he gently clamped her throat, pinning her in place, one paw on her chest. Even I could read the wolf language here: *Submit.*

The woman locked me with her maniac eyes. "He's coming for you."

Then she jerked her head under Jaxson's teeth, tearing out her own throat. Bright red blood seeped into the mossy ground.

I screamed as the nightmare unfolded. Panic whirling in my mind, I scrambled back against the opposite side of the ravine, anything to get away from what I'd just seen and heard.

What did she even mean? Who was coming for me? The faceless man?

Oh, my God.

Jaxson's body rippled, and he growled deep and low. He approached and lowered his face to mine. His honey eyes blazed, and a deep ache grew inside me. Pain stretched across my breast, and I could barely breathe.

What was happening to me?

A howl sounded through the forest, and the wolf's ears perked. He turned and took off up the side of the ravine.

I let my heart recover and then pulled myself to my feet. My muscles were tired and strained, but I managed to climb the steep sides of the embankment, yanking myself up one root at a time.

A few minutes later, Jaxson appeared, bare chested but wearing pants. My breath hitched. He was like Ares, god of war, with his blood-splattered muscles tensed and his shoulders heaving. Protectiveness and concern darkened his face. When he stepped toward me, my chest tightened and my skin burned as he scanned my body for injuries. "Are you all right?" he asked.

Physically? Or mentally? Because I was feeling messed up, either way.

"Fine," I whispered, grasping for lies. "Why would she kill herself?"

Jaxson was quiet, which I took to mean either he didn't know or shit was dire. I was betting on the latter.

"How many demons were there?" I asked.

His eyes still had a honey tint to them. "Four. All dead."

I concentrated on breathing in and out. My mind was still having a hard time wrapping itself around what I'd just witnessed.

Another howl sounded through the trees, and Jaxson froze. "Follow me. We need to go."

He took off into the trees in a blur. Hell, what now?

35

Savannah

I broke into a run after him, grimacing at my sore muscles and scratched arms. It was a short distance to the cabin, but when I arrived, I didn't see Jaxson or the others.

The hairs on my neck prickled, and my heart thundered.

The structure was a simple, single-roomed building with a couple of grimy windows and a cracked front door.

Where was everyone?

As if in answer to my question, a pack of blood-covered wolves filtered out of the forest. Light swirled around two of them, and they shifted back into human form, fully clothed. Sam and a few others were still missing. Perhaps they were still catching up.

"What happened?" Jaxson growled, stepping into view from the trees.

"I don't know," one of the Wisconsin shifter's said. "She was with us, and then the next minute, she was gone."

"Fuck!" Jaxson scrubbed a hand through his hair. His body rippled with tension and anger.

Another wolf stepped out of the forest and rose on its hind

legs. It bones popped and cracked, and its hair receded, until there was just a naked woman standing there, claws still out. Regina.

She fixed Jaxson with a penetrating gaze. "Sam was scouting ahead and was jumped. We heard her howl and she didn't respond. We tracked them—two males—to the beach and saw a boat heading north. They've got her."

I'd never witnessed a shift back into human form before, but the shock of it was instantly pushed from my mind by Regina's words. *They've got her?*

"Wait a sec. Do you mean Sam?" I asked.

Regina looked at me, anger and blame in her eyes. "The bastards took her."

The weight of that hit me, and the world spun.

Jaxson took the cabin stairs two at a time and ripped the door off its hinges. A few of the others followed, and I heard his curses from inside.

I rubbed my temples, and my heart sank. This was my fault. Sam had been taken because of me. She was the only one who'd shown me any kindness, even if she was still upset at me for wolfsbaning her. If anything happened to her, I'd never forgive myself.

I had to find her.

The others disappeared into the forest, so I stepped inside the cabin.

"—bring him to the hospital." Jaxson was crouched next to a low coffee table. Tony and two shifters were huddled around, blocking my view, so I maneuvered past them and froze. I'd seen snippets of this room in my scrying vision, but I wasn't prepared for the horror of the scene.

Syringes and empty blood bags were strewn across the floor. Two limp arms dangled from the table, each bearing tubes secured with tape. The missing man. I'd seen him in my vision as well. Tony removed the IV needles from the man's arms and lifted the body over his shoulder.

I covered my mouth as Tony carried the limp victim past me. The man was in his thirties and had purple-brown bruises where the needles had been inserted. His skin was gaunt, and his cheekbones protruded from his face. He was unconscious. Dead, maybe.

The two other shifters followed them out, and the three of them took off into the woods.

My mouth went dry as I surveyed the room. Was this what would have happened to me?

I inadvertently glanced at Jaxson. His eyes were fierce, filled with rage and concern. Was he thinking the same thing?

My gaze returned to the pile of bloody tubes. I swallowed, but my throat was sandpaper. "So they were harvesting his blood...that must have been what I saw the woman give to the faceless man, but why? What the hell were they doing here?"

"The faceless man must be a blood sorcerer," said Jaxson. "They use blood to work dark magic. But why he would drain someone dry, I don't know. Maybe he's part vampire. Maybe he's using it to summon those demons." Jaxson's body quaked with rage, and he crumpled a piece of paper in his hands and tossed it into the corner of the room.

I tried to keep the potato chips I'd eaten earlier down as I pulled my phone out of my back pocket and snapped photos of the room, focusing on the dark red ring of magic symbols in the middle of the floor. It had been drawn in blood. A few chips came up, but I forced them down again.

"This was the ring I saw in my vision," I told Jaxson. "I should ask Casey what it is, now that I've got good photos instead of blurry smudges."

"Do it. But if he gets back to you with any answers, don't tell anyone where you got the information," Jaxson muttered, his voice so low it was at the edge of my hearing.

I surveyed the wreckage. "They were expecting us. Why leave all this here for us to find? They must have been confident we wouldn't survive the demons."

"It was a message." He shot me a look that chilled my blood, then headed for the door. "Let's go."

I finished sending Casey the images, along with the question, *What the F are we looking at?*

It was definitely a day for breaking out the F-word.

Rather than follow Jaxson out, I lingered for a second, then plucked the crumpled piece of paper from its resting place in the corner. Unfolding it, I found a message written in broad strokes: *Have the Laurents really stooped so low they'd work with a LaSalle?*

Dread weighed down on me as a new thought tore into my mind. According to Jaxson, the rogue wolves had never abducted another werewolf. Had they taken Sam to punish the pack for working with me?

I shoved the note in my pocket and hurried outside. We were so in over our heads, it was ridiculous.

Regina was speaking to Jaxson. "We've scouted the area. No scent of any remaining demons."

Jaxson pointed at her and the others. "I want you all to scout out the nearest town and marina. See if you can track the rogues who escaped with Sam. Then see what you can dig up on sorcerers in the area—find out if there are any blood sorcerers milling around. I'll make arrangements for us to stay at the motel on pack lands."

Regina and the others nodded and took off into the woods, leaving Jaxson and me. He strode into the forest, tense with fury, and I had to speed walk to keep up with him, even with my boots.

"How are we going to get Sam back?" I asked.

"I'll let you know when I figure that out. Don't worry." His voice was a low rumble that sent shivers across my skin.

Even so, my irritation flared. He was trying to cut me out. "I *am* going to worry about it. Her life is on me, and I'm going to help get her back. I can scry."

Jaxson's honey eyes narrowed on me. "No. You've done enough. You wound up with blood dripping from your nose the last time, and you got caught. My guess is that wherever Sam is, the sorcerer will be there, too. He might not just kick you out of the vision next time. I don't know what's possible, but it could be very dangerous."

I stepped in front of him to stop him in his tracks. "You brought me along because I *can* scry. I saw the note, and I know Sam is in danger because of me. I'm going to do it, whether you like it or not."

He studied me for a long moment, a deep frown set on his face. When it seemed he was about to say no, I pushed. "It's worth a shot, Jax, and I *need* to help."

I'd never called him Jax before. It just slipped out.

His expression softened a little, and he sighed. "You're right, it's worth a shot. We'll get somewhere safe, and then you can try it."

Before I could argue with his presumptuous tone, my phone rang, and I pulled it out of my pocket. "It's Casey. He might have some information."

Casey's voice cut across the line. "What the hell are you doing? Are you at some sort of twisted murder scene? Shit, tell me that's not your godmother's house."

"A blood harvesting site. I'm not actually in Belmont. We found one of the abduction victims in Wisconsin. He's alive, but barely. What can you tell me about that circle of magic symbols in the middle of the floor?"

Casey's voice shook with what I presumed to be fear and outrage. "Are you out of your mind, Savannah? You have no idea how much danger you're in! I've been trying to figure out what attacked you at the fair, and the photos you sent confirm it— blood demons."

"Blood demons?"

Jaxson's body tensed at my words, though I was certain he could hear everything Casey was saying.

"Yeah. Blood demons are like vampires on steroids. If they get ahold of you, they'll drain you dry. They're apparently really nasty and nearly impossible to control unless you're an insanely strong spellcaster. My guess is that some fucked-up superpowerful blood sorcerer summoned them using a little of your victim's blood, then kept the dude around as a human juice box for the monster to feed on. That probably means the demon is nearby. You need to get out of there before it comes back."

"Yeah. Thanks for the warning, but we already shot four to death already."

"Wait, *what*?" he squeaked.

"I really appreciate all the info, Casey. I know this puts you in an awkward spot, but text me if you learn anything more. I'll be back tomorrow."

"Savannah, wai—"

I hung up and gave Jaxson a half smile. "Bad news: those things are blood demons, and the sorcerer is using people like juice boxes to keep them hydrated. Good news: we just killed four of the bastards. Five, counting the one at the fair."

Jaxson's expression darkened.

"What? That's good news, right? We know more." I cocked my head.

He grabbed my arm and silently hurried me toward the cars, but I yanked myself away. "Tell me."

He studied my eyes, then growled. "I was just wondering,

with the demons dead, what do they need the juice boxes for anymore?"

My stomach churned as we hurried back to where we'd left the vehicles. Five abducted people and five dead demons. We'd rescued one of the abductees, but that meant there were four other people who were no longer useful.

It sickened me, but I prayed that the sorcerer still needed their blood for something else.

Hopefully, our prayers wouldn't be too little, too late.

36

Jaxson

As soon as we returned to our truck, I pulled out my phone and called Billy. "I don't care about your reservations about working with the LaSalle woman—I need you up here *now*. Bring men and guns. Sam's been taken."

As I gave him the rundown, I could feel his fury across the line. He valued Sam just as I did. I depended on her for so much —intelligence, counsel, even friendship. If Sam had been harmed, I'd unleash a fucking war in Wisconsin until the perpetrators were found.

My wolf clawed to get out, and I was one hair from slipping into a rage. I steadied my hand on the wheel.

"How are you going to find her?" Billy asked, clearly enraged himself.

I glanced at Savannah as she slipped into the passenger side. She really shouldn't be privy to our traditions, but it was too late for that now. "I can do a moon calling ritual. Tonight, when the moon is at its peak. There's a spirit guide up here in the local pack who should be willing to help."

"Hopefully, that's enough," Billy growled.

Silence hung in the air. "The LaSalle girl might be able to help."

"How?"

I wasn't going down that road with him. "Meet me at the Sunrise Inn. It should be a safe base of operations. I'll call you once we know more," I said, and hung up.

Savannah turned to me with an arched brow. "What's a moon calling ritual?"

I swore. "Something you're not supposed to know about."

"Why, because I'm a LaSalle?"

"Because it's pack business, and I'm the alpha," I snapped.

She rolled her eyes. "But it allows you to track Sam?"

"Yes. If she's still alive, we'll be able to track her." I shouldn't be telling her this. Our secrets were heavily guarded, and she was on the enemy's side, even if she didn't quite realize the gravity of what that meant.

"But you can't do the thing until tonight."

"No," I snarled.

She seemed to sense I was done dispensing information and settled back in her seat. "Fine. If you can't do it until tonight, then we should scry as soon as we get where we're going. The Sunrise Inn, wherever that is. Glad to know the plan."

I ground my teeth. "Now you do. We go to the hotel. You scry. If that doesn't work, I do my thing. And we sit tight until we get a lead. The motel is on Eastern Wisconsin pack land. We'll dig in and shoot the heck out of any werewolves or demons that come calling. You don't need to worry, you'll be safe there."

"I'm worried about Sam, not myself."

"Then you'd better start."

Savannah sighed at my comment, her frustration unmistakable. She had no idea how much danger she was truly in. The goddamn sorcerer was up to something more sinister than summoning blood demons. I could feel it in my bones.

We drove in strained silence as we headed north, each of us brooding.

The moon calling ritual was something alphas could do, though it only worked when the moon was at its peak. And it was best to have a spirit guide. Like scrying, it could be dangerous to meddle with the moon mother's magic.

I would howl—not a normal howl, but a soul-empowered cry that would travel through the moonlight and summon Sam to me. If she couldn't come, then my spirit would be transported to her, and I'd be able to track her down. That was what I was counting on.

But spirit travel had its risks.

Perhaps cunningly, the sorcerer and his minions had never abducted a wolf we could have tracked. That might mean that the sorcerer knew about the moon rituals—or his werewolf minions had warned him. In that light, taking Sam had been a mistake, and I would make them pay, one way or another.

I glanced at Savannah. "To do the ritual, I'd need to go down to the shore on pack land. It's only a few miles from the inn, but it means that I'd be gone for an hour, hour and a half."

She frowned, but I could sense her unease. "You worried?"

"No." I was glad she couldn't smell lies, though she had a nose for them, all the same.

"Just take me with you."

Like hell. "It's taboo."

"Like scrying?" she asked snidely.

"One I can't break."

I didn't want to leave Savannah at the hotel, but I didn't have a choice. Some things were sacred.

The Eastern Wisconsin pack wouldn't let anyone suspicious onto their land, and Billy was heading up with reinforcements.

He might hate her family, but he would protect her, especially if the moon ritual didn't work. Then she'd be our best chance of tracking down Sam.

I just needed an hour and a half. It seemed like so little, but my gut told me we were almost out of time.

Twenty silent minutes later, we entered the nearby town. Its population wasn't more than five thousand, and its main drag consisted of a handful of restaurants and shops catering to out-of-towners passing through. We passed a pasty shop, and Savannah's stomach rumbled. She was always hungry. I glanced at the dashboard. In her defense, it was almost eight, and she hadn't eaten anything substantial all day, which only added to my irritation.

I wasn't used to looking after someone. Something also told me that Savannah wasn't the type of woman who liked being looked after. But still, she deserved better.

"I'll pick up dinner after I drop you at the motel," I offered.

She nodded but said nothing.

A few miles out of the town center, a bird-shit-blue single-story motel appeared beside the road—the Sunrise Inn. The motel was set against the woods and looked like it had been built in the seventies but recently remodeled. I pulled into the lot and parked beside Cara's Jeep.

Savannah grabbed her backpack and a bag of chips from the back seat as Cara stepped out of the motel. She was the youngest of our Wisconsin team, which meant she'd gotten stuck with coordinating logistics.

"Any news from the hospital?" I asked.

She shook her head, swinging her short, dark hair. "No progress. He's still in a coma but stable. The doctor says it might be a couple days before he comes around."

I tightened my fists, my claws itching to come out. Not that I expected him to remember much. The tortured mind was a fragile thing.

Savannah looked at me. "I guess it's up to us, then. Me first."

My stomach twisted. We were taught that scrying was dark magic with an unknown cost. I recalled her bloody nose...but what choice did we have? "Are you sure?"

Savannah nodded. "Let's do it now, before I pass out from exhaustion and hunger."

She was strong and brave, and willing to risk her life for others. No traits were more admirable in a wolf, let alone a human.

Cara passed us our keys, and I led Savannah to my room.

A smile quirked up on her lips. "A dangerous man is escorting me to his hotel and asking me to drink a strange brew. How should I be feeling about this?"

I swung the door open without a word, smelling the fear rippling off her. No matter her bravado, scrying scared her deeply.

Savannah dropped her bag on the floor and fished out the potion as I closed the door. "No taking advantage of me while I'm spying on other people."

Doubt tore at me. She was pushing on for Sam's sake, but my instincts told me this was a bad idea. "Do you want something to eat first?"

"Do you want barf on your carpet? This potion is really bad." And without a second of hesitation, she tilted her head back and took a swig from the flask. A sour expression twisted across her face. "Oh, God. It's rancid, and it burns. I'll never get used to that."

"Focus on Sam. Where is she?"

Savannah closed her eyes and wiped her lips with the back of her wrist. "Talk me through it. It's annoying, but it helps."

"You know her face. She was there the first night you came to

Magic Side. She was with you when you were attacked at the fair. Today, she bought you Coke and chips and gave you stern looks when you pried into pack business. Think of her wolf. Dark, with a patch under her eye. You saw her shift today."

Savannah's breathing stilled. The potion was taking hold.

Suddenly, she gasped and leaned back. Her hand flew to the comforter and clenched it so tightly that her fingers turned white.

The scent of her emotions surrounded me. *Terror.*

She jerked forward, and I grabbed her before she tumbled off the bed. "Savannah, are you okay?"

My heart raced as her body started to shake, and I pulled her close. She relaxed slightly, but her pulse skyrocketed, and a bead of sweat rolled down her neck. My wolf surged inside me, desperate to get out, and I gritted my teeth against the pain. He was wild and getting more uncontrollable lately around Savannah. There was something about her that drove him into a frenzy.

Savannah mumbled something unintelligible.

"Talk to me." I lightly squeezed her hand. "Are you all right?"

"I'm okay, but I see a lot of blood." Her voice was far off. A dream state.

"Where are you?"

"Concrete walls. A dirty linoleum floor."

"Is she there? Do you see Sam?"

"She's here. She's bound and on the floor, but her chest is moving. She's alive."

I gripped Savannah's hand as a spark of relief broke through the cracks. "Give me details. Anything that might be a clue to where she is."

Her voice hitched. "There's writing on the ground."

Dread crept across my skin. "Like the summoning circles?"

"No, a message. It—"

Her body quaked, and she coughed. Blood splattered across my shirt, and a red tear dripped from her eye. Panic shot through me. What was happening? A seizure?

"Savannah! Come back to me." I let my presence wash over her, a command, an imperative to return from whatever dark place was pulling her in.

She gasped, and her eyes flew open. "Holy crap, I hate doing that."

Unsteadily, she got to her feet, and then collapsed to her knees, heaving.

Guilt tore into me. How could I let her do this?

I knelt down to help, but she held her hand up. "I'm okay. Just give me a minute."

She wiped the blood from her mouth, and my nostrils flared. Her blood smelled sweet and tangy, and I wanted to taste it on her lips. I grimaced at my thoughts. Seeing Savannah in pain made my chest want to crack open, and worry clawed at my patience. "Tell me what happened."

"There was a message. For me. In blood."

"What did it say?"

"*We're watching you.* The sorcerer knew I would try scrying."

My heart hammered against my ribs, and my head began to pound. He was watching her.

Fuck.

How could I leave her to do the ritual with the sorcerer spying on her? But how could I leave Sam to rot and do nothing?

I had to handle things one at a time.

Once she was willing, I helped Savannah to her feet. It took every ounce of restraint to keep myself from licking the blood from her cheek. "Are you sure you're fine? Is there anything I can do?"

She forced out a weak laugh. "No, I'm not fine. But some

food would go a long way. And a shower, but you can't help with that."

I couldn't even manage a smile. "We're not doing this again."

She wiped her nose, leaving a smudge of blood on the back of her hand. "Yeah. Maybe that's a good idea."

37

Savannah

I shut the door to my room and slumped against it, thankful for the privacy and space to think without the wolves reading into my thoughts or watching me dry heave.

I surveyed my surroundings. The room had a light green carpet, a double bed, and a TV. Basic but clean, just like Jaxson's —minus the new blood stains and spit on the floor.

It was so conventional, like a snapshot out of my life before the nightmare began.

My mind flooded with visions of the blood demons chasing me through the forest. The she-wolf tearing her own throat out. The poor guy in the cabin, surrounded by blood bags and needles. And Sam locked in that cold room.

I'd seriously need a therapist after all this shit.

I heard Jaxson's truck start. Thank God. I desperately needed something to eat, because all I'd had today was a bowl of Count Chocula for breakfast—which was just as deliciously bad the second time—Sam's chips, and the ancient tasting protein bar from Jaxson's glove box.

Still, it had been good instinct not to eat before drinking the scrying potion. The world was still spinning slightly, my throat burned, and my legs were weak. Hopefully, the potion didn't have any long-term side effects. My stomach tightened at the thought. I'd have to ask Uncle Pete about that.

I dragged my hand through my hair and groaned when my fingers touched a clod of moss.

God, I was so dirty.

A hot shower suddenly seemed like the antidote to most of my problems.

Thirty minutes later, I collapsed onto the bed with the bag of potato chips I'd snagged from the car. Showered, hair washed, and teeth brushed, things didn't seem so grim.

I stared at the stuccoed ceiling as I popped a chip in my mouth. Typically, I never ate chips, but at the moment, they were the best thing I'd ever tasted.

Sam had purchased them.

They turned to ash on my tongue as guilt poured through me.

Someone knocked on the door.

"Just a second." I pulled on a clean pair of shorts and a V-neck shirt, then ran my fingers through my damp hair and opened the door.

My breath hitched at the sight of Jaxson. He hadn't showered yet, and the dried dirt, blood, and sweat on his thick forearms stirred an earthy desire deep within. He was all beast, powerful, rough, and sinfully sexy.

His eyes took me in, lingering on my wet hair, and his pupils dilated. But instead of jumping me, he handed me two large white takeout bags. "I brought you dinner. I wasn't sure what you liked, so I ordered a couple things."

Jaxson's voice was deep and husky, which only ratcheted up my inexplicable, animalistic desires. My cheeks blazed, and I broke my gaze from his. The aromas of whatever was inside the takeout bags had my mouth watering.

To be fair, the man had my mouth watering, too, and it was hard to tell the difference. I was really hungry. I leaned on the door, unsure what to do. "Thanks. Have you eaten? Do you... want to come in?"

His eyes flicked to my chip-covered bed, then back to mine. "No, I have to get ready. But I'll be next door for a couple hours. The zenith of the moon should be around twelve-forty-five tonight, and I'll head down to the shore."

"Are you sure I can't come?"

"You cannot come."

"Why? Do you soak yourself in wine and dance around naked? Hold a pagan orgy? Sing love songs to coax down the moon?" I twisted my hair.

A sly grin spread across his face. "And which of those would you be hoping to see?"

I blushed. My mouth had a tendency to run sometimes. "The singing, of course."

He sniffed and leaned in close. "I can tell when you're lying. I think I know *exactly* what you would like to see."

Searing heat rushed through my body—which, of course, he could also smell. I swung the door shut, but he stopped it with his hand. "I'll return soon. There will be a dozen wolves guarding the motel—Regina, Billy, Tony, a whole crew. If anything seems out of the ordinary, go to them. They'll keep you safe."

Great. I really was in werewolf witness protection. My nail beds itched at the thought, and I rolled my eyes out of habit, but in light of how things had gone recently, I was prepared to accept the situation. For now.

Jaxson pulled his handgun out and handed it to me, butt first. "Just in case."

It was a silver Glock 17 with gorgeous decorative etching that was cool to the touch. *This* was the kind of protection I liked—men handing me firearms.

I gave him a sultry smile for that. "Thanks. Good luck tonight, Jaxson."

"One more thing." His hand caught the door again as I was shutting it. "Do not scry again. Not without me there."

He locked me with his dark eyes, and I felt his alpha voodoo wash over me. I straightened my spine and fought it, but Jaxson had enough on his mind already, so I nodded.

"I promise." *Probably*. I didn't need his permission to scry.

He tensed. "I'm serious, Savannah. Don't do it."

I knew it was irrational after what had just happened, but the sharp and commanding tone of his voice only made me want to refuse. Then again, I was starving and needed this conversation to be over before my takeout got cold. "Fine. I promise I won't scry again tonight."

Satisfied, he turned and left.

Shaking my head, I shut the door and secured the deadbolt, then peeked inside the bags. Mushroom and truffle ravioli, steak tartare, and lemon-roasted chicken breast. Where had he even gotten this out here? I knew there were some fancy tourist restaurants in the area, but damn, Jaxson had nailed it.

I tore off the lids of all three and dug into them, totally prepared for the food coma that would follow. I didn't have a funky *werewolf-only* moon ritual to attend. Each bite was tastier than the last, and I groaned as my stomach filled.

Ten minutes later, I unbuttoned my shorts and leaned back against the headboard, eying the empty containers at the foot of my bed. I was hungrier than I'd thought. Exhausted from the day and the meal, I closed my eyes and drifted off.

~

I woke to the buzzing of my phone. Groggy and sore, I glanced at the clock on the side table—twelve-thirty a.m. I'd been out for a couple of hours. I found three texts on my phone from Casey, and silently cursed.

The first had come at ten-forty: *Hey cuz. I need status reports. I need to know if some freaky monster is drinking you like a cheap bag of wine.*

An hour later: *It's almost midnight. You okay? Why aren't you answering?*

The latest: *If you don't answer in five, I'm calling in the troops.*

Which either meant he was going to call the cops or the sorcerers. I wasn't sure which was worse.

Damn it, Casey.

I typed out a text: *Sorry, fell asleep. Still alive and full of juice. I'll tell you in the morning.*

As I slumped back on the bed, the rumble of engines outside caught my attention. Was Jaxson back from his ritual early? Buttoning my shorts, I climbed out of bed and peeked through the curtains. Four high rider trucks were pulling into the parking lot. I squinted as they flashed on their roof lights, which were brighter than day.

My nerves buzzed. *This is all wrong.*

I slid over the bed and grabbed Jaxson's pistol off the table just as gunfire exploded across the parking lot.

Bullets ripped into our parked vehicles. Then my window exploded, shooting glass everywhere. I dropped to the ground, landing hard on my stomach. The pistol skidded across the floor.

A black object rolled to a stop three feet from where I lay. I froze as a jet of smoke erupted from the end of the object and began filling the room with a loud hiss.

A smoke bomb?

As the gas surrounded me, tears sprang to my eyes, and my skin blistered.

I knew that scent. Not just a smoke bomb—*wolfsbane*. Scrambling across the carpet on hands and knees, I grabbed the gun and darted into the bathroom, locking the door behind me.

My pulse hammered in my temples.

This is an ambush. Think, think, think.

My eyes landed on the small window above the shower. It was only a couple feet wide. Jaxson and his wolfy goons couldn't have gotten through, but there was just enough space for me to fit.

I tucked the gun into the back of my shorts and climbed onto the toilet, then wrenched the window open and pushed out the screen. Wood cracked and glass shattered, and suddenly, there were voices coming from my bedroom. Fear and adrenaline coursed through me. I grabbed the sill and yanked myself up through the window. There wasn't enough room for me to slide my legs around, so I went headfirst. Once I had enough of my upper body dangling out of the window, gravity took control. Arms outstretched, I plummeted into the ground. Pain shot through my palms, and I rolled onto my back.

Another splintering crash and the sound of shouting erupted through the opening: "She got out the window! Go around back!"

Oh, crap. I scrambled to my feet. I'd tweaked something in my wrist, but at least I hadn't broken my damn neck.

The air was cool, and the moonlight illuminated the grassy yard that stretched to the woods behind the motel. I looked both ways—all clear—and sprinted for the trees. The ground was soft against my bare feet, but running through the woods was going to be tricky. I should have grabbed my boots, but with the gas, there hadn't been time.

I disappeared into the shadows as a man and woman

appeared around the side of the motel. They tipped their heads back, sniffing the air, and then their gazes locked onto my position.

Fucking werewolves.

I banged my shoulder against a tree, grimacing as the bark scraped my skin. Scooping up some dirt, I rubbed it on my bare arms as I darted into the trees. I had no idea if this would work, but it seemed like if I could mask my scent, I might be able to buy some time to shoot these bastards.

I slipped behind a large trunk and readied my gun.

The shifters paused beside the tree I'd rubbed against. The woman scanned the forest, searching for me.

That was all the delay I needed. I aimed and fired three rounds. Two of the bullets hit the woman square in the chest, and she dropped. Shock crossed the man's face, and his ruddy eyes landed on me. He snarled and dashed forward.

I aimed for his head and pulled the trigger. My bullet sank into a tree trunk, and I cursed. The prick was weaving in and out of trees, and I couldn't get a clear shot. Fear clawed at my heart, and I fought the urge to run.

Just breathe and aim, Savy.

The man rounded a bush and leapt toward me, and I fired twice. One bullet missed, but the other lodged in the bastard's shoulder. He crashed into the ground and growled.

I fired a few more rounds as he scrambled to his feet, shifted, and fled into the darkness.

The echoes of my pistol faded, but I could hear bursts of gunfire from the front of the hotel. I checked my magazine. Not many shots remained, but maybe I could help.

Suddenly, a branch snapped behind me. I spun to investigate, but something slammed into my chest, and I flew several feet before landing on my back with a crack. Pain flashed through me as I rolled onto my front and climbed to my knees. I tried to scream, but nothing came out.

Then a rope cinched around my throat. Terror filled me, and I clawed at my neck, trying to pry my fingers under the rope. But it was too tight. My trachea constricted, and dread settled over me as I was towed into the trees.

Just as I was about to black out, the rope loosened, and I gasped, gulping in air.

My vision cleared, and I blinked at the figure standing above me.

Terror paralyzed me as recognition dawned.

"You!" I choked.

Confusion ripped through me before something hit me square in the jaw and everything faded into darkness.

38

Jaxson

I knelt by the edge of the water on an old, weathered limestone outcrop, waiting for the moon to rise.

The spirit guide was an old woman with dark, piercing eyes. She crossed her legs and asked, "You have not done this before?"

It was only something alphas could do, and I had not been an alpha long.

I shook my head. "When I was a child, I saw my grandmother moon-call once, and my father only one time after her."

She nodded. "We'll wait for the moon to peak, but now is the time to prepare our minds. Look at the light on the waves. Become one with the reflection."

I gazed down on the slowly undulating reflections of the moon mother, who watched from high overhead.

But my mind kept going to Savannah. Worry gripped my chest, and the seer's words haunted me. *If you do not stop them, she will be dead before the full moon rises, and with her, the future of your pack.*

It was almost full moon. Two more nights. I wanted her here. But would she have been any safer from demons waiting in the forest than in the motel, surrounded by armed men and women? No.

This was for the best, but the doubt still gnawed at me. *Without her at your side, you will not discover the answers you need.*

Pain shot through the back of my head.

"Focus," the woman hissed as she shook out her fist. "We haven't begun the ritual, and you're drifting already. How will you walk through the rays of the moon and not get lost?"

I had no idea what that meant, so I tried to focus my mind on the reflection and let the guide do her work.

But I couldn't focus.

I heard thunder miles away, but it didn't smell like rain. I concentrated on that.

A mournful howl echoed in the distance.

I sat up straight, heart pounding.

Then again. Another howl, tinged with sorrow and regret.

My skin iced, and I leapt to my feet. *No.*

The woman grabbed my arm. "Where are you going?"

"My pack is in danger."

"The moon will not wait."

I cursed and ran as fast as my legs would take me.

Twenty minutes later, I skidded to a stop in front of the chaos of the Sunrise Inn.

Firemen were hosing down burning vehicles. There were bullet holes everywhere, and the entire parking lot stank of wolfsbane.

My wolf tore against my chest. I roared, and one of the broken windowpanes shattered the rest of the way.

As Tony came running out, I growled, "What the fuck

happened?" In my rage, I was barely able to hold on to my human form.

"Ambush. Half an hour after you left, four trucks pulled up and hit us with wolfsbane bombs laced with sedative. Then they laid down suppressing fire and took Savannah. All our vehicles are shot to hell, so we couldn't pursue."

"Fuck!" I screamed. "Where's Regina? I heard her howling."

"Savannah wounded another werewolf out back, but he escaped. Regina's searching the woods."

That was something. Regina was our best tracker. "Are any of our people hurt?"

"Not on our side. They knocked us out. One of the attackers is alive but in critical condition. Savannah shot her in the heart with silver bullets. We moved her to a bed, and Billy's trying to stabilize her."

"Take me there."

Silver bullets prevented us from healing but were only fatal in great numbers, or in hits to the head or heart. But when I stepped into the room, Billy stood and turned to me, disappointment and regret on his face. "I'm sorry, Jax. I tried to stop the blood loss, but she's gone."

Billy locked eyes with me, and something flashed in them —pain?

Shock dulled my senses, and I staggered forward.

Tory Lockhead lay lifeless on a pile of blood-soaked bedsheets. Another Magic-Sider. I cursed. The fucking Lockheads had been a thorn in my side since I'd become the alpha, but they were nobodies. Someone else was running the show.

If she'd lived, I would have forced the information out of her. But she was dead, and along with her, my hope of finding Savannah and Sam.

I checked her neck, my hand shaking. The twin-headed wolf tattoo. What did it mean?

A growl erupted from my chest, and I grabbed Billy. "What the fuck happened? I put you here to protect her. How many people did we have on site? A dozen?"

Rage filled Billy's eyes. "They had gas masks and hit us with wolfsbane-laced sedatives. You know who's responsible for this, Jaxson. The fucking LaSalles. They're sorcerers. They can summon demons. One of them must be calling the shots. We just got attacked with wolfsbane smoke bombs, for fates' sake. Who else could it be?"

"Fuck!" My claws erupted from my hands, and I let go of Billy, stepping back and trying to regain control. Billy didn't deserve my anger. He'd always had my back, and he'd been through enough shit to last two lifetimes. I shook my head. "These attacks are being carried out by werewolves. No wolf in a hundred miles would be caught dead working for the LaSalles."

"You are," he spat.

I tensed. "That's different."

"Is it?" he snarled. "But you're right, I can't imagine that anyone else would have the balls to work with the LaSalles. Maybe those bastards found some way to magically control them."

The rogue wolves were faster and stronger than they should be, and their eyes had been strangely tinged with red. Were they on some kind of drug or under an enchantment?

My stomach reeled. "But why? It doesn't make sense. Why would the LaSalles risk going after the girl when she was with us? Savannah's moved in with them."

"To implicate us and cover their asses! They're trying to bring the pack down, Jaxson. How better to frame us than to have one of their own disappear?"

I rammed my claws into the wall, trying to think.

Billy approached. "Don't you think it suspiciously conve-nient that out of all the LaSalles, the one who goes missing is a woman who just showed up out of the blue? They have no attachment to her—she's an easy sacrifice to bring the wrath of the Order down on us."

My body quaked with rage. It was just twisted enough to be true, but I had to be cautious until we knew for certain.

"Not a word about this to anyone, Billy. But I want our best people on high alert in case things go down with the LaSalles. Just don't tell them why."

My head spun with possibilities. Savannah was gone. Sam was gone. Could it have been the LaSalles? I wouldn't put anything past those monsters.

"Show me where Savannah was taken," I ordered.

Tony led me out back into the forest, and Billy followed. Savannah's scent bombarded my senses, and my wolf struggled to get out. I'd have to shift soon, or he might actually claw himself free. I'd never experienced him so agitated, except when my sister died.

"I need to think!" I roared at my wolf, though everyone averted their eyes.

Savannah had managed to fight off two wolves, *again*. But it wasn't enough.

I could make out the scents of Regina and the bloody trail she'd followed. She was a cunning tracker. That was a glimmer of hope.

I glanced up at the setting moon, just slightly past its peak. I wouldn't be able to try the ritual until tomorrow, and that would be too late. The attackers' timing had been perfect to disrupt the ritual and grab Savannah while I was away.

The hair on my neck rose. "They knew what I was doing and when. And it looks like they knew exactly which room she was in. We have a leak. Someone's feeding them information. That, or they're scrying on us."

Tony, Regina, Billy. I trusted them to the ends of the earth. They were as loyal as blood.

I fixed my allies with an iron expression. "For now, no one talks to anyone outside our team. Not a scrap of information gets out. Tony, we're going after Regina. Billy, you're the only one I trust to sort out this fucking mess. Someone tipped these assholes off. If it was the East Wisconsin pack, I want to know. If it was our pack, I want to know. Crack skulls and call Tony if you learn anything."

Traitors in the pack. Rogue wolves potentially working with the LaSalles. Blood demons. It was chaos.

I needed to clear my mind.

I stepped away and pulled off my clothes. My wolf rose, and the familiar snapping of my bones and tearing of muscles rocked my body.

Once the shift was over, a sense of calm settled over me, and things became crystal clear.

Traitors and trucks and logistics were two-legged problems. The fortune teller had said that Savannah would provide the answers I sought. There was nothing on earth that was going to stop me from finding her. To do that, I needed to capture the rogue wolf alive.

My paws dug into the dirt as I leapt forward through the trees.

Time to hunt.

It took all night, but we caught up with the miserable bastard just as sunlight rose above the horizon. He had lost a lot of blood and was barely able to run. He wasn't wolfborn but rather a shifter like Tony, and he wasn't even strong enough to stay in wolf form.

He stumbled out of my way, but Regina slammed him to the ground, and he futilely writhed beneath her paws.

Tony shifted into human form and started going through the man's pockets.

I padded over to where the bastard was lying belly-down, then bared my fangs and snarled in his face. He stank of piss and fear and drugs, and the sickly stench of death clung to him. Most importantly, he wasn't one of ours. As we'd expected, whoever was behind this was recruiting outcasts from all over.

After what he'd done to Savannah, the scent of his fear was delicious. I opened my jaw and pressed my teeth against his trembling throat, a mild suggestion from my wolf.

No. Not yet. Answers first.

Reluctantly, I reined in my wolf. As my bones cracked, I shifted back to two-legged form and gave a savage growl. Shoulders heaving with restrained fury, I turned to Tony. "Did the bastard have anything on him?"

He passed me a little vial, and my heart skipped a beat.

A week ago, I'd found the crushed remnants of a glass vial at one of the other crime scenes. We'd never figured out what it was.

I held up the vial and examined its contents in the light of the rising sun. Not much was left. It was bright red, like fresh blood. I popped the cork and sniffed. Definitely blood, though something was very strange about it—something that pulled at a memory I couldn't quite put my finger on.

I passed it back to Tony. "Let's stand him up."

Regina gave a low warning growl and stepped off the man. He started to crawl away, but I heaved him up and slammed him against the trunk of a tree. Tony grabbed his arms and pulled them back behind the trunk, then lashed the man's wrists with his belt.

"You'll pay for this," the rogue werewolf wheezed.

Tony rammed his fist in the man's face with a sickening crunch, and blood flowed from his nose. Grabbing a fistful of the man's hair, Tony yanked his head back against the trunk so the fucker's eyes met mine. They were bloodshot and dilated, and his skin was ashen and clammy. His hands were trembling, but not from fear.

He was a junkie, and I could smell that strange magic on him.

I leaned forward and let my alpha presence force him into submission. "Who are you working for?"

"Tory. Please, man, she's the one to talk to. I don't know nothing. She gave us the address of the motel last night. Said we had to get the redhead."

I sniffed. He reeked of Red Bull and vodka and sweat, but I also caught the scent of truth. But I was certain Tory wasn't the ringleader, just another lackey.

"How long have you been working for her?"

"A couple weeks. I met her at the Dirty Hound," he said.

I tightened my fists, and my knuckles cracked. "Who does she work for?"

"You have no idea what he'll do to me if I tell you."

"I'll do worse."

"You can't," he spat. "If I tell you, the sorcerer will let his fucking demons devour me alive. They don't just eat blood, man, they suck out your soul. I'd sooner let you tear my skin off, strip by strip, so do your worst."

Truth.

He was far more afraid of the sorcerer than me. That was bad news. But the man was a junkie, so there might be another way to get information.

I held up the vial. "What is this?"

"Shit, man, I thought I'd lost that. Let me have a taste. Just a drop on my tongue. I'll tell you what you want to know. Just a couple drops are all I need."

The freak stuck his tongue out, and I had the urge to slam his jaw up so his teeth cut it in half, but I needed him talking. "Tell me what it is. Then we'll talk."

"You haven't tasted it?" A crazed smile cut his face. "It's his blood. Sorcery in a bottle. Better than Blow, and I need some. *Now.*" He strained against the ropes as panic coursed through him. He was losing it.

I gripped his throat. "What does it do? Where do you get it?"

"Tory got it from the sorcerer. I've never met him, but he gives us his blood for our services. I'm telling you, man, once you taste it, you'll see the world in a whole new light. It makes you stronger, faster."

My breathing stilled. This was how the sorcerer was controlling the wolves? Enchanted, superpowered blood? It explained how the bastards had outrun us, had even outrun Savannah's car.

Could the LaSalles be manufacturing this, like they did wolfsbane?

"Why did the sorcerer want the redhead?" I snarled.

I doubted the junkie would know, but he was talking, and it was worth a shot.

The bastard writhed. "Don't you get it? It's all about the blood."

"I don't care what he was going to give you, why did he want *her*?"

"The blood, man, like I said. He wanted her for her blood. It's like his. He could make more of the Blow shit. That's why we couldn't just kill her."

My mind spun, and Regina and Tony eyed me. I gave a low growl.

Not a word about this to anyone.

They dipped their heads in acquiescence. The last thing we needed was word spreading through the packs about Savannah's blood.

I'd known there was something different—special—about Savannah, but her blood? Worry churned in my gut. The junkie had said that her blood was like the sorcerer's. Did that mean they were related?

LaSalles.

Billy might be right after all.

Nothing quite added up, though. Werewolves, sorcerers, demons, and blood-drinking junkies. And all of it seeming to revolve around Savannah Caine.

My heart began beating harder. "Where's the redhead now?"

The junkie's head rolled side to side. "No way, man. His demons will eat my soul."

Regina growled and stepped forward, but the bastard was beyond threats. It was time to bargain.

"I'll give you the blood and let you go if you tell me where she is. This is your only chance," I said, struggling to stop my wolf from ripping its way out of my chest.

He sniffed the air, sensing the truth of my words. I squeezed his throat, and he gurgled, "Fine, I submit. I'll tell you." Sweat rolled down his face. "We were supposed to take her to the abandoned sanitorium on Old Mill Road. That's all I know. Now let me go, man."

Truth.

"And the shifter woman, Sam. Is she there, too?" I asked.

"I don't know," he panted. "I wasn't there for that, but probably. Yeah. That's where they've been bringing people."

I turned to Tony. "Pull up whatever you can on the sanitorium and call in backup. Again, don't say a word about what you just heard. Understood?"

"What about me?" the junkie snarled. "You said you'd let me go."

"I did." I nodded to Tony, and he undid the belt. The junkie staggered back, and I tossed him the vial. "Run."

And then, in one swift motion, I set my wolf free.

39

Savannah

Buzzing. The oven timer.

I turned my head and groaned. "Alma, shut the buzzer off."

But the relentless noise continued. Why wouldn't she shut it off?

My head throbbed, and my throat burned. I tried to move my arms, but they stopped short. Opening my eyes, I squinted against blinding fluorescent light. Wooziness took hold. I tried to turn away but couldn't move.

My wrists were secured.

I blinked over and over until my eyes adjusted. Finally, I could take in my surroundings. A bare concrete room. An IV stand to my right with a blood bag attached to it. A tube connected to my arm. The buzzing was coming from the over-head light. Judging by my dizziness, I was being drained.

Panic flashed through me. *A human juice box for blood demons.*

I tried to sit up, but my wrists and ankles were secured to the hospital bed with Velcro straps. I struggled against the bindings, but they were sturdy and wouldn't budge.

This couldn't be happening. I searched my groggy mind, attempting to recall how I'd gotten here.

I'd shot two wolves in the forest. Then Billy had appeared…

Billy.

My head throbbed where he had punched me. I knew that bastard was a hateful son of a bitch, but this…he was Jaxson's brother-in-law, part of the pack.

I poured my anger into straining against my bonds. Then a woman's voice echoed outside, and I froze. A lock clicked, and the door behind me opened. I closed my eyes and laid completely motionless, trying to calm my thudding heart.

"She's still asleep," the woman said.

"Are we draining her dry?" a man asked. I didn't recognize either of their voices.

"No," the woman snapped. "Billy wants her alive. The sorcerer needs her blood."

The sorcerer? Was he here?

My stomach flipped, and I fought back the rising bile in my throat. Why would Billy be working with a sorcerer? I knew he hated the LaSalles, and I'd assumed he hated all magic and sorcerers, but clearly, that assumption was wrong.

One of my abductors tugged on the needle that was secured to my arm, and I battled the urge to flinch. I peeked open an eye. The woman frowned as she removed the blood bag from the IV stand and replaced it with an empty one. A gold ring pierced her lip, and her eyes were smudged with what looked like day-old shadow. She secured the tube to the needle that was stuck in my vein, and then the two of them left.

Fear pulsed through me, and the room spun. I glanced at the empty IV bag and strained against my bindings. How much blood could they take? The average human body had ten pints.

Fight, Savannah. Before it's too late.

Tears welled in my eyes. I leaned over and tried to grab the tube that was draining my blood with my mouth, but it was too far. A wave of dizziness and drowsiness settled over me, and I closed my eyes and drifted as I tried to fight it off.

Minutes—or hours—later, a hand slapped my cheek. "Wake up!"

I forced my heavy lids open and blinked several times. I must have passed out. How long had I been down here?

"Where the hell am I?" I mumbled.

"Eat." The woman with the lip ring and smudgy eye shadow shoved a peanut butter and jelly sandwich at me. I turned my head away, but she grabbed my hair and forced my head back. I took a bite and chewed.

Tears rolled down my face, and I swallowed the rising lump of sorrow.

A brawny man with a scar under his left eye appeared by my side. "I'd love to have a few moments alone with her. Make her pay for what she did to the others."

He grinned and brushed my cheek with his knuckles. My skin crawled, and I jerked against my bindings.

"Hands off. You can use the look-alike for your twisted fantasies. This one's too important." The woman's voice was filled with malice, and she shoved the sandwich into my mouth.

The man leaned forward and sniffed me. I strained as revulsion overcame me, but he held me down. "I wonder if her blood tastes like *his*?"

If my blood tasted like whose? Billy's? The sorcerer's? Why in the hell were they tasting anyone's blood?

Confusion clouded my mind as he detached the tube from the needle in my arm and smeared a few drops of my blood on his finger. He tasted it and jerked, closing his eyes. When he opened them, they were a deep crimson and manic.

Holy smokes.

"She's like him," he growled. "Not as potent, but sweeter."

The man looked like a drug addict who needed another fix. His nostrils flared, and a crazed grin cut his face. "I need another taste."

Crap.

He lifted the dripping tube to his mouth, but the woman snatched it from his hand. "No! Billy will kill us both. Her blood belongs to the sorcerer."

I watched in a daze as the woman secured the tube to the needle in my arm. What the fuck was going on?

The woman picked up a needle and jabbed it into a vial, filling it with something. She stepped over and lifted my sleeve. I struggled, but the man pinned my arms while she jabbed me and injected the fluid.

She flicked the needle into a metal trashcan and opened the door. "Come on. This dose of magic inhibitor should keep her down for a few more hours. I wish they'd just spring for magicuffs. Let's finish draining the others. We don't need them anymore."

As soon as they left, I glanced around the room, searching for anything I might use to get out of these bindings. There was a scalpel on the counter, but it was too far away to reach.

I grunted and thrashed uselessly against the bonds, but then an idea drifted through my sluggish mind.

Use your magic, Savy.

She'd mentioned she'd given me a magic inhibitor. Maybe it hadn't kicked in yet.

I closed my eyes and focused, searching for that feeling of cold water trickling over my skin—but it was like it had never been there.

Deep fatigue overwhelmed me, but I fought it back as my panic rose. I had to get out of here. My mounting desperation strained against my chest, and it felt like my heart was going to rip free. I arched my back and pulled against my bindings with all my strength.

"Please," I begged in a whisper.

Searing pain exploded through my arms, like my very flesh was being torn from my body. I gasped, too shocked to even scream, and felt something ripping. Was it my skin or the straps? I tried to look down, but the blood rushed to my head, and darkness swirled at the corner of my eyes.

For a second, I saw my arm as it ripped free. Something was wrong with it...

But then darkness took me.

When I came to, my head was throbbing. The buzzing of the overhead fluorescents didn't help matters. My body ached everywhere, and my cheek was pressed against something cold and hard.

Get up, Savy.

I was so tired, but I forced my eyes open. My fingers ached. I was on the floor, my arms and legs no longer bound.

Confusion washed over me. I climbed onto my hands and knees, wincing at the soreness in my muscles and joints. It felt like I'd been run over by a train.

The IV stand was on the floor, and drops of blood—*my blood* —were splattered everywhere. The needle was still stuck in my arm, but the tube looked like it had been ripped out and was lying on the floor, still connected to the partially full blood bag.

What had happened?

I used the bed to pull myself to my feet. My legs were weak, probably from blood loss. The bindings that had secured my wrists and ankles to the bed were shredded.

For a second, a vision of my hands tearing through the straps swum in my eyes, and then dizziness overcame me, and I swayed. None of this made sense. But I had to get out of there. Escape.

I listed right and stumbled. Well, this was going to be interesting.

The door was unlocked. I cracked it and listened outside, but all was quiet. Thank goodness I hadn't made too much noise.

I opened the door and slipped into a long, concrete hall that was lined with half a dozen closed doors. The place was dirty and looked derelict, and a few of the overhead lights flickered. There was no indication of which way led out, so I went with my gut and headed left.

The floor was cold and clammy, and I really wished I had my boots. God knows what was lying around to step on. At least the muscles in my legs had warmed up and were beginning to work again. I sneaked to the end of the hall and paused. Voices carried around the corner, coming my way.

Panic streaked through me. I lunged toward the nearest door, unlocked the deadbolt, and slipped inside. The room was almost identical to the one I'd been in, except there were two monitors hooked up to wires that connected to a large bed that had been adjusted upright.

"Who's there?" a woman asked, fear evident in her voice.

I rounded the bed and froze. It was like looking in a mirror— a red-haired girl in her twenties, strapped to the bed with tubes and wires stuck into her arms. Madison Lee, the girl I'd seen on TV. She was gaunt with sunken cheeks, like she'd been drained dry.

This could have been me. A wave of emotions slammed into my chest. Relief that I wasn't alone, and rage. These people were fucking monsters.

She strained against her straps in fear as I approached.

"It's okay. I'm Savannah. I'm going to get you out of here," I whispered as I undid the heavy straps binding her ankles and wrists.

The woman's body slammed into my chest, and her arms wrapped around me. "Thank you," she sobbed. "What day is it?"

I shook my head and began unhooking the wires that attached to her chest. "I'm not sure. You were taken a week before I was captured. I saw you on the news."

"It's only been a week?" She pulled out the IV in her arm. "It felt like longer. They've done awful things to me. And those creatures..."

She choked up, and I bit my lip. "Are there others down here? I'm looking for a friend, a shifter, she would have been brought in a few hours before I was. Her name is Sam."

"There were others. But I haven't seen anyone for days." The girl shuddered.

My stomach sank, but I squeezed her hand and forced a smile. "We're going to get out of here. Do you know your way around this place?"

She started to speak, but at that moment, the door behind us swung open as man in a stained lab coat stepped in. "No one is supposed to check on—"

His eyes widened with shock. I lunged forward and slammed him into the corner wall a couple times before he could react. He crumpled to the floor, crawling in a daze.

Madison kicked him in the jaw, and he flipped over.

"That's for jabbing me with all those needles," she hissed, then kicked him in the balls. "And that's for injecting me with that shit."

Crap. I hoped that magic inhibitor was the only thing they'd injected me with.

I nodded to Madison. "Let's tie him down and get some answers."

She was so drained that she wasn't much help heaving him up on the table, but for some reason, I felt like I was surging with strength.

"Fates, you're fast. What are you?" she whispered.

"A sorceress, I think. You?"

"A witch." Madison secured the arm bands while I ripped off a piece of the man's shirt and stuffed it in his mouth.

His eyes widened as I sunk my nails into the side of his face. "If you scream, I'll rip your eyes out. So be quiet and answer our questions. Got it?"

He squirmed, and when he saw it was useless, he nodded.

I slowly removed the gag, ready to shove it back in and knock his lights out if he made a peep. "Who is the asshole running the show?"

"Billy."

"No. Who's the sorcerer?"

"I don't know his name! He just sends us the blood, and I keep people alive for his pets. He doesn't make them here."

I growled. "I can smell lies."

"Then you know I'm telling the truth." He squeaked as I dug my nails in.

"What are you? Some kind of freaky doctor?"

"I just make the inhibitor. I'm not into the blood sorcery, I swear."

"Is there an antidote for the inhibitor?"

"Ah..."

I slammed his head against the table.

He groaned. "Check my pocket. Red for inhibitor. Green for stimulant."

Madison dug around in the pockets of his coat and pulled out five syringes wrapped with a rubber band, three red and two green. "Also, he's got keys."

"How do the drugs work?" I asked.

"Just inject it in your arm."

Truth. I could smell it, along with his abject terror.

"Do you trust him?" Madison asked. "They used the red ones like that on me."

I nodded. "I don't think he's lying."

She popped open the top of the green syringe, rolled up her sleeve, and jabbed it in her arm. "Here goes nothing. I want my magic back."

She offered me the other, but I shook my head. I was suddenly feeling pretty damn good, all things considered. Actually, great. Had the inhibitor they'd given me boosted my magic, somehow? Or maybe they'd given me the wrong one.

"Why do they want me?" I asked.

The man writhed against the bonds, and I started to slip a finger into his eye socket.

"Stop! Your blood is special. I think it's like his. Maybe he'll use it to make more, but I think it's something else. We're not supposed to let the demons feed on you." The man reeked of fear and piss, and I didn't think it was me he was afraid of.

Madison touched my arm. "We need to go. We're making a lot of noise."

I pushed my face close to the man's. "Where is my friend, the she-wolf you just brought in?"

"There's a werewolf woman in 5B. We were told not to drain her, just sedate."

My heart leapt. Sam was here.

"How do we find her and get out of here?"

He gave us directions to a lab, which had a door that opened to the main compound—our ticket out. If we could get to that door, we might have a chance.

I ripped his key card off his neck and shoved my shirt back in the man's mouth as he squirmed. "Let's go."

Madison nodded. "They've moved me a lot. I think I can find the way."

I shadowed her down the hall, glancing behind us to

make sure nobody rounded the other corner. We reached the end and turned right onto another hall lined with rooms.

Halfway down, I stopped and grabbed Madison's arm.

"What?" she hissed, alarmed.

I put my finger to my lips and inhaled slowly through my nose. The place reeked of mold, refuse, and neglect. But for just a second, I'd sworn I caught a familiar scent or signature. I concentrated as hard as I could, trying to ignore the sickly odors of blood and despair.

There. Recognition stirred in my chest, and I quickly moved down the hall to one of the doors. 5B. Sam.

I unlocked the deadbolt.

"Savannah?" a voice croaked. "What are you doing here?"

My heart froze.

Sam was lying strapped down to a bed. Her eyes were glassy. I crossed the room, undid her straps, and pulled her into a hug. Her body tensed, then slowly relaxed.

I scanned her quickly. She looked pissed as all hell but wasn't visibly injured. "We're busting out of here. You good to run?"

"I'm fine," she growled, and grabbed my wrist as her eyes narrowed. "Billy is behind this," she spat, her words laced with venom.

I placed my hand on her shoulder. "I know. We'll get the bastard."

Her fists were clenched, and she was visibly shaking with rage. "Let's go."

Sam jumped off the bed, and I noticed that she was limping. "You're hurt."

"I fought back. Fuckers gave me something that blocks my healing."

Magic inhibitor. Madison pulled out the other green syringe.

"This might help. It's a stimulant. I already feel my magic coming back."

Sam nodded, and Madison injected her with the stuff, then tossed the needle.

We slipped out of the room and wound our way through the halls until we reached a large door with an electronic lock. "I think this is the lab," I whispered, then tapped the quack's keycard. The door slid open, but the room beyond looked nothing like a laboratory. There were a few derelict computers on the benches, but they hadn't seen use in ages. The walls were the same pocked concrete, and a layer of dirt coated the floor—everywhere except in the center, which was covered with arcane symbols. Bloodstains were everywhere.

Different kind of laboratory.

Two confused faces turned to us—a couple of shifters, judging by their amber-tinged eyes. One was the bastard who'd tasted my blood earlier, while the other had long hair and looked rough.

Before I could react, Sam lunged for the long-haired guy, claws extended from her fingers. She slashed his face, and streaks of blood rose across his ashen cheek. He hurled her aside, but Madison charged into the room, picked up a monitor, and threw it into his chest. "Experiment on this!" she cried, and he crashed backward into the table.

The blood-licker growled and stepped toward me. The creepy look on his face had my skin crawling, but I loosened my body and raised my fists, remembering what Jaxson had taught me. When he charged, I ducked to the side, but he managed to get a grip on my bicep. I brought my other fist down onto his wrist with more force than I'd ever had, breaking his hold. He turned and faced me, his hand twitching. "Why don't you give me a taste, little pup?"

Anger flooded my senses, and oddly, the beds of my nails

itched. I sprang forward, tackling his torso. A surprised look crossed his face as we hurtled into a table with several keyboards and monitors, sending them to the floor with a crash.

He clawed at me, and pain shot through my arm.

A frenzy took over me. It was like an out-of-body experience—I could watch what was happening, but I wasn't in the driver's seat. I punched him square in the face, feeling a crunch, either from his nose or my knuckles, but I just kept punching until he slumped back and slid off the desk. I'd never felt like I had this much strength.

I staggered back from the unconscious man, wincing at the deep throbbing in my hand. There was way more blood than there should have been. His shirt and skin were shredded. I glanced down at my blood-covered hands, stunned.

Holy shit. What had they injected me with?

I turned in a daze. On the other side of the lab bench, Sam climbed off the shifter she'd attacked. His neck was twisted at an odd angle, his eyes staring blankly.

Madison was already at the service door, fumbling with a set of keys she must have found in the room or on the dead shifter. She turned to us with a wide grin on her face. "Let's get the hell out of here."

40

Savannah

Madison pushed open the back door to the lab. Late afternoon light illuminated a yard fronting woods. Freedom.

"Come on!" I cried, and we slipped outside and sprinted toward the trees. We made it about ten paces before alarms blared inside the building. Shouts erupted from the lab, and all three of us turned and tore into the woods.

We sprinted for safety, leaping over bushes and underbrush. I tried not to dwell on the fact that I was moving faster and more nimbly than seemed possible, and I wasn't wearing my speed boots. That was a future me problem, and right now, we were racing for our lives.

I heard trickling water nearby. A stream.

Howls cut through the forest behind and beside us, and two blurs flashed through the trees. Panic and fear colored my thoughts. How could we outrun them?

You can't.

I looked at Sam and the witch girl. It was my fault they were in this mess, Sam because she'd been assigned to protect my ass, and Madison simply because she looked like me. I had to make this right. If I could lead the wolves away, these two might survive this. I could tell from Sam's strained movements that the magic inhibitor antidote she'd taken hadn't yet kicked in. Sam was a fighter, but there was no way she'd have the strength to ward off these jacked-up shifters.

The trickle of water was louder now.

"This way." I grabbed Madison's hand, and we turned right, sliding down an embankment. At the bottom was a small creek, fifteen feet across.

"You two go," I whispered, pushing Madison into the water. "I'm going to lead them away."

She jerked to a stop. "No!"

"Go! They're after my blood. This is your one shot at getting out of here alive." I met Sam's eyes. "Do this for me, please. You're strong enough to get her out. Tell Jaxson what you know. Stop Billy."

Sam hesitated, then grabbed Madison's arm and waded across. She paused at the other side of the stream and nodded.

I smeared some of my sticky blood on the leaves, then took off up the stream bank, brushing against trees and making as much noise as possible. My bare feet stung as I clambered over rocks, but my resolve dulled the pain.

Once I was certain I'd put enough distance between us, I paused, chest heaving. Two howls echoed from the right, and then a crash in the forest. Close.

They'd be on me in seconds. I scanned the bank for a place to hide, but there was nowhere that they wouldn't sniff me out. My gaze landed on the stream.

Adrenaline coursed through me, and I waded into the dark water, tripping over the rocky bottom. I scrambled to a deep bend underneath some overhanging brush, took a few full breaths, and slipped under the surface just as a wolf bounded out of the trees.

The shock of the cold water made my muscles ache, but I tried to simply imagine it as my magic flowing through my body. The water was only a few feet deep, so I laid flat and held on to a large root protruding from the bank. Water flooded my nose, and my hair floated around me.

Between the murky water and the setting sun, I could just barely make out the surface. My lungs began to burn, and I fought the urge to swallow, but the burning only grew.

Just a little longer.

My fingers dug into the rocks and roots, and dizziness drifted over me. I'd always imagined I'd die in a blaze like my parents, but considering the circumstances, drowning didn't seem so bad.

A dark shape loomed overhead. A cloud, maybe. I closed my eyes. Something nudged me and then gripped my shoulder, pulling me up. Sharp but not painful.

My head broke the surface, and I launched into a coughing fit. A rock shifted underfoot, and I slipped, but a massive wolf ducked his head under my arm. My heart stuttered, and then I recognized the silver-gray fur.

Jaxson.

My shoulders slumped with relief, and tears streamed from my eyes. The wolf looked back at me with honey eyes, and I somehow knew what he wanted. I ran my hands through his fur and held tight as he dragged me from the stream.

I collapsed on the bank, and my cheek pressed into the mud as my lungs drew in haggard breaths. Jaxson nudged me with his face, and my chest tightened.

Several snarls sounded around us, but I was too exhausted to move or care. My strength from earlier had vanished, washed away in the cold water.

Jaxson bounded over me and collided with a black wolf who stepped out of the trees. They rolled several feet, and then

Jaxson pinned the smaller wolf and tore out its throat, blood spilling onto the shore.

Just then, a white wolf sprang from the forest and landed on Jaxson's back, sinking its teeth into his side. Fear arced through me. Jaxson let out a heart-stopping growl and latched onto the attacker's haunch, dragging him off. The wolf yipped, and then Jaxson's jaws sank into its neck and twisted. With a snap, the wolf collapsed, lifeless.

I blinked in horror.

I spun, looking for new assailants, but the bank was quiet apart from the gentle burbling of the stream. Heat pulsed over my skin, and I shivered and looked up.

My breath hitched as Jaxson stepped toward me, still in wolf form. Blood stained his back, and worry filled my chest, along with that aching tightness that always arose when he was near. He paused only a foot away. My chest heaved, unable to get enough air, and the itching under my nails grew again. He tilted his head, scrutinizing me with impossible golden eyes.

Jaxson tilted his head and howled, and shivers raced down my spine. The world spun as howls echoed in the distance. Some part of me knew that they were friendly howls.

Jaxson's wolf looked at me with an expression that seemed to be telling me, *Rest. You are safe.*

It was like a compulsion. The last of my strength drained from me, and I slumped back onto the bank, exhaustion weighing me down. The fading light filtered through the trees, and I closed my eyes.

41

Jaxson

I scooped up Savannah. Her skin was cold against my chest, and I breathed in her scent. Tangerines, and the taste of cool water flowing over my lips.

She smells delicious.

She was unconscious and shivering. Her clothes were still wet from the river, and she was probably in shock.

She'd sacrificed herself so that Sam and Madison could get away. She didn't even like Sam.

My wolf stirred, and my heart ached. She'd saved one of our pack.

I brushed a strand of hair from her face. At my touch, she pinched her eyebrows, and her lips trembled. Protectiveness and anger raged inside of me, and my wolf strained to break free.

I glanced down at her as I wound my way through the trees. She looked so delicate in my arms. So fragile. And so alluring. There was something about her. Maybe it was her blood.

Fuck, what was wrong with me?

She was a goddamned LaSalle...but she was also something else, and I'd have to figure out what that was.

A branch cracked, and Sam stepped out of the trees with Regina and Tony, favoring her right leg. "You all right?" I asked.

She nodded. "Just a torn muscle. I'll heal soon."

"And Madison?"

"She's a little shaken up, but she's fine."

"We've secured the sanitorium. Captured two of the blood junkies." Regina glanced at Sam and paused. "There's something else, Jax."

A cocktail of scents emanated from her—anger, betrayal, and sadness. Whatever it was, it wasn't good.

I steadied my will. "Tell me."

Sam's jaw tensed. "It was Billy, Jaxson. He was behind it all. The abductions, grabbing me, Savannah. He's been working with the sorcerer."

Her words pierced my heart, and my body shook. Regina surged forward and plucked Savannah from my arms as my vision blurred and my bones began snapping. With difficulty, I reined in my wolf. I needed to think clearly. "It's not possible."

"He's the one who grabbed Savannah and brought her in."

"Maybe he was trying to make a trade..." I growled. "For you, or for the captives. He didn't like how—"

"Jaxson. He was the one giving orders," Sam said coldly.

I read her scent. It was undeniable. *Truth.*

"But why?" It made no sense. Billy would never work with a sorcerer, even if they weren't LaSalles.

"I don't know. But he's looking for vengeance against the LaSalles, and I think he made a deal."

The world spun around me. Billy was a brother. A member of the pack. My family.

I scanned my closest confidants. Billy had once been one of them. I'd told him everything, every move...and he'd betrayed us all. For what? What was worth betraying your brother, your alpha? Vengeance?

Rage consumed me, and I turned and drove my fists into a tree. My finger bones cracked, but the pain helped focus my thoughts.

I'd show him vengeance.

"Jaxson." Savannah's voice cut through the air.

I spun to face her as she inched toward me. Savannah Caine. The root of it all, the hub at the center of the wheel trampling everything beneath its path. Why did chaos follow her like a long shadow?

The fortune teller's final warning thundered in my mind: *If you help the woman and get your answers, they will tear you apart.*

The Caine—*LaSalle*—woman took another step. I shook, barely able to contain my confusion and rage. Was she my enemy? My ally? Or my doom?

"Savannah, stop," Sam said.

But Savannah didn't listen. Instead, she placed a hand on my shoulder. A shock like cold water rushed over me, and I inhaled sharply. My muscles tightened and then gently relaxed as her touch dragged me back from the brink of insanity. Her eyes were the calm within a storm, and in them, I saw strength and kindness.

Strength. The card the fortune teller had pulled for her. Could she be that for me?

She feels our pain.

No. She couldn't. She wasn't one of us. She didn't know what it was to be pack, to be bonded.

I shook my head, trying to clear my thoughts. *Too many two-legged worries. Concentrate on the problem at hand.*

I examined her. "Are you hurt?"

Savannah shook her head. "No, but we need to find Billy. They took my blood, and the sorcerer is using it for something. We have to find out what."

I looked to Sam. "Do you know who this sorcerer is?"

"No idea," she replied. "But if Billy is working with him, I'm willing to bet he's also someone who has a beef with the LaSalles."

We wound through the forest toward the trucks we'd purchased from the East Wisconsin wolves at extortionist prices. Tony was on the phone. Savannah and Sam were behind, talking quietly. My mind, however, was occupied.

Billy must pay for betraying the pack.

I'd have to kill him to set a precedent. Bile rose in my throat. Could I kill my own brother-in-law? We'd been through so much together. How had it come to this?

Deep down, I knew the answer. It was simple: rage.

He and my sister had been true mates, I was sure of it. When she'd died, I'd wanted revenge, but Billy had wanted to tear down the world, to leave half of Magic Side in ashes. Rather than grieving her death, I'd had to keep him in check until his bloodlust had passed.

Apparently, it never had.

And now Billy had crossed the line. Gods only knew what kind of shitstorm he'd started.

Tony strode over and hung up his phone. "Our guys searched the sanitorium and found two more captives, alive but just barely. No clues as to where the sorcerer is. We caught a she-wolf who claims that Billy was the only one with a direct line to him."

"Then we find Billy."

We'd have to take him down outside of pack law. If there were a trial, the whole pack—and inevitably the Order—would know the truth about the sorcerer, the pack's role in the attacks, and that Savannah's blood was like a drug. There would be a firestorm. We couldn't risk an open trial, so Billy had to be dealt with quietly and quickly.

As soon as we reached the trucks, I fixed my shrinking inner circle with a glare. "Billy is family, but he betrayed us and put the pack in peril. He's made deals with sorcerers and demons and put his lust for vengeance above everything else. We could lose our reputation, our lives, and our alliances. From this day on, Billy is an exile. No longer family, no longer part of this pack. He no longer has rights to trial by pack law."

Scents of anger, shame, and regret filled the air. I took a deep breath. "We treat Billy like any other threat. We take him down, now. Everyone understand?"

They nodded. We all knew what had to be done.

I leaned on the truck. "Unfortunately, Billy must have known we were going to raid the sanatorium, and he probably suspects it's only a matter of time before we figure things out. My guess is that he's turned tail and gathering his allies at his cabin in the Upper Peninsula. I'm betting he's expecting us."

"Should we call everybody up? Go in heavy?" Tony asked.

"No. Billy's got a lot of friends in the pack. We need to be discreet and fast. Tony, Regina, call only the people we absolutely trust. People who are stationed up here, or who can get here quickly. And none of the dock workers. Have everyone meet at the Garden Corners Rest Area, and have them bring guns and silver."

Tony nodded. "You got it, boss man."

It was time for a reckoning.

42

Savannah

Apart from glimmers of the full moon peeking out from the clouds and the passing headlights, the night was dark.

I finished my second meat and potato pasty—a local Michigan staple—and brushed the crumbs off my tank top. Regina had given me a clean pair of jeans and a shirt, and though biker chic wasn't my style, they fit, and I was glad to be rid of my damp and blood-stained clothes.

"You feeling okay?" Sam turned and looked at me from the front passenger seat. Jaxson was driving, and he glanced at me in the rearview mirror.

She was being nicer since I'd saved her ass. Hell, even Regina and Tony had warmed up a bit. I never thought I'd see the day.

"I'm fine. Just needed sustenance. How much farther to Billy's cabin?"

"Twenty-five minutes," Sam said.

We were deep into Michigan, driving through the heavily wooded Upper Peninsula. I watched the passing trees in the darkness, and my thoughts drifted to the sorcerer. The faceless man. Shivers snaked down my spine.

What would we do if Billy didn't know where the sorcerer was?

He was after me—my blood—and I had the sinking feeling that he wasn't going to stop, regardless of whether we got to Billy.

Jaxson and Sam were talking quietly. They'd debated bringing me, but I'd had some sharp words to say about that. I'd reminded them that I'd bested four werewolves on my own and that I'd been the one to rescue Sam. If that didn't prove I was enough of an asset to bring along, I didn't know what would.

I silently reached into my backpack and pulled out the scrying potion. Would the sorcerer be there? What if he was planning an ambush with Billy? We needed more information, and I could do something about that. I leaned forward and took a swig of the potion, grimacing as I swallowed it. I knew it was a long shot, but it could make all the difference.

Settling back, I closed my eyes so Jaxson and Sam wouldn't notice what I was doing. The potion burned through my veins. I concentrated on the sorcerer, and my muscles spasmed as my mind focused and drew me into darkness.

The potion was working faster than I'd anticipated. I glanced around. It was pitch black, and the air tasted stale.

Something was different. A light shone up ahead, and I walked toward it. I was in a cave. The walls were covered in lichen and dripping with water. I stumbled on a rock and silently cursed as the sound echoed through the space. Was it supposed to do that? I'd never heard anything while scrying. The time the sorcerer had spoken to me, I hadn't actually heard his words—they'd formed in my mind like a thought, rising from my subconscious.

As I drew closer to the light, my nail beds itched, and fear took root in my heart. *He* was close. I sensed it with every fiber of my being.

My heart pounded against my chest. Last time I'd scried, it had felt like I'd been dreaming, but this...this felt so real, like I was actually here.

I swallowed my rising panic and looked around, taking in every inch of my surroundings so that I could sketch it later. There was nothing specific about this cave, though it was dark and creepy as hell.

Up ahead, the cave opened, and a small fire illuminated the space. Two passages split off in the distance, veiled in darkness. Apart from my breathing and my racing heart, it was quiet.

"Savannah," a low voice whispered.

I spun, but no one was there. Goosebumps erupted across my skin, and panic seized my chest. I couldn't breathe.

"I've been waiting for you, my darling. Come to me, Savannah."

I just needed to stay long enough to see his face. To know who he was. "Where are you? Show yourself."

A sinister chuckle echoed through the cavern. "Oh, Savannah. I told you once before: *no peeking.*"

His voice sent terror right through me, and my chest heaved as I sucked in air. I couldn't explain my body's reaction.

Instinct.

"Show your face, you coward." I spun, feeling dizzy.

Suddenly, a form appeared in front of me, gripping my arms. There was no face, though, just a black, empty, cavernous space. Horror paralyzed me, yet I managed to scream.

I tried to break the vision, but I was stuck.

The form's grip tightened, and his nails dug into my skin. This wasn't supposed to happen. This was all wrong.

"We're one and the same, Savannah. You can't escape me. I'll find you, *always.*" His voice penetrated my mind, filling my soul with a cold darkness that made me want to claw my skin off.

I kicked and wrenched my body, trying to free myself, but my blows didn't connect. Desperate, I screamed, "*Jaxson!*"

My vision went black, and two hands gripped my shoulders. "Savannah, come back to me!"

I opened my eyes. Jaxson was staring at me through the open door, fear etched across his face. His shoulders relaxed slightly when my eyes locked onto his.

Tears streamed down my face.

Jaxson pulled me toward him, cradling the back of my head with his hand. "You're safe now."

His voice was soothing, and I buried my face in his chest, trying to escape the dreadful feeling that had taken root inside me like the aftershocks of a terrible nightmare.

Once my breathing had calmed, he gently cupped my face with his palm and wiped the tears from my cheeks. His brow was furrowed, and he looked upset. "What happened?"

"I wanted to see if I could get any more clues about the sorcerer's plans, so I scried on him. He saw me and spoke to me. *Grabbed* me. I couldn't leave, it was so real..." I squeezed my eyes shut and shook my head, trying to rid the vision of his blank face from my mind.

"That's not possible," Sam said. She was crouched on the middle console, watching me closely.

"Wrong. It happened." I hiccupped and wiped my eyes.

Jaxson's hands slid down my arms, and I looked down. My heart stilled. Red streaks trailed down my skin where the sorcerer had gripped me.

Jaxson locked me with a steely gaze, and his jaw tensed. "No more scrying."

I nodded. "No more scrying."

He glanced at Sam like they were exchanging some

unspoken words, and then he returned his gaze to me. "Will you be all right? We're fifteen minutes from the cabin. You don't have to come. Sam can take you back to Magic Side."

Determination replaced my fear. "No. I'm not running. I need answers."

I was going to find out who this fucker was and destroy him.

Jaxson nodded and closed my door. He motioned to the four cars that had pulled off the road behind us, and then he slid into the driver's seat and started the engine. As he drove, he watched me with concern in the rearview mirror. I rubbed my stinging arms and looked out the window.

That was really stupid, Savy. What would have happened if I'd gotten stuck in that vision? There was still so much I didn't know about scrying, and I really had to be more careful.

Sam handed me her leather jacket. "Take this. You're shivering."

"Thanks." I slid my arms into the jacket, which was still warm, and I pulled my sketchbook and pencil from my bag. As much as my skin still crawled from the thought of that monster, I needed to draw the vision while the details were still fresh. Familiar tools in hand, I got to work, losing myself in the process.

Ten minutes later, we pulled onto a dirt road that cut through the forest. I stopped and looked at the drawings on the two papers. The faceless man stared back at me from the cavern. That was when I noticed the mark on his neck—a tattoo. My heart pounded, and I squinted at the page, trying to make out the design.

A triangle with the number thirty-seven in it. What did it mean?

I put the sketchbook and pencil away and tightened the laces on my magic boots. Jaxson had left one of his people behind at the Sunrise Inn to collect everyone's belongings once the wolfsbane dissipated, and while I hadn't had much on me to begin with, I was relieved to find my boots and my purse returned. The boots, especially—after running through the woods and sanatorium in bare feet, it was a spine-tingling relief to have them on again.

I needed to start sleeping with those puppies laced up, I decided, as if that would solve all my problems.

A light mist had started, and fog settled in the trees. Just what I needed. My nerves were already shot.

Jaxson pulled to the side and parked. The cars behind us followed, and soon, it was pitch black.

I took an unsteady breath.

Time to woman up, Savy. Get some answers.

I climbed out of the car, and Jaxson appeared before me. He slid his hand to my hip, and my heart quickened. "Stay close to me," he murmured. "I want you in sight."

He pulled out the bulletproof vest I'd used before and helped me suit up. Each time he tugged the straps tight, I sucked in a quick breath, inhaling the scent of his signature. I wished I could wrap it around me just as tightly as the vest. Then maybe the jitters would go away.

He handed me a pistol. "Things are going to get rough."

"I know."

His hand lingered for a second while his gaze lowered to my lips. My breath hitched as he turned, and I felt the sudden loss of his touch as I slipped the gun into the back of my jeans.

God, I needed to learn to control my reactions around him, but it was hard. He was dangerously handsome, and the attraction between us was electric. Every time we got close, I felt like a part of my soul wanted to claw its way out...though not in a bad way. I couldn't explain it. It made no sense and was frankly weird as hell, like a relentless pushing against my ribs that strengthened every time he came near.

Jaxson handed Sam a pistol and slid another behind his waistband. Eight shifters stepped from the other vehicles. Tony, Regina, and a couple of others I recognized from our first jaunt to the she-wolf's cabin near the lighthouse. They nodded at me, and I guessed everyone was warming up a little. That, or they expected me to die and were just being polite about things.

I took an unsteady breath.

Things would be fine. Jaxson had explained the plan of attack at the road stop. Everyone except him and Sam was going to shift. The wolves would split into two groups and surround the cabin, while we approached from the south.

The werewolves seemed to prefer attacking with claws and fangs over using guns. It made sense for fighting in the trees, where there would be a lot of cover. Plus, as far as I could tell, they were faster, stronger, and healed more quickly in wolf form.

I, however, was not a werewolf, and I had no control over the little magic I had, so I was really happy for the Glock. I touched it for good luck as Jaxson had everyone huddle up.

"You know the plan," he said. "Go quietly, and be quick about it. Take out the sentries, then breach. But don't forget— Billy is mine by right. If you see him, howl. Pursue, but don't engage. We need him alive. He's our link to the sorcerer behind this, and if he goes down, the bastard may slip away."

Everyone nodded. I could practically smell their excitement, the urgency to run.

"Stay alert," Jaxson said softly. "Billy will be expecting us."

I averted my gaze as the wolfborn stripped and shifted. The snapping of bones made my stomach turn.

"Ready?" Jaxson's voice sent shivers down my neck.

I turned and nodded. "As ready as I'll ever be."

He smiled, but I could see the pain in his eyes. This couldn't be easy for him. Billy was a prick, but he was also Jaxson's family. I really had no idea what that must be like.

With the rustling of leaves and the soft padding of stealthy paws, the wolves disappeared into the trees.

The fog seemed to blanket the forest in silence. Jaxson and Sam flanked me, and I followed their lead as we crept through the woods. My pace was slow. I didn't have wolf vision and had to gingerly step over the rocks that littered the ground. Boots of speed were great, but boots of *stealth* would have been really handy.

Gunshots resounded through the forest, followed by two howls. My pulse raced. The tension in Jaxon's shoulders was clear. He glanced at Sam, and they slowed. I bit my lip in frustration, wishing I could speak wolf.

Suddenly, loud cracks echoed through the trees behind us as bullets sank into bark. I ducked low behind a fallen trunk, unable to discern where the shots were coming from.

More gunfire erupted from the left, and bullets dug into the dirt a few feet behind me.

Wrong side of the tree.

I dove over the log, and Sam crouched beside me. Jaxson ripped off a few shots into the darkness, aiming for something flickering at the edge of my vision. Their eyes were so much sharper than mine.

My heart began pounding, and a bead of sweat rolled down my spine.

Deep breaths, Savy. You've got this.

No, I fucking didn't.

I could shoot, but I wasn't trained for gunfights in the dark. Lying on my stomach next to the fallen trunk, I suddenly had a greater appreciation for demons, which just tried to eat you and didn't shoot back.

With gasping breaths, I reminded myself of why I was there. Why I'd left Belmont and gone to Magic Side—to find out who was hunting me. I was almost there. I just needed a face and a location.

A bullet ricocheted off a rock near Sam's head.

We were surrounded.

Suddenly, Jaxson threw himself on top of me, crushing me with his weight. Though I struggled, he wouldn't budge. He grunted, and then shouting and snarls erupted around us. With my cheek pressed into the dirt, I couldn't see anything.

"Stay down! We'll lead them off" Jaxson hissed, and then he launched off me.

I glanced up. Jaxson and Sam were gone in a burst of gunfire.

A man screamed, and the sound of gurgling made me sick. I clamped my palms to my ears, fighting back the vomit in my throat. Then the shooting shifted away from me.

I peeked through the crack beneath the fallen trunk. Blurs moved through the trees on all sides. And then a canister landed ten feet away, spewing smoke.

It was the hotel attack, all over again.

Howls and shouts echoed around me. My lungs clenched, and I coughed as the gas filled the air. My eyes watered, and my skin stung.

Wolfsbane.

A man with a gas mask darted through the forest. The bastard!

I fired off three shots. The man stumbled but regained his footing. With the fog, the darkness, and now the smoke, I could barely see well enough to aim.

Screw this. I scanned the forest ahead and ran forward. I wasn't waiting for Jaxson.

I shielded my nose with the sleeve of my jacket and wound through the trees. Apart from the occasional gunshots and snarls, the forest was eerily quiet.

Light shone from ahead, and I headed toward it. I ducked

behind a bush and peered through the foliage at a rustic cabin. A single bulb illuminated the outside. How the hell this place had electricity all the way out here was a mystery.

Movement in the trees beside the cabin caught my attention. Wolves—and Jaxson. They surged forward, and my heart seized. Something about this felt wrong.

Floodlights flicked on, casting a blinding light in a hundred-foot radius around the cabin.

No!

Machine gun fire peppered the ground. I dropped as bullets flew overhead, lodging in the trunks of trees around me.

Psycho bastard prick.

I glanced through the bushes. Two wolves were down, and I didn't see Jaxson or Sam. More wolfsbane canisters soared through the air.

We were trapped.

43

Jaxson

A bullet hit Regina in the leg, and she went down.

Fuck.

It was probably silver. The bullet that had lodged in my shoulder screamed every time I moved, and the wound wasn't healing. At least they weren't hollow points.

One of Billy's men skulked through the trees ahead. I surged forward and ripped out his throat with my claws. I tore off his gas mask and tossed it to Sam, who ducked behind a tree beside me. "Put this on."

She tied her hair back. "I can't believe he's using wolfsbane on us!"

They'd used it in the hotel attack, but I'd assumed it had been the sorcerer. The fucking nerve of Billy to use that against me. After how my sister—*his mate*—had died. My body shook with rage, and my claws felt like they were going to tear out of my hands. The bastard had gone too far.

I was going to rip out his heart.

Stooped low, I charged forward, ducking from tree to tree amidst bursts of gunfire. A scream rang through the forest behind me, and I ground to a halt behind a log while bullets flew around me.

Savannah.

Protect her.

I sprang up and cursed as I raced in her direction. I shouldn't have left her alone.

A concussive force knocked me off my feet, and a jolt of agony raced up my spine as a bullet tore through my side. I rolled across the dirt as more bullets lodged in the ground next to me, then I slipped behind some rocks for cover.

Gritting my teeth against the searing pain that spread through my side, I reached my fingers into the wound and wrenched out the silver bullet. There was a lot of blood. The wound would take time to heal since it was caused by silver, and I was in human form.

My vision homed in on my attacker, and I launched myself through the air. My claws ripped into his jacket, and I pinned him to the ground. His claws tore into my side, but I ignored the pain. Savoring the wild euphoria of battle, I gripped his head with my hands. One twist, and his neck snapped.

I paused, listening to the sounds of the forest as the blood-lust filled me.

Footsteps. A shifter moving north on our right. A woman.

I stalked forward, my hunter instinct in command. The woman paused, seemingly sensing me. I burst out from the bushes as she blindly opened fire. Something tore into my chest as I collided with her. Her hands had erupted into claws, and she ripped into my face. I growled with rage as I pinned her with one hand, and then tore her throat out with my claws. The metallic scent of blood filled the air.

Sam's scream ripped through my chest.

She's in pain, but alive.

Sam was my right hand, and I fought the urge to charge

toward her. Savannah first. I locked onto Savannah's familiar tangerine scent and sprinted through the trees. I found the spot I'd left her, but she was gone.

A growl of rage erupted from my throat. I'd told her to stay put, but she never obeyed.

I'll teach her to obey.

Frustration clouded my vision as I followed her scent toward the cabin. Shit. Was she going after Billy alone?

What was she *thinking*?

Savannah

I coughed and tried to make out the shapes in the darkness. I swore I saw Jaxson moving through the forest, but it was so dark and foggy, it was hard to tell.

I'd retreated from the range lights and gunfire and circled around to the other side of the cabin. I had no idea where anyone was, and I couldn't distinguish our wolves from theirs. My plan was to shoot anything that even looked like it was thinking about charging me.

Movement drew my attention toward the cabin. The door closed, and a man slunk down the steps, making his way around back.

Holy shit. *Billy.*

I'd recognize the bastard from a mile away, even with the fog. His aura of fucking evil was unmistakable.

I sneaked around the tree line bordering the cabin and followed him. Two run-down trucks and a Honda were parked out back, and the brake lights of one of the trucks illuminated.

The bastard was running. *Coward.*

I couldn't let him get away. This was my only chance to identify the sorcerer.

I raced toward the truck as it lurched down a second gravel road. I tried the door of the adjacent Honda, but it was locked.

No, no, no.

I wrenched open the door of the second truck and spotted a set of keys in the cupholder—it was primed for an easy getaway, I guessed. I slipped onto the tattered leather seat, pressed the clutch, and shoved the keys into the ignition. The truck rumbled to life, and I fishtailed out of the driveway after Billy.

The gears were sticky and ground a bit, but I shifted her into second and then third as I floored it down the dirt road, silently praying that none of Jaxson's wolves crossed my path.

I'd already run over two wolves. Luckily, they were rogue psychopaths, or else I'm pretty sure the pack would have ended me for that alone.

The road split in two, and I slammed on the breaks.

Which way?

I leaned my head out the window, looking for any indication of the path Billy had taken, but there were tire marks on both sides.

I took a breath and gunned the gas, heading left. Desperation rose in my chest after a few minutes of driving in the darkness, and then I saw them—the red taillights.

"There you are, you bastard."

I shifted into fourth and pressed the pedal down. The truck didn't have much acceleration, but she moved.

Billy slowed and then careened left onto the highway. I didn't see any oncoming lights, so I shifted down into second and followed. The truck screeched but righted herself on the smooth pavement, and my hair whipped in the wind from the open front windows.

Billy's silhouette shifted in the driver's seat as he glanced in the rearview mirror. He seemed agitated.

I smiled and pressed the gas to the floor, pushing the old girl into third and then fourth.

A week ago, this asshole had sicced his wolves on me. Now it was my turn.

Hunt him down.

My truck lurched forward and slammed into Billy's bumper. He veered across the center line before righting himself. Adrenaline pumped through me, and I felt wild and in control.

"You want to play dirty, Billy? I'll show you dirty."

I pressed the gas and smashed into his bumper again, harder this time. He swerved and flipped me off.

If I could just get him off the road, preferably into a ditch and unconscious. Not dead. If I had to shoot off his kneecaps with silver bullets, I would, but he had information that I needed.

Billy swung in front of me. I rammed his bumper and managed to pull up beside him. "You messed with the wrong waitress, asshole!"

His ochre eyes locked onto mine, and then he grinned and sideswiped me. Metal grated against metal, and my truck lurched to the left. I cursed and righted the old girl as he slammed into me again, pushing me toward the ditch. Dread settled in my stomach as I fought to control the truck.

I released my foot on the gas, and Billy's truck shot forward in front of me and sailed through the air.

Holy—

Just then, my front right tire exploded. I gripped the wheel, trying to regain control, but I was going too fast. The truck swerved, and then flipped.

Oh, no.

They say that when you're in a horrible accident, time seems to stand still. It wasn't quite like that. I saw the pavement flip once, and then I was out.

44

Savannah

I opened my eyes and groaned. My hair hung below me, and the taste of copper filled my mouth.

The roof under me was crushed, the windshield shattered. I took a breath and moved my arms and legs, making sure nothing was broken or missing or impaled.

Every inch of my body hurt, but I'd gotten lucky. I unclicked my seatbelt and braced myself as I fell onto broken glass.

I had to find Billy.

Adrenaline surged through me, dulling the pain. I reached around and pulled the pistol from the back of my jeans, then slid out of the crushed window. Glass cut my hands, but I felt nothing.

The night was dark apart from the flickering high beams of my truck that shone down the road. I climbed to my feet. Billy's truck was in a ditch on the opposite side. The passenger door was open, and stuff was strewn around the truck—an empty soda bottle, papers, and trash.

Pistol raised and ready to fire, I crossed the road, scanning the area.

The sides and hood of his truck were dented, and the windshield was gone. I eased down the shallow embankment and peered inside the passenger door, my gun raised. I knew he wasn't inside, but I had to check. A cellphone on the seat lit up and began vibrating. The letter *D* appeared on the screen.

As I leaned forward to grab it, the hairs on my neck stood on end. I spun as two ripped arms wrapped around me from behind. Pain shot through my wrist, and I dropped the gun.

No!

Panic surged through me. I slammed my head backward and heard a crunch as it connected with Billy's face. He grunted, then threw me like I weighed no more than a feather.

I hurtled through the air and landed hard in the ditch ahead of his truck. Pain rocketed through my shoulder, and I gasped. What had I been thinking, going after him alone?

Billy grinned. "Stupid little bitch. I got you just where I need you."

I scrambled to my feet, searching for anything I could use as a weapon. I wasn't going down without drawing blood.

And then I saw it: a shotgun at the side of the ditch, halfway between Billy and me. It must have flown out of his truck when he'd crashed.

Get him talking. Distract him.

"You're a pathetic dog." I took a step forward and forced out a laugh, trying to calm my pounding heart. "A pet doing the dirty work of a sorcerer. Really, Billy? Considering how much you hate us, I never thought you'd stoop so low."

He growled, and his eyes brightened. "I can smell your fear, Savannah. You're not fooling anyone. He's working for me, and once he drains every last drop of your cursed blood, we'll both get what we want."

My chest was heaving now, but I took another step forward, keeping my eyes locked on Billy's. "And what's that?"

Fear raced up my spine, and my gaze dropped to the claws that grew from Billy's fingertips.

"Revenge." His voice was animalistic, and his body began to shake. I was out of time.

I dove for the shotgun as the cracking of bones grew louder. Cocking it with a quick pump, I rolled onto my back as claws dug into my thigh.

I pressed the trigger, and a deafening boom rang through the air. The butt of the gun kicked into my shoulder, and Billy jerked backward several feet.

I scooted away, my ears ringing and my feet sliding in the dirt. Billy clutched his shoulder, and blood pooled on the ground beside him. Releasing his hand, he looked down at the wound and snarled.

Bone splinters poked out of the ragged flesh around his bicep. I gagged and pulled myself up, cocking the shotgun and aiming it at his head. "It's over, Billy. Tell me who the sorcerer is."

He chuckled and spit. "It's not over until you and every last LaSalle is dead."

I lowered the barrel to his thigh and pulled the trigger. My shoulder jerked from the kick, but Billy screamed as he looked down at the torn flesh and muscle of his upper thigh.

I pumped the gun again and aimed at his other leg. "Where is he?"

The wound on his shoulder began knitting together, and I froze. I knew werewolves could heal, but seeing it in the flesh was horrifying. The hole in his thigh was also closing. Where were my silver bullets when I needed them?

Billy climbed to his feet. I gripped the shotgun, trying to steady my shaking hands. I was suddenly certain that I'd have to kill him, but I needed answers first.

As if sensing my fear, he smiled. "You only have one more shot. Make it count."

I raised the barrel to his head. "Tell me who he is, Billy."

"I'll do you one better and bring you to him." He growled and surged toward me.

Billy dove low as the shotgun rang out, but the blast caught him and spun him sideways. He was back on his feet in a second, hand pressed against a bloody patch where the left side of his face had been. "Fuck the sorcerer. You're dead, LaSalle."

I cocked the gun, but the magazine was empty. Billy wasn't lying—I'd used my last shot. Dread rose in my throat. My eyes flicked to the ground by his truck for my pistol, but it was too dark, and there wasn't time to search for it.

Run, Savy.

I chucked the shotgun at him like a hatchet and sprinted down the road.

A low chuckle followed me. "Run, LaSalle. I'm coming for you."

Nausea took root in my stomach, and the taste of bile burned my throat.

A truck rumbled to life behind me, and I glanced over my shoulder. Despite the damage it had suffered that night, Billy's truck lurched out of the ditch and bounced onto the road, the headlights illuminating me.

This was bad. *Really* freaking bad.

I careened right down the embankment and ducked into the woods. I was wearing my magic boots, but if he shifted, I wouldn't stand a chance.

The forest was dark, and a light mist began to fall. I tripped over a root and stumbled. With the thick vegetation, it was impossible to step lightly when I had supercharged boots. I had no idea where I was going, but I just had to keep moving and come up with a plan. Billy wasn't going to give me the answers I needed, so I'd have to incapacitate him. Jaxson would get him to talk.

My stomach lurched as a blur shot through the trees on my left. I pivoted right and slid down a gully, scraping my shin on a boulder. Bushes tangled around me, hooking on my clothes, but I clawed my way up the other side of the ravine. And that's when I saw him.

A black wolf.

Terror pushed me faster, even though my body was so tired. My eyes finally started to adjust to the darkness, and the vegetation cleared once I reached the top of the gully.

I could almost feel Billy breathing down my neck, and goosebumps prickled my skin. I weaved around trees, and then stopped short as the inky expanse of the lake appeared ahead. I stood at the edge of a cliff.

Dead end.

A low growl erupted behind me, and I turned, meeting Billy's wolf. I knew it was him. The scent, the signature, all of it filled with hate.

I stumbled back closer to the cliff as his body contorted—his shoulders and spine popped and realigned as he heaved upward in a macabre dance. Fur and fangs receded, leaving a stark-naked human standing before me. The true monster.

His eyes remained a wolfish yellow, and his face was cut with a crazed expression that made my skin crawl.

"You know what you are?" he growled.

I eased my breathing, trying to force down the panic. "And what's that?"

He began circling me. "Dead."

I flinched and started moving, so he couldn't pin me against the water and cliffs. "That's where you're wrong. No matter how much you hate me, the sorcerer needs me alive. He needs my blood. So where the hell is he? Why did he send his lap dog?"

"You'll meet him soon, if I don't kill you."

He smiled and lunged toward me. I turned, but he was too fast. He twisted my arm behind my back and gripped my hair with his other hand.

I gritted my teeth against the pain, hoping he wouldn't twist my arm any further.

"You'll be their undoing, you know?"—he leaned close, and his hot breath sent shudders in its wake—"We'll slaughter them all."

What the hell madness was he speaking?

He kicked my feet from under me and shoved me down, and I cried out as I landed hard on my stomach. Fear clenched my heart. "Get off me, you asshole!"

I kicked and clawed at the ground, grabbing a rock. Searing pain shot across my back, and my vision flashed as his claws cut through Sam's leather jacket. Anger surged inside me.

Fight.

I flipped over and brought the rock in my fist down on Billy's head. The crack reverberated through my hand.

He grunted and fell back. Rage flashed across his face, and he grabbed my ankle and dragged me toward him. I kicked him wildly with my free leg, but he backhanded me so hard, I nearly passed out.

He climbed on top of me and squeezed my throat. Blood dripped down the side of his head. "If you don't stop fighting, I'll fucking kill you, no matter what the sorcerer needs."

I'll never stop fighting.

I slammed my palms into his chest "I said, get the fuck off me!"

Time seemed to stop. Ice water flowed through my body, starting from my fingertips and toes, then spreading up my legs and arms. It narrowed to a point in my chest, then exploded through my hands.

A scream tore from Billy's throat as the force blasted into his chest and sent him flying back into a tree. Shadowy tendrils snaked around him, and he fought them off as he writhed.

My magic. I scrambled to my feet and looked down at my palms. How do I do that, again?

Billy crouched and growled, his eyes bright yellow. He was wolfing out, and I was pretty sure he was actually going to kill me.

I spun and sprinted along the ridge above the shoreline. The dark water lapped against the worn rocks below.

Billy's feet pounded the earth behind me. I leapt over a mass of twisted tree roots, fear clawing at my chest. My breaths came in ragged bursts. I couldn't outrun him—even with my boots, he was too fast.

I dipped under a low branch and glanced over my shoulder. His claws were out, and hair bristled over his arms. Billy had checked out, and there was only a monster left where the man had been.

Not good.

Up ahead, a small ravine cut through the ridge. Dread settled over me. The gap was at least ten feet across.

Could I make it?

Only one way to find out. I sent a silent prayer into the universe and launched myself over the ravine. Weightlessness took over as the dark expanse flashed by below. My feet hit the rocky ledge, and my boots absorbed the shock.

Holy crap!

But before I could celebrate, a solid force—no, *a body*—hit me from behind, expelling the breath from my lungs. Claws sank into my arms as my feet were knocked out from under me. We hit the ground hard, and a stabbing pain shot through my shoulder. I screamed as Billy and I rolled across the ground, entwined together. We came to a stop, his weight painfully pressing my back into a rock. I gasped as warmth seeped into the front of my shirt. Blood. Was it mine?

Fury flashed through me, and my mind slipped away as rage settled into the driver's seat. A burning sensation pulsed under my fingernails, and pressure built under my ribs, like my chest was breaking in two.

I was having a heart attack. My poor heart had given out from the terror, and I was dying.

Not without a fight.

My adrenaline surged, and I punched Billy in the nose, feeling it crack against my knuckles. Blood dribbled from his nostrils, and the metallic smell filled my mind. He stared down at me. Horror and confusion streaked through his tawny eyes. "It can't be."

A white-hot anger I'd never known before burned through me.

Tear his throat out.

I grabbed the front of his shirt, and rammed my other fist into his chest. That cool energy from earlier returned, erupting through my fingers in a painful flurry. Billy let out a guttural sound as his body launched backwards like a rag doll and disappeared over the ledge.

My muscles spasmed, and I collapsed. Exhaustion weighed down on me.

Get up, Savy.

I shook my head but crawled over to the ledge and peered down. Water lapped against the rocks—water mixed with blood. I could smell it, though that made no sense at all.

I gripped a tree root and climbed down the steep, rocky slope. My boots slid on the dirt, and I landed on a limestone boulder. My heart pounded so hard I could feel it in my temples.

The moon's reflection glinted on the dark water, and I scanned the shore and froze. A dark shape lay motionless at the lake's edge, rocking gently in the waves, shielded from above by an overhang.

Taking a deep breath, I stepped closer.

Blood seeped into the water from the black wolf. Billy was dead, and he'd reverted to his original form. Just like the monster who'd attacked me at the Taphouse. Wolfborn. Like Sam. Like Jaxson.

Crouching down, I gripped his wet fur and rolled his body over. Several deep red gashes cut across the wolf's chest. They looked like...

Nope.

Confusion and panic clouded my mind. I turned away and doubled over, squeezing my knees with my palms.

Deep breaths, Savy.

Billy must have scraped himself on some branches while he was chasing me. That's why I was covered in blood.

I opened my eyes and saw my reflection in the water, illuminated by the moonlight. Horror rocketed through me. Staring back up at me in the water was me. But my eyes...

Oh, my God.

My eyes were fucking glowing honey gold.

I screamed and tripped, landing hard on my butt. As I scooted away from the lake, ice chilled my veins, and panic took hold. I couldn't seem to get enough air. I clutched my heart and stared up at the starry sky. My vision blurred, but the vastness of the black expanse above was calming, like the presence of an old friend. After a few minutes, my breathing eased.

I'd just experienced a trauma. Billy had attacked me. I'd pushed him over the ledge, and now he was dead. Shock had made my mind project things that weren't real. Hadn't Jaxson told me the same thing the first time we'd met?

And he'd been lying.

I dragged myself to my feet and peered at my reflection. My eyes weren't a honey color. I sighed with relief but couldn't shake the dread that had seeped deep into my soul.

It had just been my wild imagination.

45

Jaxson

Though Savannah's scream had torn through the forest minutes ago, it still echoed in my mind.

Fury coursed through me as I growled and leapt up the side of the gully. Her scent was everywhere, clouding my mind and causing my wolf to panic. I feared that if I shifted now, he'd take over, and I'd lose control.

Why the fuck had she chased after Billy alone?

Protect her.

Anger rippled through my body, and I ran faster than I ever had on two legs. The thought of Billy's hands on Savannah sent me into a rage, and I couldn't understand it. She was nothing to me, just a LaSalle. A means to an end.

Lies.

The smells of blood and fear flooded my senses, and I slowed. The forest was dead quiet, apart from Savannah's breathing...and her heartbeat. I could feel it from twenty feet away, as if it were my own.

The reflection of the full moon shone over the lake, and Savannah moved through the trees toward me. She was wounded, terrified, but underneath it all, her alluring scent called to me.

Her eyes locked on me, wide with fear. "Jaxson!"

With a few steps, she closed the distance and crashed into my arms, her body trembling. I could smell Billy's scent on her, and my anger spiked anew. "I told you to stay with me."

She didn't answer, just buried her face in my chest. I tensed but held her tight, breathing in her intoxicating signature as her pounding heart steadied. My anger dissipated. She was alive. That was all that mattered.

I gently moved my hand up her back and felt the lacerations through her torn jacket. She flinched, and a whimper escaped her throat. Guilt pummeled me, and my body shook with fury. Billy was a dead man.

Taking a slow breath, I listened intently. Two heartbeats. Hers. Mine. And nothing else.

The woods were empty. Billy must have fled.

"You're hurt," I said, my voice rough.

"I'm okay," she whispered. "Just hold me."

I should have been calculating, planning, tracking Billy. Ransacking the cabin. Looking for clues to the identity of the sorcerer. But all of that was laughable with her in my arms. Suddenly, the battle, the danger, the stakes, none of it meant anything.

At this moment, there was only her. The scent of her hair so close to my lips. My wolf, who had been raging, was quiet. Focused. We were perfectly aligned. This was where we were supposed to be. Holding her. Protecting her. Reunited.

A part of me knew it was madness, but it was drowned by every sensation in my body.

Savannah looked up at me as she slid her hands to my chest. I could smell her emotions. The fear and panic were gone, replaced by a scent I had never encountered before. I couldn't quite name it. Rightness. Belonging.

Mine.

Her pupils spread, and her pulse throbbed against my fingertips. Could she, somehow, sense it too?

The lightness of her touch sent heat straight through me, turning my fear for her safety into pulsing desire. All I could think about was kissing her, claiming her, taking her right here under the moon.

I dragged my thumb over her bruised cheek. She winced ever so slightly but bit her lower lip. I could smell her need. Her *desire*. And I wanted to taste it.

Were we mad? Her eyes told me yes.

But they compelled me, luring me in, lighting a fire that no sanity could extinguish. I slipped one hand to her ass and lifted her. Her body was soft and inviting. She gasped and wrapped her legs around me, pushing her heat against me.

Fuck.

I had to have her. I growled, and my other hand gripped her hair as my mouth claimed hers. She parted her lips so easily, and she tasted divine, like citrus on a warm summer's day. Her fingers moved over my body, touching and exploring. I ached to feel and lick every inch of her. She kissed me hard, like she was ravenous. Her need only intensified mine, and it took every last ounce of control I had not to rip off her clothes and bury myself in her.

As if sensing my thoughts, she moaned and moved against my hardness. I could almost feel the wet warmth of her body, a drug pulling me onward. I could lose myself in her. Nothing else mattered in the world but this. Her.

Mine.

"Jaxson." Sam's voice cut through the night air, drenching my desire like ice water. She stood in the shadows of the trees, flames of shock and fear flickering in her golden eyes. "Are you mad? What are you doing?"

No bullet had ever hit me so hard. It was like an ocean wave slamming into me.

What was I doing?

Guilt, shame, and anger flooded me. I dragged my mouth from Savannah's and set her down. What had I done?

She's ours.

No, she wasn't.

Everything was wrong. The moment had been perfect. But it wasn't. Tendrils of panic twisted beneath my skin. I had to get control. Savannah was a LaSalle, my pack's enemy. The people who'd murdered my sister and driven Billy to insanity.

I scrubbed a hand through my hair and stepped toward Sam. She turned her back on me and leaned against a tree. I could smell her despair and confusion.

What had just happened had been like a heat, but far more powerful. Maybe for another of our kind it wouldn't have mattered, but I was the alpha, and she was a sorceress. A LaSalle. Not one of us.

My wolf surged inside me. *She. Is. Ours.* I forced him down with a snarl. It wasn't right.

"Where's Billy?" Sam asked, her voice pitched flat as she tried to maintain control.

I turned to Savannah. Her lips were swollen from our kiss, and her cheeks were flushed. My chest clenched, and I doused the surge of desire that ripped through me.

"Do you know?" I asked.

Anger and fear flashed across her face, and she glared at me. "He's dead."

My chest tightened as the forest spun and the nightmare coiled around me. "What? Billy was mine." My voice was icy and rough, almost unrecognizable.

Disappointment and hatred cut across Savannah's face. "He attacked me. I pushed him, and he stumbled over the ledge."

"Where?" I growled, barely able to control the emotions whirling inside of me. He couldn't be dead. She must have been mistaken.

Savannah led us through the woods. Sam didn't speak. She didn't have to.

My senses had been so consumed by Savannah, I hadn't scented Billy. But now that I'd reined myself in, it was clear as day. His scent was everywhere and all over her. I would have killed him myself for touching her, but that wasn't the point.

Finally, after a few minutes of walking, Savannah stopped at the edge of a cliff. "Down there."

I stepped around her up to the edge. Down below, Billy's body gently bobbed against the rocks. It was true. A wave of emotions erupted over me—sorrow, anger, regret. Guilt.

Sam appeared at my side. "He tripped, huh?" She arched her brow at Savannah.

Savannah's lips trembled, and she rubbed her arms. "Yup."

A lie.

We could both smell it. I scowled and dropped over the ledge. Billy's eyes were still open, staring at the sky. I knelt and closed them. Then I closed my own and let the grief bore into me.

The last thread tying me to my sister was dead. The person who remembered her best. The person who'd loved her so much, he was willing to abandon everything he believed for justice. Vengeance.

Her true mate, bound together in life and death.

I prayed to the moon mother that I would never have a bond like that, one so fierce that it could drive me to betray my pack, my kin. I was the alpha, and I couldn't risk being bound by love or desire or anything else.

I gave myself sixty heartbeats to dwell in that darkness. Then I opened my eyes and stood. I would grieve for Billy and my sister later, but for now, I needed to lead. I needed to set things right.

I looked up at Savannah, who met my eyes. In that moment, I knew for certain that she was not as she seemed.

When I'd met her, she'd been an unassuming waitress who had run down a werewolf on the road. She'd had no idea magic was real. Yet...she'd hunted werewolves and demons, rescued Sam and Madison, and now, somehow, she'd managed to take out the third strongest member of my pack. On her own.

It shouldn't have been possible.

What the hell was she? A beautiful, perilous mystery—that much was certain.

My wolf pitched in my chest, desiring to run to her. But the heat between us had been wrong, a tragic slip. I was the alpha. I couldn't let my carnal needs cloud my judgement. I had to be stronger. She was a LaSalle, and the woman who'd killed my brother-in-law. It had been self-defense, but she'd taken justice and answers from me. I had loved him once.

I couldn't let myself forget any of that.

Sam watched me from above. "I'm sorry, Jaxson."

My heart ached with regret and failure, but I buried my emotions. "Billy betrayed the pack. He signed his own death warrant."

She nodded. "There's something more you need to see back at the cabin."

I scooped Billy's body up, then froze. Several claw marks cut through his chest. He must have been wounded in the fight earlier. But he hadn't healed, which was...impossible.

Suspicion settled over me. I could practically taste Savannah's apprehension, the worry she'd tightly wound around the secret she was concealing.

I tossed Billy over my shoulder and met Savannah's blank, emotionless stare.

She was hiding something, and I was going to unravel it.

Savannah

I followed Jaxson and Sam through the forest. The two were silent. Jaxson carried Billy's body draped over his shoulder, and though I tried my hardest to focus on the ground, I couldn't help but steal glances at Billy's lifeless form.

Jaxson's demeanor was cold and distant, and I mirrored it.

What had I been thinking?

When I'd seen Jaxson coming toward me in the woods, relief had dulled my senses. I'd fled into his arms, my soul aching and broken, as if his touch could soothe my shattered spirit. And then suddenly, for one fucked-up second in my fucked-up life, everything had been right. It hadn't mattered that psychopaths were trying to drain my blood and kill me, or that I'd killed a man, or been shot at, or hunted by monsters. It didn't matter that I was covered in blood and that everything was wrong.

That moment had been right, and my body knew it. My hands and lips had moved on their own accord, compelled by his scent, his strength, and that golden light burning in his eyes.

And I'd devoured every second.

I touched my bruised lips. He'd tasted so good. That kiss had been everything, and I'd wanted him so badly—a heat that had driven me to madness. Dread coiled in my chest.

What was wrong with me?

Clearly, a lot.

I'd seen it in his eyes, and I could practically smell it on him now. He'd been ashamed that he'd kissed me.

Who wouldn't be? I'd killed a man with my bare hands, and then I'd kissed his brother-in-law.

Sam's shocked and revolted look had told me everything I needed to know: *I* was the real monster in these woods. I was just a filthy, wolf-murdering, bloodstained LaSalle, and though I'd thought that maybe Jaxson had seen through all that, that he'd seen something more, the only things he felt for me now were regret and shame.

Bastard.

My chest constricted, and heat flushed my neck. I clenched my hands and stalked along behind.

Why couldn't life let me have one moment?

It didn't matter. This was for the best. Jaxson Laurent was a freaking werewolf and my family's sworn enemy. Hell, his brother-in-law had tried to kill me, and it seemed like half the werewolves in the state were okay with that plan.

It was screwed up.

Jaxson and I could never be together. Period. I knew toxic when it hit me in the face.

The three of us stepped out of the forest onto the road. Headlights blinded me as a truck pulled to a stop, and Tony emerged.

Jaxson slid Billy into the bed, then stepped around and opened the back passenger door. I looked away but could feel his eyes on me.

So *now* he was going to be polite? Asshole.

Ignoring him, I stepped up and slid onto the back seat. Tony looked at me in the rearview mirror as Jaxson shut the door and climbed in the front. Sam got in the back with me but didn't spare a glance my way, just clicked on her seatbelt.

Was everyone going to give me the cold shoulder now because I'd killed Billy?

I killed him. Just like I'd killed the shifter at the Taphouse.

And the one at the sanatorium. My hands trembled, so I slid them under my thighs. I was a murderer, how many times over?

Oh, my God.

An image of my reflection in the water—with glowing honey eyes—flashed through my mind.

Nausea overwhelmed me, and before Tony could drive off, I opened my door and threw up on the road. The others waited as I retched, and once my spasming had subsided, I sat up and closed the door again, wishing I had a bottle of pop. "Sorry," I muttered.

Without a word, Sam handed me a piece of gum. I took it, unwrapped the silver paper, shoved the stick in my mouth, and chewed aggressively. Minty fresh. If only there was something that would take away the stench of death just as quickly as bad breath.

Jaxson's shoulders were tense in the front seat, but he said nothing. Tony pulled a U-turn, and we drove in silence.

My nerves were shot, and everything hurt, especially my back. I hadn't seen it yet, but I was pretty sure it was going to scar. Jaxson had touched it, and then we'd kissed, and...everything went to shit.

That kiss. Kill me now. Never mind the fact that I was scratched to hell and exhausted—or that I'd just killed freaking Billy—I'd never shared a more intense kiss with any guy. Well, not that I'd kissed many guys before, but none of them had tasted as good as Jaxson had.

Heat pooled in my center, and I shifted awkwardly. How could I be horny at a time like *this*?

Jaxson gripped the oh-shit handle, his knuckles white.

Damn it all to hell, he'd definitely noticed. That meant Tony and Sam had noticed, too. I was getting turned on while we were driving around with a dead man in the back. My cheeks burned, and I silently cursed.

I had to get away from these damned werewolves.

To clear my mind, I concentrated on the look of shame and horror I'd seen on Sam's face when she'd caught us kissing. That was enough to kill whatever desire had been on my mind.

They all hated me.

Ten eternally long minutes later, Billy's cabin appeared. The place looked like a war zone. Smoke still wafted through the trees, and bodies were strewn across the ground. I pried my eyes away. I'd seen enough death in the past week to last me a lifetime.

Tony parked, and we climbed out of the car. Jaxson's gaze was on me, but I stared ahead, silent and cold.

Regina appeared on the porch. She shared a look with Jaxson and then tensed. "Who did it?"

I was guessing Jaxson had just told her in wolf talk that Billy was dead.

"Me," I snapped. "*I* killed him, and I'd do it again. He was a psychopath."

My words came out in a torrent. I was just so tired of everyone silently scrutinizing and blaming me for his death. What did they expect? He was either going to kill me or hand me over to an even bigger psycho.

I shivered and suddenly felt sick again. Billy was a goddamned monster. My family may have driven him to it, but that didn't give him a pass. Evil was evil.

Regina shot daggers at me with her eyes as I climbed the front stairs. Brushing past her, I opened the screen door and strode into the cabin. I'd come here for answers about who was hunting me, and I was going to get some with or without their help.

46

Savannah

I stepped into Billy's cabin with Jaxson and the others on my heels.

The scent of cigarettes burned my nose. Maps and newspaper clippings were tacked to the walls of the dingy living room. Apart from a table and stained white couch, the place was devoid of furniture, though I spotted the canisters of wolfsbane stacked in the corner and the piles of guns scattered about.

It was an operations room. An armory.

My pulse quickened as I drew my gaze across the walls. There had to be a clue here pointing toward the sorcerer...

I froze.

Taped to the wooden boards were a series of photographs. Casey, Aunt Laurel, Uncle Pete, and a lot of people I didn't know, all arranged in a web chart like a family tree. A photograph of me eating at Eclipse had recently been added, and fear buried me like an avalanche.

Billy's words from earlier echoed through my mind: *We'll slaughter them all.*

"What is this?" I murmured, dragging my eyes to the half dozen house plans and the map of the Indies.

I'd assumed Billy had been taunting me when he'd said, *You'll be their undoing.* I never thought he'd actually had a carefully executed plan to take out every last one of us.

I ripped the photo of myself off the wall and turned. "Did you know about this?"

Jaxson was staring at Billy's plans, his expression hardened. He scrubbed a hand through his hair. "Fuck."

"I'll ask one more time," I snapped. "Did any of you know that Billy was planning to massacre my entire family?"

I scanned their faces for answers, but Tony and Sam looked uncomfortable and avoided my eyes. Regina was the only one who stared at me, her expression cold.

Anger and betrayal simmered within me. These wolves weren't my friends. If Billy had been telling the truth, then members of their pack were planning to use me—somehow—to murder the LaSalles.

"We didn't know. We knew he hated the LaSalles, but I never...I never imagined this," Jaxson said. His voice was icy and sharp. He was telling the truth, but that didn't make this all right.

I wanted to scream, to tear the cabin to the ground. "How could you let this happen? How could you not know? I was around Billy...hell, I'm lucky to be alive! You *had* to know how much he hated me and my family."

"Is it any wonder?" Regina retorted. "Your family murdered his wife. They were true mates. You can't recover from that bond. They *broke* him." She'd planted herself in front of the door, her fists clenched and gaze locked on me.

"Do you all hate my family so much that you'd just turn a blind eye to what was obviously going on?"

"Watch your words," she said. "No one had any idea it was this bad, or what he was planning."

"This is my fault," Jaxson interjected, picking up a canister of wolfsbane. "I should have suspected. But when someone is your family, it's easy to turn a blind eye to their flaws. You know that as well as anyone, Savannah."

Heat crept up my neck. "What's that supposed to mean?"

I knew what he meant—that my family were monsters who had killed his sister, and that I was okay with it. But that had happened years ago, and I didn't have the full story.

Regina crossed her arms. "It means nobody is blameless here. Not you, for sure."

"How am I to blame? I was waiting tables and minding my own business when werewolves showed up and tried to kill me!"

"Right, and then you started killing them." She spun on Jaxson. "One of whom was your brother-in-law."

Regina actually blamed me for fighting back?

"In self-defense! Are you crazy? Billy attacked me and was either going to kill me or hand me over to some psycho blood sorcerer to complete his plan of murdering my family. *I'm* the victim here, *not* Billy, and certainly not that sociopath I ran down in Belmont."

Regina's body trembled, and she lowered her eyebrows. "You didn't have to come here. And you didn't have to chase down Billy on your own. That was Jaxson's business, *pack* business, but you stuck your nose in where it didn't belong. Again. You made your choices and killed one of our wolves, so you should stand trial before the pack under the Old Laws."

Her threat hit me square in the jaw, and I flinched. I'd do no such thing.

"You're right," I shot back. "Maybe somebody should stand trial for all this. Billy planned these abductions and murders, and he had help. Maybe I should call the Order right now and let them know what I've learned about your operations. Let them know about the pack's involvement in these crimes."

Regina's claws came out, and her eyes flashed. "You're threatening our whole pack now, LaSalle?"

"Enough!" Jaxson's voice boomed through the room and made us all shrink back. "There will be no trial for Savannah. *Or the pack.* And as far as anyone outside the inner circle knows, I'm the one who killed Billy. Never speak of Savannah's role in this again."

He shot Regina and me a look that had us withering in place. His alpha signature settled over me, making my pulse skyrocket and my palms sweat. I tore my gaze from his, even angrier that he had this effect on me.

I wasn't the only one, though. Regina had submitted, and Sam's and Tony's eyes were on the ground. I could almost taste the cocktail of fear and submission that mixed within the cabin air.

"I'm assuming you three have already scoured the cabin. Any indication of who Billy was working with?" Jaxson asked his wolves.

"None. He kept his dealings with his affiliate quiet. There's nothing here but his plans for the LaSalles," Sam said, eyeing me.

Frustration mixed with my anger, and I felt like I was going to explode. I had to get out of here. Get back to Magic Side so I could warn Casey about how close the pack had come to taking his whole family out. *My* family.

I crossed to the door and stepped around Regina, who glared at me. "I'm leaving."

The screen door banged as Jaxson followed me out. "Where are you going?"

I hurried down the wooden steps, trying to get a little

distance between us. "Back to Magic Side. To my family. As far away from you people as possible."

I wasn't sure how I'd get back there. Maybe I'd steal Tony's Jeep.

"It's not safe. The sorcerer is still out there, and there may be others in the pack after you. You should stay with me on pack lands."

I spun on Jaxson. He was inches from me, and his pine scent clouded my senses. God, why did he smell so good? I dragged my eyes from his lips. How could I be so affected by him when I knew how dangerous he was? When he despised who I was? When he was ashamed of me?

My cheeks blazed. "No. And don't pull that alpha bullshit on me. I helped you find out who was behind the abductions, and now I'm done. Stay away from me, Jaxson, and get your wolves in line."

The screen door creaked, and I noticed that Sam, Regina, and Tony were on the porch watching us.

Jaxson's eyes narrowed, and his body tensed. Fear hit me like a brick, and I took a step back, praying that his wolf didn't come bursting out.

Something flashed across his face, and it looked like he was about to say something but then decided against it. "Sam, make sure Savannah gets home safely."

My shoulders eased, and I let out an unsteady breath. I'd seen it over and over, and I couldn't let myself forget it—beneath the rugged exterior, Jaxson was also a monster.

Tony handed Sam his keys, and she headed to the Jeep, casting me a look over her shoulder as she slid into the driver's seat.

I gave one last glance at Jaxson and turned, retrieving my bag from his truck. His anger was palpable, and his eyes burned into my back, sending shivers down my spine. My chest tightened as I climbed into the Jeep, but I didn't look back.

I clicked on my seatbelt and felt Sam's eyes on me. "What?"

She started the Jeep and turned up the radio so Jaxson and the others couldn't hear us. "You Wreck Me" by Tom Petty blared from the speakers, and I silently swore.

"I saw you two in the forest," she said. "That ends here. You and Jaxson can't ever be a thing. It would break him and tear the pack apart. Understand?"

My cheeks blazed. "What you saw was a mistake. Heat of the moment. There isn't anything between Jaxson and me, got it?"

"Mm-hm." She arched an eyebrow. "One more word of advice: don't tell anyone about it, and just stay away."

A deep ache lodged under my ribs, and I couldn't help but feel Jaxson's embarrassment and disgrace that Sam had seen our kiss.

My feelings for Jaxson—whatever they were—had clouded my judgement. Jaxson was dangerous. *Werewolves* were dangerous. The fact that he could instill such terror in me with a single look was a sign in and of itself.

I had to get as far away from him as I could.

As the Jeep bounced down the dirt driveway, I looked in the side mirror. Jaxson stood under the porch light with his fists clenched and honey-gold eyes burning.

I left the beautiful predator in my wake.

47

Savannah

"You okay?" Casey glanced at me as we pulled up in front of Monster Girls auto body shop.

I'd gotten back to the LaSalles' last night. They'd made me chug one of Uncle Pete's healing potions, and I was so nauseated afterward that I'd gone to bed and passed out until noon. Nightmares of wolves, blood demons, and the sorcerer had kept me tossing and turning, and I'd felt like death when I woke.

"Yup. Fine and dandy," I lied. I took a sip of my latte, enjoying the zing on my tongue that vaguely reminded me of licking the terminals on a battery, yet was weirdly delicious.

We'd stopped at Magic Grounds of Being on the way because Casey had said I looked like a zombie, to which I'd replied, *What do you expect?* Once there, he'd insisted that I try the coffee shop's signature drink, the Jump-starter.

Caffeine coursed through my veins, or maybe it was magic, because I suddenly felt full of bubbly energy. I hopped out of the car and sighed as the sunshine warmed my face.

Things were dire, probably even more so than when I'd arrived in Magic Side five days ago, but the sun was shining, and

I was getting my Fury back. Those were reasons enough to be happy.

A voice rang out as we stepped into the shadow of the shop. "Hiya, sexy!"

Looking for the source, I found an attractive woman with horns and a tail grinning at Casey. "Zara's in the garage."

I did a double take as she strode into the office, her tail swishing behind her. "*Who* is that?" I muttered.

"That, my dear, is Rayne. Hottest she-devil in town." Casey smirked as he watched her disappear into the shop.

I blinked twice at him and choked out a laugh. Not because there was anything wrong with Rayne—she was wicked hot—but because Casey looked love-stricken.

"Come on, Romeo, let's get my ride," I said, clapping him on the shoulder.

Zara was under the car on a red mechanic's creeper, her legs sticking out from beneath the front bumper. My eyes rounded with shock. The Fury had never looked so good. Its deep reddish-brown paint looked like it had been detailed, though the claw marks were still visible on the hood. They added character, I decided.

"What up, Zar?" Casey said, knocking loudly on the hood of my Fury.

I shot him a glare as Zara rolled out from under the car. "Hey, you two. Your baby is ready to go," she told me. "I was just double-checking everything. It was a lot of work for a rush job."

As she got up and wiped her stained black hands on a rag, I took in her attire: gray skinny jeans, a black crop top, and biker boots. The smudge of grease on her forehead completed the look. She was beautiful in a biker chic way, and I was sure she could kick some ass with those boots.

It seemed like she'd done a lot more than just install the magic regulator, and she didn't seem the type to hand things out for free. Worry twisted in my gut. "How much do I owe you for...?"

I didn't even know what all she'd done. What if I couldn't pay for it? Would she just keep my car?

"Your tab's been paid," Zara said dryly.

"What? How?" My mind reeled, but I knew the answer as soon as I asked. *Jaxson fricking Laurent.* It had to be.

"Jaxson ponied up. He told me not to tell you and to just say that I'd fixed it for free—but that would set a bad precedent. I don't give friends discounts, so if you need more stuff done, you'll have to pay full price. Triple if I have to steal the car first."

"Of course he paid," I hissed, feeling a scowl cut across my face. I wasn't averse to handouts—hell, I was poor and currently unemployed—but not from Jaxson. For whatever reason, he couldn't keep his meddling paws away from my ride. I already knew it was just one more way he'd weasel himself back into my life to exert his power over me. "I'd actually like to pay for it myself," I said, trying to hold my voice steady.

Zara cocked a brow and frowned. "Not possible. Money's already been exchanged, and I don't want the pack sniffing around here. I've had my share of wolves, and though they're dynamite in the bedroom, they're bastards."

An image of Jaxson in my bedroom flashed through my mind, and my cheeks burned.

Casey smirked. "Don't get any thoughts, Cuz. I think you've already got enough scratch marks on you." As he snickered, I fought the urge to crawl under my car and die.

Zara laughed and put her kit away as I tried to regain my composure.

Fine. Let him pay. Jaxson was an asshole, and he'd dragged me through hell and back, so I might as well milk the situation for all it was worth. And really, I just wanted my car. I'd worry about the strings another time. "What all did you do?"

Zara threw me the keys. "I fixed the busted taillight and replaced the tranny. This baby is a classic and tough as nails—though when I brought her in, I was surprised she would even run. That was, until I popped the hood. You've got some wicked good enchantments on her."

"Wait a second, what?" I gaped at her.

"You didn't know?" Zara laughed. "Check this out."

She lifted the hood and pulled out a little flashlight, which glowed purple when she flicked it on. She shone it over my engine, and wherever the light fell, lines of tiny, glowing symbols appeared running over the components, like the miniscule printing on medicine bottles.

"What's that?" I asked.

"Someone wove some killer enchantments on your engine that kept it running. Honestly, without them, she'd have been a pile of scrap metal years ago."

The blood drained from my head and the world spun. "My car...is magic? Did Jaxson have this installed?"

"Nah. Wolves only use aftermarket shit. These are custom. Really old-school and kinda obsessive. Like, I think you don't even have to have a working carburetor with this one, here." Zara pointed, her voice clearly bemused.

"Let me see that." Casey plucked the flashlight out of Zara's hands and leaned over the hood. "Whoa. These are some tight spells! Really precise. It reminds me of my mom's..." He stood up, slammed his head on the hood, and swore, but then he beamed at me. "Damn, Savannah. I bet your dad enchanted your car. How sweet is that?"

I shook my head, trying to clear away the shock. "But my mom was the mechanic. We spent hours working on it together. My dad said he barely knew how to change a flat."

Casey's grin reached ear to ear. "Yeah, well, I think he was tinkering around with it when you weren't looking."

My dad *had* spent a lot of time alone in the garage. I'd thought it was because he'd liked swearing loudly at the TV when the Bears played. "Holy crap."

My cousin patted me on the back. "Seems like your parents both left a little of themselves in your ride. That's really cool."

Uncle Pete's words came rushing back to me from when I'd helped him brew the scrying potion. Sorcerers put their souls into their magic, which is why they seldom gave out potions or enchantments. That meant my dad had left a *lot* of his soul in my car. And after so many hours working together on it with my mom, so had she.

As had I.

Zara closed the hood and took her flashlight back from Casey, who'd begun to inspect other things in the shop.

I wiped away a tear that slipped down my cheek. I missed them so damn much, and I wished they'd confided in me and prepared me for this bizarre world before they'd left.

I traced my fingers along the Gran Fury with a newfound sense of wonder. It seemed, even with them gone, I hadn't ever been quite alone. Not as long as I had my car.

Rubbing away the dampness from my eyes, I turned to my new friends. "So, who wants to go for a spin?"

"Hell, yes." Casey's eyes lit up. "Happy hour at Cocina del Jorge starts in twenty. Best nachos south of the Midway and microbrews on tap. Also, there's a band that sings scandalous songs at your table."

I laughed. "Jorge's it is."

He clapped his hands together. "I'll buy the first round. You coming with, Zar?"

Zara sighed like coming with us would put her out. "Sure. Technically, this was supposed to be my day off, so I'm free for a few hours. But no tequila shots." Her eyes flicked between Casey and me. "The last time we were there, your smartass cousin shot tequila out his nose and caused a bar fight with a bunch of vamp bikers."

After knowing Casey for a week, I wouldn't expect anything less. We were definitely related. "Sounds about right. Let's see what kind of trouble we can get in today."

"I call shotgun," Casey said, sliding into the front seat. Zara shook her head and cursed but hopped in the back anyway while I slid into the front.

"Hey, you can skate?" Zara hefted up my old roller blades by the laces.

Casey laughed, and I blushed as my childhood came back to haunt me. "I'm pretty good at not falling on my face."

"Hell yes." She dropped the skates. "I've got two words for you. Roller derby."

I raised my eyebrows. "Roller derby?"

She gave me a wicked grin. "Yep. This Friday. Also, the situation has changed. This is a discussion for tequila shots. Let's go."

My hands were damp with anticipation as I slid the key in the ignition.

I closed my eyes.

While my friends chatted, I thought of my mother and father, who'd tried so hard to protect me from this world. And even though they'd never told me anything, they'd done pretty well, all things considered.

There was still a faceless monster out there hunting me, but we'd shut down his organization in Wisconsin and gotten three abductees back alive. There wouldn't be any new Madison Lees on the news, and that was a win.

I took a deep breath. Today was about getting my car back and being happy. Tomorrow, I'd tackle the rest of my life.

I turned the key, and the engine purred. Pure joy shot through my heart.

My baby was back.

Thanks for joining us on this wild adventure!

Ready to sink your fangs into *Untamed Fate*, book 2? Read it now: mybook.to/Untamed-Fate

Would you like to know more about Jaxson's mysterious encounter with the fortune teller and the events that led him to hunt down Savannah? Sign up for our newsletter to get access to an exclusive, insider only *prologue story:* https://dl.bookfunnel. com/wgkpoqcjqa (you can unsubscribe at any time).

Finally, if you're interested in learning more about the archaeology and history that inspired this book, keep reading!

AUTHOR'S NOTE

Thank you so much for reading Wolf Marked!

This book was conceived while hiking in the woods in Door County, Wisconsin. When the fog rolled in, we knew we were in werewolf country. Savannah's car, on the other hand, was inspired by our own vehicle, which broke down catastrophically while visiting Linsey Hall. As of this writing, it is *still* being held hostage in an auto body shop with a busted tranny.

As archaeologists, we love to include historical tidbits and places in our stories. While Wicked Wish and the other books in Dragon's Gift: The Storm swept our characters off to Egypt and Anatolia, we wanted to stay close to home with Wolf Marked and celebrate Chicago's history.

Savannah and Jaxson visit a seer at the Full Moon Fair, which is a remnant of the 1893 World's Columbian Exposition. The original Chicago's World Fair was divided into two parts. The first was the White City, which was located in modern day Jackson Park. The central focus was fourteen great buildings constructed around a massive basin. Their white-washed exteriors and neoclassical design gave the Exposition its nickname, the White City. Despite the extraordinary effort put into constructing them, they were intentionally temporary structures. The only building that remains is the Palace of Fine Arts, which was originally constructed with a brick substructure to protect the priceless works of art on display. After the fair, it housed the Field Museum of Natural History for a while. Between 1928 and 1932, the building was reconstructed with a limestone exterior, and is now the iconic Museum of Science and Industry, which you can visit today.

The other part of the fair was the Midway Plaisance, a mile-long green space that connects Jackson Park to Washington park. It was populated with amusements, state and cultural exhibits, carnival rides and iconically, the original Ferris wheel —a 264 ft-high spinning marvel constructed to rival the Eiffel Tower. The attractions of the Midway Plaisance served as the direct inspiration for Magic Side's Full Moon Fair—though our Ferris wheel is bigger and floating in the air. If you look at the Magic Side map in this book, you can see how we intentionally mirrored the Midway and Jackson Park in the layout of our city.

You may have found it surprising for Savannah and Jaxson to wander through a reconstructed street from Cairo while at the fair, but that exhibit was one of the major attractions of the original Midway Plaisance. It provided us with a fun chance to call back to *Dark Storm* and Neve and Damian's adventures in Helwan. A fortune teller's tent was outside the original Street in the Cairo Exhibit, which served as our inspiration for Dominique (who we assure you, is the real deal). If you want to read more about how the Midway inspired our book, sign up for our newsletter at www.veronicadouglas.com/newsletter. We'll be writing an update about it soon!

Belmont, Savannah's hometown, is a tiny town in southwest Wisconsin. We chose it because it was the original capital of the state, before Madison. We wanted our book to celebrate Wisconsin as much as Chicago and figured the best place to begin was where that state itself was born. You can still visit the historic site where the first territorial legislature met in 1836. Two restored buildings remain, the Council House and the Court House. Afterwards, you can take a short stroll and look for werewolves lurking in Belmont Mound state park.

Wolf Marked is set in the wider Dragon's Gift universe created by Linsey Hall. The best part of writing in this big world is that we're able to bring in characters from other series, so you can expect a lot of crossovers between the folks from Guild City, Magic's Bend, and Magic Side in the future.

That's all the archaeological and historical notes we have room for this time around, but we'll be posting more in our newsletter.

We hope you're looking forward to reading the sequel, Untamed Fate! Read it now on Amazon: mybook.to/Untamed-Fate.

And if you'd like to chat more about the books, interact with fellow readers, and get the scoop on what's up next, join the Veronica Douglas Facebook reader group here:

https://www.facebook.com/groups/veronicadouglas

Whew! That's all for now! Thanks again for reading!

-Veronica Douglas

UNTAMED FATE

MAGIC SIDE: WOLF BOUND BOOK 2

VERONICA DOUGLAS

UNTAMED FATE

MAGIC SIDE: WOLF BOUND, BOOK 2 PREVIEW

Last week I was a waitress. Now I'm turning into a monster.

No one knows the truth, except the faceless man—a twisted sorcerer who's hellbent on stealing my soul.

With secrets and danger hot on my heels, the only one who can help me tame my inner beast is Jaxson Laurent—the Chicago alpha. Our chemistry is explosive, but the rift between our families runs too deep.

Do I dare trust him? The last time we worked together I barely escaped with my life, and if it comes down to choosing between me and his pack, I know who he has to pick.

Time is ticking, and my life is hanging in the balance. We must unmask the faceless man before he brings darkness down on us all.

An action-packed urban fantasy, Untamed Fate features a kick-ass heroine, a dangerous alpha hero, and a steamy slow-burn, enemies-to-lovers romance.

You can read Untamed Fate now on Amazon here: mybook.to/ Untamed-Fate

WOLF GOD

RUTHLESS GODS: WOLF GOD BOOK 1

VERONICA DOUGLAS

WOLF GOD

RUTHLESS GODS: WOLF GOD, BOOK 1 OF 3

Samantha

When the Dark Wolf God threatened my pack, I defied him. His retaliation was quick and brutal.

The ruthless god tore me from my life and imprisoned me in his kingdom. He's convinced I have magic that will free him from a curse.

He's as powerful as he is sexy—but he's also wrong. I'm just a wolf shifter, right?

Cadean, the Dark Wolf God

I know the little wolf's secret: she has the power to save me, or bring me to my knees. I need her help to protect my kingdom from the fae, but she thinks I'm a monster.

The truth is far worse: I'm a brutal beast that will defend my people, no matter the price.

Could the woman who wields the power to undo me be my mate? If so, I'll destroy the world just to keep her safe.

Ready to dive in? **mybook.to/Wolf-God**

ACKNOWLEDGMENTS

VERONICA DOUGLAS

Thank you to everyone who has been so supportive, especially Linsey and Ben—we could never have done this without you guys! Also, thanks for letting us borrow your car—we promise we'll bring it back soon;)

Thank you to Jena O'Connor and Ash Fitzsimmons for your patience and amazing editing skills. This book would be broken down on the side of the road without your advice.

Thank you to the amazing readers on our advanced review team! Extra special thanks to our beta readers Susie, Penny, Aisha, Charity, Eleonora, and Max—your eyes are so sharp!

Many thanks to Lauren Gardner for all of your amazing hard work. You are a lifesaver!

And finally, a huge shoutout to Orina Kafe who designed this mind-blowing cover!

ABOUT VERONICA DOUGLAS

Veronica Douglas is a duo of professional archaeologists that love writing and digging together. After spending an inordinate amount of time doing painstaking research for academia, they suddenly discovered a passion for letting their imaginations go wild! A cocktail of magic, romance, and ancient mystery (shaken, not stirred), their books are inspired, in part, by their life in Chicago and their archaeological adventures from around the globe.

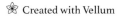

Printed in Great Britain
by Amazon

37981564R00229